Darkening Skies

Also by Bronwyn Parry

As Darkness Falls
Dark Country
Dead Heat

Darkening Skies

BRONWYN PARRY

hachette
AUSTRALIA

hachette
AUSTRALIA

Published in Australia and New Zealand in 2013
by Hachette Australia
(an imprint of Hachette Australia Pty Limited)
Level 17, 207 Kent Street, Sydney NSW 2000
www.hachette.com.au

10 9 8 7 6 5 4 3 2 1

National Library of Australia
Cataloguing-in-Publication data:

Darkening skies / Bronwyn Parry.

9780733625503 (pbk.)

Secrets – Fiction.

Suspense fiction.

A823.4

Cover photographs courtesy of Getty Images and Bigstock
Cover design by Design By Committee
Text design by Bookhouse, Sydney
Typeset in 12.75/18.5pt Adobe Garamond Pro
Printed and bound in Australia by Griffin Press, Adelaide, an Accredited ISO AS/NZS 14001:2009
Environmental Management System printer

PROLOGUE

Gil Gillespie. Mark Strelitz stopped listening to the elderly gent sharing his forthright views with him and glanced across Birraga's main street again. Definitely Morgan 'Gil' Gillespie, sitting at a table outside Rosie's cafe in broad daylight. No longer in witness protection, or wherever he'd been these past few months.

Gil was someone he needed to see, to speak with. Attempting to maintain some level of courtesy, Mark extricated himself from the conversation he'd been caught in with a promise to look into the matter further, and shook hands with his constituent before he hastened across the street.

Gil rose as he approached, the violent beating he'd endured months ago still evident in the stiffness in his left arm, his eyes narrowed with the same wariness he'd always carried. Growing up they'd never been close, the gulf between their lives too great, and Gil's experiences since then had given him few reasons to

1

trust easily. Three years in prison, then fifteen managing a pub in inner-city Sydney and trying to keep it out of mafia influence. A stark contrast to Mark's life – studying at university, managing the family pastoral company and grazing properties, and six years serving his outback region as an independent member in federal parliament.

But Gil's stance against the mafia in Sydney and their connections in Dungirri, when he'd returned a few months ago, had earned Mark's respect. He'd held the mafia at bay for years but they'd used bent police and local thugs with grudges to get at him, almost beating him to death.

Mark held out his hand. 'Gil! I didn't know you were back.'

'I just arrived.'

'It's good to see you. Everyone was worried for a while there.' Worried he wouldn't survive the night, after he'd been flown out by air ambulance following a police raid to rescue him. 'You're well?'

Mark could have bitten his tongue. Small talk, awkward and out of place with Gil, who rarely practised the social customs that had become natural to Mark.

Nevertheless, Gil answered with only a hint of irony, 'Much better.'

'Great to hear it.' Mark paused. Forget polite enquiries. He had to grasp this opportunity, find answers to the questions that haunted him. Answers only Gil could give him. 'Gil, would you have a few minutes? There's a matter I've been wanting to discuss with you.'

Gil hesitated. 'Yeah, I guess so. I don't have to be anywhere until six.'

'Thanks. My office is just round the corner – shall we go there?'

His staff had gone home and the electorate office was deserted but for the two of them. The afternoon sun through the west-facing windows overpowered the air-conditioning, so Mark poured cool drinks and showed Gil into his office.

Mark looked down at his hands, at the glass in them. What happened in this conversation could change everything. Probably *would* change everything.

'Gil, I need to ask you about the accident, with Paula.' The event that tied them together. Eighteen years, half a lifetime ago for them, but not for Paula Barrett, her vibrancy extinguished forever when the car smashed into the tree.

Gil stilled, wary, but Mark ploughed on. 'I've never regained my memory of it,' he explained. 'The medicos think I probably never will. It's just a black hole in my head. But the thing is . . . ever since the other month, when you were here, I've had dreams, quite often. Always the same – a bloody kangaroo glaring at me in the headlights, a horrendous crunch as we hit the tree.' He paused and took a mouthful of the cold drink, his throat tight. Then he looked Gil straight in the eye, determined to uncover the truth. 'The scene I see – it's always from the driver's seat. I was driving that night, wasn't I?'

Gil stood abruptly, walked to the window and gazed out. 'It's just a dream,' he said.

'I have to know for sure, Gil. I don't know if what I'm dreaming is a fragment of memory or just my imagination. I don't remember anything between my birthday the week before and waking up in the hospital. But seeing you again has triggered something in my head. The dream keeps coming again and again and again, and I need to know whether it's real or not.'

'Leave it, Mark.' Gil still didn't look at him, his back rigid, his low voice a rough warning.

A warning Mark ignored. He rose from his seat and pressed harder for an answer. 'Can you swear to me that you were driving, Gil? Can you do that?'

Gil finally turned to face him. 'It's ancient history, now. Just let it be.'

No denial. There would never be a denial. The truth was there in Gil's unwavering dark eyes and Mark felt the shift in his life, in what he understood about himself, almost as a physical sensation. 'Why?'

Gil didn't respond.

'Damn it, Gil, why?' Mark demanded. 'Why did you tell them it was you?'

Gil let out a slow breath, and the words came with it, tumbling out after years of silence. 'I didn't. The old sarge – Bill Franklin – was the first one there, and by then I'd got you out of the car and was doing what I could for Paula. I couldn't get to her through her door so I was kneeling in the driver's seat, and Franklin just assumed at first I'd been driving. Then Paula died at the scene and they didn't know if you'd make it, and everyone was angry, and although Franklin knew by then it was you, not me – well, I guess he figured it was better to blame the feral kid than the town favourite.'

It made sense; more sense than the lies told and maintained for years. 'But why didn't you say something?'

4

'I was just a kid, an outcast, and way out of my depth.' Gil grimaced, and for a moment Mark saw the shadow of the isolated youth in the hardened man. 'It was . . . made clear to me that I was to carry the blame. And then the first night in the remand centre, the threat was delivered – comply, or Jeanie would suffer. I thought I had no choice. The days went by and you never said anything to contradict the story. No-one would have believed me without your back-up, and I couldn't risk anything happening to Jeanie.'

Jeanie Menotti – the one adult who'd given Gil a chance, employed him at her Truck Stop Café, demonstrated her belief in him. Whoever was behind the cover-up had threatened her to gain Gil's compliance. Mark clenched his fists tightly, the harshness of Gil's experience worse than he could have guessed. And all his fault.

'Gil, I wish I knew what to say. "Sorry" is nowhere near enough.'

'You don't need to say sorry or any other shit,' Gil said, hard and blunt. 'It's done and gone years ago, and you weren't involved. They stuffed up the rigging of evidence, and the conviction was quashed. I don't have a record. There's nothing to fix. There's no bloody *point* in bringing it up after all this time.'

No point? Gil had served three years in prison before being able to prove that the damning blood-alcohol report couldn't have been his blood.

'There is if it was my fault,' Mark said firmly, no doubt in his mind. 'Had I been drinking, Gil? Was I drunk?'

Gil ran a hand through his hair. 'You weren't drunk,' he said. 'I was hitching and you offered me a ride. I was only in the car ten minutes or so before the smash. Paula had a bottle of something, offered it around, but you didn't have any.'

'That doesn't mean I wasn't already over the limit.' It didn't mean that the blood-alcohol report wasn't *his*.

'I saw no sign of it. Look, Mark, the accident was just that, an accident, no-one's fault. Not yours or mine or Paula's or any bloody kangaroo's fault. So don't go being all high-minded and doing anything stupid.'

Stupid? No, he wasn't about to do anything stupid. But justice mattered, truth mattered, and it was his responsibility to clear Gil's name and make the truth known.

The black hole in his memory swirled, a chasm that might yet swallow his life.

ONE

Twenty-four hours on a plane followed by a hot, sleepless night, packing quickly in the early morning and almost nine hours on the road from Sydney to Dungirri, and still Jenn Barrett's brain grappled to make sense of yesterday's out-of-the-blue email and the phone message that played on a continual loop in her mind on the long drive.

'Jenn, it's Mark Strelitz. I hope you get this before you hear it on the news. I need to tell you . . . Gil Gillespie came back to town again last week and I finally had the chance to talk to him about the accident. I still have no memory of it because of the head injury, likely never will. But, Jenn – I was driving, not Gil. I have to set the record straight and make sure the investigation is reopened.'

Memories and emotions she'd long ago buried crawled out of their graves and whirled around the stunning fact of Mark's revelation: *he* had been driving when her cousin Paula was killed eighteen years ago. Mark, not Gil Gillespie.

Mark, whose friendship had been the one steady rock in her adolescence. Whose affection she'd eventually rejected. Who had been one of the reasons she'd caught the bus out of Dungirri at seventeen, the day after Paula's funeral.

So much for her vow, back then, never to return.

The gravel road wound through the last kilometre of the thick, dry, Dungirri scrub, and the old familiar tension coiled around her spine as she crossed the low wooden bridge over the creek and into the town.

A willy-willy stirred up dust and dead leaves and swirled across the road ahead of her. Dust and death. They still clung to Dungirri, the terminal illness of economic and social decay evident in boarded-up shop windows, long-empty houses and scarcely a soul in sight, the main street almost as dead as the cemetery she'd just passed.

Why the hell had she agreed to come back to this godforsaken hole?

Because of the desperation in her Uncle Jim's voice in his phone message last night, the pleading of her cousin Paul's email. Proud men, both of them, not the kind who could easily ask for help, but out of their depth with this sudden news and worried how Paula's father Mick would respond.

But Jenn hadn't come back just for their sakes. *She* needed to find out the truth behind Mark's unexpected confession. Unexpected and very public – at a brief lunch stop in a roadhouse somewhere along the way she'd seen the news of his press conference this morning blaring out from the TV – his shock resignation as an independent member of parliament, and the reopening of the police investigation at his request.

She gritted her teeth against a wave of nausea. Greasy takeaway food on top of jetlag, fatigue and stress hadn't been one of her better decisions.

'Get a grip,' she muttered. 'It's only bloody Dungirri. You can sort out this mess and then leave again.'

Approach it like a story. Use her skills as a journalist. Be objective, rational. Behave as if Paula hadn't been her cousin, sister, friend. As if Mark were just another politician with a convenient case of amnesia.

At the end of the block, a couple of cars were parked outside the Dungirri Hotel, a 'For Sale' sign attached to the upper veranda, and across the road, a sign advertising ice-cream stood on the path in front of the old general store.

Undecided about what to do or where to go first, she turned into the street beside the shop and parked in the shade of a tree. As she climbed out of the air-conditioned car, the dry December heat hit her, sucking moisture from her skin. Her legs and back stiff from hours of driving after a day in planes yesterday, she walked back to the corner to stretch her muscles.

Apart from slight movement in the leaves on the trees along the street, nothing stirred in the hot afternoon. A bulldozer parked across the road marked the recent demolition of Jeanie Menotti's Truck Stop Café, burned in a fire. A gaping hole in a once-familiar streetscape.

Old habits resurfaced but she refused to allow her gaze to linger on the dilapidated buildings of the Dungirri showground, or the grassed area of the overgrown show ring where she and her parents had once camped while visiting family. Where everything had changed in one terrifying, soul-ripping moment, condemning her to five years in her Uncle Mick's uncaring guardianship in Dungirri.

A crow rose above the showground, black against the bright sky, its harsh caw so desolate in the stillness that Jenn had to close her eyes against the wave of old grief.

Dust, desolation, death – that about summed up her memories of Dungirri.

Steeling herself against the temptation to simply turn around, walk back to her car and drive away, she eyed the hotel from across the street. Time hadn't been kind to it, and she would bet that the accommodation was basic. She could decide later if she would risk staying there, or head into the larger town of Birraga, sixty kilometres further west.

Right now she needed to bury her memories again, find her objectivity and focus on making some sense of this mess. Sitting in the car, she jotted on a notepad the facts as she knew them from her Uncle Jim's emails over the past few months and the news reports she'd seen. Fact one: Gil Gillespie's return to Dungirri almost three months ago. Fact two: Gillespie's revelations of connections between the Calabrian mafia Russo family from Sydney and the Flanagans, local shady business family and thugs led by wealthy businessman Dan and his sons. Drugs, blackmail, coercion – all the usual organised crime, and she'd seen more than enough of it, all the world over. Fact three: Her cousin Sean's involvement with the Flanagans and the Russos, and his assault on Gillespie, believing him responsible for their cousin Paula's long-ago death.

She paused with her pen on the page so long that the ink ran, forming a blot. There lay the crux of Jim's and Paul's concerns – how Mark's confession would impact on Paul's brother Sean, guilt-ridden and in prison, and on her Uncle Mick, Paula's father.

She didn't give a fraction of a damn about Mick, but the others – yes, maybe she did. Or maybe this was just personal, about her own needs, her own questions.

Fact four: Gillespie's return to the district from witness protection a week ago, Mark's meeting with him and subsequent public confession and resignation today, after informing the Barretts privately yesterday.

And in that line of her scrawled writing lay the focus of most of her questions and her journalist's scepticism. What the hell had gone on during that conversation between the two men? Exactly what had prompted Mark to throw away his career so abruptly?

She tossed her pen and notebook on to the passenger's seat and yanked the car door shut. The best place to find the truth was at the source. And the source, in this case, lived fifteen minutes beyond Dungirri.

She ignored the catch in her breathing and started the car. Ask questions, investigate, find the truth. She'd been preparing herself for this meeting all day, thrusting her fond, youthful memories of the boy she'd been half in love with firmly into the past; they were irrelevant now.

The three blocks of the town's main street disappeared into her rear-view mirror and the road ahead ran straight west into the flat, mostly cleared farmland towards Birraga. Only pockets of scrub and the eucalypts lining the road remained, the paddocks brown and withered in the summer sun.

All familiar, this road she'd travelled hundreds – probably thousands – of times. She battled the unsettling sense of being thrust back eighteen years in time by looking for the changes. The old O'Connell wool shed, flattened in a storm when she was a kid, had been replaced by a new steel machinery shed. The Dawsons had installed solar panels on the homestead roof. The property next door to them had new fences.

Small, incremental changes. Nothing that disturbed the shape of the land; the paddocks stretching for kilometres, the cone of Ghost Hill towering over the plains, the green smudge of trees in the distance marking the Birraga River, snaking its way across the country.

A kilometre or so before Ghost Hill she slowed, shifting down a gear, indicating for the turn-off even though there were no other cars around to notice.

As she made the turn on to the dirt road, a wave of nostalgia caught her unawares. The kurrajong trees still shaded the short row of mail boxes and the tilting corrugated-iron shelter where she'd waited, day after day, with Mark and Paula for the school bus into Birraga High. Despite all the frustrations and unhappiness of her youth and her Uncle Mick's resentful guardianship, she, Paula and Mark had shared good times and a strong friendship.

'A long time ago,' she murmured, steering her thoughts away from the past, concentrating instead on avoiding dust-filled potholes and the deep tyre ruts gouged in the last rain. Five kilometres along the track the gates of Marrayin Downs stood open, and she turned into the tree-lined driveway.

A dusty white ute was parked in the shade of an old red gum in the wide drive-circle across from the century-old homestead, and she pulled up behind it. Mark? His property manager? It was unlikely to be her Uncle Jim over here – he managed another Strelitz property just south of Dungirri. And her Uncle Mick probably hadn't stepped foot on the place since his dismissal had forced them to leave the manager's cottage nineteen years ago.

She spared a single glance towards the old cottage, half-hidden in its grove of trees. No vehicles, no signs of life. Turning her back on the house she'd once lived in – never a home – she straightened her shoulders and walked across the drive to the main homestead.

The deep shade of the vine-covered veranda created a refuge from the heat and her steps sounded on the timber boards with a mellow, half-forgotten resonance.

Long gone were the days when she would have simply called out and walked in through the front door. Instead, she pressed the doorbell, heard its chimes echo in the house. Heard, too, footsteps inside. The silhouetted figure she glimpsed through the leadlight window beside the door hurried – but not towards her, the back door slamming seconds later.

Strange. Definitely strange. The figure was stockier than Mark. Although she hadn't seen him in person for eighteen years, she'd seen him often enough on the TV news, and he'd maintained his lean fitness. Perhaps it was the manager or a housekeeper. A ten-thousand-hectare grazing property needed staff to run it. Or perhaps a lover or friend – she had no idea of Mark's current domestic arrangements. A few women had been linked to him over the years, by his side at formal functions. One of them might have caught his heart.

She pressed the doorbell again, heard it echo through the house. No response. Uncertainty tightened the tension in her spine and she glanced again at her watch – it was after six o'clock. According to Mark's office manager in Canberra, he'd left straight after this morning's media conference. Unless he'd stopped on the way, he should be home by now.

Huffing in frustration, she followed the veranda around to the back of the house. The east wing was new since her day, as were the French doors opening off the eat-in kitchen on to a large, multi-level terrace tiered down the slight hill. She quickened her steps, the low sunlight glinting on the jagged glass in the doorframes. Smashed glass, open doors, a man who'd run away on her arrival . . . her senses snapped to alert.

Nothing moved among the outbuildings beside the house that she could see. In the few minutes she'd waited on the veranda, he'd disappeared.

She hesitated, considering her options. Find the manager? She assumed there was one, but he could be anywhere, mustering, fencing, checking dams. Phone the police? She was three steps towards the kitchen phone when she caught the first whiff of smoke, and she whirled around, scanning the view for grassfire in the paddocks, or bushfire in the distance. Either could be deadly in the dry summer heat.

The second whiff of smoke drifted from behind her, from the house, and a fire alarm suddenly began to beep, high pitched and loud. Underneath that sound a car engine roared to life somewhere – possibly down by the old wool shed.

Her sandals crunched on the broken glass on the kitchen floor. She could see the smoke now, thickening in the passageway behind the main rooms of the homestead, the light starting to flicker with a garish glow when she turned into the passage that led to the office.

The door was open, the room a mess, burning papers were scattered on the desk and floor, fire already eating the desk chair, the armchairs, and climbing the curtains.

And on the floor behind the desk she could see two feet, clad in dusty leather boots, lying motionless, close to the flames.

&

Nearing the end of the long drive from Canberra, Mark skirted around the edge of Dungirri, dodging the main street, turning back on to the Birraga road a kilometre from town. He didn't intend to avoid Dungirri for long, but he planned to go home, shower and change, check his messages for anything he couldn't ignore and then head back to face the Friday-night crowd at the pub. There were usually a fair few people there; tonight, with the announcement of his resignation, he expected the pub to be crowded with people talking about it. About him.

Better to face them today, rather than later. His electorate covered a huge area of outback New South Wales, including larger towns such as Birraga and Jerran Creek, but in Dungirri they'd known him all his life. And they'd known and mourned Paula. If there was anger and a sense of betrayal, it would be strongest here.

Beyond Dungirri, out of the scrub, the road stretched flat and mostly straight ahead, the late-afternoon sun strong between the flickering shadows of the eucalypts along the road. He passed the rough track that led to the old Gillespie place a few kilometres from town. Somewhere along this section of the Dungirri-to-Birraga road he'd picked up Gil Gillespie one evening eighteen years ago. There was nothing in his memory to tell him where and why. Nothing but the gaping hole caused by the head injury he received in the accident, permanently erasing several days from his short-term memory. Days he would never recover. And while he'd been unconscious in hospital, Gil had been threatened and subsequently confessed to being the driver of the car.

Ghost Hill rose out of the flat plains, still some distance ahead. No matter where he travelled, that first sight of the hill beckoned him home.

Yet today the view of the hill seemed hazy, despite the clear afternoon air. Perhaps his eyes were just tired . . . He blinked a few times to refocus them, and scanned the landscape as he drove. Yes, definitely a grey, smoky haze. Worrying, in this summer heat. But from where?

Coming over a slight rise, he located the faint plume of smoke on the horizon – and he instantly pressed harder on the accelerator. If it wasn't on Marrayin Downs, it was close to it. He turned on the UHF radio and switched it to the emergency channel.

'. . . *Seven-four-one-five on Dungirri One Alpha. We're responding. ETA seventeen minutes.*'

Seven-four-one-five. As a volunteer with the Rural Fire Service he knew every one of the local IDs. Even if he hadn't recognised Paul Barrett's voice, he would have known it was the captain of the Dungirri brigade.

Another voice reported in: *'Firecom, Birraga Two Alpha responding. ETA Marrayin thirty minutes.'*

Marrayin. His property. And the Dungirri tanker was at least fifteen minutes away.

This time Mark floored the accelerator.

From the main road he couldn't pinpoint the location of the fire. The trees at the corner of the road obscured the view, but as he sped down the dirt track the glimpses across the landscape gradually revealed the worst: not the paddocks, not the wool shed or the shearers' quarters, not the machinery sheds, but the homestead itself. His home.

Smoke spilled from the house, flowing across the driveway and garden. A few metres along the veranda from the main entrance, flames blazed out from the French doors of his office, the doorframe, the veranda and the roof above it well ablaze. The old, dry timber in parts of the house would burn quickly and easily – and spread if it was not controlled rapidly.

He drove around the side of the house, straight down to the shed that held the fire trailer, permanently ready with a tank of water and a pump, and swung his vehicle around to reverse in. Focused on his objective, he didn't see the woman running from the house until she was almost at the shed.

Recognition hit hard. Jenn Barrett.

Jenn, *here*, with no warning; no chance to prepare himself for this first meeting in years, no way to know her thoughts, and no time to find out.

Jenn, with dishevelled hair and dark soot smeared across her face and her light shirt.

He caught her by the arms and she gripped him, her breathing raspy, urgent but not panicked. 'Mark! Jim's inside, hurt. I've moved him out of the office, but I can't—' She caught sight of the fire extinguisher on the shed wall and left his hold to unhook it from the brace, continuing over her shoulder, 'He collapsed again and I couldn't move him. We have to get him out.'

Jim Barrett. Inside the burning house. All the other questions spinning in his head had to wait. Even Jenn, with smoke-scented hair, a red burn on the hand that had rested briefly on his arm and the thousand tangled emotions between them, would have to wait. He yanked open the back of his vehicle and grabbed his RFS kit bag. 'Where is he?'

'The living room.'

He took the extinguisher from her and set off at a run but she kept pace beside him, explaining in between gasps, 'I closed the doors but that won't last long. The fire's taken hold. The kitchen extinguisher wasn't enough.'

The broken glass of the kitchen door partially answered one question, but smoke had spread in the room beyond it and the enclosed back veranda, leaving no time for details. The light breeze might keep the fire to the front of the house, but there was no guarantee of that.

Adrenaline pumped in his veins and fifteen years of training and experience with the volunteer RFS kicked in. 'Stay outside,' he said, grabbing the fire blanket and his protective jacket and hat out of his bag.

She *hrmphed* – so many years since he'd heard that particular intonation of stubborn disagreement. He knew she would follow him in. No point wasting precious time trying to argue with her. Yet. He handed her the jacket and hat. 'On. Now.'

The solid doors and mud-brick walls of the original four-room homestead separated the living room from the first addition, providing some protection from the blaze in the office. Some, but not total. As they dodged around the oak table in the dining room, Mark could hear over the din of the alarm an ominous crackling in the roof cavity, and saw the plaster work in the corner of the ceiling start to smoulder.

They had a minute or two, maybe less, to find Jim and get him out.

The knob of the living-room door was still cool to the touch, but nevertheless he opened it warily, holding Jenn back with one arm lest she dash straight in. The smoke was thicker in the room but he could see Jim sprawled on the thick rug, motionless, a cream damask cushion underneath his head dark with blood, a large patch of the sleeve of his cotton shirt burned to blistered skin. At least, unconscious, he wouldn't feel the pain.

'I had to move him. We have to move him.' Jenn dropped to her knees beside her uncle, quickly checking his pulse.

Smoke trailed in around the door to the office wing, fire already charring the edges of the door and the cornices above. Mark gave it a blast with the fire extinguisher to slow it down, before checking through the doors to the veranda. The roof out there already burned. No safe exit that way.

He dropped the extinguisher and knelt next to Jim. 'We'll cover him with the fire blanket. I'll carry him. Can you support his head?'

Jenn nodded and slipped into position, ready to lift. Mark manoeuvred one arm under Jim's back, the other under his legs, murmuring, 'Sorry, mate, this is going to hurt.'

'Not much choice,' Jenn said, her mouth drawn in a grim line.

He nodded. They had to move him quickly – and hope they did no more damage. He looked at Jenn. 'One, two, *now*.'

Jim, over six feet and packed with the muscle of sixty years of physical labour, was heavy on Mark's shoulders as he carried him back through the dining room. Jenn used the extinguisher on the flames that licked and danced along the cornice. Both quickened their steps in the rapidly intensifying heat, their focus on the exit.

Smoke smarted his eyes and scratched his throat. Jenn's eyes were red, and she tried to stifle a cough but she didn't stop or slow her pace. In the marginally clearer air in the kitchen they both drew deeper breaths. A dozen more steps and they were outside on the paved terrace, and Jenn coughed again and again.

Beyond the incessant beeping of the smoke alarm, sirens sounded in the distance as Mark exhaled a long breath. He nodded towards the table on the lower terrace, protected from the sun by shade sails above. 'We can put him there. He'll be safe for the moment till the RFS crew can help him.'

'I told triple-0 to send an ambulance, too,' Jenn said, still as level-headed and cool in a crisis as she'd always been.

They gently laid Jim on the wooden table, and Jenn immediately put her fingers to his neck to check his pulse again.

'He's not breathing.'

Hasty fingers tore at the buttons on Jim's shirt and for the first time, her voice caught with a note of panic. 'Damn it, he's *not breathing.*'

TWO

As Mark breathed into Jim's mouth and Jenn counted compressions, she tried to picture the bald head and androgynous features of a first-aid training manikin instead of her uncle's pale face and greying temples, but reality wouldn't budge.

Mark's head lifted and she pumped Jim's chest again. *One . . . two . . . three . . .* 'Come on, Jim. Breathe.'

Somewhere beyond the immediate focus of her attention, she was vaguely aware of a vehicle stopping nearby, of voices and doors slamming and the thud of running boots.

A firm hand gripped her shoulder and a male voice spoke beside her. 'Jim. Shit. How long has he been out?'

She didn't take her eyes from her uncle, and Mark didn't break from the CPR rhythm. 'Unconscious – longer than fifteen, twenty minutes,' she guessed. It felt like hours since she'd arrived, but it couldn't be. 'Not breathing – I'm not sure, a minute or two.'

Three more compressions. *One . . . two . . . three . . .* She felt the flutter in Jim's chest, heard the faint intake of breath.

The man moved her aside with gentle firmness, his fingers already taking Jim's pulse. 'We'll look after him. We'll need to defib, Beth.'

Beth? Jenn glanced up. Beth Fletcher. It had to be. In the orange jacket of the State Emergency Service. No longer the quiet, reserved schoolgirl that Jenn remembered. The girl Jenn had thought back then would end up marrying Mark. But Ryan Wilson's ring glinted on her finger as she readied the defibrillator with quick, expert movements.

Beth gave her a quick smile of recognition. 'Hi, Jenn. Stand clear, everyone.'

Jenn took a couple of paces back and found herself standing beside Mark.

'Beth and Karl are trained as Community First Responders,' Mark said in a low voice, while they watched them work on Jim. 'For Dungirri incidents, they can be on the scene quicker than the ambulance from Birraga.'

Jenn nodded, not trusting herself to speak. They applied the charge to Jim's chest, and a few moments afterwards Karl gave a quick thumbs-up. She closed her eyes and breathed in deeply. He'd be okay. He had to be okay.

They heard another emergency vehicle arrive, switching off its siren before it reached the house.

Mark rested a hand on Jenn's shoulder for a brief moment. 'That'll be the RFS. I'll get the trailer and join them.'

Beth and her colleague bent over Jim, giving him oxygen, bracing his neck, brisk, professional and calm.

'They don't need me here,' she said. 'I'll help you with the trailer.'

She guided him as he reversed his LandCruiser back to the trailer tow hook, then helped him lift and nudge the trailer across to fit over the tow ball. With fire consuming the house they slipped straight back into old rhythms of working together, as if no time had passed, as if there was no awkwardness hanging between them.

As he squatted to plug in the electric cable, he finally glanced up and asked, 'Do you know how Jim was hurt? How the fire started?'

'There was someone else here. They went out the back when I rang the doorbell. I heard a car somewhere beyond the shed, then I smelled the smoke and found Jim in your office. At first I thought . . . I thought it was you.' She didn't know why she'd said that, and she swallowed again, her mouth dry from the smoke and the fear and all the reactions she had yet to process.

She couldn't see his face as he quickly pulled on the protective clothing from his kit and the jacket she gave back to him. 'Jim's fit and strong, Jenn. He's not going to give up easily. Can you stay with him? And get Beth to look after your hand.'

'I'll come and help.'

He paused for an instant, with his hand on the driver's door, looking at her. 'Not without proper protective gear and training, you can't. Stay where it's safe, Jenn. This isn't your place.'

This isn't your place. As he started the vehicle and slowly pulled the trailer out of the shed, her overcrowded thoughts noted the words. He'd meant them as protection, not exclusion, but they were truthful. Marrayin had never been, would never be, her place. She'd only ever wanted to leave. But it *was* his place, the homestead and the landscape, the community that even back then he'd dedicated himself to serve. Wound through his identity, essential to his spirit.

Right now the best thing she could do for her uncle was to keep out of Beth and her colleague's way. And Mark was right – she wasn't dressed for fire-fighting. The burn on her hand smarted, as did the one on her foot where the straps of her sandals had been no barrier to the heat of burning paper in the office. She had boots in her car, but that was too close to the fire and might be lost.

What Mark would lose, however, dwarfed to insignificance the potential loss of her car and a few clothes. She walked around the side of the house, standing well back and out of the worst of the smoke to assess the situation. The single-storey homestead was large, but the fire seemed contained within a few rooms of the original central structure and around the office, and the RFS crew concentrated their efforts there. So far, the long wings on either side were unaffected. She hoped the doors she'd closed as she'd retreated from the fire had slowed the fire's spread.

She ducked back in through the kitchen to the family room beyond it. The smoke wasn't too thick here yet, but the low sunlight from the western window highlighted the haze, with small particles floating in the sun's rays.

The pine cabinet she remembered stood in the same place, with its eclectic mix of family treasures. It held nothing of monetary value: a worn, patched teddy bear; a scratched and dented flute; a linen tablecloth embroidered by Mark's grandmother – pieces of family history that insurance could never replace.

As she opened the cabinet door the house shuddered with a rumble; part of the structure collapsed, showering her with dust and shattering several of the window panes.

It took just ten, fifteen, twenty seconds to lay a few things on the tablecloth and draw the corners together in a bundle. A crackling growl crawled along the ceiling above her – the force of the collapse must have blasted fire through the roof cavity. No more time. She ran for the external door, her eyes watering heavily, and barrelled into a yellow-coated fireman, a wall of muscle.

He swore and gripped a hand around her arm.

'I'm okay,' she said, but he kept hold of her arm, through the door and into the fresher air outside away from the house.

She dragged a hand across her eyes to relieve the stinging, and focused on the fireman to see her cousin Paul's face, framed by the protective helmet. Tall and straight and serious, the image of the war-hero grandfather both he and Paula had been named after.

'Jenn! What the hell were you thinking, going in there?'

'There were three rooms between me and the fire.' That was what she'd been thinking, and it had seemed logical, a few minutes ago. Maybe smoke was addling her brain. Paul snorted and continued to walk briskly around to the terrace. 'Paul, your dad—'

'Mark just told me. Thanks for getting him out of there. But don't you dare go near the fire again, not for anything, you hear me?'

She might have reminded him she wasn't a kid anymore, but they'd reached the table where Jim lay, an oxygen mask on his face, and Paul's attention had switched to his father.

'He's breathing okay, Paul, and his heart-rate and blood pressure are stable,' Beth said. 'The ambulance will be here in a couple of minutes. Do you want to go in to Birraga with him?'

'I can't yet. Jenn, can you go with him? I'll come in as soon as I'm finished here.'

'I don't—' *I don't want to.* Jenn bit back the words and nodded. 'Yes. I can do that.' Her fingers closed around her car keys in her pocket, and she handed them to Paul. 'If my car is okay, could you bring in my bag? I'll need my wallet and my phone if possible.'

Paul nodded, giving his father's uninjured shoulder a brief squeeze before he turned away, stony-faced, back to his duties.

Jenn watched her uncle's chest rise and fall. Too many years since she'd seen him, and age and worry had greyed his hair, carved lines into his face. Barrett men didn't do emotion but Jim had always been kind to her in his own way. Unlike his brother and sister-in-law, who had scarcely given a damn about the orphan niece in their care.

She wasn't much good at emotion either – dealing with it or expressing it – but she reached out and gently clasped his rough, work-worn hand, avoiding the bruising that darkened his knuckles. 'Your boys still need you, Jim,' she murmured. 'So, don't you dare die, you hear me?'

∝

A jet of water hit the corrugated-iron roof in a roar of hissing steam, the sounds melding with the rumble of pumps and engines and the rolling thunder of the flames into a nightmare cacophony, drowning out all but the most immediate thoughts.

Sweltering in his fire-fighting gear, Mark targeted his hose at the burning rubble inside his office. Beams and twisted iron from the collapsed roof piled high on the remains of furniture and walls.

The RFS crews from Dungirri and Birraga aimed at the roof with their higher-pressure hoses, fighting to control the fire spreading through and consuming the old wooden beams. The entire original section of the homestead might be lost, maybe more. The knowledge drove them all – as did the forecast threat of westerly winds during the evening, and dry paddocks all around that a single ember could ignite.

Mark blasted water on to a sheet of corrugated iron to cool it before dragging it aside to reach the burning remains of bookshelves underneath it. He worked systematically: douse them; extinguish the flames and embers; tackle the next pile. The adrenaline pumping through his body and the years of training kept him moving, working in the cocoon of heat and smoke and noise. Beyond awareness of the fire, the other fire-fighters and the work they did right now, he didn't *think*.

He made himself *not* think of Jenn facing the fire, unprotected, with only a fire extinguisher. Nor of Jim, his friend, mentor, valued employee, lying so still.

In the remains of the formal living room, the antique dresser stood scorched amid the ceiling debris, the glass doors smashed, dented Royal Agricultural Show trophies and the charred remnants of champion ribbons strewn around. A century and a half of Marrayin history. Fifty years of Strelitz history. Gone up in flames.

Mark dragged his eyes away from the blackened awards. Fight the fire before anything else was lost. Questions, emotions and picking up the pieces had to wait.

When his tank of water ran dry he backed out of the house, coiling the hose as he went.

Paul Barrett, seemingly everywhere in his supervision of the fire crews, came to join him by the trailer. 'You going for a refill?'

Mark nodded.

'Birraga West brigade's almost here,' Paul said, always serious, never one to waste words. But the strain that had entered their friendship since their meeting yesterday showed in the stiffness of his body language. 'The breeze is picking up, so we'll probably get spotting. Can you move Jenn's car and then look after any spots? I'll send someone to help.'

The ambulance appeared from around the back and edged around the far side of the garage, its emergency lights flicking on as it headed away, along the driveway.

'They're taking Dad to Birraga,' Paul said gruffly. 'I don't know if we can save the house, but at least he's alive and stable.'

'Whatever he needs, just do it. I'll cover any extra expenses.' He'd manage it, somehow, even without the parliamentary salary that had kept Marrayin and the other properties going these past years.

Paul had no shortage of the Barrett stubbornness. 'We're not a bloody charity.'

Mark understood that it was pride talking, and grief, and anger. 'He's employed by Strelitz Pastoral, Paul, and covered by workers' comp, and he's also a valued friend.'

'And what if he did it?' Paul challenged. 'Lit the fire?'

Mark looked him squarely in the eye. 'I don't believe that any more than you do. Listen, I know all the Barretts have got good reason to be pissed off with me, but Jim is no arsonist. If he was, he'd do a damn sight better job of it than this.'

❧

Jenn hated hospitals. She especially hated Birraga hospital, and the hazy, shock-shadowed memories of a helpless child watching paramedics and nurses work frantically on her mother's bloodied body, the harrowing images of her father's death playing repeatedly in her mind, raw and inescapable.

An adult could deal with it, she told herself now. *She* could deal with it. Put those memories in their rightful time and place and keep her perspective on the present. But the redeveloped emergency department remained too small to escape the sights and sounds of loved ones being assessed, and the hard plastic chairs could never be comfortable.

With nothing to do but wait and keep the memories at bay, she itched for her phone, her laptop, even a notebook and pen to write down *this* story, the objective facts and events so she could de-personalise it, make sense of it all. *The home of former federal MP Mark Strelitz was today badly damaged in what is believed to be a deliberately lit fire. Property manager Jim Barrett, 65, of Dungirri, was injured and is in a stable condition in Birraga hospital. Detectives are . . .*

Here. The man asking for her at the nurses' station wore a plain white shirt and dark trousers, but the weapon on his hip marked him as police even before he approached and introduced himself.

'Jennifer Barrett? I'm Detective Sergeant Steve Fraser.' He gave her a firm handshake and a cop's assessing look. 'How's Jim doing?'

Jim – not *your uncle* or *Mr Barrett* or something similarly formal. Small towns, rural communities – she hoped he didn't only know Jim because of his youngest son's arrest and conviction. 'He's still unconscious. They're taking him to radiology for scans now.'

'Good. Can you spare a few minutes to tell me what happened?'

'Yes.' Anything had to be better than just sitting and waiting.

He ran a quick eye over the others in the emergency department – the kid with the broken arm and his father, the dizzy elderly lady and her daughter – and indicated the exit.

'There's a garden outside where it's quiet. Let's talk there.'

Close to the solstice, it wasn't yet dark, the light tinged with gold. Long shadows stretched across the grassed area between hospital buildings. The sweet scent of honeysuckle hovered in the air. Detective Fraser chose one of the outdoor tables, and although she would have placed him in his mid-thirties, with a toned and fit-looking body, he eased down on to the bench seat with a suggestion of weariness in his movements.

'So, Ms Barrett, I presume you're *the* Jennifer Barrett? International award-winning journalist?'

She inclined her head. 'Yes.'

She didn't ask how he knew. Not many people recognised her outside the frame of a TV screen, but Dungirri was a small town and some of the older folk probably still proudly claimed her as one of their own.

'Jim's spoken of you,' Fraser said. 'And sometimes I have time to watch the news. I guess you're here because of Mark's announcement?'

'I am. I have questions I want answered.'

An almost-grin cracked the hard lines of his face. 'You and me both,' he said dryly. 'So, take me through what happened today. What time did you arrive at Marrayin?'

He didn't make notes but he listened attentively while she recounted the events in order, facts only, clear and precise. A detective who referred to Mark by his first name might be a useful contact, so she would give him the information he needed now, freely and fully.

'You said you saw the intruder?' He interrupted her to clarify. 'Can you describe him?'

'I only saw a silhouette, blurred through the textured glass in the window. I had the impression of a man in a light-coloured top and darker trousers, but I can't give you more detail than that.'

'How long after you saw him did you enter the house?'

'Maybe three or four minutes. I went around the back to see if he or anyone else was there.'

When she described finding Jim, barely conscious, and dragging him away from the fire, the panic she'd suppressed at the time rose again and threatened her steadiness.

'Take your time,' the detective said, and she regained control by concentrating on him, on observing his body language and responses to assess how he interpreted what she told him. Usually she asked the questions; she knew the techniques, the tricks, the ways to draw a subject into saying what they didn't want to say.

Steve Fraser was cool and confident, and although he listened carefully he didn't necessarily believe her. He listened to find the holes in her story.

'You seem pretty familiar with the place,' he said, when she told him about remembering the fire extinguisher in the kitchen and using it to slow the fire.

He might be on first-name terms with some of the locals now, but he couldn't know all the history. 'When I was a teenager, my uncle worked on the property and we lived in one of the cottages. Paula and I were good friends with Mark. We used to spend a lot of time in the homestead.'

'The three of you were friends? But you didn't go into Birraga with them on the night of the accident?'

'No, I didn't.' Clear and truthful, and she could give him a legitimate reason why, even if she kept the real reason to herself. 'A friend of Paula's was playing in a band at the Royal Hotel and she wanted to see him. I wasn't eighteen, and anyway, I had other things to do.'

'Did you see them before they left?'

She recognised the real question: Did she know if Mark had been drinking? 'No.' Another truthful answer. 'I saw him about five o'clock that afternoon. But I was out when he came to pick up Paula around eight o'clock.' Out on purpose. Sitting by her mother's grave in the Dungirri cemetery, walking home afterwards in the last light of the long summer day.

'You lived with Mick and his wife?'

'Yes. They were my guardians after my parents died.'

Fraser grimaced in a show of silent sympathy. Clearly he knew Mick. 'Why Mick and not Jim?'

The explanation she'd been given, time and again, remained carved in her memory. 'A single father with two teenage sons was not considered a suitable placement for a twelve-year-old girl.'

'Was Mick as wrecked then as he is now?'

More sympathy, or a leading question to assess her and establish her history in the district? 'I haven't seen or spoken to him since I left Dungirri after Paula's funeral. I'd have described him then as a bitter non-achiever who blamed his lack of success on everyone and everything but his own weaknesses.'

Damn it, a little more emotion there than she'd intended to reveal. Yes, she was bitter, too. But she'd left it mostly behind her, hadn't let it hold her back from achieving her goals.

Fraser had to have noticed, but kept his expression bland. 'What about Mick's wife? I've not heard much about her.'

'Shotgun wedding, hopeless marriage,' Jenn answered without emotion. 'Doctor Russell had half the women in Dungirri doped to oblivion on anti-depressants, and Freda was one of them. Paula remembered her when she was younger, more together, but I only knew her as a vague, absent woman. She died some years ago.' Unmourned, as far as Jenn was concerned. She'd sent flowers to the funeral out of respect for Paula's memory. That was it. She shoved away the unexpected spike of old anger and pinned the detective with a firm gaze. 'I don't see how these questions are relevant to your current investigation, Detective.'

He shrugged off the rebuff. 'As a result of the new information Mark provided to the Police Commissioner yesterday, the investigation into your cousin's death has been reopened and

I'm preparing a brief for the Assistant Commissioner. Given Mark's public announcement this morning, I have to consider that the fire may be connected. So, everything is relevant.'

Especially the presence of two of Paula's relatives at the scene before witnesses arrived. Oh, yes, she could read him. The sympathy, the soft approach. He wanted her to slip up, to incriminate herself or Jim.

'My uncle has suffered a head injury, presumably inflicted by the man I saw. Jim's worked for the Strelitz family for many years. There is no way he would have lit that fire.'

Fraser lounged against the back of the bench. 'Sweetheart, I can't tell you how often I hear friends and family protest that so-and-so *couldn't* have committed a crime. Jim was there, he has motive, and he also has a history – he and his boys laid into Gil Gillespie when he first came back to town a few months ago.'

Oh, that very deliberate *sweetheart* annoyed her. Exactly as he intended. She unclenched her teeth and aimed to correct the record.

'I'm not sure what you're talking about, Detective. It was Sean and his mafia mates who assaulted Gillespie. Not Jim and Paul.'

He dismissed her objection with a shake of his head. 'You obviously aren't up to date with all the family news. Days before Sean's "mafia mates" got hold of Gillespie, your male relatives had an impromptu welcome-back party for him when they ran into him at the pub. Luckily for them, Gillespie refused to make a complaint.'

Jenn swallowed back her humiliation. 'If Jim had issues with Mark, he'd have it out with him face to face, as he apparently did with Gillespie, not inflict wanton destruction.'

'And what about you? You were there, and it could be said that you have motive, too.'

His goading words sparked her overload of stress and frustration into barely contained rage. 'Detective,' she said coldly, choosing her words with care, 'I'm an experienced journalist. In the same way that you most likely know how any number of corrupt actions *could* be taken, although you wouldn't take them yourself, I know exactly how the reputation of a man like Mark Strelitz could be dragged through the mud and left there, whether the police investigation finds him lily-white or not. So, believe me, if I wanted to destroy Mark, I'd choose a far more effective way than setting fire to his house.'

Before Fraser could answer, his phone beeped and a single glance at the screen wiped the smug grin from his face. With a quick apology he excused himself and moved away to take the call.

Jenn dropped her head into her hands at the table and fumed. That damned cocky, good-at-his-job detective had undermined her control with a few well-placed barbs. And she'd let him rile her and probably come across as a vindictive bitch, although she'd meant to stress the opposite. There *were* strategies she would never take. Not even if Mark proved to be a lying, manipulative bastard, responsible for Paula's death.

CS

The bright white lights of the hospital blurred Mark's vision after the half-hour drive in the darkness, his tired eyes gritty from smoke and his gut churning. Now the buzz of engines and pumps and voices in his ears had become machine beeps and the clattering of medical trolleys and the low urgent voices of the emergency department, dealing with someone in crisis.

The elderly woman sleeping on one bed, and the child with a wrist brace sitting up in another clearly weren't the crisis. It took him a moment to locate Jenn, standing by a wall, staring at a curtained-off cubicle, her arms wrapped tightly around herself and her face as white as the bandage on her hand.

Once, he would have simply taken her in his arms and hugged her. Now, he stopped two paces from her, with no idea how she would react to him away from the urgency and commotion of the fire.

'Jenn?'

Deep in her thoughts, she turned her head slowly. 'Mark.' She bit at her lip. 'He's deteriorating. Skull fractures. Major brain damage. Paul's . . .' She nodded towards the cubicle. 'Paul's saying . . .' Her face crumpled into grief, and she held her hand against her mouth to halt her pain from overflowing, unable to say the word.

Saying goodbye. A hard lump formed in his throat, his mouth dry and tasting of ashes. He reached a hand out to touch her arm, but Jenn flinched and turned away, struggling for composure.

The rejection tore at him even as he understood it. His own sorrow at her news added to the other losses twisting painfully in his chest, and he wanted to strike them away, pound out his frustration, shout a denial. Not Jim. Proud, hard-working, knowledgeable Jim. He should have retired soon, had years yet to play with his grandkids, see his youngest son reform and do him proud like his eldest. Not this.

One of the monitors in the cubicle began an insistent beep and the curtain billowed outwards as people moved within. Jenn took a hasty step forward, but then stopped as a woman said, 'He's arresting again. Get the crash cart.'

'Paul?' Another woman spoke gently.

'No. He wouldn't want it.' Mark almost didn't recognise Paul's voice, low, harsh, cracking. 'Let him go.'

Jenn's shoulders shook, and when Mark put his arms around her this time she turned into him, burying her face against his shoulder, sobs racking her body. She wasn't thinking, and he could have been anyone, just then, but they stayed that way while a solemn nurse slipped out from behind the curtain and someone switched off the beeping machine, and there was only silence except for Jenn's muffled sobs, and the gulping breaths of Paul, struggling not to cry.

THREE

In the staff kitchen Mark stirred a heaped teaspoon of sugar into each mug of coffee. Sugar for shock. Whether it was medically sound or an old wives' tale, he didn't care. They'd all had an emotionally and physically draining night, and weren't yet ready for the long drive home. The boost of caffeine and energy wouldn't hurt.

He carried the three mugs back to the small meeting room a nurse had shown them to. Just outside, Paul spoke on the phone with his wife Chloe, stoic and withdrawn, while inside the room Jenn wrote on a notepad she'd borrowed from the nurse.

Hadn't that always been the way she'd coped with challenges? Transform them into written words; order, arrange and analyse the events and the issues. Report objectively and thoroughly. Even in high school, that had been her trademark style – and her strategy to rationalise her emotions.

He'd seen her on television regularly, the familiar passion for her work enlivening the features she'd always thought plain beside Paula's prettiness. She still kept her chestnut hair long, caught back in a practical ponytail, and although she often wore basic make-up for the harsh eye of the camera, she wore none now. But plain? No, in his eyes she'd never been *plain*.

She barely looked up as he placed her mug on the table, but he could see the moisture on her cheeks, the tightly held damp tissue she still needed.

'The detective will need a statement,' she said, the flatness in her tone amplifying rather than belying her emotional turmoil.

'Steve sent a message a few minutes ago that he's on his way,' Mark told her. 'But the written statements can wait, Jenn. You can do it tomorrow, or whenever you're ready.'

'I need to do it now.'

He stood by the window, looking out on to the dimly lit garden between the hospital buildings. He mentally made lists of things to do, people to notify, the words and phrases to include in his witness statement – anything to avoid grappling with his own response to Jim's death.

Emotionally there'd been a great deal for one day: the media conference first thing this morning announcing his resignation, the reaction to it, the long drive home, the fire, Jim's injury and death . . . and Jenn, sitting at the table a metre from him, back in his life, bringing with her the unsettling strangeness of being so near and yet so distant from the one person who'd ever understood him completely.

Nostalgia for his long-gone youth? No, not just that. Their friendship had been close and deep. Despite the different paths they'd taken and all his life experiences since then, he sometimes missed that closeness.

But he'd travelled a long way from the idealism of his youth, and even if some of the girl he'd known remained in the successful, highly respected journalist, Paula's ghost and his role in her death stood between them now.

He heard the gentle clunk of her mug against the table, and the breathy intake, not quite controlled. 'I keep thinking I shouldn't have moved him,' she said, grief shadowing her blue–grey eyes. 'I knew he had a head injury. He shouldn't have been moved.'

Mark pulled out a chair opposite her and straddled it. *This* he had been over a hundred times already while making the coffee, rationally cataloguing every alternative, every what-if. But no other course of action had been possible. 'Jim didn't die because we moved him, Jenn. He died because someone bashed him on the head at least twice and broke his skull.'

'Paramedics couldn't have got to him in time,' Paul said from the doorway. 'I'm glad he wasn't left in that fire.'

So was Mark. There'd be plenty of nightmares, but at least Jenn would be spared additional gruesome images on top of the ones that might still haunt her.

Firm footsteps approached along the corridor, and Steve Fraser tapped on the door before entering. Uncharacteristically solemn, he expressed his condolences to Paul and Jenn briefly but with sincerity. No longer the cavalier, cocksure detective who'd first worked in the district two years ago, Steve's voluntary return after personal failure and his subsequent work had earned Mark's respect, despite his sometimes flippant manner.

Jenn accepted the condolence with a nod of acknowledgement, but as she laid the pen aside on the table and watched Steve, her lips pressed tightly together. Wary, or fighting for composure? Mark couldn't tell.

'I'm sure we all want to get to the bottom of what happened,' Steve said. 'I know this is a bad time, but I'd like to go over a few things with you all, if that's okay.'

Yes, Mark wanted to piece together the events, find the person responsible for Jim's death. None of the rest of it mattered, compared to that.

Paul and Jenn nodded mutely, and Steve dragged out a chair and sat down. 'The first thing I want to know is, why was Jim there? He doesn't normally work at Marrayin, does he?'

Not a line of enquiry Mark wanted Steve to waste time pursuing, and it could be easily dealt with. 'He works for Strelitz Pastoral. He manages the Gearys Flat property—' Damn. He should have said *managed*, past tense. With a twist of pain he continued, 'But the Marrayin manager left last month, so Jim's been keeping an eye on things there whenever I had to go away. He could have been there for any number of reasons – checking water or stock, dropping off mail or supplies. I've notified WorkCover,' he added. 'They're sending an investigator in the morning.'

At the end of the table, Paul broke his silence. 'He was resigning.'

'Resigning?' It shouldn't have surprised him; shouldn't have felt like another knife twisting in his chest. They'd parted cordially enough on Wednesday after Mark had told Jim the news, but even then he'd noticed the new strain tensing the previously comfortable friendship. If he'd been thinking more clearly, had less on his mind, he might have expected it.

'It's because of Sean,' Paul continued. 'He was already on suicide watch before Dad saw him yesterday. Guilt at what he did to Gillespie is eating him hard. Harder now he knows that Gillespie was innocent. Dad promised to stay in Wellington for a while, to be close to Sean. Help him get through his sentence.' His face haggard, Paul ran a hand through his hair. 'I guess I'll have to do that now.'

Mark rose and went to the window again, leaning on the sill and staring out into the darkness. He'd only thought to do the right thing. Clear Gil's name, have the investigation reopened, find out if he was responsible, and take whatever punishment was demanded of him. If he'd kept quiet, or handled it differently, Jim wouldn't have been at Marrayin today. And now the Barretts – all of them, Jim, Paul, Sean and Jenn – were paying the price of that decision.

α

Sean at risk of suicide? Jenn could hardly imagine the cheeky, irreverent cousin she remembered falling so deeply into depression. But then, she couldn't imagine him getting mixed up with organised crime and beating Gil Gillespie almost to death with a metal pipe, either, and yet he'd done that and more back in September. Jim's emails hadn't been full of detail, but from a cafe in Tashkent she'd looked up the court reports of the evidence and Sean's guilty plea at his committal hearing, the words distant and unreal, unconnected to her. Only Jim's diligent cards and notes every birthday and Christmas – not her own efforts – had kept the family connection alive after she'd left Dungirri behind her at seventeen.

And in the phone message she hadn't heard until her plane landed in Sydney last night, Jim had pleaded with her to come. Now there was only Paul and Sean – Sean suicidal in prison, and Paul overwhelmed with responsibility. Jenn shut her eyes against the light, swamped by the desperate desire to wake up, somewhere, anywhere else. Family . . . God, she didn't know how to do family.

Paul sat at the end of the table, holding his grief behind a face carved into stone, still wearing his grimy RFS T-shirt and fire-fighting trousers. Hard-working, dependable Paul. Their fearless Grandfather Barrett would have been proud of his namesake. Whereas she . . . she'd fought some hard battles in some of the world's hellholes using words as her weapons, but she'd chosen those battles. Not this one.

She owed it to Jim to try. She might be a failure at family but she had other skills, and unearthing the truth might help them all.

Would it help Mark? He stood by the window, tense and silent, his once-white business shirt discoloured by soot and sweat. The brown-haired, brown-eyed good looks of his teenage years had deepened in maturity, but the media images she'd seen over the years didn't capture the intense reality of his presence. The five o'clock shadow, dishevelled appearance, and the large, work-roughened hands emphasised his authenticity.

Authenticity? The word had sprung to mind, but did it still apply? The truth used to be important to him. The law used to be important to him. Truth, honour, compassion, conciliation, justice: the values that had defined him in his youth. Or so she'd once believed. She didn't know what she believed now – about his sudden confession, and the convenient amnesia – but although he'd lost his career today, his home, and a friend, evidence of his concern for others was there in the mug of coffee in her hands, in his quiet presence.

They'd all fallen silent, each deep in their own thoughts. Even the detective, who might simply be giving them space but who seemed almost as drained as the rest of them.

Paul pushed his chair back suddenly and stood. 'I can't stay here,' he said. 'I have to tell the kids about their grandpa, after I see Mick. And I've got to get to Wellington by the morning to tell Sean.'

Jenn almost offered to go with him but he was already walking towards the door on his way to his wife and family who knew him far better than she did. He paused with his hand on the doorframe, desolation in his eyes. 'Catch the bastard who murdered my father, Fraser.'

They all listened to the heavy tread of his fire-fighting boots take the thirty paces down the corridor to the exit.

Answers. They all needed answers, and she needed to *do* something, make some order of the jumbled thoughts in her head. Focus on the questions and establish the facts . . . and take the lead and prod the detective away from any more irrelevant questions about Jim.

'Detective, as I told you earlier, when I went into the office, there were papers on the floor and the desk and the filing cabinet drawers were open. It gave me the impression that the intruder had been searching for something.'

45

Fraser gave her a sharp look that said he read her tactic, but he took the prompt anyway. 'Did Jim say anything to you? Did he tell you that there was someone there and that he was attacked?'

'He was barely conscious. He only said a few words, and they were mumbled. But he did say "fight", and if you look at his hands you'll see some bruising on his knuckles. And I think you'll agree, Detective, that it's very difficult to hit oneself on the back of the head hard enough to do serious damage.'

Fraser conceded the point with a slight nod. 'Okay, let's assume for the moment that Jim confronted an intruder – the person you reported seeing leaving the house. Have you any idea what they might have been searching for, Mark? Were there valuables in the room? A safe, maybe?'

Mark turned slowly, considering the question. 'No, nothing valuable. There's no safe in there. And the computer equipment is nothing special – a few years old.'

And now it was just piles of molten plastic and metal. Jenn hoped he had a sound back-up system in place. 'What about files or documents?' she asked, tossing an unapologetic look at Fraser. 'Filing cabinets and paperwork wouldn't usually be the first place a thief looks for valuables. Are there any parliamentary papers or reports someone might want to get their hands on?'

'Not at the house. Confidential papers stay in Canberra, or are locked up in my office in Birraga. But there's been nothing sensitive lately.'

'What about—'

'Did you—' Jenn spoke at the same moment as Fraser,

continuing when he stopped, her train of thought running on an express line. 'Did you have anything relating to the accident?'

'Yes. A copy of the police file.'

Fraser forgot police etiquette and swore. 'How the hell did you get one so quickly? Archives told me two weeks.'

Mark shook his head. 'I've always had it. I requested it a month or so after the accident.'

'Why?' Jenn asked. It had never occurred to her back then to ask for the police report. Gil Gillespie was already in prison, having pleaded guilty to drink driving. There'd been nothing more to find out.

Mark wrapped both hands around his coffee mug, leaning back against the window with so much weariness in his face that she almost felt guilty asking questions. 'It was just after I got out of hospital. I couldn't remember anything. I hoped something in the report would prompt my memory, bring it back. But it never did.'

She dropped her gaze from his. If the amnesia was a lie, he was telling it convincingly. She wanted him to be telling the truth. Maybe he was.

'Please tell me,' Fraser said, 'that you have a back-up copy of that report somewhere safe.'

'Several electronic copies. With off-site back-ups. But Steve, I've been over it again, several times this past week. There's nothing in it that contradicts the official story.' He shifted his gaze to her. 'Jenn, if you know anything, anything at all, please tell Steve.'

'I don't. I've already told him that I didn't see you that evening, so I'm no help.' No help to anyone, Steve or Mark, in piecing together what had happened. She needed to get it all straight in her head, line up the facts. 'The report says Gillespie was driving? And drunk?'

Mark's legal education showed in the careful way he chose his words, as though he were on the stand in court. 'It states he was the driver, yes. And that he recorded a blood-alcohol reading of point one-four.'

'But there was some mix-up with the blood test, wasn't there?' she pushed, remembering the reasons for Gillespie's release from prison. Reasons she'd been angry about at the time. 'That's why his conviction was quashed after a couple of years. An error recording the time, wasn't it?'

'At the time the test was recorded as being taken here at the Birraga hospital, Gil was, according to the custody records, still in the Dungirri police cell, sixty kilometres away.'

Still those precise, factual words. Nothing she couldn't find out from public records. But all that precision highlighted what he hadn't said. He hadn't agreed that it was an error. If it wasn't an error . . . her sluggish brain processed that slowly. If it wasn't an error, someone had deliberately framed Gillespie.

Steve took advantage of her pause to reassert control of the conversation. 'Mark, you made a very public announcement this morning, and although you were circumspect in your comments to the media, I've read the statement that you sent to the Commissioner that details your concerns and the conversation with Gillespie. This afternoon someone *allegedly*—' Jenn caught the warning look he shot at her, 'broke into your office, went through papers and set fire to the place. Maybe they're unconnected, but in the absence of other evidence or explanations, I'm thinking not.' He paused and aimed a questioning tilt of the head at Mark. 'Who knows that you have the report?'

'I haven't spoken of it to anyone since I received it. But I presume some police and perhaps some others around at the time may have known I'd requested it.'

'*Perhaps some others?*' More subtext . . . and Fraser nodded and seemed to understand.

She didn't. Yet. 'The statement you sent to the Commissioner – can I see it?'

For a moment, she thought Mark would say yes. The instinct was there, a flicker in his brown eyes. But the moment passed and he shook his head. 'The matter's with the police now, Jenn. I made my public statement.'

Oh, that stung. Caution or distrust? Did he think she would race to publish it?

'Paula was like a sister to me,' she objected. *And you were my closest friend.* 'I have a right to know.'

Mark met her gaze but remained silent.

Fraser stood and broke the moment. 'I'll keep you informed of the investigation's progress, Ms Barrett, when I have the facts. Will you stay in Birraga tonight? Or would you like me to arrange a lift for you to Dungirri?'

Interview over. Smoothly, politely done, but she wouldn't get anything more from Steve Fraser tonight. If she'd been somebody other than Jennifer Barrett, journalist, maybe she would have. But in this circumstance her reputation worked against her, not for her. Fraser and Mark were toeing the professional, legal line, and neither of them would be easy to budge.

She would respect that if it didn't frustrate her so much.

But if Jim's death was connected even slightly to the long-ago accident she would keep pushing until she uncovered the full story. Just not right now. Not when she was so exhausted from the mix of jetlag, smoke inhalation, adrenaline letdown, shock and grief that she could scarcely think straight

She dragged a strand of hair away from her eyes, the movement giving a sharp, painful reminder of the damaged skin on her hand. Tomorrow. Tomorrow she would ask questions. In the meantime, she needed to arrange somewhere to stay for the night.

'I can drive you to Dungirri, if that's where you want to go,' Mark offered quietly. 'I brought your things from your car.'

Forty minutes in a car with Mark? Nothing about today had been easy, but she would rather drive with him than the detective or some night-duty constable allocated the task – and maybe she would be able to get a better sense of the man he'd become.

He watched her, waiting for her response, and she wondered if he thought she would reject his offer out of hand.

She nodded. 'Thank you. I planned on staying at the pub, assuming it's bearable. But I haven't booked.' She couldn't stay with Paul and Chloe, not unannounced, not tonight when Paul needed his wife and family and privacy to grieve.

'They'll have a room for you,' Mark said. 'It's nothing flash, but it's clean and well kept.' He made an attempt to smile, a ghostly shadow of his old grin that twisted in her heart. 'In other circumstances, I'd offer you a guest room at Marrayin, but I'm sure you've breathed enough smoke for tonight.'

'Yes. Thank you.' They were dancing around each other, being polite, and as he escorted her to his LandCruiser, controlled and distant and so unlike the easygoing friend of her youth, the unexpected sorrow of that loss hit her almost as hard as her uncle's death.

❧

The headlights illuminated the black ribbon of road ahead, a tunnel in the dark night. Beside him Jenn sat silently in the passenger seat, staring out the window away from him.

He didn't intrude on her grief with any attempt at small talk. Nothing he could say could ease such sorrow – hers or his. He steered his own thoughts away from the quagmire of feeling on to the solid ground of planning and practical needs. There would be plenty to deal with: the workers' compensation inspector, house-insurance assessor, arson investigators and safety inspectors as well as the police questions about both the fire and his confession. The days ahead would not be easy. And the media would have hold of the story by morning, relishing another dramatic turn to the news of his resignation.

The road began a zigzag around some old property boundaries and the headlights shone on a large old gum tree, dead branches stark against the black sky.

'It was there, wasn't it?' Jenn broke the silence as he shifted down a gear to negotiate the next curve.

'So I was told.' On his release from hospital he'd stopped there, seen the rut dug into the dirt by the wheels, the scar on the tree, the broken stump of the low branch that had speared through the windscreen.

'What I don't understand,' she said, turning to face him, 'is why Gillespie is making these accusations now about you being the driver, after eighteen years? And why you believe him?'

Mark kept his eyes on the road. 'He didn't make any accusations. I had to drag it from him. When he came back to town a few months ago it was the first time I'd seen him since the accident. He never said a word about it. But the information that came out then about the Flanagans and their mafia connections, about the corruption and coercion that's infested this district for years, got me thinking about the inconsistencies. It haunted me, Jenn, and I don't know if it's the shadow of a memory or just my subconscious at work, but I kept dreaming about swerving to avoid a kangaroo. When Gillespie walked out of witness protection a week ago and came back here, I confronted him about it.'

'What makes you think he's not lying? He gains from this, and you lose.'

'I believe him because it makes more sense than the official story.' He shifted back up a gear as the road straightened again, and the words to answer her question formed into logical sense. 'Jenn, I was barely eighteen years old and I'd had that car for less than a week. Paula was with me. What eighteen-year-old guy with a girl to impress lets someone else drive his new car? I know I tried to be a decent person, but I wasn't a bloody saint.'

'Do you really have no memory of it?'

Ghost Hill rose on their left and it might as well have been between them. *Do you really have no memory of it?* They'd asked him that repeatedly at the media conference this morning, suspicious, eager to find any hint of a lie.

He couldn't read her expression in the darkness. 'Are you asking as a journalist, or as an old friend?'

'Does it matter?' she countered. 'Are the answers different?'

'No, they're not different.' Her scepticism didn't surprise him. They hadn't spoken in eighteen years; he'd never had a chance to explain. She'd gone by the time he returned home from hospital, her only farewell a note in a 'Get Well' card. 'I don't remember any of it,' he said. 'The accident and the few days before it are gone. The doctors said that they weren't laid down in my long-term memory, so I'll never get them back. I don't remember my eighteenth birthday. I don't remember—' He risked a quick glance away from the road to make eye contact with her and made his second confession for the day. 'Jenn, I don't remember getting together with Paula, although everyone tells me we did. I don't understand how or why, because although I was always fond of Paula, what I do remember is you and me. I know we were young, but our friendship was important to me then and if I hurt you, I'm truly sorry.'

She didn't respond. The road stretched ahead into the night, the rear-vision mirror black. No, not much point in looking back, it was past and done with and there was only the narrow path to move forward on now, wherever it took him.

But he remembered the horror of that first day when he'd woken up in the hospital and overheard someone refer to the Barrett girl who'd died . . . and his guilt-ridden relief when he'd discovered that it had been Paula, not Jenn, in the car with him.

CR

He genuinely didn't remember. Either that, or he was an excellent actor and a bastard determined to manipulate her emotions. Maybe it would be easier to believe that, to be angry, than to face the truth that *she* had been the one who had hurt *him*. The emotional tumult of that last day with him hung in her memory, even if it was wiped from his. But few people made it through teenage years without at least one episode of romantic drama and heartbreak, so what did it really matter, now?

The scattered lights of Dungirri came into view as they topped a slight rise. A sight she'd come to loathe, that last year after her Uncle Mick had slacked off at Marrayin one too many times and they'd had to move into town. At Marrayin there'd been plenty of places to escape the manager's cottage, and Mark's parents hadn't minded her and Paula making use of the homestead family room and library to study. But in Dungirri there had been only the small weatherboard house in its untidy, overgrown yard and the constant sullen presence of her uncle and aunt.

If it hadn't meant leaving Paula alone to deal with Mick and Freda, Jenn would have left Dungirri long before she did. She'd stayed only because of her cousin, their plans to leave together as soon as Paula finished high school the goal that kept her going. That, and Mark's friendship and support. They'd been close . . . no wonder the story about him and Paula puzzled him. At least she could set him at ease about that.

'The thing with you and Paula . . . she wasn't your girlfriend. She was keen on a guy from another town, but one of the Dungirri boys was pestering her, almost stalking her. So, the two of you decided to pretend to be together to discourage him. That's all it was.'

He slowed as they reached the first scattered houses of the town. 'I'm glad I didn't hurt you. I sometimes wondered if that was why you never wrote, never phoned.'

She hesitated, seeking words to explain. 'Your future was based here, and that was everything you wanted. My future was elsewhere, and I was passionate about what I wanted to do, what I wanted to be. I still am. We were just kids, Mark, but we both understood that.' She forced lightness into her voice. 'So, no hearts broken. Not even fragile teenage ones.'

Lights blazed from the pub, and a dozen or more four-wheel drives and utes were parked in front of it and in the side street. Through the open doors of the front bar she could see that most of the tables and the bar area were full.

'Busy night,' she commented.

'Yes.' Mark swung the vehicle in to reverse park on the opposite side of the road. 'Plenty to talk about.'

His revelations this morning, and his resignation. The fire. Jim. Plenty of reasons for a small community to gather.

'I'll just grab my bags and go in the side door,' she said. 'There's no need for you to come in.'

'Yes, there is.'

Mark's response didn't surprise her. His political reputation for staying the course and mediating and negotiating through conflict took a kind of courage that he'd always had. Always accepting responsibility and never walking away from difficult situations.

He offered to carry her duffle bag but she slung it over her shoulder, her laptop bag in her other hand. 'Habit,' she said so that she didn't seem rude. 'Some of the places I travel, I like to keep my things close.'

Entering through the side door, she caught sight of a young woman cleaning up in the back bar, the chairs already on the tables. Mark went straight to the servery window off the front bar and caught the attention of the young Asian barman. Definitely someone new to town – other than Johnno Dawson's Filipina bride, there'd been no Asian people in Dungirri in her time.

Seeing Jenn and Mark in their grimy, ash-covered clothes, the barman raised a concerned eyebrow. 'Mark! We heard about the fire – are you okay?'

'I'm fine, thanks, Liam. Jenn needs a room, at least for tonight. Have you got one for her?'

'Sure.' Liam took a key from the drawer. 'Room two's upstairs on the left. It's the nicest one. You can fix up the bill in the morning, Ms . . .' He gave her the I'm-sure-I-recognise-you look she was gradually becoming more accustomed to. 'Ms Barrett, isn't it?'

'Yes. Thank you.' A shower, a bed, peace and quiet – she craved all of it.

'I'd better go in,' Mark said, his voice low, indicating the front bar, where the rumble of conversation was gradually slowing. 'They'll want to know about Jim. Do you want it known, yet?'

He was asking her permission – family permission – to tell them. Not that she had any right; that was Paul's role, not hers. But Paul wasn't here, and a bar full of locals who knew Jim far better than she did were waiting on news.

She nodded. 'Let's go tell them.'

She left her duffle bag in the hallway and walked into the main bar beside Mark. The chatter fell silent, and all eyes turned to face them.

She scanned the small crowd: maybe thirty, forty people. There were guys in RFS T-shirts – the crew who'd been first on the scene – and a couple of people in SES overalls, including the young man who'd worked with Beth on Jim. She knew the face, although in a much younger form. One of the Sauer boys; Karl, Mark had called him earlier. She'd babysat the Sauer kids a couple of times.

Other faces held that similar disconcerting familiarity of kids she'd known, now adults. And the older ones – yes, they'd aged, some more than others. George Pappas and Frank Williams now with white hair and the faces of old men.

And every face watched Mark, wary, with a hundred questions waiting to be asked. A few people nodded at Jenn, one or two with subdued smiles. She checked the room again for her Uncle Mick – no sign of him. Good. Maybe it was cowardly of her, but she was relieved Paul would be the one to tell him of his brother's death.

Frank Williams cleared his throat. 'Mark. I'm sorry about your place. Is there any news on Jim?'

She felt Mark's eyes on her, his hand light against her elbow. He'd do it for her if she couldn't. But some part of her wanted to take the responsibility, do Jim this small service and tell his friends.

Words. Just words, and there were a thousand phrases she could use.

'We've just come from the hospital,' she said, more steadily than she'd expected. 'It won't be announced officially until Sean and Mick are informed, but I'm sorry to tell you that Jim's injuries were too severe. He . . . passed away a little while ago.'

Passed away. Stopped breathing. Died. Expired. Departed. She could think of a hundred synonyms and none of them came close to expressing the sense of desolation gradually engulfing her numbness. How could a man she hadn't seen in so long leave such an emptiness?

Murmurs of shock, denial and dismay rippled around the room. Frank squeezed his eyes shut, a brief battle for control evident in his features, but he succeeded, stepping forward and taking her hand between his.

'Jenny, I'm sorry for your loss. Jim was a good man, a good friend.'

The *Jenny* threatened her composure. She could almost hear Jim saying it, in his voice so like her memory of her father's. She hadn't been Jenny since she left Dungirri. But that was half a lifetime ago, and she wasn't going to fall to pieces in the front bar of the Dungirri pub.

Do the right things, say the right things. 'Thank you, Frank. He valued his mates. I know you will all miss him.'

'Has anyone told Mick yet?'

'Paul's telling him now,' she said.

'Tough on the lad. I'll head over there and see if he needs some support. Your Uncle Mick can be . . . unpredictable.'

A tactful way of saying 'prone to drunken rages'. Yes, she knew that.

Frank clasped her hand again, eyes brimming with earnest sympathy. 'If there's anything we can do, Jenny, anything at all for you or Jim's lads, you just ask.' He turned to Mark. 'And you too, Mark. When the police are done and you start to clean up out there, you give us a hoy. I'm sure there'll be plenty of people who'll be happy to come out and help.'

A significant public statement of faith and friendship, and Jenn watched the response of those gathered. Some nodded, others were less approving. It seemed to touch Mark, his voice catching as he shook the man's hand with quiet dignity.

'Thank you, Frank. I appreciate the offer.'

Johnno Dawson shoved away from the bar, beer schooner waving unsteadily in his hand as he lurched across the room. 'Yeah well, that depends. What the fuck's the story, Strelitz? Have you always been a lying prick, or is that bastard Gillespie blackmailing you?'

The tension thickened the air, and no-one moved, no-one spoke. Except Mark. He took a single step forward, his unwavering gaze on Johnno. Firm, not aggressive, his words clear and deliberate.

'No, Johnno. Gil's not blackmailing me.'

The screen door thwacked behind her, and a man in black leathers stepped inside, lifting a motorbike helmet off his head. Gil Gillespie. Except for the absence of insignia or tattoos, he carried the hard air of the roughest biker. Most of her contemporaries had steered clear of him as teenagers, although she'd always suspected that his bad reputation exceeded reality. But still not a man she'd ever want to have as an enemy.

He threw Johnno a brief, withering look. 'Oh, shut it, Dawson. I'm not frigging blackmailing Mark.' He tossed a nod to the watching crowd. 'Mark's telling the truth. Although he's a bloody idiot for saying anything at all. It's in the past. I told him there's no point bringing it all up again.'

The two men faced each other, equal in height, Gillespie slightly broader in build than Mark's lean, muscular frame. Their similarities and contrasts struck her: same age, different backgrounds, different personalities, yet both with an unshakeable strength – acquired by one through years of adversity, the other from an inner core of integrity and emotional intelligence.

'The point,' Mark said, with the formidable calmness of certainty, 'is that you went to prison for a crime you didn't commit. That needs to be set right.'

Gillespie gave a shrug. 'The way I see it, there was no crime, and that's what I told Fraser today.'

No crime? Jenn stepped in front of him as he started towards the bar. 'My cousin died that night, Gillespie.'

Too late to rephrase her words, she remembered that this was the man Sean had almost killed. She saw recognition in his face and his dark eyes considered her coolly. Yet he spoke politely enough. 'Sometimes accidents happen. A swerve to avoid a 'roo, a blown-out tyre – it's happened to all of us. Believe me, Jenn Barrett, I'm more than sorry about Paula. But her death – I doubt that was a crime. It was what happened afterwards that was the crime.'

He walked around her, conversation finished, and all those who'd been watching fell back a step, clearing his path to the bar. He went behind it without hesitation, saying to the barman as he passed through to the kitchen, 'You got those figures for me, Liam?'

She had no clue why that prompted a whole new round of whispers and hushed discussion, and she didn't bother trying to figure it out, but at least attention drifted away from her and Mark. A headache pounded alongside a million conflicting thoughts, the room suddenly hot and stuffy, and a whiff of smoke from her own clothes made nausea rise.

'Are you okay?' she heard Mark ask as the room wavered in front of her eyes. 'Can I get you something?'

'No. Thanks. I'm just going to . . .' She could scarcely form a coherent sentence. Go upstairs. Wash. Sleep. Maybe even cry. Not necessarily in that order. 'I'll phone you. Tomorrow.'

It was what happened afterwards that was the crime.

Tomorrow. Tomorrow she would find out what Gillespie meant, and what Mark and Fraser had alluded to earlier. She would demand answers from them. Answers about the old crime and the new – Paula's death, and Jim's.

The homestead lay dark in the moonlight. Jagged remains of the roof speared into the midnight skyline around the two original chimneys, still standing. Tomorrow, after the arson investigator and insurance assessor had been, he'd check what might be salvageable. But tonight the house was out of bounds, surrounded by police tape.

The empty manager's cottage, over in a grove of trees a hundred metres from the main house, would have to be his residence until the homestead was habitable again – if it ever was.

Unable to settle, he set to work, selecting basic camping gear from the storage shelves in the garage. A camping lantern provided good light in the machinery shed while he checked over the generator. With the power line to all the outbuildings and the cottage running off the main house, he'd be reliant on the generator for days, maybe longer.

When he'd loaded it on to the back of the farm ute he went in search of some rope to tie it down for the short trip – and noticed for the first time, on one of the benches, a cloth-wrapped bundle.

The knitted lace edging on the tablecloth – yes, he knew what it was. But how the hell had it got here?

He cleaned the grease off his hands with some metho and rinsed them at the water tank before he undid the loose knot in the vintage fabric and opened it out on the seat of his car.

A lump formed in his throat as he lifted out each item. His grandfather Josef's flute, salvaged from the wreckage of his family home in Poland, bombed in 1939. A teddy bear, pieced from scraps of sheepskin by his grandmother in a displaced-person's camp after the war. A photograph of the two of them, teenage sweethearts reunited in a migrant camp in Sydney. Josef's war medals, the tablecloth itself, embroidered with the delicate flowers of the old country during the voyage to the new country, and the necklace of black opal he'd made his wife from the first gems he'd found at Lightning Ridge.

Jenn. It must have been Jenn who found them, saved them. No-one else here would have understood their significance, but she'd known the story of each item, had even interviewed his grandfather for a piece she'd written for an essay competition.

He folded the cloth neatly and wrapped the treasures in a plastic bag, protected from dust and grease. His grandparents had created a new life with little more than these few belongings, their courage, determination and their love. His own trials today were insignificant beside theirs. He would find his way through, and as they had rebuilt the struggling property they'd purchased, he would rebuild Marrayin, with similar determination and hard work. But alone.

The grove of trees around the manager's house blocked the haunting sight of the homestead's altered outline, but there were more than enough poignant memories at the cottage. With thoughts of Jenn fresh in his mind as he unpacked the ute he could almost see her here, working at the desk by the window in the room she'd shared with Paula, or reading in an old armchair on the veranda.

Not much point remembering any of that. Jennifer Barrett had travelled a long, long way from Marrayin.

By the time the eastern sky began to lighten, he had the generator connected and running, and power to light the house and recharge his phone and laptop. Although he'd put a camping mattress and swag in a bedroom, he gave up any idea of sleeping and had a cold shower instead to wash away the ash and smoke. The day ahead would be busy, and before the investigators arrived he needed to go and feed Jim's dogs and bring them back here.

The sun edged over the top of the scrub as he drove into Dungirri, turning to the right a block before the pub, intending to take the causeway across the creek and the short cut to the

Gearys Flat property that Jim had managed for more than a decade.

But as he drove along the quiet, narrow street an elderly woman ran unsteadily out from the garden of a house, her pink floral dressing gown clutched around her, waving at him to stop.

Esther Russell, panicked and crying.

He caught her in his arms but she flailed at him, trying to grab his hands.

'It's Edward. Oh, Edward. You must help him. I just found him and I can't . . . please, you have to come. He can't be . . .'

Mark sprinted up the driveway. The Russells' house had once been the grandest in Dungirri, a Federation residence on a two-acre block, bordered by hedges. Now the once-extensive gardens were dead, dying or overgrown, with only a small area of lawn and garden beds in front of the house maintained.

Doctor Russell lay in his maroon dressing gown by a straggling rose bush, his walking stick a few metres away, the garden hose still dribbling water into a freshly weeded border.

Mark dropped to his knees beside him, felt his wrist for a pulse. Nothing. He reached to check again at the neck, and stopped. The old man's eyes stared blankly, his face lifeless above the twisted, torn collar of his pyjamas, with bloodied scratches and a rough red mark around his neck.

Not a heart attack or stroke or something one might expect in an elderly man. He'd been strangled by a garrotte. Murdered.

Mark stood up carefully, towering over the lifeless body of the doctor who had taken the blood sample in Birraga hospital after Paula's death and certified it as Gil Gillespie's blood – when Gil was sixty kilometres away locked in the Dungirri cell.

Edward Russell was dead, and so was any chance that he would finally reveal the truth of whose blood he had taken that night long ago, and why he'd lied about it.

FOUR

The couple in the room next to Jenn's were having a damned fine time. Unfortunately, their bed creaked and the bed frame thumped rhythmically against the thin wall. Jenn dragged the lumpy pillow over her head to shut out the noise and the daylight, and wished she was still asleep. Seven hours of stifling, restless sleep wasn't enough, and her body clock was still on Central Asia time, convinced it was the middle of the night.

Jim was dead. The knowledge kept hitting her, each time freshly painful, each pain the sharp pointer of a hard truth: she had never acknowledged, to him or to herself, how significant he'd been in her life. Too late now to finally understand and be grateful for his stable, quietly supportive presence throughout her years with Mick and Freda, even though he'd had two boys of his own to raise alone. Too late to remember that there had always been some small, meaningful gift for Christmas and her birthday; to remember the silent rock of his strength in the aftermath of Paula's death.

He'd found expressing emotion difficult, had never to her knowledge used the word 'love' . . . but Jim had done his damnedest to be *family*. And she'd repaid that real, selfless love by leaving, by scribbling short notes once or twice a year, by being too busy with important stories to heed his unspoken need for help when Sean had lost his soul and all sense and done the unthinkable.

Somewhere just outside the window, a kookaburra cackled maniacally, long and loud. It might as well have been cackling at her. She felt like shit, physically exhausted and aching; emotionally a writhing mess of sorrow, anger, regret, guilt and self-loathing.

And next door in room three they were still at it. *Thump, thump, thump.* Oh, yes, life always went on around sorrow, but she wasn't in the mood to feel happy for them. In room one on the other side, a mobile phone rang. And rang. Someone muttered a few swear words before it stopped.

Jenn groaned and reached for her own phone to check the time. Seven o'clock. No way now to get back to sleep. She tossed off the sheet and dragged herself upright. Whether she was ready or not, her day had started. Jim was dead, and she'd left it far too late to return the support he'd given her. But Paul . . . Paul had his own family, as well as the responsibility of Sean and Mick, and maybe it was past time she shouldered her share of that responsibility.

The thought of checking on Mick made her nauseous.

Bathroom. To the left around the veranda. Another shower might help rid her body of the memory of smoke and ash and refresh her mind enough to face the day. And Mick.

She pulled on jeans with the singlet she had slept in before venturing out through the French doors into the daylight and the view of anyone passing on the street. About as much privacy here as staying in a camping ground . . . or a refugee camp. She'd done the latter more than once for work, and intellectually she knew she had no cause at all to be grumpy about the comparative luxury of the Dungirri pub. But she indulged in the self-pity anyway, wishing for the privacy and comfort of four stars instead of the shared 1960s bathroom with its faded pink and black tiles.

Just outside the bathroom she heard a door slam below, and caught sight of a woman in police uniform running down the street. A police officer running? Her instincts kicked in, honed in places where a running police officer signified danger, and she leaned over the veranda rail to see where the woman ran. The road past the school; a short street with a dozen or so houses, leading to the dirt road that crossed the creek at the causeway. An SES vehicle came around the corner past the pub and took the same road as the policewoman.

Common sense told her that here, in Dungirri, it was probably something mundane, like a car getting bogged in the sand on the causeway. Not a bomb or a shooting or an insurgent strike. No danger, and nothing to do with her.

No excuse for avoiding Mick. Better do it before she chickened out entirely. She showered quickly and returned to her room to dress, heading downstairs within ten minutes.

In the back bar – called the bistro these days – self-serve breakfast ingredients were laid out on a long table: a selection of cereal, juice, fruit and bread alongside a toaster, coffee plungers, teapots and an urn. Whoever ran the place obviously believed in a reasonable quality of coffee.

It had been too long since she'd eaten a decent meal, and caffeine deprivation had already set in, but her stomach still roiled.

As she paused in the doorway, someone pounded down the stairs, two at a time. Gillespie, his phone to his ear. 'She's still at your place? Good. Keep her safe. I'm on my way.' As he passed Jenn and headed out the door, he added, 'Yeah, there's trouble.'

A motorbike roared to life moments later and sped off.

Jenn hesitated. A policewoman running, the SES who also doubled as paramedics, and 'trouble' involving Gillespie and someone close to him. Too much coincidence for fifteen minutes on a Saturday morning. And given Gillespie's connections to Paula and Mark, and the attack on Jim last night . . .

Breakfast had to wait. The bike had already disappeared from view, so she followed the direction the police officer had taken.

The SES vehicle, a police car and a ute blocked off the road outside Doctor Russell's house. The once-trimmed hedge around the large garden had grown high and wild, hardenbergia and honeysuckle threading rampantly through it, effectively hiding the grandest residence in Dungirri from view. Jenn had been inside that hedge just twice, both times sent away without stepping foot in the house. Although Barbara Russell had been a kind, quiet girl in the same year at school as Paula and Mark, Doc Russell did not permit his only daughter to mix outside school with her social inferiors, and Mrs Russell rarely defied her husband's wishes. According to the doctor's rigid social hierarchy, the Barretts were somewhere near the bottom, and even Mark didn't rate highly due to his Polish grandparents' refugee background. Barbara might as well have been the princess in the tower.

Jenn stopped across the road, where she could see in through the open gates along the driveway. The police officer she'd seen earlier was just outside the gate, speaking on her phone, but Jenn's attention zeroed in on a policeman straightening up from draping a blue plastic sheet over something on the ground. A body. It had to be a body. The doctor? Or Mrs Russell? The doctor must be well into his eighties and his wife some years younger – Barb had been a late baby – so maybe this was an entirely natural event.

But 'natural' didn't mesh with Gillespie's *Yeah, there's trouble,* nor his dash to keep someone safe.

She didn't notice the man in the shade of the trees at the corner until he moved into the sunlight and walked towards her.

Mark. Mark, on a Dungirri street first thing in the morning instead of at home at Marrayin. Another puzzle.

They met halfway, outside one of the more modest houses on the other side of the road. Mark must have been home since last night, because he'd changed and washed away the soot and grime, and shaved. But in his drawn face and the shadows under his eyes she didn't see much evidence of sleep or rest.

'Do you know who's . . . ?' she asked.

'It's the doc,' he said. 'I was on my way to look after Jim's dogs when Esther ran out on to the road. She'd just found him.'

'So, it was you who called the police?'

'Yes. That's Kristine Matthews, the local sergeant.'

Jenn could read the signs. A police sergeant, finishing one call, immediately making another. And the sergeant's offsider covering the body with a plastic sheet and tying crime-scene tape across the driveway. Both of them – and Mark as well – tight-lipped, with solemn faces and tense body language.

'It wasn't a natural death, was it?'

Mark's momentary pause told her the answer even before he said, 'No.'

Trouble. She couldn't yet see how or why the old doctor's death was significant, but the sunshine and twittering birds in the garden in front of them seemed out of place, a too-stark contrast to the grimness of the scene across the road.

'How—' She caught herself and didn't finish the pointless question. 'You're not going to tell me that, are you?'

His brown eyes looked straight into hers. 'No.' Direct, but there was no offence in that intense honesty. Of course he wouldn't tell her – a journalist – what he'd seen until after the police had decided which details to release. If then.

But he didn't move away, or offer any other comment. He just turned away from the road, rested his forearms on the fence-rail beside her, and waited.

Waited for her to ask a question he could answer.

Why would anyone want to kill Edward Russell? No, that would only invite conjecture. Besides, the doctor had been an arrogant, misogynistic, prejudiced old bastard. A general practice in Dungirri, rostered on call at Birraga hospital, one of only three doctors in the district back then. He might have retired now but . . .

Birraga hospital. Gil Gillespie. Trouble. A puzzle piece snapped into place.

'He signed the blood-alcohol report, didn't he? The one that convicted Gillespie.'

'Yes. That's on the public record.'

With nothing happening across the road, she also turned away from it, resting an elbow on the rail to face Mark.

'It's less than twenty-four hours since you held that media conference and already someone's burgled your place, Jim's dead, and now the man who certified that disputed report is dead. That's a lot of coincidences, Mark. In fact, it might lead one to suspect that someone is trying to tie up loose ends.'

Shadows crossed Mark's face as he considered his answer. 'I knew there was a possibility that the public announcement might send those behind the corruption running scared, but I wanted to make sure that Gil's name was cleared without doubt,' he said. 'I weighed it up, assessed the risks, made my decision, and made the announcement. Because if there were to be any repercussions, I expected them to be targeted at *me*.' His tightly clasped hands betrayed his tension but his voice remained even. 'I was wrong. Mrs Russell is grieving for her husband, and Jim . . . I'm so very, very sorry, Jenn, that he got caught up in this. You and Paul and Sean, Chloe and the kids – he's such a huge loss to you all.'

Some of his media critics had assumed that because of his self-control, his compassion was scripted, a mere performance. Others viewed his compassion and honesty as weaknesses. Jenn knew better – both about the boy he'd been, and the man she'd watched from a distance. She knew that he cared deeply about people and issues and put others' needs first. And that his outward control masked not an absence of genuine emotion, but his own deep feelings that he kept to himself, alone, private.

She knew that he grieved for Jim. 'You reminded me last night that moving Jim didn't kill him,' she said. 'Your announcement didn't kill him, either.'

'Not directly, no,' he conceded quietly, but the weight of responsibility still clouded his eyes. 'Although I can't help but think if I'd just gone to the police would things be different? I need to ensure that there's no more risk to anyone.'

She focused on him, putting aside the immediacy of her own jumbled emotions of the past day, and tried to consider the events from an objective perspective. 'Listen, Mark, I may have flung a thesaurus of swear words in your direction when I first received your messages, and questioned your sanity yesterday when you dropped your resignation bombshell so publicly, but thinking about it rationally, of course you did the right thing, the right way.'

She'd covered political scandals, criminal investigations, old crimes and corruption aplenty and was more than familiar with the hundreds of ways the truth could be obscured. 'We both know that if you'd done it quietly,' she continued, 'if you hadn't resigned, chances are the reopened investigation would have been swept under the carpet, bogged in bureaucracy or become a juicy media scandal muddying the facts. And all the while whoever's behind this would have heard about it anyway, and they'd still be cleaning up – but with a whole lot less police and public scrutiny.'

After a long moment of reflection on her words, Mark pushed up from the fence, stood straight, close in front of her, raising a hand as if to brush her cheek the way he'd done, so long ago. He dropped it, but he didn't drop their eye contact.

'Thank you, Jenn.'

Simple words, from a complex man. As she stood there, close to him, she remembered, understood now, why few people forgot an encounter with Mark. 'Personable', 'charming' – no, the words they often used didn't come anywhere near the truth. When Mark Strelitz looked at a person, he saw them. Not just eye contact, but a total focus and awareness, instinctively seeking the person beyond the face and words. Right now he saw *her*, Jenn, not the public persona but the girl she'd been and the woman she'd become. An intensity of connection that worked both ways – if she opened her eyes enough to see it.

He was a private person, but not secretive. It was all there, in his eyes, the depth and complexity, the compassion and integrity that defined him.

And he'd driven the car in which Paula had died.

The growl of a motorbike engine coming closer provided a welcome distraction from the uneasy jangle of her thoughts.

Despite the helmet she recognised Gillespie on the bike, with a young girl riding pillion behind him in T-shirt and leggings, a long dark ponytail hanging down her back. They stopped near the police sergeant, who hugged the girl and called over the constable to escort her around the side of the house and inside, avoiding the plastic-covered heap in the driveway.

But it was the sergeant and Gillespie who interested Jenn. She couldn't hear their words, but their body language spoke volumes. Unguarded concern on the sergeant's face, very little space between them, Gillespie's hand gentle on her shoulder.

Intimacy.

Gillespie at the pub, seven a.m. phone call, policewoman leaving hurriedly . . . it all added up. They'd been in room one, next to her.

'Gillespie and a *cop?*' she muttered in a low voice.

Mark folded his arms, unsurprised by the scene they'd just witnessed. 'Yes. Kris and Gil fell for each other pretty hard when he first came back to Dungirri, a few months ago.'

'But wasn't he caught up in the mafia?'

'Not through choice,' Mark said. 'And we've had our own tangled web of organised crime around here for a long time, Jenn. Gil might have walked a fine line sometimes through necessity, but it seems he stayed on the right side of the law.'

Unlike Sean, who'd fallen for the promises and the money and the power of corruption and committed acts she couldn't reconcile with the boy she'd known.

Maybe there was more to Gil Gillespie than she'd thought.

'Who's the girl?'

'Long story. The short version is, Barbara had a daughter, adopted out as a baby. Barb died of cancer a few years back, the adoptive parents died, and Megan is here with her grandparents.'

'And Gillespie?'

'Is her father,' he said calmly.

Jenn stared at him, searching for signs that he was joking. Gil Gillespie and the cop was hard enough to figure, but Gil and Barbara Russell . . .

'How the hell did *that* happen?'

For the first time since she'd been back, she saw a flicker of his old grin. 'The usual way, I presume,' he said. 'It seems Barb didn't share her father's prejudices. Two decent, lonely teenagers can find a lot in common, given the opportunity.'

A hazy memory re-emerged: a summer night, teenagers gathered at the swimming hole on Dungirri Creek for an impromptu party, and Barbara joining the crowd, a little upset, a little defiant, a little nervous. Someone said she'd argued with her father and walked out. She'd been just as much an outsider as Gillespie, and no-one quite knew how to treat her. Except, perhaps, Gillespie, who lived and worked cutting timber with his violent father a few kilometres from town, and rarely had the chance to mix with his peers.

Two lonely teenagers, something in common, and the opportunity . . . she remembered seeing them talking, sitting together on a log at the edge of the crowd. One night, one party – it had to have been then, because Gillespie was arrested the next night – and now there was a teenage girl.

Oh, there but for the grace of a functioning condom . . . She felt her cheeks suddenly heating. Damn it. Why the hell was she blushing over something so long ago, so natural and normal for the teenagers they'd been?

She slid a glance at Mark, but he watched the couple across the road, deep in his own thoughts, oblivious to the memories fresh in hers.

That long-ago afternoon, just after his eighteenth birthday, in the old shearers' quarters, the sweet, shy, gentle loving between them, and the heart-tearing sorrow that followed it when she told him she was determined to leave Dungirri soon . . .

He didn't remember anything about that week. None of it. That bittersweet afternoon was gone, wiped from his mind along with the memories of the accident and Paula's death.

cç

Two decent, single adults could find a lot in common, too. Not only sex. And in the case of Kris and Gil, Mark could see the strengthening of the deep physical and emotional attraction he'd witnessed develop between them during Gil's return to Dungirri back in September. Respect, friendship, intimacy, commitment, love – it was all there, in a lively match of temperament and personalities, of values and ideals. No wonder Gil had voluntarily left witness protection to return to town again last week.

All the more reason Mark needed to stand his ground and see Gil's name completely cleared. He owed it to Gil, and he owed it to Kris, one of his closest friends, to do what he could to enable their relationship to flourish.

He and Kris had never been lovers – never *wanted* to be lovers, either of them – but their friendship had sustained them through some of Dungirri's darkest times, since she had arrived in the district five years ago. He trusted her completely: as a police officer, as a community leader, as a friend. In the twenty or so minutes since she'd arrived on the scene at the Russells', she'd spoken sympathetically with Esther, handed her to the care of Beth and Karl from the SES, instructed her constable, Adam, and made calls and given orders. Other than conveying the basics of the situation, Mark hadn't talked with her. Some time he'd undoubtedly get a good-hearted blasting from her for making his public announcement without warning her first, but for now all her concern – and his – focused on the murder of the doctor and its implications.

Gil rode off, and Kris strode across the road to them, a frown narrowing her eyes. A frown directed at Jenn.

Mark made the introductions, although it was clear that Kris had already figured Jenn's identity.

'The police will release a media statement later this morning, Ms Barrett. Until then there will be no comment.'

Jenn matched every ounce of Kris's professional firmness. 'Sergeant, you needn't worry. I'm in Dungirri for personal reasons, and I'm just as invested in discovering the truth in this matter as you are. It's family business, not work, and I'm not at all interested in rushing to be first on the morning news with no more than a headline about a suspicious death.' She gave Kris a restrained but genuine smile, one capable professional woman to another, and then turned to Mark. 'When you're finished here, can you let me know? I'll need to get my car from your place.'

Of course she'd want her car. He mentally juggled timeframes and tasks. 'I'll have to wait for Steve Fraser, so I'll probably be here at least an hour yet, maybe longer. Then I still have to go out to Jim's place.'

'To feed the dogs?' She had never been one to stand around idle, so it didn't surprise him when she offered: 'I could do that, if you can lend me your car. I can probably still tell one end of a dog from the other.'

One problem solved. In the building heat of the morning, the likelihood of the dogs being out of water had become a major concern. Even if they refused to take food from a stranger, they'd at least have access to fresh water. She'd been around the station dogs enough in their youth, and Jim trained his working dogs well, so Mark didn't worry about how she'd handle them.

Mark passed the keys to his ute over to her without hesitation. 'Thanks, Jenn. The dog run is around the back and the feed's in a bin in the machinery shed.'

'I'll find it,' she said. 'I'll be back soon. Assuming they don't eat me.'

With a flash of her old, wry grin, she took the keys and headed over to his ute, practical and focused, and for a moment it was Jenn the teenage girl he saw, not the television journalist, and the summer heat on the breeze and the scent of dry grass brought a hundred memories of working together at Marrayin tumbling back.

As the ute did a U-turn and took the corner into Gearys Road, Kris shook her head. 'I'd heard she was Jim's niece, but I still can't quite get my brain around seeing Jennifer Barrett here in Dungirri. She lived here for a while, didn't she?'

'Yes,' Mark replied. 'At Marrayin for some years when Mick worked for my father, and then in town.'

'Does she know anything more? About what happened?'

'I don't think so. She was only seventeen at the time, Kris, and she and Paula were close. I left messages for her the other night, before the media conference. Like everyone else, she believed Gil was responsible for the accident.'

'Yeah.' Kris blew out a long breath, and leant against a tree. 'I heard about your resignation on the radio while I was driving to a suicide at Jerran Creek. I couldn't call Gil right then to find out what the hell was going on, but when he got back from

Sydney last night I extracted the details about the conversation you two had last week.'

Extracted. He'd have felt some sympathy for Gil if he didn't know that the man was more than capable of meeting Kris's assertiveness head-on and deflecting it.

But he needed to set matters straight. 'I'm sorry, Kris. I knew it would be a shock to you, but it seemed the best way to handle it.' He made an attempt at a grin, but it probably looked more like a grimace. 'I've challenged the government – both parties – often enough about honesty and accountability. I don't plan on being a hypocrite.'

'You've never been that.'

A simple statement, from a woman who didn't bullshit, and for a moment gratitude clogged his throat.

Her phone beeped and she glanced at the message, then tucked it back in her pocket. 'I can understand why Gil kept quiet, all these years,' she said. 'I don't necessarily approve, but I can understand his take on it – that to speak out would do more harm than good. Especially since you don't remember it, and few would trust his word over yours.'

Privilege. She spoke no more than the truth, but he hated how the world worked, how he'd benefited from an accident of birth when others – when Gil – had struggled against prejudice and injustice every step of the way. Mark had recovered from his injuries, gone on to university, made a life and a career for himself, while Gil had gone to prison, just a youth, alone and friendless in a violent environment. It shouldn't have happened that way, and it made a mockery out of the principles he'd tried to live his life by.

'The investigation was corrupt, Kris.' He couldn't keep the anger from his tone. 'Those involved in framing him have to answer for it – for threatening an eighteen-year-old youth and sending him to prison for something he didn't do.'

She nodded in agreement, and her gaze settled on the doctor's body, just visible in the driveway. 'Was he one of them, Mark?'

'I don't know.' And that was the honest truth. 'To all appearances he was an ethical man. A defender of moral decency.' He had a folder filled with letters from Doctor Russell in his office, demanding parliamentary action on a wide range of issues.

'But he certified a blood-alcohol sample as Gil's when it wasn't.'

'Yes.' Mark could see no grey between the black and white in this case, no greater good to be served that could defend the magnitude of the lie, and he couldn't fathom the doctor's reasons.

But he *had* done it, certified the form when Gil was sixty kilometres away – and the only other patient who Mark knew with certainty was at the hospital at the time was him. If the well-over-the-limit blood sample proved to be his, then criminal responsibility for Paula's death lay squarely with him.

❧

Driving down Gearys Road suited Jenn's restless mood better than waiting around, either outside the Russells' or back at the pub.

At Gearys Flat, a couple of kilometres from Dungirri, the 1930s homestead Jim had lived in was as well kept as Marrayin, except that instead of terraced gardens there was mown grass and a sturdy wooden swing set and a treehouse not unlike the one Jim had built for his boys when they were small.

Jenn had helped out mustering here a few times long before Jim became the manager, so she knew the place a little. The driveway, homestead, garage and assorted sheds to the rear of the house were all standard rural layout. As she drove around the back and parked near the large machinery shed, three border collies rushed at the fence of the dog run, barking.

Despite volunteering to do this, it had been a long time since she'd had anything to do with dogs, and somehow she had to get these ones to trust her. She walked slowly over to the fence, talking to them in an even voice, letting them watch her and take her measure while she took theirs. Three females of assorted ages. One grizzled around the jaw and thicker in the middle, but still the dominant dog. One quieter, holding back, wary. The third a half-grown puppy, all legs and bounce and excited barks.

The oldest and the youngest sniffed her hand through the wire and she spent a few more moments talking to them, light and easy, encouraging the timid one closer. Undoubtedly not the way Jim had talked to them, although he had always been a bit soft when it came to his dogs. Working dogs, yes, but mates, too. Unlike Mick, who'd treated his dogs more as barely tolerated slaves.

'How about I get you some food and water, hey? You hungry? Want some munchies?'

Three dog dishes stacked on top made locating the feed bin in the shed easy, and next to it sat a full sack of food with feeding guidelines on it. Not that she had any clue how much each dog weighed, but it gave her a rough idea. As she wasn't sure when they'd last been fed, or when Mark would be out again to collect them, she added extra. It surely wouldn't hurt.

She found a metal bucket upended on a post near the tank stand and filled it with water, the precious liquid noisy as it bubbled into the bucket. Just as well she'd come: the bowls in the run were empty, and the temperature was climbing. They were dependent on her, those innocent, trusting dogs. Not the kind of dependence she sought – her lifestyle was way too erratic to ever consider that kind of commitment – but today she could do this task for Jim, and take one weight from Mark's shoulders.

With feed bowls stacked in one hand and the water bucket in the other, she approached the gate to the run, the dogs running backwards and forwards along the fence. She had a vague memory of Jim feeding his dogs once – they would have been different ones, long-gone now – and giving them a command to sit and stay before allowing them to eat. With her hand on the gate latch, she tried telling them to sit, and with a second, firmer command, they did.

She felt as ridiculously pleased with herself as the puppy looked.

The puppy wasn't so good at the 'stay' part, jumping around her, but she managed to get the bowls down on the ground without spilling the dry food, and all three dogs began to wolf down their meals when she told them to eat. Innocent, trusting, and oblivious to death and murder. They would miss Jim when he didn't come home. The two older dogs looked up frequently, both keeping an eye on her, and looking for their pack leader.

She opened the gate into the larger, grassy part of the enclosure and spent a few minutes tossing well-chewed balls and a piece of knotted rope for the younger two dogs while the older one sat beside her, permitting a back scratch. She envied them the simplicity – eat, play, work, sleep. Not to mention free, no-obligation back rubs.

The dog suddenly tensed under her hand, and the other two stopped tugging at the rope, all ears turned towards the house.

She heard a car door slam. A neighbour? A visitor? Maybe Paul's wife, Chloe. Jenn rounded the dogs back into the smaller enclosure and latched the gate securely. As she headed towards the house, she saw someone in the kitchen. Definitely not Chloe.

Shit.

She reached for her phone, well aware she stood, fully visible, in the open yard.

The man crossed the kitchen in front of the window. Her Uncle Mick. Bitter and self-absorbed, he'd managed some affection for his daughter but never for Jenn. She'd avoided him as much as possible even when they lived in the same house, but now she had to confront him.

Shit. Shit. Shit.

She dropped her phone back into her pocket. Mick might well have reason to be at his brother's home. For all she knew, he might live here – although probably not, since Mark hadn't mentioned it.

She walked around to the front of the house, and found the door open, the lock jemmied with a crowbar. In the kitchen, he had half-filled a cooler with meat and other food from the fridge and was rummaging in the pantry cupboard, leaving discarded tins and packages strewn over the floor.

For all that he was a broken old man, her anger boiled over. 'For God's sake, Mick, he's been dead for less than twelve hours and you're here stealing his *food?*'

He barely glanced at her, but she saw recognition and contempt register in his bloodshot eyes. 'He doesn't fuckin' need it now, does he?'

His callousness about his own brother stunned her, and for a moment words failed her.

He yanked open another cupboard, and muttered, 'Yes.' Bottles – wine, spirits, a six-pack of beer, went into his cooler. He opened a bottle of Scotch with an inch or so in the bottom and took a swig.

She followed when he wandered out into the dining room, bottle in hand. Jim must have been in the midst of doing some accounts, for there were papers on the table, a chequebook and a laptop.

Mick unplugged the laptop and tucked it under his arm.

Food was one thing – he'd been right, Jim didn't need it now – but valuables were another thing entirely.

'Leave it, Mick,' she warned. 'That's for Paul to deal with it.'

'Get out of my way.'

'No.'

The smell of alcohol assaulted her nose as he approached but she stood her ground, one hand reaching for her phone, the other held out towards Mick. Her heartbeat thudded but she didn't let him see her rising anxiety. 'Take the food, but give me the laptop. It stays, Mick.'

'Don't you fuckin' tell me what to do, you little bitch.'

He shuffled forward and took another slug from the bottle, tipping it up to drain it but keeping his eyes on her. Hate-filled eyes, devoid of reason, just like the last time she'd faced him, and belatedly she realised that he'd positioned himself where he almost blocked her path to the door, the table inches to her right hemming her in. Stand her ground? Try to dodge around him? She didn't dare give him power by dropping her gaze to her phone; dialling triple-0 wouldn't do much good way out here, anyway.

He spat straight into her face. 'You should be dead. It should have been you, not her. You should have died with your goody-two-shoes fuckin' mother. My bloody brother Pete couldn't even get that fuckin' right. It's all your fuckin' fault.'

At seventeen, she'd almost believed him. At thirty-five, she knew the ravings of a mad alcoholic bastard, but still . . . still his barbs hit, derailed her concentration for an instant. First her parents, then Paula, then Jim . . . he was screwing with her mind.

Get out. She had to get out, get away from him. She pushed past him, but before she reached the doorway crashing pain hit the side of her head and the bottle bounced against her arm before shattering against the doorframe. She instinctively raised her arm, turned her head to protect herself from the flying glass, but shards stung her. Head swimming, unsteady, she couldn't move quickly enough, and Mick grabbed her wrist, jerking her around with surprising strength, throwing her stumbling back against the sharp edges of the door.

'You should have burned instead of Jim, you bitch,' he said, and in her blurred vision all she could see was his fist, flying towards her face.

FIVE

Mark jumped out of the SES truck the moment Karl pulled to a halt behind Mick Barrett's ute. Around the back, the dogs barked. Closer – inside the house – a woman's cry rang out.

The uneasiness that had been nagging at him since he'd seen Mick drive down Gearys Road blazed into full-blown alarm and he pounded up the front steps and into the house. A thud and another gasping cry led him to the kitchen just as Mick raised his arm to swipe another blow at Jenn, who was scrambling to her feet, blood on her face and arm.

'Leave her!' Mark bellowed. Fury raged red in front of his eyes as he grabbed Mick's arm, hauling on it, shoving him away from Jenn and forcing his body between them.

The old man snarled and with unexpected strength wrenched out of Mark's grasp. He stood for a few seconds, panting like a raging bull, venom in his eyes. 'You killed her. You bloody killed my girl. You and that bitch.' With a roar he swung, fists flailing. Mark dodged the blow and locked his arm in a choke hold around Mick's neck, dragging him backwards, swinging him around to slam him against a wall and holding him there.

Heat and revulsion and wrath pounded in his head along with his heartbeat. The image of Jenn, bloodied, flinching as she tried to deflect the blow played again in his mind, and he barely resisted the urge to ram Mick's head against the wall, repeatedly. If Mick had gone for him, he'd have understood it, but to attack Jenn – that was unforgivable.

'Jesus, what the—'

One glance at Karl confirmed he had grabbed a first-aid kit before following him. 'See to Jenn while I get this mongrel out of her sight.'

'I don't need seeing to. I'm okay,' she said behind him, but the breathless shake in her voice belied the words. 'Just keep the bastard away from me.'

'I will,' he vowed. 'I'll get him outside and then call Kris. She should be able to send someone down.'

'Don't bother the cops yet,' Jenn said, lifting her hand to her head and wincing. 'They've got more important things to do right now. They can pick him up later if they need to. He won't go far.'

Mick struggled in Mark's grip and let loose a stream of abuse, continuing as Mark and Karl dragged him out of the house and down the front steps. Mark held him face-first against the side of the SES vehicle, and signalled Karl to stand back.

Days ago, when he'd visited Mick to inform him about the accident, the man had been drunk and morose and slow with it, as usual. But without alcohol dulling his system, he became mean and unpredictable. And right now, Mick didn't have enough alcohol, despite the fumes on his breath. Whatever happened here, Mark wanted Karl as a witness, but not involved.

'I'm going to give you a choice, Barrett,' Mark said roughly, only just keeping his fury in check. 'You can get the hell off my property right now, or I can ignore Jenn's wishes and call Kris Matthews to come and arrest you for break-and-enter and assault.'

Twisting around to spit at his face, Mick missed and hit Mark's T-shirt. 'Fucking lying murdering bastard.'

Mark gritted his teeth and hauled the man around to face him. 'If you want to have a go at me, then do it. But I swear, if you ever touch Jenn again, I won't hold back. You understand me, Mick? She had nothing – *nothing* – to do with Paula's death. Or Jim's.'

He let Mick go, and stepped back half a pace. For a moment, he thought Mick would swing at him, but the old man must have thought better of it.

'I'll fuckin' have *you* for assault.'

'Then I'll see you in court. And you can be sure I'll explain how I dragged you away from belting Jenn.'

'Bastard.'

Mark folded his arms and regarded him coolly. 'Yes, I can be, and on this I will be. So get out of my sight and off my land before I change my mind and hold you here until the cops come.'

'Sonofabitch. You'll fuckin' get it, Strelitz. You'll fuckin' get it one day, you will.'

Mark clenched his jaw, but didn't waste his breath responding as Mick shambled to his ute, still muttering threats.

Karl stepped beside Mark, phone in hand. 'I recorded pretty much all that. Just in case he tries to make trouble.'

'Thanks. Can you go inside and take care of Jenn? I want to make sure he actually leaves.'

'I'll follow him up to his place. You look after Jenn. Last time she saw me, other than last night, she was babysitting me and I put tadpoles into her glass of water. So, she might have more faith in your abilities.'

For Mark, the cheeky, perpetually scabby-kneed boy had long disappeared in the capable young man Karl had proved himself to be through thick and thin, but perhaps he was right – Jenn didn't know that side of him yet.

The kitchen was empty, but the water pump was on and from outside the bathroom door, Mark heard a tap running, a sniff and then a few swear words. When the water stopped running, he tapped lightly on the door. 'Mick's gone, Jenn, and Karl's following him to make sure he stays away.'

'Good.' He heard another sniff, a nose blow, the gurgle of the sink emptying.

'Are you okay?'

'I'll live.' She pulled open the door. 'Nothing broken except some skin.'

Nothing broken maybe – but puffy eyes, red marks on her face and jaw, scratches still seeping blood, and a damp facecloth wrapped around her forearm, which she held against herself, upright.

The sight of those injuries made him wish he *had* slammed Mick's head into the wall. But his anger at Mick wouldn't help her and he tamped down the violence simmering within him.

'Come and sit down and let me check you over.'

'I'm not . . .' Her hesitation telegraphed her reluctance.

Have a man touch her after Mick's assault? He understood her hesitancy. 'Would you prefer me to see if Beth can come? Or Kris?'

'I'm okay. Really. Although maybe this cut could do with some tape or something. And I think there might still be a bit of glass in here.' She indicated a place just above her elbow. 'But can we go outside? It just feels . . . not right, being in Jim's house.'

With Karl's first-aid kit, they went out to Mark's ute in the backyard and she sat on the tailgate while he unwrapped a sterile dressing pack and laid out the contents. The dogs watched, noses pressed up against the fence.

'What happened?' Mark asked as he took the facecloth from her arm to examine the cut.

'I was out here with the dogs,' she said flatly. 'I saw Mick through the window. I went around the front and saw he'd broken in. He was helping himself to the contents of the kitchen. Then he took Jim's laptop. We had words. He told me I should be dead. Then he threw a bottle at my head.'

Every one of those staccato sentences raised a dozen questions, but the last worried him most. 'At your head? Did it hit you?'

'Not hard. Just bounced off the side of my skull and then hit the doorframe. That's when it smashed.'

Not hard. Bounced. Definitely worrying. He stepped back a small pace so he could see her eyes and her responses. 'Does your head ache? Do you feel woozy or nauseous?'

She looked straight back at him, direct, focused, and well aware of his examination. 'I'm suffering from caffeine deficiency, sleep deprivation and the remnants of jetlag, and I'm royally pissed off with the universe right now. But no, I'm not about to collapse from bleeding on the brain or concussion.'

He wanted to believe her. But the red marks, the bruising beginning on her jaw and face meant there'd been at least two blows to her head in addition to the bottle. He didn't waste his breath suggesting the hospital, yet, although he'd make sure that someone kept an eye on her for the rest of the morning.

'Do you want to formally report the assault to the police?' he asked.

'I don't know. Probably not. It was stupid of me to confront him. I should have remembered how much he hates me. I do remember it. The day after Paula died, he made sure I understood that it should've been me, with his words and fists.'

The day after Paula died . . . Everything kept coming back to that one event. For a moment he didn't dare look at her, didn't dare touch her, his gaze focusing only on the disinfectant wipe as he carefully laid it on the plastic sheet.

'He assaulted you then?' he asked quietly, anger building in his gut again.

She nodded. 'He was drunk, angry and looking for a scapegoat. I was crying in my bedroom and didn't run fast enough. Fortunately, Jim came along and stopped him.'

Mark pressed the first steri-strip across the cut on her arm. The reality of her bruised and bleeding now, as an adult, was bad enough, but imagining the teenage Jenn in the same state, vulnerable, grieving and alone, disturbed him deeply. That he'd known nothing about it, had failed to help her when she'd needed a friend, sat uneasily in his soul. 'Did you report him then?'

'No. Maybe I should have, but what would've been the point? He was grieving for his daughter. I doubt they'd have even laid charges.'

Given what he knew now about the man who'd been the Dungirri police sergeant at the time, the man who'd helped frame Gil, she was probably right. 'Is that why you left Dungirri?'

She paused imperceptibly, but in that moment he both wanted her answer and dreaded it.

'After Paula's funeral, there was no reason to stay.'

No reason. He focused on the task at hand. Of course their friendship had not been enough reason. *He* had not been enough reason. They'd just been kids with different goals and no defined relationship to bind them.

No reason for his distracting physical awareness of her proximity now, either. No reason other than nostalgia, memories, fondness and pheromones.

They both fell silent as he put the last steri-strip on the wound and covered it with a dressing. He flushed the small cut near her elbow with saline, her skin smooth and warm from the sun, and the small fragment of glass washed out, a brief sparkle amid a trickle of diluted blood.

She slid off the tailgate while he packed up the first-aid gear, but the tension from being so close to her didn't dissipate with the increased distance.

He couldn't allow himself to spend time thinking about why. If it turned out that he bore responsibility for Paula's death, it would obliterate any remnants of their friendship, destroying his past as well as his future.

☙

Jenn hunkered by the fence of the dog run, their warm tongues licking her fingers through the wire. The dogs' enthusiastic attention seemed surreal in the circumstances, but she stayed there, wishing the playful contact could restore some badly needed equilibrium.

She couldn't think straight, her ability to objectively assess a situation totally derailed by the onslaught of unfamiliar and conflicting emotions. The reality of Mick's physical attack had hit her as she sat on Mark's ute, her reaction so disorienting that she'd almost succumbed to the temptation to turn into Mark's arms and weep. Except that he was the cause of at least half the confusion in her head.

Mark, who'd dragged her bastard uncle away from her, the rage and power of that moment kept in check, directed by reason, all his interactions with her afterwards unfailingly calm as he responded to her needs.

A man who . . . damn it, that was the crux of it. A man, not a boy. Standing close to her, tending to her arm with a gentle, considerate touch, his masculinity had inundated her, throwing her even further off balance than her uncle's attack had.

Maybe she'd been half in love with Mark as a teenager. More than half. He'd been a rock, understanding her, challenging her, supporting her in her efforts to shape her own life. Caring for her. But she wasn't a lonely, lost teenager anymore. She'd carved her own life, worked hard for her successes, learned from her failures, and she didn't need a man to lean on emotionally. She didn't need Mark.

She rested her aching head against the high fence and breathed deeply. With some peace and quiet, she'd sort the mess in her brain into its proper place. She had to find Gil Gillespie, ask him about the accident. Do what she could to help Paul and Chloe arrange Jim's funeral. Then return to her apartment in Sydney and her work.

First things first. 'Can you give me a lift back to the pub?' she asked Mark. 'I need to change. And maybe find some coffee.'

'Of course,' he agreed instantly, but underneath the courtesy she heard the rasp of fatigue. Exhaustion carved fine lines in his face, his skin drawn beneath his natural tan. All the signs of a man who hadn't slept much recently.

'Have you eaten?' A simple topic to deal with. Practical, logical, nothing to do with emotion. 'You could probably still get breakfast at the pub.'

'I could do with some breakfast,' he admitted. 'But I have to speak with Steve first. I'll come up to the pub after I've seen him.'

She collected the food and bowls while he put the dogs in the back of the ute and fastened their leads. She paused for a moment to watch the firm but easy way he handled them – remembering him with the first dog he'd been given sole responsibility for, to train from a pup. 'Your old Sammy – I suppose he's long gone, now?'

'Sammy?' He shut the tailgate but she caught his wistful smile as he went to the driver's door. 'Yes. He made it to sixteen, but he died just before I was elected to parliament. I haven't had the time since then to give to a dog.'

But he would take on Jim's dogs, if Paul couldn't. The fact that he'd remembered them, seen to their needs despite everything else happening, spoke volumes.

When they arrived back in town they saw four more police vehicles parked outside the Russells' house, and a young constable blocking the street, directing them around to the hotel via the main road. Mark parked in the shaded side street beside the pub, ensuring the dogs in the tray of the ute were protected from the sun and filling a plastic container with water for them.

'Are you sure you're okay, Jenn?' he asked as she turned to go inside. 'I'd be happier if you were assessed properly, in case of concussion.'

'I'm fine,' she insisted. 'I promise, if I get a bad headache or start feeling woozy I'll let someone know.'

He didn't like it, judging by his frown, but he didn't argue. 'I should be back in an hour,' he said. 'Then I'll take you to collect your car.'

Inside, the breakfast buffet was still laid out in the bistro, the only guests a couple of young tourists so absorbed in each other they scarcely glanced up when she entered. They must have been in room three. Scandinavian, by the sound of their accents and blond looks. Young and in love and travelling the world, and as oblivious as the dogs to the violence and murder outside. They didn't notice her blood-stained T-shirt.

The rich aroma of freshly brewed coffee hit her nostrils and almost, but not quite, overpowered the smell of blood and antiseptic clinging to her skin and clothes. The thought of food didn't tempt her, but the caffeine craving kicked in and she longed for some kind of normality and comfort. Just as soon as she'd cleaned up.

In the solitude of her room her composure wavered, but she caught the beginnings of self-pitying thoughts and stopped them. She would *not* let Mick, a miserable failure of a man, determine her emotional state. No way in hell. Now the initial shock of their confrontation had passed she'd square her shoulders, ignore the bastard, and get on with achieving her objectives.

In the bathroom, she dragged the bloodied T-shirt over her head and dumped it in the bin. A quick wash, a fresh T-shirt and assertive thinking restored her sense of self and purpose, and she gave her reflection in the mirror an affirming nod. Mick might have bruised her face but that would heal quickly enough, and he couldn't touch the core of who she was.

As she made her way down the staircase, she could see in the hallway the young barman from last night talking with the Scandinavian tourists. Liam, Mark had called him. He indicated something on the map they'd spread out, his easy courtesy and helpfulness drawing warm smiles from the couple. Their conversation finished as she reached the bottom of the stairs, and the couple passed her to go upstairs. Liam greeted her cheerfully and followed her into the bistro, busying himself clearing their table.

She heaped several spoonfuls of coffee grounds into a plunger. 'I didn't think Dungirri had anything to offer tourists,' she commented to Liam. 'Were you showing them the thirty-second tour, or the way out of town?'

He shook his head good-naturedly. 'Oh, there's plenty of potential for eco-tourism here. They're interested in wildlife, birds in particular, and asked where to camp. I suggested the Ghost Hill campground.'

'There's a campground there now?'

'Yes. Near the river. Birraga Council has just finished it. Water tanks, outdoor kitchen and composting loos.'

'And mosquitos and deadly snakes,' she added dryly. And memories. A popular camping spot for the local teenagers – without facilities, back then – she'd camped there numerous times, with Mark and Paula, with Jim's boys, sometimes with a crowd of local kids. Brief escapes for her and Paula from the depressing, sullen atmosphere of their home, and for Jenn reminders of better times, camping with her parents on their infrequent leave together from her father's army duties.

But none of those memories was relevant to here and now.

She carried her coffee mug and a bowl of fruit and yoghurt out to the courtyard, and found Gil Gillespie sitting at a table, his laptop in front of him and one hand around a large mug. An old, spreading kurrajong tree cast dappled light and shade over his face, so that she couldn't read his expression clearly as he watched her approach, but the four-cup coffee plunger beside him was almost empty. Without asking permission she sat on the bench seat opposite him.

If she'd been the easily intimidated type, his scowl would have done it, but she doubted that the lover of the local police sergeant posed any serious threat.

'I'd say good morning,' she began, 'but that's a debatable statement. Especially for the Russells.'

'Yes,' he said slowly, taking a long look at her face. 'You been walking into doors?'

The bruises must be coming up. Great. 'Not a door. My uncle. For an alcoholic, he has a mean right hook.'

'Yeah. He does. Seems to be a Barrett speciality.'

'It's a deficit in the Y chromosome.' She bit her tongue as soon as the words left her mouth. He had every reason to mistrust, even hate her family, given his encounter with Mick, Jim and the boys when he'd first returned to town, days before Sean had tied him to a chair and gone at him with a metal pipe. His experiences with the Barretts called for something more than flippancy. 'Gillespie, I'm not proud of what they did. As for Sean . . . I can't comprehend how he . . .' With the shock and pain of Mick's attack still reverberating, the horror of her cousin's brutal actions constricted her throat and her words faltered. 'I'm sorry . . .'

'You didn't do it,' Gillespie interrupted bluntly. 'You weren't there. Sean's crimes are his responsibility, not yours or Paul's or Jim's.'

Despite the harshness of his voice, his generosity of spirit, if not forgiveness, surprised her. She pushed the peach slices around in her bowl, searching for the right words.

'You must regret ever coming back to Dungirri.'

He shrugged. 'I came back to pay a debt. Found more than I expected.'

The police sergeant. And the dark-haired girl on the back of the bike.

'The girl – your . . .' She still couldn't get her head around that. 'Barb's daughter – is she close to her grandparents?'

'Megan's fond of them. She's made the relationship work, despite difficult circumstances.'

And clearly she had made her father proud. Beneath his hard-edged, taciturn manner she began to suspect a soft heart lurked. Well beneath.

But contemplating Gillespie's complexities wouldn't get the answers she needed to the questions raised in the past two days.

'Doctor Russell's death – do you think it's connected to the accident and Mark's announcement?'

His face closed and he studied the laptop screen, hitting a couple of keys. 'No comment.'

'Jesus, Gillespie, I'm not interviewing you.' Frustration rushed the words. 'This isn't about a story. It's about my cousin's death. And perhaps Jim's. You're the only witness to the accident and I need to know what really happened.'

He considered for a long moment before he answered. 'I was hitching on the Birraga road. Mark gave me a ride. I'd fought with the old man for the last time and walked out for good, so I wasn't in any mood to be sociable. Paula had a bottle of something and offered it around, but neither of us had any. I saw nothing to suggest that Mark had been drinking. I was in the back seat with my eyes closed, when all of a sudden Mark swore, the car swerved, Paula screamed, and then we hit the tree. That's it. That's what happened.'

Paula screamed. Simple, stark words, and she could *see* Paula's face transformed in terror. 'Did she . . . was it quick?'

'Yeah. I don't know what they told you. A low broken branch came straight through the windscreen. I tried . . . I hardly knew what I was doing, but I did try. Although I think she was gone the instant the branch hit her.'

There was more information in those few sentences than anyone had ever told her, and tears flooded her eyes. Embarrassed, she dragged the back of her hands against them, and struggled to find her voice.

'Thank you.' Not enough, for what he'd tried to do. For the horror he'd faced, young and alone in the night. In the hardened, mature man across from her she could see reminders of the too-wary boy he'd been, a solitary youth who'd had to deal with the shock of death and injury – and the subsequent events that changed his life forever.

She struggled to pull her thoughts together, to pull herself back on track. 'You said last night that the only crime was what happened after the accident. What did you mean by that?'

'Off the record?'

'Yes. You have my word on it.'

'Falsification of evidence, intimidation of witnesses, conspiracy to pervert the course of justice.' There was nothing soft in the anger glittering in his eyes, and his clipped phrases contrasted with the marginally gentler tone in which he'd described the accident.

'Intimidation? Is that why you lied? Why you said you were driving?'

'I didn't say it. The old sarge assumed that I was driving to start with, then he decided to stick with that.'

'But you pleaded guilty. Why?'

'Well, it wasn't because I wanted to go to prison.' As dry as a desert, he wasn't making it easy for her.

'Were you protecting someone?' she persisted. 'Were you protecting Mark?'

'Mark? No. He's always been a decent bloke, but I wouldn't have gone to jail for him.'

'Then who? Was there someone else in the car?'

'There was no-one else in the car. Listen, I'm not going into detail now. Let's just say that I was only a kid, powerless, and I'd made enemies. Threats were made against someone who mattered, and I had good reason to believe they'd be carried out unless I complied. I've told Fraser that, and—' He waved a hand at the laptop. 'It's all in the statement I've just sent to him.'

The statement he wouldn't let her see, probably for the same reasons Mark had given her. But she refused to be dismissed. 'Who made the threats?' she pushed. 'The old sergeant?' She dug in her memory for the name of the arrogant, bigoted cop who'd picked on the easy targets to make himself a big man. 'Franklin, wasn't it? Bill Franklin?'

He snorted. 'If it had only been Franklin, I could have had him charged for wrongful arrest and police brutality. But he was only ever a tool, way out of his depth.'

'So, who was behind it?'

She wanted to hear Dan Flanagan's name, but Gillespie kept his guard up.

'I've got no proof of who was behind it. Or why. Threats were delivered by messengers. Things were insinuated, not stated outright. What I believe and what I can prove are two different things.'

We've had our own tangled web of organised crime around here for a long time . . . Mark's words from earlier this morning added substance to Gillespie's near-cryptic comments, and made her wonder what the hell had been going on in the district, what Gillespie had been caught up in, while she'd been absorbed in preparing to escape the place.

'You said you'd made enemies. Dan Flanagan, right? How?'

'Back then I collected some information. Used it to . . . *dissuade* Flanagan from sending his thugs to collect protection money from Jeanie Menotti's business. Not anything that would have stood up in court, but enough to damage his business if I'd been able to get it to an uncorrupt cop.'

Jeanie Menotti's Truck Stop Café, where Gil had worked part-time as a teen. Burned out back in September. She'd bet it was Jeanie he'd been protecting, that he'd gone to jail to keep her safe.

His phone beeped and he glanced at the message, closed his laptop and tipped the thick dregs from his coffee mug on to the adjacent garden.

She had seconds before he walked away and not enough answers. 'I read that Dan Flanagan's sons were arrested with Sean and the Sydney mafia guy – Sergio Russo, wasn't it? But I don't understand how the Flanagans are connected to organised crime, now or then, or why the Sydney mob came here.'

'Vanna Flanagan. Dan's wife. She's the connection. Her maiden name was Russo.' He rose to his feet, tucked the laptop under his arm, picked up the coffee mug and plunger. 'And I pissed off one of the Russos in Sydney. They wanted payback, and the Flanagans were happy to help.'

With no farewell he left her, walking back into the pub through the bistro door.

She swallowed some of her own cooling coffee, her thoughts sprinting to round up scattered recollections. Vanna Flanagan. Tall, elegant, impeccably dressed, the owner of a chain of beauty salons across northern New South Wales – one of them next door to the *Birraga Gazette* office. Wife of Dan, a Birraga businessman with interests in many areas, and a substantial advertising account with the *Gazette*. Mother of Brian and Kevin, loud, obnoxious boys a few years older than her, arrested with Sean two months ago after the assault on Gillespie.

A year on the crime desk of a Sydney newspaper early in her career meant she knew of the Russo family. Whispers, shadows, hints and hearsay – but nothing ever definitively connecting prominent property developer Vince Russo or his brother Gianni with the crimes of the day.

It seemed absurd that the small-town Birraga Flanagans could be connected to the Sydney Russos. Laughable, almost. And yet . . . there *had* been a few whispers about Dan Flanagan when she'd hung around the *Birraga Gazette* office as a teenager. Only whispers, nothing concrete, nothing said in front of her.

Certainly nothing printed. Not with his advertising dollars keeping the struggling regional paper alive.

But perhaps those whispers held substance. Perhaps there had been a shady underworld back then, capable of framing a young man and getting away with it for years.

She carried her empty dishes into the bistro and went upstairs to her room. She opened her laptop. Research. Go back to the sources, reconstruct events, piece together the connections and the relationships. Her skills and talents, the exact same approaches she took in her work could be applied to this.

But it had never mattered quite so personally before.

SIX

The forensic team from Inverell that had been on its way to Marrayin to investigate the fire stopped first in Dungirri to assess the Russell crime scene. The senior officer, Sandy Cunningham, grilled Mark on every movement he'd made while in the Russells' garden and house and took his fingerprints and an imprint of his boots, although the footprint in the garden had a very different tread pattern from his.

When they'd finished with him he joined Steve and Kris beside Steve's car.

Steve was on the phone, but Kris greeted him as he approached. 'Karl told me what happened. If Jenn's up to a few questions, I'll go and see her, since I can't do anything else here.'

He well understood Kris's frustration at being kept at arm's length from the murder investigation, her itch to be doing something constructive. And knowing that she would see Jenn and keep an eye on her injuries would ease at least some of his concern. 'She said she wouldn't report it, but maybe if you talk to her she might. She's at the pub.'

'Good. Mick's not usually a problem but he's been crankier and occasionally unstable lately, since Liam and Deb at the pub clamped down on serving drunks.'

'He threw a bottle at her and struck her several times because she wouldn't let him take Jim's computer. I had to haul him away from her. He's becoming more than unstable, Kris. He's downright dangerous.'

'Shit.' She bit at her lip. 'I'll have to find some way to curb him. An assault charge would help.' Her face grew darker as they watched the unmarked mortuary van reverse into the Russells' driveway. 'I hate the sight of that van,' she confided. Then she shook her head, as if to shake away the image – or the moment of vulnerability – and it occurred to Mark how many qualities she shared with Jenn. The tough armour covering a caring core. The determination to take charge of her life and do her chosen job with thoroughness and commitment. The independence and resilience.

'Steve hasn't eaten and I'm guessing you haven't, either,' Kris said, interrupting his thoughts. 'Tell Steve I'll ask Liam to leave some breakfast out for the two of you. See you up there.'

She headed back along the road to the pub, taking one last glance through the gates towards the doctor's body as she passed.

Mark didn't watch them load the body, leaning on the bonnet of Steve's car instead while the detective finished his call.

'Did I hear Kris say something about breakfast?' Steve asked as he pocketed his phone.

'Up at the pub. Presumably the usual basic breakfast, but anything will be good as far as I'm concerned.'

'Yeah, well personally I'd prefer a croissant in a Parisian cafe with a gorgeous blonde and a weekend in front of me with no work to do, but that sure isn't going to happen anytime soon. Let's go. We can talk as we walk.' Steve shot him a glance as they set off. 'You know I'm going to have to ask you about your movements this morning?'

Exactly the first question Mark expected. Underneath Steve's various masks – charm, informality, off-handedness – lay a thorough detective, more than committed to his job. 'I left Marrayin a little after sunrise, maybe six-thirty or so. I drove to Dungirri, turned right on to Gearys Road, and saw Esther Russell run out on the road just outside their place.'

'Did you see anyone else? Any vehicles on the Birraga road?'

'No. No-one in Dungirri, or on the road. Which leaves me,' he pointed out, 'without an alibi.'

Steve acknowledged the fact with a nod. 'Let's hope someone saw you. Or the killer. Adam's checking all the houses nearby now. Did you happen to step on the garden?'

'No, I didn't. The footprint isn't mine. Or Esther's – her feet are tiny.'

'Yeah. And I'm no religious scholar, but I haven't heard of angels leaving footprints.'

They walked the last few metres to the hotel in silence. Mark paused to check on the dogs in the back of the ute – still in the shade, still with plenty of water. Inside the pub, he paid Liam for the buffet breakfast, and after pouring himself coffee and filling a bowl with muesli and fruit, he followed Steve out to a table in the back corner of the deserted courtyard. No sign of Jenn or Kris.

For the first few minutes they both concentrated on eating, Steve hoeing in to his food as though he hadn't eaten for days. Mark *hadn't* eaten decently for days – a meat pie on the road yesterday didn't count as decent – but he had no appetite, and ate only for necessity.

After polishing off a bowl of cereal and a thick slice of bread with jam, Steve leaned back in his chair, a coffee mug clasped in his hands, as casually as if they were relaxing at a barbecue. Except there was nothing relaxed in his eyes, and he launched straight back into the business at hand. 'Both you and Gillespie implied yesterday that Russell might have known the truth about the blood sample.'

Mark could read exactly where Steve was going. 'That could provide a motive for murder. So, I could be a suspect, if I believed Russell's evidence might incriminate me. Gil Gillespie could be a suspect, if he *was* the one who was driving that night and wanted to cover it up. And whoever organised the corruption might want to silence Russell, if he knew part of the truth.'

'Now you're playing detective,' Steve said, the dry humour friendly enough. 'But Russell's death *could* be purely coincidental. Someone else may have a reason to want him dead. Doctors can have angry patients – misdiagnosis, medication allergies or side effects, even an unsympathetic bedside manner can breed resentment.'

'He wasn't universally loved,' Mark agreed. 'He was very old-fashioned, and he certainly wasn't known for sensitivity.

But other than the blood-alcohol report issue, I'm not aware of any significant questions over his actions. He was living quietly in retirement. And I know that a spouse is often the prime suspect, but Mrs Russell has been with him for close on fifty years, and they loved each other, despite his bad temper. I don't see her ending his life, even out of mercy. I certainly don't see her strangling him with a garrotte.'

'There'll be an autopsy. Cause of death seems obvious, but I've been surprised before. They'll screen blood samples for drugs, check his organs and such.'

'You'd better hope they put the right name on the samples this time.'

'Yeah. Maybe the doc didn't look at what he was signing. Maybe he did. But Gillespie can be thankful that the custody records were complete, and contradicted the hospital's. That's what got his conviction quashed. There was no other evidence suggesting culpability.'

'Yes.' Mark had noticed the absence of other evidence in the transcript of Gil's committal hearing. The blood-alcohol report and Gil's guilty plea – made under duress – had ensured a speedy conviction. Which left far too many questions unanswered.

Straightening and stretching his arms, Steve asked, 'Speaking of police records, can you send me a copy of what you have?'

'I'll email the file to you this morning.'

'Thanks. I've been hassling the archives staff, but their files are missing. They can't find anything in the computer files – there was a basic system back then – or paper files. And the blood sample itself is apparently long gone.'

The last thin hope Mark had held for a speedy resolution disappeared, and he swore silently. 'No chance of DNA analysis, then.'

The look Steve gave him had a dose of compassion in it. 'No. No nice clear answers there. But add together Doc Russell's death, missing police records, the fire at your place yesterday and Jim's murder, all less than twenty-four hours after your announcement, and I'm smelling a hell of a lot more than just smoke.'

'It has to be someone attempting to destroy any evidence relating to Paula's death – the police report, what Russell knew. Believe me, Steve, if I'd known there was a substantial risk to anyone, I'd never have spoken to the media yesterday.'

'I believe it. I wouldn't have thought a crime this old would provoke this response. I'll keep an open mind, but I want a list from you of all the people who might have some knowledge of the accident and its aftermath. Names, Mark – anyone, from police stationed here at the time, to paramedics, to nurses at the hospital.'

Mark already had several names listed on the note app on his phone. 'Bill Franklin was the sergeant based at Dungirri at the time.'

Steve nodded. 'I checked on Franklin yesterday. He went up to the Northern Territory after he retired. A couple of years ago, he drove off into the bush in Kakadu and disappeared. His car and campsite were found, but no signs or sightings of him since and his bank accounts are untouched. The Territory cops are referring it to the Coroner for an inquest.'

The wild country in the Kakadu National Park could kill a man quickly, and in the vastness, remains might never be found. A crocodile, a snake, a wild boar, or even heat stroke or a heart attack – plenty of things could go wrong for an old man alone and a long way from help. Mark mentally struck through Franklin's name on his list.

The second contender was definitely still alive. Dan Flanagan. Everything Mark knew about the man pointed to the likelihood that he'd been the one behind the cover-up, yet in the same way the police had not been able to pin anything on the patriarch of the family despite arresting his sons, Mark had no evidence, no link, nothing solid to prove Dan's involvement.

'Bill Franklin wasn't the brightest guy,' Mark commented carefully. 'Someone with more influence, more ability to fix things must have been involved.' He didn't mention Flanagan's name. He didn't need to.

'There are several avenues of enquiry I'll pursue, don't worry. People with influence, as you put it. Although I have to say, Gil has plenty of suspicions about who was behind setting him up, given the enemies he'd made, but all the threats were delivered by hired thugs, so he doesn't have any firm evidence. Which reminds me, Mark, I want to talk with your parents. They retired to the coast, didn't they?'

People with influence. No evidence against Flanagan. His parents. Steve's connection of the three ideas caught him unawares, but the frankness in the detective's study of him made clear his train of thought. As prominent and active landholders in the district, his parents *had* been influential. Rationally, the possibility that they'd arranged to frame Gil to protect their son had to be considered, but Mark's every instinct insisted it was a waste of time. Service, integrity, decency – values not just drilled into him throughout his upbringing, but demonstrated in everything Len and Caroline Strelitz did.

'They do a lot of overseas charity work,' he told Steve. 'At the moment they're in Bolivia, building a school in an isolated village without phones or mobile reception.' He thumbed through the contacts on his phone. 'They have a satellite phone but it died, so I'll send you their email address and mobile number. Good luck getting hold of them. I spoke with them last Sunday. They might go into a larger town this weekend to check their messages.'

'Did you happen to ask them about the accident?'

'Yes. They were shocked and worried. But it was a bad line; we couldn't talk for long. I got the impression they'd never had any doubt that Gil was driving.'

'But they're not rushing home to stand by you?'

'I doubt it.'

Steve raised an eyebrow. 'You don't get along?'

'Yes, we do.' How to explain his parents to someone who'd never met them? Too complex to try, and not relevant to the situation. He shrugged and opted for a simpler, close-enough comment. 'I'm thirty-six now, not eighteen, and even then they encouraged my independence.' Not an entirely adequate phrase to describe their distracted affection and the consequent physical and emotional self-reliance that Mark had formed from a young age, but it would have to do. 'They handed control of the family company to me some years ago and moved to the north coast. Their charity work is a full-time job, though, and they're often away. They're very dedicated to it.'

'Dedicated' – there was another inadequate word. Passionate. Driven. Although what drove them he'd never been entirely sure. All the commitment and energy they'd once put into building Marrayin they now poured into building schools, hospitals and clinics in isolated corners of the world.

Steve's phone, lying on the table, beeped with a message, and he heaved a frustrated sigh and thumbed a response. 'I'll have to go in a minute,' he said, putting the phone down again. 'But before I do, how do your folks get on with the Flanagans?' He dropped the name almost casually, as if it were of no importance.

Mark kept it brief. 'Coolly polite. When they meet in public. But they try to avoid meeting at all.'

'How come?'

'I don't know the full story. But I do know that back in the long drought in the early eighties, Dan Flanagan specialised in irrigation equipment, and he started buying up land and properties that were heavily in debt and had to be sold. My father didn't say why, but he believed that some of Flanagan's actions were, at the very least, unethical. He established Strelitz Pastoral and outbid Flanagan on at least three places, including the Gearys Flat property.'

'Some rivalry there, then.'

'Yes. Definitely not business associates. Of any kind.'

After Steve left, Mark considered again the idea that his parents might have framed Gil to protect him – and he rejected it as swiftly as he had the first time. Not only because they weren't here, now, and couldn't possibly be responsible for

Edward Russell's murder, but more importantly because the idea of them framing Gillespie ran counter to everything Mark knew and believed about his parents' characters.

Dan Flanagan had to have known, if not masterminded the whole business. It had been there in his behaviour, especially since Mark's election to parliament. The jocular pretence at friendship, the confident grins – oh, yes, he'd known. But the one thing Mark didn't understand was *why* Flanagan had never used the information he held against him. And he wondered if he would try to use it now.

SEVEN

The blackened ruins of the homestead's central wing stood against the brilliant blue of the sky, the reality of the destruction making Jenn's breath catch in her throat.

Never her home, but still she'd loved the house, the heritage grace of the old sections, the rambling additions of successive generations and owners, the whole place rich with history and stories. In Marrayin's glory days, a hundred years ago, there'd been a whole community here – a family, household staff, station workers – with the buildings to house them. A self-reliant village, like so many large properties isolated from towns. As a girl she'd been fascinated by the history, spending many long hours reading the old account books and wandering around the outbuildings, imagining the kitchen maid in the dairy where the machinery shed now stood, the stableboy working with the family horses in the main stable, now the garage, and the grazier's daughters playing tennis in long white frocks.

But now there was only Mark.

'I'm camping in the manager's cottage for the time being,' he said as he parked beside her car. 'The east wing of the homestead might be livable, but I'm not sure yet how much damage there is.'

'You won't be employing another manager?'

'No. Not for here, probably not at Gearys either. I prefer to be hands-on. I just couldn't do it while I was an MP. Now I can again.' And although he'd been silent and preoccupied most of the drive from Dungirri, that last sentence – *Now I can again* – rang with a quiet pleasure she hadn't heard from him since she'd returned.

Mark and Marrayin. Every memory of him mustering cattle on horseback or motorbike, hot, sweaty and filthy after a day fencing or calf-marking, or half-covered in hay and chaff after carting feed during dry spells, came with an awareness of his deep contentment, his joy and fulfilment in the hard work and its rewards. He'd been passionate and committed in his parliamentary career – she'd stood in the shadows in the public gallery when he'd given his influential maiden speech, and all her colleagues agreed he'd achieved significant respect for his actions and achievements – but nothing she'd seen or read in the past six years hinted at the same kind of serenity. Some people thrived on the cut and thrust of debate, on power plays and negotiations, on political tactics, manoeuvrings and victories. Not Mark.

If his intellect, his detailed comprehension of complex rural issues, his natural leadership skills and his commitment to service had led him to stand for parliament, it must have come at a personal cost.

Mark belonged here, at Marrayin.

She stood in the drive-circle beside her car and surveyed the damage to the house. 'You will rebuild it, won't you?'

'I hope to. I'll have to wait for the building inspection and the insurance decision. And for the outcome of the police investigation.' He shot her a sideways glance. 'If I'm found culpable for Paula's death, there may be a prison sentence.'

Mark in prison? Her mind blanked and refused to process the thought. At what point had she shifted from anger and suspicion to wanting him to be innocent? Even at her angriest, her most doubtful of him, at no time in the past forty-eight hours had she imagined him behind bars.

He stood by the back of the ute, gently rubbing the ears of one of the dogs, and when she didn't respond he said, 'I'll accept the findings and the outcome, Jenn. Paula was important to me, too.'

She found enough coherence in her brain to string some words together. 'I know she was. So, now we just have to work out what actually happened.'

'Yes. Although Steve's first priority will be Jim and Doc Russell. We can't know for certain if they're linked, but I'm hoping those investigations will shed light on the old crime.'

So was she. Because no matter what the level of public interest was, no police command was going to allocate many of their scarce resources to an old car accident that might, or might not, have been caused by a man with an otherwise unblemished record.

A white car turned into the driveway. Insurance, WorkCover or police – whichever, Mark would be caught up with them for some time. Jenn checked her watch. She just had enough time to get into Birraga library before it closed; she wanted copies of the accident reports from their archives of the *Gazette*. She planned to investigate the accident, too, and that was a good place to start. She'd known all of the *Gazette*'s small staff. She'd find out from the archives what had been reported, and – just as importantly – what hadn't, and armed with that information she would ask them why.

ॐ

'We don't hold the hard copies here anymore,' the young woman at the library's information desk told her. 'They're in the Regional Archives Centre in Armidale. But we do have the papers on microfilm. Which year do you want?'

Tucked into a corner in the reference section near several large printers, the small booth with the microfilm reader trapped warm air and received little of the flow of cool from the air-conditioning.

'Can't wait for digitisation,' Jenn murmured, threading the microfilm through the rollers and under the lens. The rollers squeaked as she fast-forwarded through the months of papers, the images and text flashing across the screen in a scratchy blur.

She slowed as she scrolled through the three editions in the second week in December and paused with a wistful smile at her Friday column, 'Youth Matters', celebrating its second anniversary. Started during her first week of work experience when she was fifteen, she'd badgered the editor Clem Lockrey to keep it going, providing copy every week, and before long it became a regular column. All those afternoons through years ten and eleven at Birraga High, hanging out at the *Gazette* office, making herself useful, drafting advertising copy, assisting with research and proofreading items eventually paid off when Clem gave her a desk, a modest wage as a part-time office assistant and the occasional by-line when she transformed Birraga Council's media releases into coherent articles. And 'Youth Matters' had gradually moved from page eight to page four.

She skimmed her very last column, 'Cool things on the World Wide Web', with some amusement at what had seemed cutting edge then, and pressed the button to scan it to email. Maybe she'd do a retrospective piece on it some day.

She scrolled through Friday's classifieds and sports pages to reach Monday's edition. Front-page news, as she expected.

The headline took up a third of the page: 'FATAL SMASH KILLS GIRL'. The rational, distanced part of her brain focused on the clunky phrase. One of Larry's, probably. Headlines weren't his strength.

But the headline didn't matter. She couldn't stay distanced and she braced herself as she scrolled the page up on the screen to study the photos and the story. Staring out at her was a four-column image of the smashed car at the crash site, with an inset photo of Mark in school uniform.

Birraga High School captain Mark Strelitz was airlifted in a critical condition to the John Hunter Hospital in Newcastle following a single-vehicle accident on Saturday evening on the Dungirri road that claimed the life of Paula Katherine Barrett, aged 18.

Lead with the most important fact – and in the way of small-town newspapers and the social strata of the district, Mark's injuries made more significant news than Paula's death.

Jenn ignored the twinge of resentment on Paula's behalf. Selling newspapers was always the purpose, not assuaging the feelings of a few family members.

The only child of graziers Len and Caroline Strelitz, Mark suffered head injuries and remains in a coma. Speaking from Newcastle, Mr Strelitz expressed his gratitude to police, paramedics and nursing staff for their care of his son, and his sorrow for Miss Barrett's death.

Build sympathy for the victim – and already, in this first report, Mark had been presented as victim, not offender.

Morgan Gillespie, also 18, of Dungirri, has been charged with culpable driving occasioning death and was remanded in custody. Police allege Gillespie had a blood-alcohol reading of 0.14.

A statement from the senior sergeant at Birraga added the detail that the car had *'apparently swerved off the road and collided with a tree'.* Coming after the mention of the blood-alcohol reading, it reinforced the perception of Gillespie's guilt.

The next statement, from the principal of Birraga High School, expressed shock at the tragedy. *'Paula was a delight to teach and a valued member of our school community, loved by her peers and always supportive of younger students.'*

Jenn's eyes watered and she had to dig in her bag for a tissue. Good old Mr Howie.

The final paragraph was in italics, indicating an editorial comment on the story, and as Jenn read she had to press the tissue against her mouth to suppress a sob, tears now spilling over.

The deceased woman is the sister of the Gazette's *Youth Matters columnist, Jennifer Barrett. The staff of the* Gazette *express their deepest condolences to Miss Barrett and her family.*

The screen became a blur, and she had to look away, wipe the tears running down her face. It had to be Clem who'd added that. The main article had Larry's old-school style, and his technically incorrect reference to an eighteen-year-old woman as a 'girl'. But that reference to Paula as her sister – that was Clem, bless him, and it harked back to an editorial she had proofread for him about extended families and foster-siblings and complex care relationships. And he'd argued in that article that often the legal relationship didn't matter as much as the relationship of the heart.

God, she had to pull herself together before she started to howl. The grief shouldn't still be this fresh and raw – it had to be just her fatigue and the shock of the past days' events throwing her emotions off kilter.

She heard a librarian informing other patrons that closing time was in ten minutes. Ten minutes. Hiding in her corner and howling wasn't an option. She dragged a dry tissue over her eyes and made them focus on the machine. Print. Scan. Email.

She quickly scrolled through the next couple of editions but saw little that related to the accident, other than a brief mention of Mark remaining in hospital in Newcastle. And then she was out of time. Wishing that small community libraries had the staff and funds for longer opening hours was wasted effort. She'd just have to wait until Monday to look for mentions of Gillespie's committal hearing.

After placing the microfilm back in its box, she collected her pages from the printer, glancing over them to check they'd printed all the text. She stopped abruptly, her eye drawn to the photo of the accident.

The low quality of the microfilm made the image grainy and she stared at it, blinking salty eyes to try to make out the detail. No, to be certain she needed the original image. Now she just had to find out if Clem or Larry were still around, and if she could get it.

⟡

With the arson investigator, WorkCover inspector, insurance assessor, police forensic officers and Steve all arriving, the driveway soon filled with vehicles. Mark answered their initial questions and then left them to their work. Stand around passively watching while they picked over the remains of his home? No, not when he had a property to run, and no-one to help him do it.

Jim's dogs leapt with ears-up eagerness on to the tray on the back of the quad bike. They knew Mark and accepted direction from him, keen to work. Out in the sun-hot paddocks checking water troughs, dams and stock, his physical restlessness found some ease. He wished he could spread that ease to the crowded, racing activity of his thoughts, but planning what needed to be done on the property only added another layer to the discordant chorus of concerns in his head.

The sale of two hundred steers just before the manager left a few weeks ago meant that Marrayin wasn't heavily stocked at present, but he had heifers to move from one paddock to another, this season's calves to be marked and, he discovered when he reached the east river paddock, a mob of feral goats and a trampled fence to deal with.

He prioritised tasks, made plans. First priority – phone Karl and offer him some casual employment. He'd already proved to be a good worker. Mark would have to go over his finances and see if he could juggle things to offer Karl something more permanent, or at least regular. Like most rural communities, limited employment opportunities in the district meant that Dungirri's younger people left for larger towns and cities, but if the town were to have a future, it needed people like Karl to stay. Mark would do what he could to enable that.

He rode along the river and up past the stockyards to the three long-empty workers' cottages, and the old shearers' quarters. He left the quad bike under a tree to check inside. There was some basic equipment and tools stored there, plus a fridge in the old kitchen for days when a few people were down here working. And there were memories.

Jenn kept coming to his thoughts, each part of the property holding recollections of working, playing, and exploring the landscape with her. Always Jenn stood out more than Paula, although he could still see, too, the warmth of Paula's smile, hear her teasing him with the cheeky confidence of their four weeks' age difference. He never minded, because she needed all the confidence she could find within. But Jenn, for all her reserve and emotional armour, had a stronger sense of self and certainty. From horse riding to mustering, school work to journalism, if she set her mind to something she usually succeeded.

But she'd never smiled enough. She still didn't. Granted, there hadn't been anything to smile about since yesterday and no reason for her to smile at him now, but he wished he could see her again as she had once been, whooping with exhilaration after a good gallop, or sitting here on the old shearers' kitchen table, sweating from a day's work in the yards, tossing her head back to glug down a bottle of water, laughing as he tipped it to spill on to her face.

He blinked hard to dislodge the image. Nothing but dust and daydreams here now, and he had no time for any of them. Fatigue descending on him, he moved leaden feet out into the sunshine again. At the tank stand he splashed water over his head and face and gulped several mouthfuls from his cupped hands, pouring some into the enamel dish kept there for the dogs and placing it down for them.

Beyond the sound of their slurps he idly tuned in to the usual background noises – the ever-present buzz of insects; a flock of galahs squabbling; a few cattle in the large wool-shed paddock mildly protesting another's transgression. But those last sounds were coming from the wrong direction. Unless the cattle were behind the wool shed . . .

He called the dogs and started the quad bike. The track from the road to the stockyards passed the disused wool shed and he rode up there, expecting to see the beasts come into view. Instead he found a gate that should have been shut swinging wide open, and around twenty young steers calmly grazing along the roadside.

Hadn't Jenn said last night that she thought she'd heard a car down this way?

He stopped on the track. *Damn it.* It would have been easy enough for the arsonist to leave his vehicle here and approach the house unseen, able to ensure that no-one was around before he broke in.

To preserve any tyre tracks or other evidence at the gate, Mark went back to the stockyards and out on to the road across the stockyard grid. On his command, the two older dogs, Maggie and Rosie, flanked the cattle but he kept the youngest one, Dash, at his heel, and between them they made short work of moving the cattle into a paddock across the road.

On his way back along the road up to the homestead Mark stopped to close the wool-shed gate, avoiding touching it where someone might ordinarily handle it. Twenty cattle milling around the gate had churned up the track and obliterated tyre prints, but if there were fingerprints on the gate, he wanted them saved for the crime-scene officers. As he dropped the chain over the hook, something small and white caught his eye in the grass near the base of the gate post. He knelt to see it better. A cigarette butt. He didn't smoke. Jim didn't smoke. It might not be relevant . . . but it might.

When he arrived back at the house the crime-scene officers were packing up their gear, but on hearing his suspicions Sandy Cunningham sent his offsider down to see what she could find.

'The arson investigator has finished and so have we,' Sandy told him. 'You can go into the safe parts of the house to salvage things, but not that whole front part – what's left of the roof could be unstable. Wouldn't be anything worth salvaging in there, anyway, I'm afraid.'

The insurance assessor, a solemn man in his fifties, echoed the warning. 'I'll arrange for a structural engineer to come out on Monday. You can go into the kitchen, and that east wing from the second room down, but the rest is unsafe. I'll be in touch early next week with the report.'

The kitchen and the east wing – three guest rooms and a sitting room – were all that remained. He might as well keep to his plan to stay in the manager's cottage.

His boots crunched on the gravel driveway as he walked along in front of the house to see the state of his bedroom through the remains of the veranda. Yes, they were right. Nothing much left there but charred memories.

Who? Who had broken in, searched through his papers, fought with Jim, and set the office alight? Who had known the property well enough to enter via the wool-shed gate? He still refused to believe that Jim could have been responsible for the fire. Mick? Perhaps. He knew the place – but then, so did plenty of other people. There had been tens, possibly hundreds of people over the years who had worked on or visited the property. Shearers, when they'd still run sheep; livestock truckers every few months; station hands and fencers; fuel and feed-truck drivers . . . the list went on and on.

No easy answers there. He veered his thoughts to practicalities and plans. Clothes. He had Canberra clothes down in the cottage – not much use here, but at least he'd have a suit for the funerals. He needed work clothes and some everyday gear, and food, since the perishables in the fridge would be well gone from the heat. Bedding he could get from the guest rooms. Likewise some furniture. Computer equipment could come from his office in Birraga. And he'd need fuel for the generator since the fuel truck wouldn't be out this way again for at least a week.

'Bit of a bloody mess, mate,' Steve said behind him.

'Yes. But I've got enough left to get by. It could have been worse.' Jim's death still cut sharply into his emotions, but at least Jenn was okay, when she so easily might have been killed.

'I've just heard from Adam,' Steve commented. 'Mick Barrett's in the clear for this. Adam was throwing him out of the pub yesterday evening at the time your intruder was lighting fires. And this morning Frank Williams was watering his garden before six and he saw Mick in his house across the road. Frank went over to check on him, because he was on something of a bender last night, and made him coffee.'

'You couldn't get a much more reliable alibi than Frank.' Retired accountant, president and driving force of the new Dungirri Progress Association, and member of numerous community groups in the district – he was a man Mark respected a great deal.

'Nope. It's as solid as a rock.'

Unlike his own, non-existent alibi. Steve gave no indication that he seriously considered him a suspect, but the fact that no-one could confirm his whereabouts before either crime hung in Mark's awareness.

'I'll need to go into town to get some supplies and more fuel for the generator,' he told Steve. 'If you don't need me anymore.'

'No. I'm heading back to Birraga myself. Got a few things to follow up.'

He didn't offer anything more and Mark didn't ask. Police business, and for all that Steve had been more open with him than a stranger might have, he had no role in the investigation other than as a witness.

Mark respected the law and the judicial process. But two men had died, and he'd do whatever he could to ensure that no-one else did.

⁜

The front door of the *Gazette* office was closed and locked – not surprising on a Saturday afternoon. But the vintage sports car parked outside was typically Larry, and through the window Jenn could see the overhead fan circling. She rapped on the window using her old signature rhythm for after-hours entry.

When Larry pulled open the door he stared, mouth dropping open, for a good three seconds.

'Jenn Barrett?' Incredulity slid into pleasure, and his face lit up with a wide grin. 'Jenn bloody Barrett, what the hell are you doing here in the back of beyond? Come in, come in.'

The computer screens on the desks were bigger and the office chairs had morphed from dark brown to muted green–grey upholstery, changes that seemed reflected in Larry himself, carrying extra kilos, his hair grey and receding.

'So, look at you, living the dream, hey? Foreign correspondent, travelling the world.'

'The fantasy doesn't bear much resemblance to the reality,' she said. 'Long hours, a lot of travelling, and no glamour. Just as Clem warned me. Is he still around?'

'Clem? Retired five years ago. Then had a heart attack a couple of years back when he was out fishing with some mates. Not a bad way to go.'

For a quiet man who'd struggled with his health but loved fishing and the outdoors? 'Not a bad way at all,' she agreed, 'but I'm sorry he's gone. I would have liked to have seen him again.'

Larry poured her a mug of coffee from the ever-warm pot and waved her to a seat by his crowded desk, moving a couple of manila folders to a side table behind him as they sat. 'So, where has the intrepid Jennifer Barrett been reporting from lately?'

'Central Asia. Tajikistan, Uzbekistan, Kyrgyzstan. Doing a series of reports about gas and water issues.'

His chuckle bubbled, just as she remembered it. 'Jeez, Jenn. No need to go all the way to the 'Stans. If you want to do stories on gas and water rights, we've got plenty of them here.'

She nodded in agreement. Here and everywhere. Energy, water, food production – fundamentals for twenty-first century living, and potential battlegrounds for control and exploitation. 'At least you don't have several nuclear-armed nations vying for control of the resources.'

'Maybe not. Yet. But where there's money and big business involved, there's always a story to tell.'

His knowing grin and hints piqued her interest but she quashed it and moved on. 'There's only one issue I'm interested in here, Larry.'

Lounging back, hands clasped behind his head, under the pretended casualness he watched her shrewdly. 'Mark Strelitz and his out-of-the-blue resignation.'

'Yes. What do you know, Larry? What's your reading of it?'

'I could ask you the same thing. I'm not the one who knows him well.'

'*Knew* him well,' she corrected. 'As teenagers. There's been plenty of water under the bridge since then.'

'Actually, more drought than floods round here,' he teased her lightly. A classic Larry avoidance strategy.

'If I wanted a rainfall report, I'd look it up online,' she said. 'What's your take on Mark's resignation?'

'You can look that up online, too. Breaking news goes out digitally now.' His eyes sparkled with the pleasure of sparring with her again.

She took a sip of the strong black coffee and considered him carefully. 'I didn't ask for the paper's take on it. I asked for yours.'

'Why? Are you covering the story?'

'No. I'm on leave. Paula was my cousin, so this is purely personal for me. And I'm asking for your opinion because you've been here all these years, you know Mark, his work and what goes on in this district far better than I do.' Unblinking, she kept her eyes on his. 'And because you reported the accident originally.'

He didn't shift in his chair, or look away, or fidget with anything. He held her gaze steadily, serious now. 'I did.' But that steadiness when he'd teased her a moment before, along with his brief answer alerted her.

'Tell me about it,' she said.

He gave a casual shrug. 'There's not much to tell. Wolfie and I were covering Carols by Candlelight at Anzac Park when Clem paged us. We went out there, but it was dark and not much to see since the police wouldn't let us close. The ambulance had gone, Gillespie had already been arrested, and the cops were just waiting for the forensic people. Wolfie took a few shots with the telephoto lens, and that was it. I put the report together mostly from the police statement.'

'I don't suppose you still have Wolfgang's photos?'

'The photos?' He rubbed his chin, thinking, then shook his head. 'Nah, I doubt it. He was still shooting film back then, so it would have been negs or hard-copy prints, and there's not enough space to keep such old files. Clem did a big cleanout before he retired.'

All reasonable, on the surface. And she would have believed him, if she hadn't glimpsed Mark's name on the folder he'd moved out of sight, and seen the edge of a printed photograph not quite tucked in. Of course there'd be a file – paper or digital – relating to Mark. There would have been one well before his election, covering all his community involvement. And knowing the kind of newspaper man Clem had been, in any cleanout all documents relating to Mark would have gone into that file. Even at a paper as small as the *Gazette*. *Especially* at a paper this size, serving a regional community that had overwhelmingly elected Mark as their federal representative, twice.

Larry could be telling the truth. Maybe the photos *had* been discarded long ago. She knew from her own experience helping out in the office that filing had not been the strength of any of them. So she didn't challenge him on it. Yet.

'What's Wolfgang doing these days?' she asked. 'Is he still around?'

'Yeah. Rumour has it he makes a bit on the internet from his photography, but God knows how, since every second person has a digital camera now and thinks they're a porn artist.'

'Erotic art photography. The good work is quite different from porn.'

'It's all just boobs and bits, if you ask me.' He grinned. 'But then, I've never been accused of being an artist. He never tried to drag you into his sleaze, did he?'

'No.' Larry's teasing and innuendo had bordered more on sleaze than Wolfgang's polite distance. 'He knew I was under eighteen, and he never discussed that work with me. A couple of people – a year or two ahead of me – did model for him after they left school. I heard the money was good but it didn't tempt me. I knew the career I wanted. Having nude images of me floating around wouldn't have helped it.'

'Always were single-minded, weren't you?'

'I still am.'

'And now you're asking questions about a long-ago accident.'

'It seems that the wrong man went to prison. I want to find out why.'

'I'm not so sure Gillespie was innocent. It's a damned shame that Strelitz decided to fall on his sword. But I doubt they'll turn up anything new after all this time, let alone anything substantial enough to charge him.'

'Did you hear about the fire at Mark's homestead last night?'

'Yeah. That's why I'm here, on a sunny Saturday afternoon. Jim Barrett was your uncle, wasn't he?'

'Yes.'

'I'm sorry, Jenn. I didn't know him well, but he showed a lot of dignity during the police business around his son being charged with attempted murder. Do you know anything more about the circumstances? Or about the incident in Dungirri this morning?'

Sometimes she shared information. Other times she kept what she knew close, and right now she didn't plan on enlightening Larry about anything she'd seen. He could use his own sources and skills. Instead she showed him one of her sweetest smiles. 'I'm sure the police will release a statement in due course.'

He laughed out loud. 'Oh, Jenn, you have grown up, haven't you, honey?'

Not many people called her 'honey' and got away with it, but she let it slide this time. For all his faults, she owed him for his early encouragement and belief in her. 'I've learned from the best, Larry.' She rose from her chair. 'Now, I'd better let you get on with reporting the news.'

With a promise to catch up for a drink some time, she headed for the door, turning back as she pulled it open. 'By the way – the photo of the car at the accident site in the newspaper? The inset image of Mark is partly over the rear wheel. I was only looking at it on microfilm, so not great quality, but it kind of looks like the rear wheel isn't there.'

Standing by his desk, he held his mug to his mouth and his Adam's apple bobbed with a swallow, but she could have sworn no coffee passed his lips. Yet after that tiny pause he answered easily enough, 'Can't say I noticed anything at the time, Jenn. It was dark except for the police lights, and Wolfie had to use the zoom. Might have just been a bit of rock or brush or something in the way.'

'Probably. I just wondered. Seemed an odd thing for a head-on smash with a tree. See you later.'

She let the door click shut behind her and stepped out into the hot, glaring sunlight. Saturday afternoon in Birraga? Definitely a contrast to last Saturday in Tashkent. Most of the main-street shops here were already closed, save for the independent supermarket and the takeaway further down the block. A couple of utes had stopped in the middle of the road, the drivers leaning out their windows to have a leisurely yarn together.

She paused under the awning next to the *Gazette* office to wipe dust off her sunglasses, casually reading the signs in the window as she did. No longer Vanna's Beauty Salon, the Bellezza Viva Day Spa exuded elegance and promised comfort, relaxation and renewed vitality – five days a week and Saturday mornings. But although the 'Closed' sign hung in the door and the blinds were drawn, she heard a phone ring inside and the murmur of a voice answering it.

She'd parked a few doors down, in the partial shade of a street tree, but the interior of her car still blasted a wave of heat when she opened the door, and she sat for a couple of minutes with the air-conditioning on high and the window wound down to make it bearable, using the time to do a quick web search on her phone for Wolfgang's phone number. Movement outside caught her eye: Larry, coming out of the *Gazette* office.

There was no sign of his trademark smile or relaxed manner. Instead, he was hunched, his face tight, every movement betraying physical tension as he fumbled in his pocket for his keys and got into his car.

A man troubled. Stressed. And, she had the distinct impression, afraid.

EIGHT

The pump at the Birraga fuel depot chugged as the petrol poured in to the last of Mark's four twenty-litre plastic containers in the back of the ute. He had plenty of diesel at Marrayin, but the generator ran on petrol and the tank at the homestead was running low.

Another vehicle pulled up on the other side of the bowser as he finished. Normally he'd nod and say g'day, but today . . . today he was no longer a federal MP, duty-bound to serve his constituents, and his natural reserve and desire for privacy won out.

But if he'd hoped to avoid curiosity, questions or censure by not looking at the other driver, all three hit him when he walked into the depot shop and saw his name plastered in four-inch letters on the front pages of the major newspapers beside the counter: 'STRELITZ SCANDAL'. 'STRELITZ FALLS: POLICE INVESTIGATE'. 'STRELITZ "FORGETS" DEATH'.

Newspapers. They'd been the furthest thing from his mind today. But the headlines didn't surprise him.

Jared, who'd worked at the depot for more than a year and usually greeted him cheerfully and chatted about politics, now gave him an uncertain nod, his gaze skittering to the newspapers.

Ignoring the elephant in the room impossible, Mark sought for suitable words to acknowledge it. 'We'll all have answers when the police finish their investigation,' he said.

Frowning, Jared rang up the sale and gave him the account docket to sign, breaking his silence to ask, 'Will there be an election now?'

'A by-election, yes. Probably in about six weeks.'

'Any idea who'll run?'

The tension within Mark unwound a fraction as they settled into an almost-normal conversation. 'No. The major parties will nominate candidates, I'm sure, but I don't know who, or if any independents will stand.'

'Yeah, well, let's just hope *he* doesn't,' Jared replied darkly, jerking a thumb out the window to the other vehicle at the bowsers.

Flanagan. Dan Flanagan, impeccable in moleskins and a blue shirt, filling up his top-of-the-range Land Rover. The very picture of rural wealth and confidence – and of a man who rarely did actual physical work.

Mark couldn't avoid him, and on one level was fiercely glad of the opportunity to confront him. He just had to step carefully.

Flanagan greeted him with a smile, as if they were friends. 'I was very sorry to hear of your resignation, son, and the reasons for it. I trust that the police investigation will absolve you of any blame.'

Mark didn't bother to return the smile. Flanagan often called him 'son' but today it grated more than ever and he was in no mood to tolerate the man's pretence of friendship. 'I trust that you will inform the police of any information you have regarding the accident.'

'But why would you think I know anything about it?' Flanagan infused exactly the right amount of friendly puzzlement into the question. Too exact. Mark had spent enough years in politics to recognise the signs of a man lying through his teeth.

'I saw the news reports at the time,' Flanagan continued, with that same, smooth, faux concern. 'And there was discussion about it, of course – such a tragic event, in a small community like this, with that pretty girl dying and you so seriously injured. Everyone was shocked and worried.'

Inside the Land Rover, one of Flanagan's grandchildren squealed with laughter at a game they played. Leaning casually against the vehicle, Flanagan could almost have been an ordinary country grandfather, taking the kids out for an ice-cream.

Unless one knew the truth about him. In the wake of his sons' arrests in September and the police investigation into drug distribution, extortion and violence, more than a few people had come to Mark with stories of blackmail and threats, seeking his advice about going to the police. He'd encouraged them all to do so.

He'd never trusted and certainly never liked Dan Flanagan, but now he discarded any pretence of courtesy and drove straight to the point.

'Gil Gillespie was framed, Dan. And more than one person had to have been involved in it.'

'I really don't know what you're talking about, son,' Flanagan insisted. 'Gillespie pleaded guilty, according to the newspaper reports. I understood it was a straightforward case. I confess I was glad to see the young hooligan behind bars. Culpable driving causing death is a serious offence.'

'So are extortion, drug trafficking, arson and attempted murder.'

If he'd hoped to rattle Flanagan, it didn't work. The man sighed and nodded, with a reasonable impersonation of sorrow.

'Yes, they are. My wife and I are devastated that our sons are in custody, and all our energies are focused on proving their innocence and securing their release.'

His *former* wife. A member of a prominent Sydney mafia family. Flanagan had a habit of ignoring inconvenient truths. Mark stuck to the facts. 'The judge apparently agrees that the police have sufficient evidence linking your sons' activities with their cousins' organised-crime operations to commit them for trial.'

But not enough to incriminate Dan . . . yet. And although his power in the community had been reduced by his sons' arrests and the exposure of their illegal activities, Mark didn't doubt for a moment that Dan Flanagan still had ways and means to influence events to his liking.

Flanagan studied him for a moment, but his tone remained that of a friendly, paternalistic advisor. 'I'm sure, with your legal education and passion for justice, you believe in innocence until guilt is proved. Evidence can be manufactured, Mark. And sometimes those of us in leadership positions in the community make dangerous enemies.'

There it was. Despite the ambiguous words and cordial delivery, the threat came through loud and clear. Mark had no doubt the man could still be dangerous.

'If someone has a grievance with me, they should take it up with me. Not with anyone else. I'm the threat to whoever is behind this, because I will do everything in my power to ensure that the truth is uncovered, and that those responsible for concealing it are called to account for their actions.'

'Very worthy of you, son.' Flanagan couldn't entirely hide the amused edge of sarcasm. 'I wish you nothing but the best in your endeavours.'

He didn't specify the best of what. Failure, probably. But Flanagan's confident double-speak signalled more than refuted his involvement in the cover-up, at least at some level.

'Thank you, Dan. I'm sure the outcome of the police enquiries will be well publicised.' With that pointed courtesy, Mark turned away and walked to the driver's side of his ute, starting the engine and pulling out without looking back.

cⱾ

Back bar of Impies. 6.15 pm. Pretend surprise. W.

The text message from an unknown number arrived half an hour after Wolfgang had brusquely denied during their phone call the possibility of still having any images from the accident. Had he remembered some – or changed his mind about his answer to her question? *Pretend surprise* – the instruction sent her imagination into overdrive. Larry's nervousness, Wolfgang's caution – whatever she'd stumbled on, she'd better be alert.

A few minutes after six o'clock she arrived at the Imperial Hotel and studied the blackboard menu for counter meals in the back bar. She needed to eat. Preferably something healthy. She ordered the chicken salad and a mineral water and found a vacant table by the wall.

Ten past six. Too early for Saturday-night crowds, just twenty or so people relaxing on a hot evening. She drew a notebook from her bag and opened it on the table. Few people approached a woman dining alone, writing in a notebook, and it gave her the perfect excuse to spend some time with her face down, ostensibly working, while she unobtrusively kept an eye on movements in the bar.

Although one or two faces seemed familiar – perhaps people who'd been at Birraga High in her day – most of the small crowd concentrated on their friends or on the sport playing on the large TV screens, and no-one recognised her.

Wolfgang walked through the door at six-seventeen. Tall, a leather waistcoat buttoned over tattooed skin, faded jeans – unchanged but for the lines chiselled on his weather-hardened face and some loss of muscle tone. He was still striking, still sensual in his rebel-artist way, although he must be well past sixty. He greeted a couple of people, propped on a bar stool, made a dry joke with the barman and ordered a beer and a packet of chips without once looking in her direction.

The rumours whispered in Dungirri, long ago, that he'd escaped the East German Stasi in Berlin in the 1960s took on a whole lot more credence. Most people – people other than dissidents, spies, undercover cops, actors and investigative journalists – didn't have the skills or experience to carry off a charade so convincingly.

She continued to doodle on her notepad, wondering about him. Although he and his wife, a potter, lived closer to Dungirri than Birraga they'd generally kept to themselves, and aside from the spy rumours and hushed references to pornography, the locals – at least the older locals – had mostly regarded them as drop-out hippies who didn't belong in Dungirri. She'd learned a little more about him through his part-time photography work for the *Gazette* – but not much.

When she casually glanced around again Wolfgang had swivelled on the stool and was watching the action on the TV screen on the wall to her left. She let her gaze drift to him, smiled in recognition, and he saw her then, and performed a credible double-take. With his slow, crooked grin he slid off the stool and sauntered over to her, beer in hand.

'Jenn Barrett. Almost didn't believe my eyes. Who'd have thought you'd come back here?'

She stood and he enveloped her in a bear hug, kissing each cheek and then her mouth, tasting of beer and salt and marijuana.

He winked. 'Couldn't do that when you were sixteen.' Dragging a chair out, he put his beer on the table and sat down, to all appearances settling in for a catch-up yarn. 'So, what have you been up to, kid? Other than what we see on TV.'

She played it as relaxed and easy as he did. 'Work, work and more work. An apartment in Sydney I don't see much of. I was based in London for a couple of years, covering Europe, more recently in Afghanistan for a year or so. And I've just come back from three weeks in Central Asia.'

'I saw the ad for your report. Tuesday night, isn't it?'

She nodded. 'Part one this week, part two the next.'

'So, is it what you wanted it to be? The career?'

The question took her by surprise. Was it? She let some mineral water cool her throat. 'I'm happy with what I've achieved so far. But there's always more to do, and journalism is a rapidly changing field. Technology is making it the best of times and the worst of times, as far as news and current affairs are concerned.'

'Yeah.' Forty years in Australia and it still came out more like *ja*. 'For art, also. Good times and bad.'

'How is Marta?' A quiet woman, Jenn remembered from their few meetings, with an unpretentious beauty that Wolfgang had often captured on film.

The energy in his face drained, so that it became merely skin stretched over bone, a skeleton in waiting. 'Gone.'

'Oh, I'm sorry, Wolfgang.'

'Cancer, five months ago. Bastard of a disease.'

In the echoing flatness of his voice she understood his joviality of a few moments before as the pretence it really was – not only a performance for any malicious observers, but a courageous pretence of being alive, of being *okay*.

In the face of his grief, words deserted her and she closed her hand over his on the table. He squeezed her fingers for several seconds before he broke the contact to raise his glass and sip his beer.

'You want something to write about, Jenn? Do you know how many women in the bush – young women, often – have a double mastectomy because they can't afford to spend weeks or months in Sydney or Dubbo or Tamworth having chemo and radiation? We were okay because we live pretty frugally, had a bit put aside, but working women, women with kids or caring for parents – and guys with other cancers, other illnesses, it's the same. There aren't enough choices and they're too bloody tough.'

His concern for others touched her, and she automatically saw possible angles, approaches and questions – but she already had plenty to write about, projects in the works, leads to follow, and none of them had anything to do with Birraga or Dungirri. 'I'll mention it to one of my colleagues,' she told Wolfgang. 'He does a lot of work on rural issues.'

The waiter brought over her salad, and with the interruption Wolfgang checked his watch and then drained his glass. 'My pizza will be ready to pick up, so I'll leave you to your dinner. Good to see you, Jenn.'

Leaning over, he gave her another surprisingly strong hug, holding her tightly, burying his face in her hair. 'There's a USB drive in your bag,' he murmured into her ear. 'Be careful what you do with it. There's danger, Jenn.'

The next moment he was strolling away, returning his empty glass to the bar, then walking out the door with only a raised hand in farewell. And she found her vision blurring with unexpected tears.

❧

Sorting files did little to improve Mark's mood. Sorting files, carting boxes for storage, running the shredder – activities that kept him busy but didn't occupy all his thoughts. Apart from the intermittent burr of the shredder, his Birraga office was quiet, the last sunlight of the day slanting through the west-facing windows into the reception area where he stacked boxes of correspondence and resource material to take to Marrayin, and bags of shredded material for recycling.

Like Marrayin, this building had a history, and that was one of the reasons he'd chosen it for his electorate office. Originally a bank built more than a century ago, it still had most of the original features: the long, solid cedar counter, the large fireplace behind it that they never used, and the walk-in safe, built sturdily enough to deter bushrangers back when there'd been gold in Birraga.

Tellers, bank clerks, accountants, customers – generations of local people had known the building, transacted their business over the counter or in the manager's office. It had always seemed to him fitting to continue that connection and honour the traditions and the history, so he'd left the counter in place, and the safe and the images of historical Birraga, although the other former bank buildings in town had been gutted and modernised to fashionably bland office style.

Mark carried another box of files to the growing pile by the door. To make additional room he pushed aside the chairs and coffee table and the stands with information leaflets about various government services. There'd be more boxes yet. Despite his resignation, he still had work to do – correspondence to respond to, referring constituents to other assistance, and sending submissions to parliamentary inquiries, albeit as a private citizen now.

His phone vibrated in his shirt pocket and he checked the screen before deciding to answer. Jenn.

'I might have something,' she spoke as soon as he answered, crisp, quick. 'Some info about the accident. Are you at Marrayin?'

Curiosity and wild hope flared. 'No, in Birraga. In the office.'

'Good. I've just left Impies. Have you got a functioning computer there? I need to look at some files.'

'Yes. You know where my office is? The old bank in Burke Street, just off the main street.'

He caught the lilt of amusement in her voice. 'I'll find it. See you in five.'

Of course she'd find it. Birraga's business district consisted of two blocks. He opened the front doors of the building and tried to still the questions circling in his mind by loading the first of the boxes on to the tray of his ute, parked immediately outside.

Jenn turned into the street and pulled in beside the ute. Stepping out of the car, she slung a small leather bag across her body and stood for a moment studying the graffiti scrawled across the front wall below the windows.

Amusement curved her mouth. '"Lying batsard"? That's a new twist on an old insult. Or a dyslexic vandal.'

Mark carried another box to the ute and slid it on to the tray. 'I can understand why people think that way.' And so he'd left the graffiti there, instead of spending time cleaning it off this afternoon. 'The I-don't-remember explanation from politicians is more than overused.'

'Yep,' she said dryly. 'You may be the only politician in the history of the world who has used it legitimately.'

He replayed her words again in his head to make sure he'd heard them correctly. Confident, unequivocal, unambiguous. His mood lifted. 'You believe me.'

'Yes, I believe you. Otherwise I wouldn't be here.' She clasped her bag closer to her body and glanced up the street. 'Might be best if we go inside.'

Observing her caution, he closed the door firmly behind them.

When she saw six years worth of paperwork stacked by the door, her old quicksilver smile lit her face and she teased, 'Have you been waiting for the filing elf, Mark?'

Despite everything, he couldn't help but grin in return. 'Are you volunteering?'

'Oh, not me. I'm all for the paperless office. Not that I've achieved it, yet.'

'Me neither.' He held open the tellers' gate for her. 'Come on through to my office, and tell me what you've found.'

'Does the police file have photos of the accident site?' she asked.

'One. Not very clear.'

'I think I have more. And I want to see them.'

More photos of the accident . . . he couldn't see why that might be important, but he didn't press her. She'd come to him, and he valued the trust and the renewed ease between them despite the circumstances.

As he led her towards his office, from outside came the sudden rev of an engine under strain, and a movement beyond the high, timber-framed window caught his eyes – a small flash of light flying through the air, and the crash of glass breaking.

He bolted back for the door and yanked it open. Flames spread over the back of his ute, the boxes well alight, heat already radiating.

'What the—' exclaimed Jenn, just behind him.

No time to say the words. A Molotov cocktail. And four twenty-litre plastic containers of fuel on the back of the vehicle, less than three metres from them.

He slammed the door shut, grabbed her hand and dragged her behind the timber barrier of the counter, pushing her down to the floor and dropping on top of her as two explosions in quick succession blasted glass, bricks and flames all around them.

NINE

She didn't want to open her eyes; she just wanted to curl into the foetal position and scream and scream to block out the echoing all-too-familiar noise in her head – the multi-layered instantaneous sounds of a car exploding; plastic, metal, tearing, burning, bursting through the air, sounds playing again and again and again from her memories and nightmares, the images of her father, her mother—

No. Not this time. The panic in her brain didn't quite dull her awareness of here and now, of memory and reality. No images, other than the fire on the tray of the ute. No-one in the car this time.

Breathe. She had to breathe and think and—

Her brain snapped back into full mindfulness. Searing pain in her left ankle. Heat. A roar underneath the ringing in her ears, acrid smoke clogging her nose and mouth. She opened her eyes to the hell of wild orange flames in the swirling dust and smoke. Like yesterday. Not like yesterday. Flames all around her. A heavy weight on top of her, immovable. Panic surged again and she struck out with her hand, tried to move, tried to shout, anything to get out of here.

The weight on her shifted and strong hands rolled her back, closer against the counter, and it was Mark thrusting a handkerchief into her hand, lightly pressing her fingers and the cloth against her mouth. Mark, protecting her with his body. The flickering light reflected in his eyes, and on the blood trickling down his face.

'Are you hurt?' He gripped her shoulder, his face tight as he rapidly looked over her for injuries.

Part of her still reeled in panic but rationality started to regain control. They were alive. They might have a chance. She tried to move her ankle, couldn't help wincing, but it functioned. 'I can walk.'

Walk or burn – the stark reality left no choice. Fire was quickly surrounding them, the brochures and information sheets near the window dispersed by the blast, a thousand lit matches among the debris of wood, brick, paper and plaster. Flames grew everywhere. One of the chairs at a desk already flared high, and she could hear the growl of fire in the reception area as a choking black smoke filled the room.

Mark coughed, and waved in the direction of his private office, where they'd been heading just seconds ago. 'Extinguisher by the door. Wait here.'

Gulping in a breath from the clearer air near the floor, he crossed the room in a crouching run beside the counter, kicking burning debris out of his way. He had the extinguisher off its hook within seconds, blasting a spray of flame suppressant around, dousing flames between her and the door.

She shifted to a crouch, her weight on her good foot, bracing herself to move.

'Keep down,' Mark called, and she crawled along the floor for the length of the counter, her head low, through the smoke and heat towards him.

With the door closed, she couldn't see if whatever was beyond was alight, but they could not stay here. As Mark continued to douse the flames around them, she reached up to touch the door handle – warm but not blistering. Mark motioned her to the protected side of the door, and signalled her to pull the handle as he readied a blast from the extinguisher.

There were no flames directly behind the door, no sudden back draft, and she limped after him into a corridor, dragging the door closed behind her. To their right, the door to his office was open, with fire taking possession of the room and smoke swirling into the corridor.

Mark sprayed around the doorway of the office with the extinguisher, clearing it temporarily of flame, and with his shirt tail wrapped around his hand, he grasped the handle and yanked it closed.

The shut doors gave them slight protection, dulling the sounds and softening the garish light. There was less smoke here, but she struggled to draw breath, her throat and lungs still raw from yesterday now not coping with burning-fuel fumes. A coughing fit took hold of her, doubled her over, made her gasp for air between racking coughs. Pain and smoke blurred her vision, dark spots danced before her eyes, and her knees hit the floor, then her hands. *Crawl.* She'd have to crawl out of here. If she could.

She could hear Mark coughing, his own smoke inhalation as bad as hers.

Her lungs screamed for air and her injured ankle scarcely worked, buckling under her weight so that Mark had to half-carry her, but she forced herself to move, and they staggered together down the corridor, a green exit sign dimly visible through the smoke. He dragged her the last few metres, fumbled for awkward seconds with the lock before it finally gave, and pushed her out into the fresh air of the back lane.

'Careful – steps,' he said, his arm a vice around her waist, the only thing preventing her from falling down the steep stone stairs.

The air was cooler on her face, but she couldn't breathe it, and the stairs faded out of focus and then out of her vision as she slipped into blackness.

⳥

Mark caught her weight before she collapsed to the ground. His own chest struggling for air, fear for her safety and pure adrenaline kept him going, lifting her and forcing his legs to carry her beyond the burning building. His eyes glued to her face, he watched intently for signs of breathing, of a pulse. She *had to* breathe. He had to make her breathe. Ten seconds, fifteen . . . far enough away to be safe for now, he dropped to one knee, then the other, lowering her to the stairs leading into another building.

She moved her head, coughed, muttered a swear word, and the surge of relief at seeing her taking in air almost made him light-headed.

'Hold still, Jenn. You're safe.' The words grated against his raw throat. 'You're safe now.'

She tried to push herself up anyway but groaned and closed her eyes and he shifted so that he cradled her head in his arm.

He could hear sirens in the distance but his vision centred on her, nothing else. Her hair fell back from her face, faint bruising visible on her jaw and cheek from Mick's assault, and her lips moved as she tried to swallow. He kept his fingers lightly on her wrist, monitoring her pulse. Other than her ankle, he could see no injuries from the explosion, no burns, but she'd collapsed, fainted, and that worried him.

Her reddened eyelids fluttered open again and she looked straight up into his face. 'Mark. You're bleeding.'

'I'm okay.' He wiped a new trickle of blood off his cheek with the back of his hand. His head pounded, every breath clawed through his throat and lungs, his eyes stung, but it didn't matter. He had to get an ambulance for Jenn.

Lifting her head gently, he moved from under her. 'Just lie here, Jenn. Get your breath back. I'll go for help.'

'I'll be fine,' she protested, but he didn't wait to argue with her.

He pulled his phone from his pocket to call an ambulance but he could hear sirens of emergency vehicles approaching. Ignoring the drumbeat throbbing in his head, he forced himself to run up to the main street to direct them around to the lane. About to turn the corner, he almost barrelled into someone running towards him. Steve Fraser. He'd probably come straight from the police station in the next street after hearing the explosion.

Steve grasped him by the arm. 'Mark! Thank God. Is there anyone else in there? There're two cars.'

'Jenn's out – around here.' When he turned he saw her sitting up and clasping her ankle. So much for resting. 'Need an ambulance.'

'Already coming,' Steve said. 'Call went straight in when I heard the explosion.'

Echoing his words, the resounding crash of structure collapsing rolled through from the street, and the back door to his office building blew open, less than twenty metres from Jenn. If the fire spread . . .

Jenn clambered to her feet in the few seconds it took Mark to reach her, Steve close behind him.

'Just strained,' she insisted breathlessly when he put his arm around her to take some of her weight. 'Not broken. I can hop.'

By unspoken agreement, one on either side of her, Mark and Steve supported her, almost carried her, so that even her good foot hardly touched the ground as they hurried up the lane to the safety of the main street. Mark flagged down the ambulance as it approached and it pulled in beside them.

In the flurry of questions and oxygen masks and monitors, Mark sat on the old stone gutter and kept Jenn in his sight while a paramedic helped her on to a gurney and attended to her. Gary Meadows, the senior paramedic, gave him an oxygen mask and hunkered beside him to inspect the wound on his head.

'Do you know what hit you?' he asked.

'No idea. Could've been anything.' A piece of glass, fragment of brick or wood or metal. Something larger would have knocked him out or killed him.

'We'll take you both down to the hospital. Doc Cameron will want to take a look at you.'

Scans and observations for the next few hours – standard drill for head injuries, and he'd go along with it for a short while because he understood the risks and wasn't stupid. And because they'd take Jenn there, and he would stay until assured she wasn't badly injured.

Mark inhaled more of the oxygen and attempted to slow his adrenaline-loaded metabolism. His pulse rate and blood pressure still spiralled higher than normal, chafing for action. His thoughts raced just as fast, questions of who and how and why spinning without answers, but he kept coming back to the one stark fact: Jenn could have died. She could have died or been badly burned or injured more severely in the blast. He scarcely believed that they'd both come out of the inferno alive.

She lay on the gurney, her hair dark against the white pillow, eyes closed, but even with the oxygen mask obscuring much of her face he could see her wince as Gary's offsider wrapped a brace around her ankle.

He started to stand, to go to her, but Gary pushed him down with a firm hand on his shoulder.

'I can see another cut on your head, round the back here.'

Mark acquiesced only because he had no place by Jenn's side. She'd shown clearly enough over the years that she didn't need or want him.

Now that Gary had drawn attention to the back of his head, he registered the small stinging pains against the background of other aches.

Gary made quick work of checking and cleaning blood from the cut and although his professionalism never faltered, in the absence of his usual steady chatter Mark sensed the new distance, as if their many years' acquaintance and their several seasons together on the Birraga cricket team no longer counted.

Something cool pressed against his skin, and Gary confirmed he had more than the current incident on his mind when he abruptly asked, 'I don't suppose the blow to your noggin has knocked your memory back?'

'It doesn't usually happen like that,' Mark explained. 'The memories are gone, never laid down in my long-term memory.' And he had to live with that empty space, rely on others to fill in the gaps. Like an ambulance officer who'd been at the scene. 'Were you on duty, the night of the accident?'

'Me? No. It was a month or two before I moved to Birraga.'

'Do you know who was?'

'Shorty Cooper, I think. Not sure who was with him. Might have been the guy I replaced. Sad case, that was. Depression, stress, trauma – I don't know what the problem was but it got to him bad and he ended it.'

Dead. Another potential witness no longer able to talk. Coincidence or something else? Mark's suspicions kicked up a few notches. Even more so because Shorty – six-foot-five Will Cooper – had left the ambulance service after a year or two, taken over his father's car yard, and married Dan Flanagan's daughter.

❦

Closing her eyes to regain some sort of equilibrium didn't shut out reality, or Mark's conversation with the ambulance officer. Gary, he'd called him. It shouldn't surprise her that Mark was on first-name terms with just about everyone.

It got to him bad and he ended it . . . One of the paramedics who attended the original accident was dead? She opened her eyes, gripping her fingers tighter around her bag containing the newspaper reports and Wolfgang's images. Larry evasive and scared, an ambulance officer dead, and Wolfgang telling her to be careful? And all three of them witnesses to the scene of the accident.

Rationally, that added up to quite enough to invoke suspicion, justify questions. But, off kilter from the shock of the explosion and close escape, the uneasiness rising within her didn't need rational justification.

Gary and his colleague were doing paperwork at the door of the ambulance. She beckoned to Mark and pushed the oxygen mask up as he rose quickly and came to her side, resting a hand on the edge of the gurney, but not touching her. For all that she could cope alone, didn't need anyone, a small part of her craved that human connection, and noted its absence.

Not important. The situation had become life-and-death last night, with Jim's passing, this morning with Doc Russell's, and now even more imperative with Mark's and her close call. Her voice was still as croaky as a crow's but that gave her an excuse to whisper, 'Where did Fraser go?'

'Not far. Just over there.' He nodded towards the intersection. 'Talking with a constable.'

'Tell him to come to the hospital. With a laptop. Please. We need to see – to copy – the images. Before something else happens.'

The harsh line of his mouth and unsmiling eyes reflected her unease. 'Yes. I was thinking the same thing. I'll go and tell him.'

He left his oxygen mask on the mattress and walked away, responding to Gary's protest with the assurance he'd be back in a minute.

'We'll get you both down to the hospital,' Gary told her, as they readied the gurney and loaded her and it into the ambulance.

Birraga hospital. Again. The prospect made her even more nauseous than the smoke inhalation did and she had to fight the wild urge to scramble off the mattress and escape the ambulance to the open space outside. She bit her lip, willing the tears of desperation away. Just for a couple of hours. Just until she could breathe comfortably. Just until Mark's head wound was examined and X-rayed, because she doubted he'd stay at the hospital if she didn't. She'd worked among death and danger in war zones and natural disasters; she'd confronted criminals and powerful people and unravelled corruption and vice. Birraga hospital contained nothing that threatened her.

Except her memories and the pain of her past.

She caught a glimpse of Mark through the open door, and heard Gary ask, 'Are you okay to ride in the front?'

'Yes, sure.' He stepped into her view, hand on the door as he looked in at her. 'You're okay in there?' She wasn't, but she nodded anyway, and he added, 'Steve'll come as soon as he can.'

Gary filled in more paperwork during the short distance down the main street to the hospital. It was just three minutes before the ambulance stopped outside the emergency department. Gary slid the gurney out into the fresh air, and Mark was waiting, walking in through the automatic doors alongside her.

Conscious of his head injury and the pallor beneath his tan, she wanted to protest that he should be lying on the gurney, not her, but in her distracted state she'd left it too late, and they were already inside.

At least the nurse who'd been on duty last night recognised her and directed Gary to take her to the cubicle furthest from the bed where Jim had died. Mark took a seat by her side instead of following instructions to take the next bed. Dishevelled and grimy with dust and ash, his eyes reddened with irritation, blood drying on his neck and shirt – he had to be feeling as shitty as she did, but even in boyhood he'd put others first. Put her first.

A rare man, Mark Strelitz, and she should be thanking him for saving her life, for getting her out of the inferno, for staying with her . . . yet the words were sucked in to the whirlpool of her emotional overload and she hated her own inadequacies, her failure at something so simple.

He waited until the nurse left them before he asked in a low voice, 'Do you want to tell me what you've found?'

Facts. She could deal with facts. Grasping the distraction, grateful for it, she wriggled up to a sitting position, the pain in her ankle sharp but bearable, her breath only catching slightly with the movement. Much better, being upright, rather than the disturbing vulnerability of lying flat on her back, helpless.

She unzipped her bag, sending a quick thanks to the universe that it and the evidence it held remained intact. If they'd made it as far as the office, if she'd put the drive into Mark's computer before the blast, chances were it would have been lost.

She had her fingers on the printed newspaper pages when the nurse – Mark called her Rhonda – returned, pushing a small trolley with monitors. Jenn zipped her bag closed again.

Rhonda checked their details with friendly efficiency and ran through standard observations for blood pressure, pulse, oxygen levels and responsiveness.

'Both of you put those masks back on for a little while,' she instructed. 'Doc Cameron's on her way in. Would you like me to pull these curtains closed?'

'No, please don't,' Jenn said quickly. Just the thought of being shut into a small space, even by fabric, almost had the panic chemicals surging in her head again. Space and clear view versus privacy – tonight she'd take the space. Particularly since there were no other patients around at present; the Saturday-night drunks mustn't have got around to damaging anyone yet.

Rhonda left them alone, walking out of the main emergency room to the kitchen beyond, and only when she was out of sight did Jenn open her bag again. She took out the copy of the *Gazette*'s front-page article, double-checking as she did that Wolfgang's USB drive was still safe.

She passed the page to Mark. 'Take a good look at the photo.'

He leaned forward, elbows on his knees, studying the page. Like her, his gaze gravitated to the corner of the image where the tarpaulin covered the front of the car. Where Paula had died. His eyebrows tightened and she saw him swallow.

'Not there,' she said gently. 'The back of the car.'

He stared at it for several seconds before he noticed what had caught her eye. 'That's an odd place to put the inset picture, isn't it?'

'Yes. It's very amateur – not aligned with anything, not centred. It's almost covering the back tyre. Except . . .'

He finished the sentence for her. 'Except that where there should be the edge of the tyre, you can't see it.'

'That's right. It could just be the quality of the photo – night scene, zoom lens. But the emergency spotlights seem to light that area well, and the wheel arch is sharply in focus.' So sharp that Wolfgang might have intentionally centred the camera's focus on that exact spot.

Mark thought it through aloud. 'The tyre could've been flat. Or if I'd swerved sharply, perhaps run over something, it might have buckled.'

She'd gone through the same ideas herself. 'Yes, either of those possibilities could explain it. But they don't explain why the inset image is positioned to obscure it, or why Larry Dolan at the *Gazette* became very cagey when I asked him about it. Or why Wolfgang Schmidt warned me to be careful when he slipped me a USB drive with the images he took at the accident site. That's what we need to look at. There has to be something there. Something that somebody wanted covered up.'

She fell silent as the door swished open again. *Be careful.* Oh, yes, she'd be careful. People had died. Others were frightened. And someone who had convinced a man like Wolfgang to stay silent all these years had to be a significant threat.

⚘

The ring of lights in the CT scanner whirred around his head, a bright reflection of the infinitely circling concerns occupying his mind. The head injury was the least of his worries. The throbbing and nausea were dissipating now the toxic smoke was clearing his system and he doubted that the scan would find any skull damage or internal bleeding.

He couldn't find any pattern, any logic to the events. A Molotov cocktail thrown at his ute had more in common with the graffiti – an expression of anger – than with the more specific search for papers in his office at Marrayin, or the murder of Doc Russell.

Unless the arsonist knew about the fuel on the back of his ute – fuel that turned the crime from attempting to fire-damage a vehicle to a near-fatal explosion.

Dan Flanagan had seen the fuel containers.

The scanner ceased its whir, and the technician slid him out of the machine. She had barely finished unclipping the head brace when Mark swung his legs over the side of the examination table and stood, more than ready to return to the emergency room and Jenn.

'Whoa, there,' the technician said. 'You'll have to wait for the wheelchair. I'll call for the orderly now.'

The technician had been a few years behind him at high school, and now managed the small department servicing the region. She was highly regarded by her colleagues and Mark trusted her abilities. 'Unless you saw something nasty on the scans, I'll walk back.'

'The radiologist in Newcastle will look at your scans – hopefully tonight,' she said, properly giving nothing away. But she didn't object again to him walking the short distance down the corridor alone, and in that he had an answer. His head was likely fine. Now he just had to make sure Jenn was.

In his absence Steve had arrived, and was waiting restlessly by the nurses' station while Morag Cameron – Mark could hear the doctor's soft burr of an accent – spoke with Jenn behind drawn curtains.

He heard no anxiety in the voices, so with nothing to be done there for the moment, he beckoned Steve into the room they'd talked in last night, closing the door. Outside the window a few late visitors passed through the garden on the way to the wards.

Steve dumped his laptop case on the table and dropped into a chair. 'Morag will have my head if you're supposed to be in bed and connected to monitors.'

'I'm okay. I'll do the right thing and stay and do the hourly obs.' More because he wanted Jenn to stay than because he thought he needed it, but he dragged out a chair and was glad to sit rather than stand.

'Good. I'll have someone on protection duty here overnight.'

'Is that really necessary?'

'Yes. Already arranged. Even before the Feds phoned and asked for it.'

'I've resigned from parliament. I'm not their responsibility anymore.'

'Your electoral office was just firebombed. I don't think they're splitting hairs about your resignation date. They're probably sending someone up tomorrow. It's going to be a real party,' he added dryly. 'There's a couple of Ds from Sydney homicide arriving tonight, and a few extra uniforms from around the district. And, as well as the Feds' protection squad, I've had the agent from their drug squad on the phone. She's the one who was here a few months ago, working on the case against the Flanagan brothers.'

'I remember her.' Cool and efficient and a stickler for process. Also, if he wasn't mistaken, with a healthy suspicion of Dan Flanagan and a determination to find reliable evidence to tie him to his sons' criminal activities. With officers from homicide, plus the locals, the investigation would be revved into high gear – and their presence would, he had to hope, deter any further acts of violence. 'The sooner we sort out this mess, the better. I'll write up a statement straightaway. Not that I saw anything useful.'

'Yeah, so you said. Molotov cocktail, fuel-laden ute, *kaboom*. Forensics are on their way too. They'll check if that's all it was.'

If that's all it was. 'I've got no evidence to suggest that the explosion was anything but a combination of circumstance,' Mark said, weighing his words with care. 'An aggrieved person striking out, unaware of the fuel load. But there *were* a couple of people who knew about the fuel. Jared at the depot. And I saw Dan Flanagan there, too. We spoke briefly.'

Steve raised his eyebrows. 'How long ago was that?'

'About four o'clock. I went straight to my office afterwards.'

'Did he say anything of interest?'

'You know what he's like. He said nothing that couldn't have been entirely innocent.'

'Hmm. I'll find a reason to have a chat with him, check what he was up to this afternoon.' Tapping his fingers on the table, working things through just as Mark was, Steve asked, 'Do you happen to know what information Jenn Barrett has found?'

'Something that may be odd about the crash site. She has some images on a memory stick. That's why she came to my office – to use my computer to view them.'

'Good. We could do with some leads.' Steve patted his laptop. 'Let's see if she's finished with the doc, and take a look at these images, then.'

When they walked back to her bed, Jenn was sitting upright, her natural, restless energy returning along with some colour to her face.

Morag Cameron glanced up from writing notes at the nurses' station and pointed her pen at him. 'Mark. Oxygen. Now. And leave it on until I've seen consistently improved levels.'

Constrained breathing and unfamiliar weakness still dragging at him, he didn't argue, but he pulled up chairs for himself and Steve beside Jenn's bed before he slid the plastic mask over his face. He needed to be functioning at his best and he'd do what he had to.

Morag filed her notes and left the quiet emergency department. Silence settled, only distant sounds from outside drifting in. While Steve booted the laptop, Jenn showed him the image from the newspaper.

'Is this in the police file you have, Mark?' he asked.

'Not that one. The only one in it is taken more from the front of the car, on the other side.' He found it harrowing to look at every time, despite the blurriness, with the low tree branch stabbing through the windscreen, and his imagination filling in the vision his head injury had wiped clean.

'Does it report on the damage to the car?'

'Describes the impact damage at the front, consistent with hitting a tree. No mention of other damage. I emailed a scan of the file to you not long before Jenn arrived at my office.'

'Good. Thanks. I'll go through it tonight.'

Mark doubted that the detective planned to sleep. With homicide detectives arriving shortly, there probably wouldn't be much sleep for any of them.

Jenn had the USB drive ready, and plugged it in as soon as Steve logged on and passed the laptop to her.

'There're two folders,' she murmured. '"Strelitz" – that'll be the one.'

Steve leaned forward to view the screen. Mark stood, resting a hip against the bed to look over Jenn's shoulder.

Jenn noticed, and angled the laptop towards both of them. 'There must be twenty or more photos here. Let's see . . .'

Image after image filled the screen, the Corolla his parents had given him for his birthday a red splash of colour against the darker, night-lit shades of trees and road around it, the blue tarp covering the passenger side of the car another stark contrast. Where Paula had died.

'There!' said Jenn, pointing at the screen. 'This is the photo Wolfgang used in the *Gazette*. Let me just zoom in.'

'Jesus,' Steve muttered under his breath. 'Why the hell . . .'

The lower portion of the image grew larger and clearer as Jenn zoomed in. There was no rear near-side wheel, only the drum, and a gouge in the half-metre of gravel between the edge of the road and where the drum rested. Mark's thoughts paralleled Steve's: how the hell could a front-on collision with a tree impact a rear wheel? Gil had never mentioned anything.

'I'll get on to Gillespie,' Steve said, his jaw tight, quick anger starting to rise. 'He must know something more than he's said.'

'Not necessarily,' Mark said as he lifted his oxygen mask, Gil's words from their conversation last week replaying in his memory: *I'd got you out of the car and was doing what I could for Paula. I couldn't get to her through her door so I was kneeling in the driver's seat . . .* 'Gil said he was on the other side of the car, on the driver's seat when the sergeant arrived. He might never have seen this side of the car.'

The last half-dozen images Jenn clicked through were quickly shot variations of the same angle, with the empty wheel well clear in all of them.

Mark smothered the flicker of hope with logic. 'It doesn't change anything,' he argued. 'I might still have been drinking. I might have run over something on the road and damaged the wheel.'

'Perhaps,' Jenn conceded, 'but why did they go to so much trouble to conceal it? It's not mentioned in the report, not mentioned in Gil's committal hearing. And why did Wolfgang suggest there's risk in knowing about it?'

A good question, and Mark considered it. Wolfgang was a man who kept to himself, so although they lived only a few kilometres apart Mark had little real knowledge or sense of him. Intelligent. Wary. Reserved, under a socially polite, artist façade. Reclusive, in that neither he nor his wife joined community activities, although they donated modest amounts to them.

Criminal? Other than the faint odour of marijuana wafting around him, Mark had seen or heard nothing to suggest it.

'This Wolfgang who gave you these – big bloke?' Steve asked. 'Lives outside Dungirri, off the main road and wears leather like a Viking?'

'Yes,' Jenn answered. 'Wolfgang Schmidt. He used to work part-time for the *Gazette*. Where do you want me to copy these images to?'

Steve began to reach over to take the laptop, then sat back again with noticeable self-restraint. 'Just copy them to the dropbox,' he said. 'That'll back them up to the server later.'

As she copied the folder across, from his view over her shoulder Mark read the name of the second folder: 'Bohème'. The faintest spider-web of a memory brushed the edge of his awareness but vanished before he could grasp it.

'Open the Bohème folder, Jenn.'

'Just about to,' she said.

Most of the files listed were named in some sort of code: six numbers, two or more letters. Dates perhaps – but if so, some related to the 1970s, long before digital photography. More than forty files, all images.

Jenn clicked on the first file.

'Shit,' said Steve.

Mark shifted slightly so that the glare from the overhead light didn't fall on the dark, under-exposed image. A black-and-white picture of a naked woman lying among cushions on a bed, her arms above her head . . . tied? . . . her legs spread wide. Nothing subtle or artistic or beautiful. Mark found the implied power of the photographer over the powerlessness of the woman repugnant.

'I don't . . .' Jenn shook her head and opened the next file. Then the next, and the next, working her way through the list.

More of the same kind of image, but with different women, different positions, their faces out of shot, some covered by blindfolds. A few included a naked male in the frame – but never a male face – and intercourse occurring. Intercourse – or rape? Mark saw little evidence of pleasure, and his disgust and anger increased with each image.

'I thought this guy was supposed to be some type of artist,' Steve objected. 'This is just porn. Bad bloody porn.'

Mark didn't argue the definition. 'But why did Wolfgang give these images to you, Jenn? Along with the accident photos?' he asked.

'I don't think . . . Listen, I've seen some of his work online. I researched erotic art for an article years ago. He does beautiful images, respectful, often in the natural environment, showing reverence for both people and nature. This stuff – it isn't even well framed, or properly in focus. There's no skill in this.'

'You're suggesting someone else took them?' Steve asked.

'Yes.'

Steve's phone burst into an incessant ring, and he swore and excused himself to take the call, answering it with a 'Yes, sir,' as he walked out the emergency-room door.

With a little more space, Mark pulled up his chair again. Not only could he see the screen better, he could see Jenn's face too. Brows drawn in concentration, she gnawed at her lip as she stared at the file list. The oxygen mask hung around her neck, forgotten. As he'd forgotten his. He didn't put it back on.

'If it's dates – years and months – some of these images are decades old and must have been scanned from originals,' she said. 'There're no clothes to date fashions, but the hairstyles . . . see, this one could well be the seventies. Can't really see her face, though, or her make-up. And see the last-modified dates? Looks like the files were created or modified on two consecutive days – July thirteenth and fourteenth – almost five months ago.'

Five months ago. Before Gil Gillespie had returned and the Flanagans' criminal activities had been exposed. Forty years after the first image was taken, if the date codes were correct. The woman in it might be in her sixties now.

'Can we take a look at the accident folder again?' Mark asked. He leaned forward to see more clearly, resting a hand on the bed beside her. He'd become accustomed to the smell of smoke that hung around him – both of them – but he caught another waft of it, and Jenn's hand moving on the track pad still wore the dressing from yesterday. Stark reminders of the dangers they'd survived. Of the dangers she'd faced that all, ultimately, came back to his announcement and the accident with Paula. The accident images and these images, Dan's veiled threats, Wolfgang's caution – he had to ensure her safety from whatever had been unleashed.

Jenn looked up from the screen at him, eyes narrowed by her frown. 'All the accident images were created around the same time as the other folder. July. Why July? Did anything happen then?'

'I can't think of anything significant. It was before Gil returned.'

'July. Five months . . . oh, shit. Marta died five months ago. Wolfgang's wife. He told me at the pub. They'd been together forever.'

He now remembered skimming the obituary. He'd known Marta only a little better than he'd known the more private Wolfgang. There'd been an exhibition of her work at the Birraga Art Society five or so years ago – the first local recognition of the talent in their midst. From their brief meetings he recalled a shy, self-effacing woman, who'd studied under a master potter in Germany before emigrating decades ago. And in the rubble or whatever remained of his Birraga office he had a set of her coffee mugs, the rich brown decorated with the salt-glaze technique in which she'd specialised.

'So, if Marta's death prompted him to scan the old photos, why?' Jenn thought aloud.

She sat there in the hospital bed, still with irritation reddening her eyes, dust and ash marking her T-shirt, and asked him why a man had delayed taking action on incriminating photographs until the woman he'd loved was gone.

'Perhaps he was protecting her. If these images represent illegal activity, then their existence is a threat to whoever's behind it. Gil was intimidated into pleading guilty because someone threatened to hurt Jeannie. If Marta was threatened, or Wolfgang was afraid they'd get to him through her, that might have kept him quiet.'

'Until it didn't matter anymore.'

'Yes.'

'We need to talk to him.'

'Yes. Or Steve does.' If Steve didn't, Mark would. He made that a silent vow. He had to find out from Wolfgang where the danger came from, so that he could protect Jenn, protect them all from it.

'But we still don't know what the connection is between the images in the Bohème folder and the accident.' Jenn's gaze drifted back to the screen, and the list of files. 'Okay, there're two – three – here from the year of the accident.' Her fingertips brushed over the track pad as she selected the files, and they opened in quick succession, one after another, tiling on the screen.

A woman, kneeling naked on a patterned carpet with her hands tied behind her, her head forward in submission, dark hair falling loose around her shoulders. Two more of the same woman, from different angles, curtains on a floor-length window visible in one, only a little of her face visible in the last, her face turned and shoulder raised as if flinching from something.

Mark's breath froze in his chest. 'Zoom it. There.'

As that portion of the image grew, so did the eyes of the woman, and the scar on her shoulder became clear. The scar she'd carried since she'd been thrown from a bolting horse at a barbed-wire fence when Mark was just a kid.

'Oh Jesus . . . oh fuck,' breathed Jenn. 'Is that—'

The ice in his chest spread, and the room around him narrowed to just those few square inches of screen, to the image that he could find no way to comprehend.

'Yes,' he said somehow, his voice strangled inside his head. 'That's my mother.'

TEN

Mark stayed silent a long time, his gaze fixed on the screen, on the image that felt to Jenn like a punch slamming into her gut every time her eyes were drawn back to it. Caroline Strelitz. Beautiful, self-assured, capable; as at home on a horse mustering cattle on the plains as presiding over an elegant dinner table or a meeting of the Dungirri Country Women's Association. And kind and encouraging to two girls lacking a strong female role model. She'd never been motherly or physically affectionate – neither of Mark's parents had been demonstrative, even towards him – but Caroline's practical advice on a few occasions, her down-to-earth expectation that a girl could – should – be whatever she chose to be, had stuck in Jenn's mind all these years, a reinforcing echo when she'd needed it of her own mother's principles.

To see Caroline in such a position of capitulation, of degradation, made absolutely no sense, and felt like a violation. She passed the laptop to Mark.

'I'll have to phone them,' he said at last, closing down the screen, as if he too had seen more than enough. 'I'll have to ask her what this is about.'

She didn't envy him that conversation. 'Where are they?'

'South America. This year they're building a school in Bolivia. Last year it was a clinic in Chile. They spend most of their time on charity projects in out-of-the-way places.' He exhaled a tight breath. 'I doubt I'll get on to them straightaway. I haven't even been able to tell them about the fire at Marrayin. I'll have to leave another message, but at least they might have time to get over the shock of it all, to prepare themselves before they call me back.'

Not a conversation any man should have with his mother, prepared or not. Also, she wondered whether giving them time to prepare a response in these possibly sordid circumstances might take them further away from the truth, rather than closer to it.

Damn it, when had she become such a cynic? Caroline and Len Strelitz had always been active, respected members of the community, both taking on leadership roles in numerous spheres. Caroline in the CWA, on the Dungirri Shire Council before it amalgamated with Birraga, and on the Birraga Hospital Board; Len in the Rural Fire Service, in the local branch of the Farmers' Federation, and in livestock research programs in conjunction with Harry Fletcher, the local veterinarian and Beth's father.

The Fletchers. Aside from her brief encounter with Beth, Jenn hadn't thought of them in years. They'd been close friends of Caroline and Len. Probably their closest; they'd certainly visited Marrayin more than anyone else in the time Jenn lived on the property. Barbecues, dinners, informal visits – hardly a week went by without them getting together. And Beth had stayed at Marrayin when her parents went to conferences overseas, a significant indication of trust by her protective parents. If Caroline had confided in a friend, it would most likely have been Beth's mother, Sylvia.

'If you can't get on to your folks, would it be worthwhile asking Sylvia Fletcher?' she suggested.

'Maybe. But it's not the kind of topic I want to broach with anyone other than my mother initially.'

'The police will ask questions. Steve will . . . if you tell him you recognised her.' Would she tell Steve, if Mark didn't? No, not yet. Not tonight, anyway.

Mark dropped his head on to his hands and rubbed his uninjured temple. 'I'll tell him.'

One more horrendous task on top of everything he'd already faced. The deep lines of fatigue on his face and the dust streaking pale lines in his brown hair gave her a glimpse of how he would age in ten, fifteen years. Had he slept at all last night? She doubted it.

'Why don't you leave it until morning?' she said gently. 'You look exhausted.'

'No, this could be something key. Steve needs to know. But first I'll phone and leave a message for them.' He reached to the pocket of his shirt. 'I'll go outside where it's quiet.'

'I'll go through the images again while you're doing that,' she said. 'I'll see if I can piece together any pattern, make any sense of the file names.' Like the two-letter code after the numerical section of the file name. Her fingers itched to open the laptop again, but she'd wait until Mark left. In her distraction earlier she hadn't properly registered the file names on his mother's photos, but now she recalled seeing the suffix 'CN'. Caroline Napier? All the locals knew her maiden name – half of them had called her by it – as generations of her family had held another prominent grazing property west of Birraga, at least until drought and illness took their toll.

'Will you be okay here for a few minutes?' Mark asked.

'Of course,' she said, but he hesitated for a moment until Rhonda returned, carrying a box of dressings.

'Doctor Cameron said the radiology reports shouldn't be long,' she told them as she crossed to a storeroom.

The pain in Jenn's ankle had eased considerably and once the X-rays confirmed that it wasn't fractured she would leave, as long as Mark's scans didn't reveal any problems. Getting back to Dungirri might be difficult tonight – she assumed her car would be a smoking wreck – but even a night in a Birraga motel was preferable to a night in the hospital. She'd coped, so far, because of the distraction of Wolfgang's images, but the prospect of staying all night here, in the dark and quiet with nothing to occupy her thoughts except the memories of both her mother and Jim dying in this room . . . she couldn't bear to contemplate it.

She pulled Steve's computer back on to her lap and skimmed the list of files again. No other files with the suffix 'CN', but one with a longer alpha/numeric code, ending with six letters – CNLSGM. From the year of Mark's birth, if she interpreted the date code correctly, and among the earliest images. More initials? It could be. CN for Caroline, LS fitted Len Strelitz, but she couldn't think of anyone with the initials GM.

She opened the file. Another black-and-white image. A party scene. If her mouth hadn't been dry she'd have whistled. Some party. In the corner of the image, a man sat naked, playing a grand piano. Not surprisingly, Jenn didn't recognise the slim torso and buttocks, or the semi-dressed couple draped over the piano groping each other.

But in the centre of the image, Caroline stood, young and pretty in a clinging seventies-style halter dress, a champagne glass in her left hand. The man holding her from behind had his face buried in her neck, one hand possessively low on her abdomen, the other cupping her breast. Unsmiling, her face was turned away from him, towards another man. Len Strelitz. Len, leaning against a wall in a half-unbuttoned shirt, drinking from a wine glass, his face tight with anger.

CNLSGM – she'd been right. Caroline Napier, Len Strelitz, and GM . . . who the hell was the man embracing her in that predatory, controlling grasp? She could see no sign of a ring on Caroline's hand, but Len's reaction and her pleading look at him signalled their interest in each other.

No-one else in the image seemed worried by, or even aware of, the undercurrents between the three in the striking tableau. Around them, the piano player, the groping couple, and a quartet of people sitting on the floor with a guitar and a bong partied on, oblivious.

'Definitely not a CWA meeting,' Jenn muttered to herself. 'Just what kind of craziness did you get caught up in, Caroline?'

Sex and power, mixed with alcohol and drugs. A combination that could rapidly become dangerous, particularly in the absence of trust and respect.

The bell in the reception area pierced the quiet, jerking her back to awareness of her clinical surroundings. On the reception side of the nurses' station, Rhonda spoke with someone before buzzing them in to the emergency area through the connecting door.

Steve, not Mark. The small flutter of expectation died before Jenn even recognised it.

The detective strode across the room, took his seat beside the bed and resumed the interrupted discussion without wasting a syllable. 'Mark said you'd found a photo of his mother.'

With the permission implicit in Mark's sharing of the information, she opened the later image and turned the screen to Steve. He whistled under his breath. 'That's her? Mrs Strelitz?'

'Yes. You've not met her?'

'No. I don't think they visit here often. Not when I've been here, anyway.'

A purely pragmatic curiosity got the better of her. The more she knew about the detective, the more effectively she'd be able to work with him. 'Have you been based here long?'

'Me? No. I usually work out of Dubbo. I was called in to work on the Sutherland kiddie abduction a couple of years ago. And again last year when Ryan and Beth's little girl was taken. Thankfully that worked out better than the first one.' The guarded solemnity in his face dissolved into a sardonic twist of his mouth. 'Hell knows why they asked me back but I've been temporarily filling a two-month vacancy for six months now.'

In a hotel in – where had it been? London? Moscow maybe? – she'd skimmed the few terse lines in her uncle's email telling her the news of the death of Mitch and Sara Sutherland's daughter, experiencing a detached twinge of sorrow for them before the next email and pressures of work distracted her again. A year later, after a week working in Southern Sudan she'd caught up with her emails, and Beth's daughter was already found, safe and well. Jenn had dozens of dead Sudanese children to write about so Dungirri news again slipped to the back of her mind, nothing to concern her.

But this man, with his cynicism and no connections to Dungirri, had walked through hell with her former schoolmates and neighbours.

She put the discomfort in her chest down to after-effects of smoke inhalation and ignored it. 'So, why take a posting here in the backblocks? Surely there must be plenty of other detective postings.'

He leaned back casually in the chair, hands in his pockets, legs outstretched, and his crooked grin was half-sardonic, half-boyish. 'Oh, a stint in purgatory is supposed to be good for a sinning soul. And it's a long way from my father.'

She recognised it as a measured, strategic admission, not so much relaxing of any personal guard but designed to gain her trust. Steve Fraser was playing a role and wasn't about to reveal anything truly personal. Nevertheless she asked, 'You have daddy issues?'

'Assistant Police Commissioner Fraser issues.'

She recognised the name. 'He's your father? The tall, dour guy?'

'Yep, that's him. He sure isn't renowned for his sense of humour.'

Daddy issues, indeed. The disconnect between her knowledge of Steve and the stiff, formal and yes, decidedly humourless senior officer who appeared in media briefings . . . not hard to imagine a chasm of issues, there.

Steve grinned and shrugged his shoulders. 'Maybe I should have bucked the family tradition and joined the army instead of the cops.'

'My father was in the army.' She didn't mean to speak, but the words were gone, unable to be recalled. Just words. Nothing to do with the memories of an exploding car and her mother's death in this room. She would not, could not, allow those memories to overwhelm her.

'Barrett. Isn't there a Barrett on the Memorial Hall roll?' Steve asked.

'That's my grandfather, Paul Aloysius Barrett. He earned a Distinguished Conduct Medal and lost a leg in Vietnam. He died just before Paul and Paula were born. Hence their names.'

'Ah. Honouring a hero in the family. But you escaped that.'

She shrugged. 'Not entirely. Jennifer Pauline. I came a year later, though, and it was already confusing enough with Paul and Paula.'

'Your dad was the only one of his sons who followed him into the army?'

'Yes. If he stayed here it would have been either the timber mill or agricultural work. The army paid more and provided better training.'

'Was your mother a local?'

Don't ask about my mother. Not here. Not now. 'No.' She kept her voice just steady enough to offer the bare minimum. 'An army nurse he met at Puckapunyal. But my family history isn't relevant,' she pointed at the laptop, 'to this.'

'Old crime in a small town,' he said mildly, 'in my experience, that makes everything, current and past, potentially relevant.'

In her experience, too. Damn him for being right. But once again she deflected the focus away from herself. 'Wolfgang must believe the roots of this crime go back years, because he also included this image. That's Caroline, and Len over on the right.'

Steve raised his eyebrows, spent long moments studying the photo of the party, then reached over to the track pad to flick between the two images. When she told him about the file-name code – dates and initials – he asked to take a look himself and she reluctantly passed his laptop back to him.

Without the distraction of the computer, she shifted restlessly.

She could hear Rhonda's voice in the triage room, talking to another woman, soothing a sobbing child. Just as a nurse had soothed her when she'd been twelve, desperate to reach her dying mother, incoherent with shock and terror.

Oh, crap, she couldn't do this. She pushed the cotton blanket back and swung her legs over the edge of the bed, reaching for the crutches Rhonda had brought a while ago.

'Hey, you okay?' Steve asked, dumping the laptop on the bed, moving to her side.

'Yes. Just a sane, rational adult woman on the verge of a panic attack.' Her strangled attempt at a laugh didn't sound exactly *sane*. 'I just need some fresh air and space. *Now.*'

Without comment he handed her the crutches, helped her steady herself, then, tucking his laptop under his arm, he walked with her out to the ER reception area and through the glass doors to the almost-deserted foyer beyond.

Mark. She almost burst into irrational tears the second she saw him. He and Morag Cameron broke their conversation and crossed swiftly to her.

'I'm fine,' she said to forestall their questions. 'I will be fine. Just . . . Doc, I hope you've got good news on those X-rays, because I'm checking out.'

'No fractures,' Morag said. 'But I'd like you to stay overnight, under observation.'

'No. No offence, but I can't do it.' She felt ridiculous. Maybe if she explained, they wouldn't all think she was losing it. She leaned on the crutches, her injured foot resting lightly on the floor for balance. Words, just words, and rational ones at that, if only she could get them into a clear, concise order. She sucked in a breath. 'There's a few too many bad memories. Not just Jim. I saw my mother die in there when I was twelve. My father was killed . . . they both died . . . the car-bomb explosion . . . I'm not usually emotional, but . . .'

If she opened her mouth for one more word she would howl. She dropped her head, feeling the pain in her lip as she bit it, desperate to keep the sobs building in her throat from escaping. Control. *Control.* She *had* to pull herself together and stop this stupid overreaction.

A hand clasped her shoulder, then became an arm around her, and she knew it was Mark because of the scent of smoke on his clothes. And because the ghost of the teenager she'd been knew she could rest her head against his shoulder. Just for a moment.

'It's okay, Jenn,' he said, with the gentleness that had always been his strength. 'Breathe. Cry if you need to. We'll find somewhere else to stay tonight. You're going to be fine.'

She meant to move away from him after that moment but she stayed, her wet cheek dampening the soft cotton of his shirt, his arms firm and warm holding her. Part of her was twelve again, running away in distress from the hateful house and the nightmares, lost in never-ending bush in the dark . . . before the boy found her, wrapped a rug around her, lifted her on to his horse and promised to teach her about the land so that she could always find her way, and never feel so lost and alone again.

⁓

Midnight came and went, and still Mark lay awake, his thoughts too crowded and active to allow him to slip into sleep on the hot, still night. Starlight shone through the narrow window above the bunk bed, and occasionally the headlights of the police car making a sweep of the caravan park flashed into the room, the officer exchanging greetings in a low voice with the one on guard outside the cabin.

In the main room of the cabin Jenn slept in the double bed, peaceful for now. He could see her through the door she'd insisted he leave open so the slight breeze from the overhead fan could flow into the tiny bunkroom. At times she turned, or caught her breath or murmured something in her sleep, but the wave of panic that had caught her in the hospital had dissipated once she was out in the fresh air and calm of the night.

With Birraga's only motel full with a tour group, and the hotels too insecure in Steve's opinion, the caravan-park cabin had been their only choice.

In the morning he'd make arrangements to take Jenn to Dungirri and return to Marrayin, but even if he had access to a vehicle now he had enough sense not to risk a long drive in the dark after the minor injuries of the explosion. And he could not have left her alone in the hotel in Dungirri tonight. Besides, Steve would be back in the morning, with the homicide detective and prints of all the photographs so that they could go through them all properly, one by one.

Mark checked his watch, the time glowing in the darkness. One in the morning. In Bolivia his parents were fifteen hours behind – ten a.m., Saturday. If they were travelling into the nearest small town from the village they might already be there, might have checked their email. He reached for his phone. No messages.

He closed his eyes again. Exhaustion, physical and mental, overwhelmed him. His mind was fruitlessly dragging all the unanswered questions around and around. He needed to stop thinking, get some rest.

His senses leapt to full alert as Jenn caught her breath again and made a small sound into the pillow. But she turned on to her side and settled without waking, curled under the sheet, one arm clutching it to her chest.

Thirty seconds, perhaps a minute he'd held her tonight before she'd regained her equilibrium and limped away with a murmured apology; not much longer the night before when Jim had died.

He couldn't ignore it any longer. All the friendship, the affection, the *love* he'd felt for her in their teens – none of it had faded. And neither would the memory of those few minutes of closeness. The pride, resilience and independence that had enabled her to survive and triumph over a difficult youth remained, stronger than ever, and he doubted she would reveal that much vulnerability again, allow him close again. She'd leave Dungirri as soon as she could – and who could blame her? Her wounds cut too deeply and she had nothing to hold her here, nothing she cared about enough to stop her from going. Just like last time, he would have to let her go. And just like last time, she would leave an aching void in his life.

He rolled on to his stomach and punched the lumpy pillow into a better shape. With one arm flung over it, he rested his face against it, and just for a moment allowed himself to remember the warmth of Jenn in his arms and the trust and connection between them.

He woke with sunlight streaming through the window on to his face, the sound of running water in the small bathroom and the quiet rolling crunch of a car pulling up on the gravel outside. Sitting up hastily, he narrowly avoided hitting his head on the low bunk above, but relaxed on hearing Steve greet their guard-duty officer.

He yanked his smoky, ash-stained jeans on again and didn't bother to tuck in his rumpled shirt before he answered Steve's knock on the cabin's sliding door.

Steve handed Mark a plastic bag as he walked in. 'Kris said she sent some clothes for Jenn around last night, and here's my contribution. Clean jeans and T-shirt. Thank me later. Sorry I didn't have any socks washed, and I ain't lending anyone my jocks.'

'We can all be thankful for that,' Mark joked in return. A shower and fresh clothes would help to clear the grogginess in his head and wake him up properly. Six hours' sleep hadn't quite made up for days of sleep deprivation. Coffee might help, too – the empty mug in the sink said Jenn had already had some. He refilled the still-warm electric kettle and set it to boil, found the remaining two mugs in the cupboard and emptied a couple of instant-coffee packets into them.

Steve dropped a bulging folder on the table and pulled out one of the chairs. 'That's the printouts of the photos. Not for sharing around, but maybe you or Jenn might recognise more people. I only recognised one. Nothing to pin on him, of course, but wherever there's a hint of trouble, he's there somewhere.'

Mark took the enlarged black-and-white photographic print Steve passed him. The door of a house, a large bush to one side of it, and two men on the porch, exchanging a joke as if they'd just walked out the door after an enjoyable time.

It took him only a second to identify one of the men. 'Dan Flanagan,' he said. 'But he's a fair bit younger there. What's the date code on the file?'

'The file names are on the backs of the photos. That one doesn't have initials like the others, but it has a precise date – day, month and year.'

Mark flipped it over. 'Two months before the accident. Around the same time as the photo of my mother. But there's no indication here what the connection is.'

'No. You're good with faces and names – any idea who the other bloke is?'

Mark stared at the man's face, a vague fraction of memory again dancing in and out of his mind, never quite solid enough to grasp.

The latch on the bathroom door clicked and Jenn limped out, her dark hair wet around her shoulders, the borrowed blue T-shirt loose over a pair of jeans. Her face had more colour than last night's pallor, and although her eyes still carried some strain, the redness had gone. She'd left the crutches by her bed but seemed able to put weight on her injured foot, albeit briefly.

Mark drew out a chair for her. 'How are you feeling this morning?'

'Better than last night. Somewhere approaching human. And you?'

'About the same.' He passed her the photo. 'We didn't look at this one last night. Do you recognise the man on the right?'

'That's Dan Flanagan on the left, isn't it?'

'Yes.'

'This other guy – he's familiar. But I can't remember . . .' Her brow furrowed as she focused, deep in thought. 'He can't be from Dungirri, because we knew everyone there. Must be Birraga, or the region—' Her eyes widened. 'The bank. Not the one your office was in, Mark. The one in the main street, on the other side of Vanna's salon from the *Gazette*. He was senior, the manager or deputy manager or something. Mc-something. Irish.'

Mark placed him, now, with sparse recollections of seeing him around town. Not part of his parents' social or business circles, as far as he'd been aware. Marrayin's accounts were with a different bank. 'McCarthy?' he asked, the name coming to mind, but not quite right.

'Maybe . . . No, it was McCarty,' Jenn said, emphasising the hard 't'. 'I remember now. Gerard McCarty.'

Mark realised the significance of the name the same moment she did. GM. They both reached for the pile of photos but it was closer to him, and he quickly flicked through to find the early one of his parents at the party, and laid it on the table. 'The question is: is this also him?' He didn't voice the bigger questions – about the relationship between his mother and the man, and the implication of the sequence of photos that there'd been some connection, some cause-and-effect, for more than eighteen years, from before his birth until the accident.

'Could be him,' Steve said. 'Can't see his face, though. Is this guy still in town, Mark? I haven't run into him.'

'That bank closed its Birraga branch while I was at uni. He must have gone somewhere else, because I can't recall seeing him since then.' Gone, and with him any immediate answers. An internet search might find his current whereabouts, but whatever Steve planned officially, Mark also intended to discover what he could.

Steve's phone beeped, and with a quick glance at it he rose. 'I have to go. Briefing with homicide and the boss in five minutes. I'd appreciate it if you two could go through each image today, see who you can identify. I'll be in touch again later this morning. Jenn, the constable can run you back to Dungirri and you to Marrayin when you're ready, Mark. We can only spare one officer at present to protect you but she can stay with you today.'

'No,' Mark objected. 'I can arrange a ride home for us, and I'm not convinced there's a threat to my life. The most likely scenario is that last night's attack was aimed at my car, not me. Vandalism, not a murder attempt. If it hadn't been for the fuel, I'd have only had a damaged ute.' The fact that Dan Flanagan knew of the fuel worried him, but the chances of Dan organising a murder attempt in an hour or two had to be slim, and if Dan really wanted him dead, surely there were far more effective ways to accomplish it. 'You must have higher priorities for the available officers,' he continued. 'I know how thinly they're spread even when there aren't two arson attacks and two deaths to investigate.'

He could see Steve wavering, the harsh realities of perpetual short-staffing an undeniable issue. 'Okay. For the moment. I'll see what the Feds have to say. Maybe they've got some resources to spare. I'll let you know.'

Mark stood on the cabin's porch as Steve drove away, followed by the constable in the marked police car. When he turned inside again, Jenn was watching him, photos spread out on the table in front of her.

'Are you thinking what I'm thinking?' she asked.

'I'm thinking that I should be able to hire a car from my mechanic. He keeps a couple of loan cars for customers. And then I'm thinking that it's not much of a detour to Wolfgang Schmidt's place on the way home.'

She smiled, the austere lines of her face softening into a beauty that had only deepened in the years she'd been away, and that made his chest tighten.

'Great minds think alike,' she said.

ॐ

Jenn almost didn't recognise in Mark's mechanic the pimply, pipsqueak kid who'd been a couple of years below her at Birraga

High, but Ian remembered her – or at least knew of her local connections. Word had travelled and in the circumstances Ian didn't object to being called on a Sunday, and quickly offered to bring around a vehicle. He arrived within ten minutes, with a blue Pulsar sedan. More than ten years old and a little dented and faded in the paintwork, but mechanically sound and clean – and automatic, so she didn't need a functioning left foot to drive it.

'How much to hire it for a few days?' she asked, reaching for her credit card, determined to refuse to let Mark pay. He had his LandCruiser at Marrayin, and only needed to get to it. She needed to have a car until her insurance company provided a proper hire car or a replacement car, and out here that would probably take days.

'No charge,' Ian said. 'Use it for the whole week if you need it. It's bloody terrible what happened to your cars. That kind of shit doesn't belong in Birraga.'

Didn't belong anywhere. But she kept seeing it again and again and it didn't matter if it was Birraga or Baghdad or Beirut – the combination of anger, violence and weapons was a human speciality, both individually and collectively.

The cynicism brought a sour taste to her mouth and she reminded herself that decent people like Ian still existed, people who'd go out of their way to do a favour for someone they hardly knew. And people like Mark, who stood up for their ideals and dedicated themselves to serving their communities, to bringing communities together rather than ripping them apart – negotiators and peacemakers who too often became the target of an assassin's gun.

She shivered, despite the growing heat of the day, thankful that Mark lived here, in western New South Wales, and not in some place where war and hatred raged. She smiled, shook Ian's hand and wished him the best.

While Mark showered, Jenn washed their mugs, stuffed their smoky clothes into a plastic bag, and hobbled around to sweep the cabin floor. She picked up the car keys when he emerged from the bathroom.

'I'll drive. You can check your emails and phone messages on the way.'

He didn't object. 'Thanks. Can we go past my office? I'd like to see how bad the damage is.'

When Jenn pulled to a stop beside the barriers closing the street, they both stared silently at the rubble. Little remained of the building apart from the back wall and a small portion of the front wall, the angle of the latter looking precarious with no internal beams to support it. What the fire hadn't destroyed the demolishers would have to pull down. Her car was a shell of blackened metal and Mark's ute was unrecognisable. She made a mental note to call her insurance company this morning.

The lone policeman on duty recognised Mark and strolled over, leaning on the side of the car to chat through the open window.

'G'day, Mark.' He nodded in her direction. 'Morning, Miss. Can't let you any closer than this, sorry. Walls might collapse.'

'No worries, Todd,' Mark said. 'I just wanted to get an idea of the damage.' From some well of internal strength, he dragged up a grin. 'We left in rather a hurry last night.'

'Too bloody right,' Todd replied. 'Must have been some blast. Arson squad will be here soon to take a look. Hope they find some evidence so we can catch the bastard.'

Todd didn't mention it, and Mark didn't either, but clearly visible in the middle of the blocked-off street sat a chunk of the base of a brown bottle. Jenn had seen enough Molotov cocktails thrown to know you gripped it at the base with your dominant hand, lit the taper with your other, and flung it, hard.

She waited until she'd completed a three-point turn and was back on the main street again before she said, 'There might be fingerprints on that piece of bottle.'

Mark glanced up from his phone. 'Yes. But fingerprints aren't helpful unless they can be matched on a database, or to a suspect.'

'You're right. And real-life crimes aren't solved as easily as on TV, in a one-hour program.' She heartily wished they could be, but the gulf between reality and fantasy grew even wider with the added complication of isolation. The autopsies on Jim Barrett and Edward Russell would be held in Newcastle, hundreds of kilometres away. The arson investigators were travelling from Tamworth – again. The forensic team was coming from Inverell – again. And Steve, the lone detective in a district of hundreds of square kilometres, was trying to cover it all, with Kris Matthews and the dozen or so other uniformed officers stationed at Birraga. 'Please tell me you have an email from your parents, explaining everything.'

'Nothing from them yet,' Mark said. 'I'll check my phone.'

She drove silently while he dialled and listened to message after message, the line of his mouth tighter with each one. At one point he had to hold the phone away from his ear, the abusive yelling loud enough for her to hear.

Graffiti on his office door, the firebomb, abusive messages . . . 'Are they all like that?' she asked as he cut off the message.

'There's a few,' he acknowledged, without being specific. 'My standing in the community took a nose-dive yesterday.'

'Would you like me to vet them for you?' That, she could do for him. Spare him the pain of listening to them all.

'No. Thanks. I have to go through and save them all. And if my parents have phoned, their message might be in the middle of the others.'

The sun was still low enough in the morning sky to cast shadows from the trees lining the road, the kilometres flickered by. The tree at the site of the accident seemed more benign in daylight than in darkness, its long-dead branches grey against the startling blue sky. As the Birraga River began its curve to skirt around the base of Ghost Hill, she slowed, looking out for the pottery sign on the other side of the road and the track leading into the large pocket of scrub, a few hundred hectares that had never been cleared.

The sign for the pottery had gone, only a bare post with empty hooks remaining, but she saw it in time to make the turn without hard braking. The track had deep ridges of sand and she had to take it slowly, keeping the car to one side so that the undercarriage didn't drag down the centre ridge, and it was a constant struggle to keep the car straight.

Some men might have commented, criticised or offered to drive. Mark didn't. Even when teaching her to drive in Marrayin's paddocks he'd never belittled her skills or undermined her confidence. Unlike many men she'd met over the years.

He finally finished listening to his voice messages and lowered his phone. 'Forty-eight messages, but nothing from my parents,' he said. 'They can't always get into the nearest town easily. Maybe later today or tomorrow.'

Disappointment dropped her spirits low. Probably not as low as his, although he hadn't expressed frustration. Only that hopeful '*maybe later . . .*' She tried to be positive. 'Wolfgang should be able to give us some answers.'

The sandy track running through the trees ended at a gravelled parking area in front of the mud-brick pottery studio. An open shed on the side protected a large brick kiln, with a wood pile beside it. Thirty metres beyond the studio the house stood on the other side of the wide clearing in the scrub, a vine-covered pergola providing cooling shade around it.

'Have you been here before?' she asked Mark.

'Only once, I think. I was just a kid. They were living in part of the studio then, still building the house.'

The blinds were drawn over the studio windows but the door was open. Leaving the crutches in the back seat, Jenn walked unaided beside Mark along the paved veranda, and knocked on the door. With the contrast of bright sunlight outside and shade inside, at first she could see nothing, so she called out, 'Wolfgang? It's Jenn Barrett.'

Her eyes adjusted to the light. A showroom area inside the door, shelves lining the walls but only a few pieces of pottery remaining – plates and bowls and mugs. Packing materials were spread on a central table, sealed boxes stacked on the floor. In the work space beyond were two kick wheels, work tables, two large sinks, along with more shelves, some holding clays, glazes and tools, and a couple holding unfired pottery.

But no sign of Wolfgang.

'He's probably at the house,' Mark said. 'Are you okay to walk that far?'

She nodded. 'Sure.'

A gravel pathway led to the house, taking a straighter route than the curving driveway. Sunshine beamed, birds flittered and chattered in the native garden, and a stumpy-tailed lizard scuttled away at their approach. A peaceful retreat from the world – no wonder Wolfgang and Marta rarely ventured into town.

She opened her mouth to comment, but the loud report of a gunshot cracked through the air, and a bullet sprayed the gravel in front of her feet.

ELEVEN

They set off at a run to the house, Mark crossing behind Jenn to protect her exposed side, his arm around her waist as both support and body shield.

The shot had come from the wooded slope to the east of the house. A second shot went wide. A third ricocheted off one of the pergola posts. But then they were at the house, the building providing cover.

Mark supported her as she limped further along the paving under the pergola, her face twisted in pain. Watching her, he almost didn't see the trail of blood.

Ants milled around the first drops; flies buzzed at the larger, sticky puddle and the bloodied hand prints on the open door.

Jenn caught her breath. 'Wolfgang—'

A shot sounded from inside the house, then a second. It was hard to tell, but Mark didn't think it was in their direction, and the nearby windows stayed intact.

Mark pushed Jenn down between two large half-barrel planters. 'If you've got your phone, call for help,' he whispered. She nodded, her fingers at the zip of her leather bag.

He stepped over the pool of blood, saw the trail criss-crossing the open-plan living area, and Wolfgang slumped by a panelled glass door, barely gripping a hunting rifle that pointed out through one of many shattered panels. The cushion stuffed under his abdomen was sodden with blood. The phone on the floor beside him also had blood on it. Mark hoped that meant he'd already called for help.

Wolfgang mumbled something in German, and squeezed the trigger again, the reverberation echoing in the house.

Mark dropped down to crouch on the floor, using the sofa as cover to get to the injured man. Sunshine streamed through the French doors, stifling the room and intensifying the sharp stench of blood.

'Mark?' Jenn called.

'I'm okay,' he called back. She had to be safer in here with him and a rifle than outside alone. 'Come in but stay low. Wolfgang's hurt.'

'Keeping bastard . . . up there,' Wolfgang muttered as Mark heard Jenn edging into the house. 'More ammo . . . laundry . . . cupboard.'

Mark risked a quick glance through the remains of the glass door. The cleared area around the house and studio stretched more than fifty metres before the scrub began again. Good bushfire protection, and a long way for a sniper to cross in clear view. Movement on the edge of the scrub caught his eye. He took the rifle from Wolfgang's limp grasp, and raised it to his shoulder. Balancing the weight, he aimed and fired, holding steady against the rifle's recoil. The sniper ducked back into the trees.

Mark slipped to the other side of the doorway, where he had a better line of fire and wasn't reaching over Wolfgang. In his peripheral vision he saw Jenn drop to her knees beside the injured man, sliding a box of ammunition clips across to Mark. Enough to hold the sniper for a short while until help came – assuming he didn't have friends nearby.

'Help's coming, Wolfgang,' Jenn murmured, taking his hand. 'The ambulance won't be long.'

'Won't . . . make . . . it.'

Mark kept his eyes and the rifle trained on the trees in the distance, but he heard the despair in Jenn's unsteady voice.

'Of course you're going to make it. You have to be all right. I need answers to questions, Wolfie, and you're the only one with them. So, you just lie still and keep breathing and they'll have you in hospital in no time.'

'Bohème club . . . sex . . . taught Dan . . . develop . . . photos . . .' The words trailed away, his breathing becoming hoarse gasps.

'Shush, Wolfie. No need to talk now. You can tell me later,' she lied. 'You'll be fine to tell me later.'

The sniper moved again, a white shirt against the brown grass, and Mark waited one second before he pulled the trigger so that he could get a look at the man. A bush hat shading his face, jeans belted over a generous gut. Mark fired just to the right of the man, sending him back behind the tree.

He reloaded, and in those brief seconds he saw tears running down Jenn's face, Wolfgang's closed eyes and grey face and he heard the deathly slow, faltering breathing.

But he murmured again, and Mark had to strain to hear: 'Club . . . convent . . . went bad . . . blackmail . . . hurt Marta.'

Jenn gulped, choking back a sob, in her eyes a silent, desperate plea to Mark before she leaned over Wolfgang, hugging him, stroking his cheek. 'Don't try to talk, Wolfie,' she whispered. 'Just stay with us.'

'Marta . . .' He exhaled the single word, and fell silent.

Mark blinked away the moisture in his own eyes, training the rifle's scope on the figure weaving up through the trees, away from the house. Away from Jenn. If the man turned and doubled back, Mark would shoot to kill.

He didn't move until the distant figure topped the rise and disappeared, and the faint wail of sirens became a loud blare outside the house.

And all those long minutes Jenn talked softly to Wolfgang, holding him and soothing him, stroking his face as his life drained away.

⁂

The senior detective from homicide gave all the orders. What she lacked in size she more than made up for in authority, coordinating the police response on the scene with cool, no-nonsense efficiency.

Jenn sat on the timber edge of a raised vegetable garden, shivering despite the sun's heat, watching half a dozen uniformed police gear up in protective vests to start searching the area for the sniper while the detective grilled Mark over by the studio. Unlike the younger detective constable who'd briefly interviewed Jenn, every subtlety of her body language and tone telegraphed scepticism and suspicion.

Beth came out of the house, the orange trousers and navy T-shirt of her SES uniform incongruous on her petite figure, the large first-aid kit looking heavy in her hand – and of no use to Wolfgang.

Beth crossed the dry lawn and knelt beside her. 'How are you holding up, Jenn? Would you like me to clean up your hands?'

Jenn held out her arms, Wolfgang's blood smeared almost up to her right elbow. 'Thanks.'

While Beth spread out a plastic sheet with saline and wipes and set to work on her hands, Jenn watched the interchange between Mark and the detective. Mark stood his ground, his courteous manner remaining firm despite the detective's forceful style. Although she couldn't hear the words, it seemed Mark calmly repeated his story, again and again, answering every question without hesitation.

Noting the direction of her attention, Beth cast a glance over her shoulder towards them. 'Don't worry about Mark. He's been in parliament for six years. He can hold his own.'

He could hold his own against the toughest journalists, too. Jenn knew his reputation, had watched interviews. He wouldn't crack because he wasn't hiding anything. But the detective had yet to realise that. 'Do you know where Steve is?' she asked Beth.

'He's not here.' Beth dropped her voice. 'I think he's off the case.'

'Off the case? Why the hell would she—'

'He's friends with Mark, friends with Gil. Maybe she thinks he's too close to it.'

Or maybe their very different styles clashed. 'If he called her "sweetheart",' Jenn mused, 'he'll be busted down to constable. Or buried.'

'Oh, I think Steve's smarter than that these days.'

So did Jenn. But regardless of the reason, if Steve was off the case, chances were she and Mark would be sidelined, and denied information. She narrowed her eyes against the sunlight, planning. 'I need to talk with you later, Beth. Will you be home this afternoon?'

'All day, as long as there are no call-outs.'

'Good. Thanks.' She stood up, testing her ankle, putting her full weight on it and holding it. Painful, yes, but bearable. 'I'll talk to you later.'

She walked across the grass at a reasonable pace without favouring her ankle, concentrating on not grimacing despite the pain. As she reached Mark and the detective she held out her hand with such assured confidence that the detective accepted the invited handshake automatically.

'Detective Haddad, isn't it? As Mark will have told you, I'm Jennifer Barrett. I'm sorry to have kept you waiting.'

Dark eyes raked over her, set to drill. Haddad knew exactly who she was. 'Ms Barrett. I hope I don't need to remind you that this matter is a police investigation and the details and name of the deceased are not yet released to be broadcast.'

Jenn met the rigid formality with another serve of imperturbable courtesy. 'Detective, I'm sure Steve Fraser has briefed you about my family connections to this case. You have my word that I will respect the investigative process. I have no wish to have my family's tragedies become the centre of a media storm.'

'That makes two of us,' Haddad replied, infusing the few words with a chilly warning. 'Mr Strelitz,' she continued, turning to Mark, 'a forensic officer will be here shortly. He will require your fingerprints, and the clothes you are wearing. Please wait in the garden until he arrives. Ms Barrett, I—'

'Are you arresting me, Detective Haddad?' Mark spoke over her.

She didn't make that mistake. Not in front of a journalist who could have it on national news bulletins within an hour. 'You were in possession of a loaded, recently fired weapon at the scene of a fatal shooting. I expect your full cooperation in the investigation.'

'Which I have already given and will continue to do so,' Mark responded evenly, with no sign of offence. 'Naturally your priority is to conduct a thorough investigation. I'll go home and change – it's only a couple of kilometres from here – and you can send an officer to collect the clothes.'

Jenn didn't feel inclined to be so polite, but she took her cue from Mark's assertive, win–win approach. She could understand the detective's perspective: two people found at the scene of the crime with no other witnesses and, as yet, little evidence to support the existence of the sniper.

'If you want my clothes, too, you can have someone collect them at the hotel in Dungirri. As I promised the detective constable, I'll write up my statement today, including the few words that Wolfgang spoke before he died. I think they may be relevant. If you give me your business card, I'll email that to you as well as to Steve Fraser.'

Haddad nodded curtly. 'Thank you. I may need to speak to you again later. Which hotel are you staying at?'

A city woman who obviously hadn't looked around Dungirri yet. 'There's only one,' Jenn replied. 'You can't miss it. But here's my card with my mobile number.'

'Thank you.' The detective tucked the card in her pocket without looking at it and walked away, a mental dismissal as she moved on to her next problem.

'She's just doing her job, Jenn,' Mark said, too easily reading the annoyance she thought she'd concealed.

'I understand that. The scary thing is, I look at her and see aspects of myself.'

Oh, the detective could probably be polite and friendly, even charming if necessary, just as Jenn could. But Jenn also recognised the single-minded focus, the total absorption in the work, and she wondered if Leah Haddad had any life outside the job.

08

Someone had been in the cottage. Mark stood in the open doorway after Jenn dropped him at Marrayin and surveyed the sparse contents of the living room. He didn't have much in there – the few camping chairs and a folding table he'd brought down from the shed, a couple of boxes from his Canberra apartment – but the chairs had been moved to reach the boxes, and they were open, the books and papers no longer neatly packed. In the bedroom he saw the telltale signs of interference: the door of the wardrobe where he'd hung his Canberra clothes ajar, a kit bag holding his few remaining casual clothes gaping open, the camp bed slightly out of position.

Not vandalism or destruction, but a search. For what? The old police report? If so, the intruder went to a great deal of effort to locate a document that contained so little.

The gun locker in the laundry remained locked, and appeared undamaged. Mark keyed in the code, and breathed easier on seeing his laptop and hard drives exactly as he'd left them. He had most of his files backed up on external servers, but with the damage to his home office and Birraga office, this was the extent of the technology left to him until he could replace the destroyed items.

The jeans and shirt he'd washed out late on Friday night flapped on the line in the breeze. He unpegged them, sunlight warm, and changed on the back veranda, folding his discarded clothes – Steve's clothes – in a pile for the officer to collect shortly.

In the dog run at the end of the yard under the trees, Jim's dogs watched his every move. Next priority, feeding them. He let them out, and Dash and her mother Maggie bounced around him, jostling for pats and attention. Rosie came for a wary sniff and a pat but then kept a cautious distance.

Mark crouched down, letting them close to nuzzle him and lick his hands, building their familiarity with him. 'If you girls could talk, you'd tell me who was here, wouldn't you?' Dash barked twice and pawed at him. Mark ruffled her head and rose, keeping up the one-sided chatter. 'Really? He didn't feed you? And you haven't eaten since yesterday? Poor starving puppy.'

After they'd eaten he threw some old tennis balls he found in the shed for them to chase, and they brought them back again and again. This, *this* he'd missed all the years of commuting to and from Canberra, of travelling all over his huge electorate. He found himself grinning with the sheer, simple pleasure. But when a ball bounced off a tree branch and rolled towards his LandCruiser, Maggie lost interest in chasing it and instead gave the vehicle her total attention, crouching low to sniff some scent underneath the car, behind the front wheel.

Mark called her off and strolled over to take a look. It wouldn't be the first time a possum or a rat had found its way into an engine bay, or a snake curled under a car. A rat with a taste for rubber and plastic could do hundreds of dollars of damage to a vehicle.

When he hunkered down to peer underneath the chassis, he noticed a few footprints beside the vehicle, a few scuffs in the dust. Scuffs that went a fair way underneath. Scuffs too large to be a possum or a rodent.

He lay on his back, wriggled under . . . and froze. No possum. No rat or snake. A human hand had wired the pack of explosives and the detonator into place.

TWELVE

Jenn carefully descended the stairs from her room and hesitated at the door to the courtyard. Sunday lunch at the Dungirri pub seemed to be popular. An inexpensive buffet selection, a barbecue in the courtyard, and free face-painting for kids had brought out the families, and most of the tables in the courtyard were taken up with groups of families and friends, mostly adults and teens sitting down while the children ran around.

When she'd dropped Mark at Marrayin they'd agreed to meet here for lunch but she hadn't expected the place to be bustling with activity and people. Dungirri people. The likelihood of finding a quiet table and having an uninterrupted talk over lunch fell somewhere below zero.

The door into the front bar opened and a man backed out, carrying a tray loaded with glasses, two large jugs of soft drinks and a couple of schooners of beer.

'Jenn! Hello! We wondered if we'd see you today. Chloe and the kids are out there with my lot. Come and join us.'

It took her a moment to place the familiar face. Andrew Pappas. Andrew and Sean had been the only two other Dungirri kids in her year at high school, and he still had the broad grin and the easy charm she remembered. Some of the Birraga kids had picked on him because of his Greek background, but in Dungirri's much smaller community the kids knew each other better, had to rely on each other, and the only teasing tended to be good-natured.

'Thanks, but I'm meeting Mark,' Jenn said. 'Have you seen him?'

'No, not yet. Come and say hi while you wait.'

She hardly felt social, but refusing would be churlish. No matter how far behind she'd left Dungirri, how rarely she thought of it, in the way of small towns they still regarded her as belonging, as one of them.

'Look who I found inside,' Andrew announced as they came to the first large table, shaded by two umbrellas, and within seconds she found herself drawn into the circle in a hubbub of greetings and hugs and introductions.

Andrew's father George embraced her and kissed both her cheeks. 'So much more beautiful than on the television. But we are very, very sorry about Jim. He was so proud of you, wasn't he, Eleni? So proud. Always he told us when your reports would be on.' And Eleni kissed her cheeks, too, and squeezed her hand, and Andrew's wife Erin – no longer a fourteen-year-old with braces – hugged her and introduced an assortment of kids too quickly for Jenn to remember names. And finally Chloe,

Paul's wife – whom Jenn had only ever seen in a photograph – stepped forward with red-rimmed eyes, a brave smile and her hand outstretched.

'It's great to finally meet you, Jenn,' she said. 'Paul has very fond memories of you.'

'It's good to meet you, too. I'm sorry I didn't call to see you yesterday. I should have, but things . . .' Did she really have an excuse? She'd thought about visiting Chloe but had too easily found other 'important' things to do. But if she'd put family first, if she hadn't gone racing off to the library, if she hadn't pushed Larry and Wolfgang for the photos, might Wolfgang still be alive? One more thought for her conscience to fret over. 'I got distracted,' she finished lamely.

'It's okay, no need to apologise.' Chloe waved at the chair beside hers and invited Jenn to sit. 'I heard about Mick, and of course about the fire in Birraga. I phoned the hospital when I heard, but you'd just left. Are you okay? You weren't hurt?'

News of Wolfgang's shooting mustn't have travelled this far, yet, and she didn't spread it. 'I'm fine. But how are you doing?' Better late than never in acknowledging the family's sorrow. Marginally. 'Jim's such a huge loss to you all.'

'Yes.' The word had a small waver in it but Chloe held her composure. 'The kids were very upset yesterday. A pretty torrid day, all round. Paul had to go and see Sean, of course, but it was hard without him here.'

'Have you heard from Paul today? How's Sean?'

'They're taking it hard. Both of them, but especially Sean. Paul's going to stay in Wellington for a few more days. He's allowed to spend a couple of hours each day with him. They'll find out tomorrow if Sean will be given a day release to attend the funeral.'

The funeral. Another ordeal to get through. Two ordeals: Jim's and probably Wolfgang's. 'Do you know yet when it will be?' she asked.

'We'll have to wait for the—' Chloe dropped her voice as a boy left the other kids and came towards them. 'The examination. That will be tomorrow, Steve said.'

Depending on what the autopsy found, Jim's body might not be released for days, or longer. The case was the same with Wolfgang. She might have to return to Sydney and then come back to Dungirri in a week or two, or maybe longer. Or extend her leave. Just the thought of more than a week here made her gut knot further, but she still had to find the truth behind the accident and Paula's death.

The young boy, not quite a teenager – the image of his father at the same age – leaned against Chloe, an arm around her shoulders, comfortable with the physical affection in a way Paul hadn't been, back then. Jim had raised his boys the best he could, but physical affection hadn't been part of his repertoire of skills.

'This is Calum, our eldest,' Chloe introduced him. 'Calum, this is Aunty Jenn, your dad's cousin.'

Calum gave her a fleeting smile and said, 'Hi, Aunty Jenn,' before turning to his mother. 'Mum, I think Ollie's getting edgy again. He's gone all . . . tight. Do you want me to take him to the car?'

'No, it's okay. I'll come and talk to him.' Chloe pushed back her chair. 'Sorry, Jenn. Ollie's on the Asperger's scale. He finds crowds and noise hard to process. He usually copes okay with this, but today he's without his dad or granddad. It's a big change for a kid who needs routine.'

'If you want us to take Dana and Calum for the afternoon, just let us know,' Erin offered from across the table, and Jenn felt the odd one out, inexperienced with family and kids and this relaxed type of socialising.

'Here, Jenn, try some of Deb's sourdough,' Andrew said, passing a platter piled with slices of bread. 'She's the cook. She and Liam are friends of Gil's.'

Friends of Gillespie? That explained why he seemed to be making himself at home. She took some sourdough, the butter melting into the fresh bread. The light-hearted, affectionate chatter of the Pappas family flowed around her, snippets of conversations drifted from other tables, kids with Spiderman and butterfly-painted faces raced around, and over at the barbecue Karl Sauer flipped steaks and sausages and flirted with a young woman. A pleasant Sunday afternoon in a country pub. The Dungirri Hotel had made it to the twenty-first century.

But there was no sign of Mark, already more than half an hour late.

She checked her messages and emails again. Nothing. Uneasiness crept up between her shoulders. Anything could have delayed him – he'd said he had a few jobs to do at Marrayin before he came in. But the uneasiness wouldn't dissipate. She excused herself from the table, planning to phone him. She'd limped halfway across the courtyard when Kris Matthews came in through the side gate and scanned the crowd, looking for someone. Looking for her.

Their eyes met and Kris walked briskly towards her, her skin pale, her face tight. Not good news.

'I need you to come down to the police station,' Kris said quietly, her words laced with urgency. 'Now. With the photos Steve printed.'

'Something's happened? To Mark?'

'Yes. My car's just outside. I'll tell you as we drive up there.'

⁂

In the small bathroom in Kris's residence behind the police station, Mark splashed cold water on his face. He couldn't quite stop his hands from shaking. If not for Maggie's curiosity, he'd be a dead man. He would have got into the LandCruiser to go and meet Jenn, turned the ignition key . . . and died.

The certainty of it hit him harder than all the other dangers he'd survived over the past few days. Rescuing Jim, the attack in Birraga, the shooting this morning – he could have died in those, but whoever was behind them hadn't necessarily been targeting him, intending to kill him.

That someone could so cold-bloodedly wire explosives and a detonator into his car, to explode on ignition . . . it meant planning and acting for a single outcome: his death. Premeditated murder.

Jim Barrett, Doctor Russell, Wolfgang Schmidt. His would have made the fourth death in three days. And they all led back, in one way or another, to the accident eighteen years ago – and to whatever had gone on before it. They had to find answers, and find them soon, to stop the killer.

He'd brought the dogs with him, chaining Maggie and Dash on the front veranda and Rosie on the back and they barked a warning as Kris's car returned. He gave his face one more splash with cold water. *Focus.* Work through the facts. Piece together everything they knew. The answers – or at least leads to them – had to be there, somewhere.

Kris and Jenn came into the kitchen through the back door, and before he could speak, Jenn – reserved, undemonstrative Jenn – thrust the folder with the photos at Kris and crossed straight to him, into his arms, burying her face against his shirt, her body trembling, tension wound tightly along her spine.

Even as he closed his arms around her, he shot a questioning glance over her shoulder at Kris, but she shook her head slightly and slipped past them to the passageway that led to the police station.

'It's okay,' Jenn said into his shirt, as if she'd seen that exchange, 'I'll be angry in a minute. Really, really pissed-off angry with whoever did this. It's just . . .' She pushed away from him, scrubbing at her eyes to wipe the dampness away. 'Holy crap, Mark, that was way too close. Kris said if it wasn't for the dog, you'd be . . .'

Her attempt at anger falling short, she stood a metre from him, hugging herself, and pressed a fist against her mouth, unable to say the word.

Dead.

Although he wanted nothing more than to hold her, to be held, to affirm life and love and humanity, he recognised his adrenaline reaction was an hour older than hers, and for him the racing, gut-slamming what-ifs had finally slowed. She still had to process the fright, the shock, and all on top of this morning's trauma.

'I'm alive, Jenn. They tried and failed. Thanks to Maggie's good nose. She'll get the best bones every week from now on.'

His attempt to lighten things had no effect. She stared at him, eyes wide, struggling with her distress.

'I can't lose anyone else, Mark. I can't. My parents, Paula, Jim . . . everyone I loved. I can't lose you. So, you've just got to damn well stay alive and safe.'

I can't lose you. Still in shock, her natural guard lowered, her thoughts and emotions were probably as raw and tangled as his. But her confession hit him like an electric shock – part stun, part pain, partly a jolt of energy and life into emotions he'd suppressed for years.

C&

She was babbling like an upset kid, when *he* was the one who had narrowly escaped death and must be feeling the shock. Where was her control, her consideration?

There were questions in the brown eyes that studied her for a long moment, but whatever he was feeling, he kept it to himself behind a gentle smile and a light response. 'Believe me, I'm going to do my best to stay alive. Definitely my preference over the alternative.'

How could she be angry, or fall to pieces, faced with his calm courage and humour?

She relaxed a fraction, the worst of the initial shock wearing away. She had to get herself together and ready to deal with the challenge they faced.

'So how do we keep you alive? Where to from here?'

'Steve and Kris are in the interview room,' he told her. 'We're going to work through everything we know so far.'

'Steve's still on the case?'

'Yes and no. Ordered off duty today. Now called back on for temporary protection duties. For me.'

She immediately saw the advantage. 'So, we can work on the case with him.'

'Yes. For this afternoon, at least.'

Doing something, anything, practical to keep him safe might help her forget the moments of sheer terror when she'd thought him hurt – or worse. She made a credible attempt at a grin. 'Let's go and work, then.'

The police station was tiny, a few rooms joined to the cottage and all built a century or so ago, when policing was a much simpler business.

In the small interview room, Steve laid the photographs out in date order, covering the table. Kris wheeled in a whiteboard from her crowded office and positioned it against the wall, making best use of the limited space. Mark brought in a couple of the plastic chairs from the reception area and Jenn sank on to one of them, giving him a grateful smile.

Mark pulled up the chair next to her. With the four of them around the table, the room was crowded and she was acutely aware of Mark only inches away. On the surface he appeared calm, composed, but she sensed the tension in him, humming like a tightly drawn string.

Jenn hauled her brain into journalist mode. Much easier to deal with the firm ground of facts and process, questions and answers, than the quicksand of emotions and unknowns.

First, establish the playing field. 'Is Detective Haddad coming?' she asked.

Steve glanced up from sorting the photographs. 'Not yet. Not for a while. She'll be busy with forensics and the Feds for at least a couple of hours.'

'Mark said you were ordered off duty. Why?'

'Because I've already been on for eight days straight. Nasty domestic-violence case earlier in the week. I was supposed to be rostered off Friday and over the weekend.'

'Did Haddad order it?' She was beginning to feel like an interrogator, and Steve noticed, shooting her a glance that told her he'd only respond if he chose. But he answered her question.

'Nope. Regional Inspector's orders, not Haddad's. She's got lead on the murder investigations, though. I'll be "local liaison". So, since I've been called back in to babysit Mark, I plan on doing my job.' He gave a wolfish grin. 'First time I've been given official permission for my local liaisons.'

Kris snorted. 'In your dreams, Steve. You don't have time for that kind of liaison.'

Jenn watched the good-natured humour flow between them. Colleagues and friends. Given the tough investigations they'd dealt with in the past couple of years, the trust and respect for each other must have been earned, and Mark's ease with them reflected the same regard. A good sign that she could trust them.

'Yeah, well, I'd dream about it if I had time to sleep,' Steve retorted. 'So, let's get cracking and get this bastard identified and locked up.' The humour vanished and he stepped to the whiteboard, picking up the pen to draw a circle in the centre of the board, jotting the words 'fatal accident' inside it. 'Okay, let's assume that this is the connection – the accident in which Paula Barrett died. Now, up here – because we don't know yet how it's connected – we've got the series of photographs of sexual activity, over years.'

'The Bohème Club,' Jenn said. 'Wolfgang called it that.' She took out her notepad. 'Here are the words he said – I think I've got them right. "Bohème club" and "sex". "Taught Dan . . . develop . . . photos".'

'A sex club in Birraga?' Kris mused. 'Hard to believe.'

'Yeah, well it *was* the seventies when those photos start,' Steve pointed out. 'Sexual revolution, free love, the pill and no AIDS.'

Beside her, Mark added, 'Plus the demographics were different then. Larger population, on average much younger. While a lot of young people went to the city for university, a much higher proportion of them came back to work in the district than is the case now.'

'Okay, so ripe conditions for sexual experimentation, I guess.' Steve scrawled 'Bohème Club' on the whiteboard. 'And someone photographed it. What did Wolfgang say about developing the photos?'

Jenn repeated the words, 'Taught Dan . . . develop . . . photos.'

'That's got to be Dan Flanagan,' Steve said, and no-one disagreed. He laid his finger on the image of a younger Dan. 'But why would Wolfgang teach Dan to develop photos?'

Jenn had already thought it through. 'They're not the kind of photos you could get commercially printed, then or now. Wolfgang was a skilled photographer and developed his own images, so he'd be the obvious person to ask, wouldn't he? He had the equipment, the skills, the dark room already set up. Maybe he was part of the club. He said something about it going bad.'

'The combination of Dan Flanagan, sex and bondage is definitely bad,' Kris said dryly.

Mark rested his elbows on the table, his fingers intertwined tightly. 'We need to find out more about this club. Who was in it, where they met. I need to know how my parents were involved.'

'Have you had any word from them yet?' Steve asked.

'Nothing yet. I'll check again in a little while.'

He spoke evenly enough, but again Jenn felt the underlying tension in him. The sooner they had some response from Caroline and Len, the better. In the meantime, they had to keep following the leads they had.

She tapped on some of the words she'd written. 'Wolfgang mentioned a convent. But it can't be the Birraga convent – that's in the centre of town next to Saint Joey's, and the nuns were still there into the nineties at least.'

Mark nodded in agreement. 'Sister Brigid moved out last year, into the nursing home. She was the last nun in the convent. She might know if there was ever another convent, though.'

'I'll get someone to ask her,' Steve said.

Jenn reached for the image of Dan Flanagan and Gerard McCarty emerging from the doorway. With the lens zoomed on them, not a great deal of the building showed. 'In the meantime, does anyone recognise this place? Have ideas where it might be?'

'There's really only the doorframe, isn't there? Maybe colonial era, if you look at the brickwork over the door,' Kris said. 'But, do you know what strikes me about the image? The other photos – they're taken nearer the subjects, in the same room. This one isn't. It's a surveillance photo.'

It was obvious when compared with the other images. Jenn kicked herself for not noticing before.

'I agree,' Steve said. 'So, who's doing the surveillance? Wolfgang? And why?'

Jenn looked at Wolfgang's last words, searching for a pattern, significance, possibilities. 'He mentioned blackmail. "Club, convent, went bad, blackmail, hurt Marta." I assumed someone was blackmailing him, threatening Marta. But I don't know – maybe he was blackmailing them?'

'Or gathering evidence against them,' Mark suggested quietly.

'Finding a way to take back the upper hand,' Kris agreed. 'Information becomes power. That was Gil's strategy when he couldn't do anything else.'

'Is Gil around?' Mark asked. 'Does he know anything about this aspect of Flanagan's activities?'

'He'll be back in a couple of hours,' Kris said. 'He's taken Megan and Esther Russell to Esther's sister in Dubbo. He's worried about Megan's safety.'

Megan. Gillespie's daughter. Jenn still had difficulty believing it – the rough, wrong-side-of-the-tracks youth now the unexpected father of a teenage girl. And the lover of a police sergeant. That, she found easier to believe; although friendly, Kris had a rock-solid core, tough without being harsh, and, Jenn had the impression, a strong but pragmatic sense of justice, of right and wrong.

Steve stepped up to the whiteboard again, tossing over his shoulder, 'You can bet I'll be grilling Gil the minute he gets back. You can use your subtle feminine wiles on him after I've finished with him, Kris.'

'Nothing subtle about my interrogation techniques,' she retorted with a grin.

Jokes, black humour, teasing, sarcasm – Jenn had seen them used again and again between teams of soldiers, doctors, aid workers . . . a protective mechanism, armour for dealing with unceasing death and darkness.

His sense of responsibility never faltering despite the humour, Steve slid back into serious mode in an instant. 'We've got a lot to cover, so we'll need to divide tasks. Jenn and Mark, you two grew up here, and Mark's got a good eye for faces, so I want you to go through each photograph and see if you can identify anyone else. Also, I need a full list of anyone who might have had some involvement with the accident or the aftermath. Kris, you and I need to start checks on the main players, including Wolfgang. I want to know more about him, and where he fits into this. We need to map connections, starting with working out who in the district would know how to wire up a car bomb.'

'They wouldn't need to know,' Kris pointed out. 'There's probably a thousand sites on the internet with instructions.'

Jenn's fingers gripped tightly on her pen. The heat of the room pressed in on her, and she had to fight the instinct to run, to get out of there. 'Someone knows,' she said, and even to her own ears her voice sounded choked. 'Someone around here knew, well before the internet existed.'

Steve and Kris waited, eyes on her, but Mark's hand rested on her shoulder, connecting with her, giving her strength. In the face of disbelief and threats she'd stayed silent for more than twenty years. But now it mattered, now she had influence and respect, and with the spotlight on past events the truth might be uncovered. As long as she had the courage to crack open old wounds and speak out.

'My parents died in a car-bomb explosion. Just up the road at the showground. My father knew explosives from his army work, and the Coroner ruled it as a murder–suicide. I was only twelve years old, and no-one believed me that it couldn't have been.'

❧

She'd never believed . . . so that was the reason for the forbidden topic of her parents' death. He'd only been thirteen when the wild-eyed, too-wary girl moved into Mick's cottage and started to catch the school bus with Paula. *Be very gentle with her*, his mother had said, and he read the local papers and knew the stories going around – that Peter Barrett hadn't been himself when he'd brought his wife and daughter from the Holsworthy army base to Dungirri for a Christmas family visit, so despondent that he'd rigged his car to explode.

So, Mark had been polite and friendly to the new girl, avoiding any mention of the incident, and even threatening to use his fists a couple of times on schoolmates who tried to taunt her. But it was months before she'd begun to let anyone, even Paula, see beyond the hard shell of emotional armour. The only time Mark had made any comment about her parents' deaths, a few years later, she'd responded coldly that he had no idea what he was talking about.

A heavy concern for a young girl to carry, alone. And she still carried it, behind the forced toughness that protected her from the world. That protected her from the hurt of caring. That kept her alone.

Three months ago, before Gil's return to Dungirri and the exposure of the district's dark underside, before Jenn had walked back into his life, he would have continued to believe the Coroner's report about the death of Peter and Susannah Barrett. But now . . . He kept his attention fully on Jenn, only peripherally aware of Steve and Kris on the other side of the table. 'You believe they were murdered?' he asked.

'Yes. I was there.' Her voice stayed flat, dead. 'We'd camped at the showground over Christmas. Jim lived just across the road back then. It was early morning and we'd packed up ready to go. Mum went to dump the rubbish in the bins and I went to the loo. As I was walking back I heard Dad call out, "Come, on honey, we've got to get on the road," as he got into the car. And then it exploded. I was thirty metres or more away, but Mum was much closer. And Dad . . . I saw—' She stopped, swallowed hard. 'He didn't stand a chance.' Her breathing rapid, she shoved her chair back and stood at the small window, hugging herself as she stared out.

Mark exchanged glances with Steve and Kris, but they stayed silent, giving her a moment. Although he'd always known she'd been there at the time, he couldn't imagine seeing it, watching a parent die in that way. No wonder she'd withdrawn, refused to talk about it. And no wonder that his close escape this afternoon had distressed her. She didn't have to imagine what could too easily have happened.

She turned abruptly to face them, blue–grey eyes burning with feeling. 'If he wanted to blow us all up, why didn't he wait twenty seconds longer until we were in the car with him? Why explosives, when he could have shot us, or killed us quietly in any number of ways? He was a career soldier, for God's sake; he knew how to kill effectively. A car bomb set off prematurely doesn't make sense on any level. Except murder.'

Except murder. The little Mark had known about the incident shifted into a new light. The Flanagan family's intimidation and corruption business stretched back decades. Given the suggestions of vice, sex and perhaps blackmail going back further – to before he was born – perhaps the Barretts' deaths did warrant review. 'You're right. It doesn't make sense. But is it linked to any of these other issues? Kris, Steve – can we get hold of the reports from the time?'

'The Coroner's report will be available, but it might take time,' Steve said. 'I don't think they're on computer that far back.'

'You said no-one believed you,' Kris asked Jenn in her straightforward but respectful way. 'Did the police interview you?'

Jenn dragged a strand of hair back, sagging against the wall by the window. 'I remember a policewoman at the hospital, but I was pretty distraught. She came again the next day with a detective but . . . well, looking back now, their questions were all leading questions. My parents had been arguing, hadn't they? My dad was in a bad mood, wasn't he? I was just a kid, though, and I didn't realise for a while that everyone was blaming Dad.'

Kris winced. 'You didn't speak to anyone else? Your uncles? A counsellor? A teacher?'

'Mick. Once.' Bitterness hardened her words. 'He told me to shut the fuck up and that if I spoke about it again he'd have me locked up as a loony. I saw the school counsellor once. She told me I was making up stories because I didn't want to believe my dad had tried to kill me and I had to accept it. Jim . . .'

She shook her head. 'I don't know what Jim thought. He just said things had got complicated for Dad, but the best thing I could do for him and Mum was to leave it, get on with my life.'

Complicated? An ambiguous term from a man who, in Mark's experience, had always been honest and didn't mince words.

'The Coroner's report won't be much use,' Jenn continued. 'I requested a copy years ago. According to his commanding officer, my father had suffered mood swings and irritability since returning from a UN mission in Afghanistan a month before his death. It was years before the war, a mine-clearing mission after the Russians pulled out. My parents' marriage was under some strain, and there were witnesses here who said he was acting out of character and argumentative.' Tense, shaking with constrained emotion, she pushed herself away from the wall. 'I need some fresh air.'

Mark rose to go with her but she shook her head as she passed, and he let her go.

Steve waited until her footsteps receded before he asked, 'What do you reckon, Mark? Do you remember much about it?'

Restless, he went to the window she'd been standing by only moments before, the security grille and mesh blurring the view of the Memorial Hall next door. 'I'm only a year older than Jenn. My parents and I were visiting my grandfather in Lightning Ridge for Christmas when it happened. I remember a fair amount of hushed talk, conversations broken off suddenly when I came into the room.' And now he wished he'd been the kind of kid to eavesdrop – or at least to push for more answers. 'I stayed with my grandfather for another few weeks, as I usually did over summer. When I came home, Jenn had come to stay with Mick's family in the cottage at Marrayin, and my mother asked me to be kind to her. All the talk among the Dungirri kids was that her father had killed himself and her mother, and that he'd tried to kill her. I felt pretty bad for her.'

'Did you know her parents?' Steve asked.

'Not really. He'd joined the army and left before I was born. They'd visited town a couple of times. I remember Jenn at a Dungirri Christmas Tree party once – we were maybe eight, nine years old.' Funny how he'd noticed her, even then. A quiet, pretty girl with brown plaits; she'd joined in a few of the games with her cousins but then drifted to the shade of a tree, absorbed in the book she'd received from the Santa who'd visited the party.

Steve took notes. 'Do you know who her parents' friends here were?'

'I don't remember much at all. Peter seemed more like Jim than Mick. Reliable, steady. Her mother – I can recall her sitting with some of the older women at that Christmas party. Esther Russell, Eleni Pappas, Jeanie Menotti—' The mention of the last name sparked a thought. 'We should ask Jeanie.' He indicated the photos, still spread on the table. 'We should ask her about all of this. She's been here all her life, and people trust her, confide in her. She doesn't gossip, but it may be that she'll have some more pieces of the puzzle.'

'I was thinking the same thing,' Kris said. 'I'll go and call her, see if she can come down.'

Would his mother have confided in Jeanie? About sex and bondage and perhaps blackmail? He doubted it, doubted she would have shared that kind of secret with anyone – except, perhaps, his father.

He closed his eyes, everything that had once seemed solid in his youth shifting now he viewed it from a different perspective. His parents were close, loved each other . . . but what if the underlying stress that had always characterised their relationship stemmed not from financial worries or the demands of running a large enterprise, but from something far more personal?

The image of his mother haunted him. Bondage and discipline, dominance and submission – some couples might seek that kind of edge in a relationship, might be happy, might love those roles, but every instinct said that his parents weren't among them. Respect, honour, fidelity, love, compassion, service – those were the values they lived by, and in everything they'd been equal.

He clenched his fists tight on the window sill, anger burning, threatening his control. Someone must have compelled his mother to that ultimate submission, and he needed to know who, why and how – and he needed to see them pay for it.

Wolfgang's photos and words implicated Dan Flanagan, or at the very least suggested his involvement. Although the police had yet to come up with hard evidence, Mark believed Flanagan was responsible, through his sons and associates, for decades of extortion, corruption and blackmail.

The possibility that the extortion had extended to sexual services affecting his mother and other women sickened him, angered him. But if Peter and Susannah Barrett had been murdered, if Flanagan was somehow responsible for that and for the shadows Jenn had carried in her eyes since she was twelve years old, then he deserved nothing short of the harshness of life in a maximum security prison, and Mark would do everything in his power to make that happen.

THIRTEEN

Jenn sat on the back step of Kris's place, rubbing the ears of Rosie the dog, who, after some reservation, had come to lie close to her. The soft warmth of Rosie's fur, the gentle pressure of the canine body against her hip and the simplicity of patting a trusting dog began to work their calming effects on her whirling emotions.

She'd doubted her father. The realisation hit hard. On one level she'd believed in his innocence all along, but beneath that . . . at some point in her twenties she'd started to doubt, and she'd not pursued the issue as an adult. He *had* come home from Afghanistan a changed man. It was supposed to be a training mission, to train local forces in ordnance recognition and basic mine-clearance techniques following the end of Soviet rule. But in the couple of weeks between his return and their Dungirri visit, she had memories of him telling his mates, with the macho, laugh-it-off attitude of so many men, that there'd been a few close calls. His hands shook sometimes, he took to roaming the house at night and although he tried to be happy, even at twelve she'd recognised it as a performance.

Post-traumatic stress? Possibly. Probably. Maybe his army records could tell her. The evidence given by his commanding officer in the Coroner's report certainly suggested it. And perhaps that's why she hadn't pursued it. That, and because it would have meant returning to Dungirri, and she hadn't been ready to do that.

But the arguments between her parents had only started during those few days in Dungirri over Christmas. Rosie nudged her hand, reminding her to keep patting. She dug her fingers into the soft fur again, massaging gently while she tried to think, to put things in order. Those arguments – they'd been subdued, disagreements rather than fights, frustration rather than anger, her mother's patience stretching thin. Hushed exchanges when they thought Jenn was out of earshot or asleep. Some tension between them, but not enough to erase all their smiles, their tender touches. Her mother had always had a nurse's faith in the importance of touch, of physical connection, and she'd taught her tough soldier husband the power of gentleness.

Now Jenn thought about it, whatever issue worried them, it wasn't marital strife. That last night, after she'd gone to bed, she'd seen them through the mosquito flap, standing together in the moonlight, holding each other, laughing lightly, kissing long and deeply. Joy and contentment, not despair or depression. She'd fallen asleep happy.

Eight hours later they were both dead.

'How could anyone think it of him, Rosie?' she murmured. 'How could I have doubted him?' The dog sat up, licked her face and Jenn snuggled her cheek into the fur, her arm around the gentle animal. 'He loved her, Rosie. He loved me. No way could he have wired the car to kill us and then kissed her like that.'

She stayed there, hugging the dog, the old confusion and uncertainty dissolving. And although fresh sorrow for her parents and their cut-short lives welled, she didn't need to cry. They'd lived and loved and laughed, and now she had those memories back, untarnished, unshadowed.

Except for the knowledge that her father's reputation had, in his death, been maligned. That, she would restore. Once they'd untangled the murky past, once they'd found the truth about Paula's death and Mark was safe, then she'd keep digging and asking questions and working to clear her father's name. She had the skills, the position and the persuasive powers to make the authorities sit up and take notice. Rosie licked her face again, as if in agreement with her thoughts.

The sun had shifted, eating away the shade of the porch, and the heat prickled on her skin, hot on her head and Rosie's fur.

'Come on, Rosie girl. I'll move you to the end there, where it'll stay shady.'

She refastened Rosie's chain to another post a metre away, and moved the water bowl close, giving her another pat.

Standing here on the back porch, she could see the back of the Memorial Hall next door, and beyond it the creek, curving around the edge of the Dungirri scrub that butted close to town. Scrub Road ran north from the main street along two short blocks of houses, past the old O'Connell house on the corner of Mill Road and on to the vast dry forest that had, when she'd lived here, given Dungirri a timber industry – and double the current population. That the town still survived after the timber mill's closure surprised her. That people voluntarily stayed – people like Mark, like Paul and Chloe, Beth and Ryan, Andrew and Erin – perplexed her.

She'd left the back door open, and Rosie stiffened as Maggie and Dash barked at the sound of a vehicle approaching. Through the screen door she heard Mark's command to the dogs to lie down, and they quietened.

'Jenn?' She heard the concern in his voice, and the hesitation. She went back inside and met him in the kitchen.

'Are you okay?'

'Yes. I am. Rosie and I have been getting acquainted.'

He stood a metre from her but his smile touched her, as if he understood how soothing the quiet time with Rosie had been. 'Good. That's Leah Haddad arriving. She wants to do a formal interview with me. Will you be okay for a while? Kris said to help yourself to coffee or food.'

'I'll be fine. I might . . .' She might what? She wanted more solid information before she saw Haddad again. 'I might go up and see Beth. She's in the old O'Connell place, isn't she?'

'Yes, that's right. Can you tell her what's happened? She'll want to know.'

'I'll tell her. Ryan – I was surprised when Jim told me they'd married.' The sweet, shy girl and the rough-lad-turned-boxer who'd been only marginally less on the outer than Gil Gillespie when they were all kids. 'Is he . . . do you trust him, Mark?'

'Yes. Absolutely. I doubt that Beth will know anything about Bohème, although if there were any rumours circulating among our mothers' friends she may have heard something. But Ryan's old connections go a little deeper into Birraga's rougher side. He may have heard things.'

'I'll ask – but don't worry, I'll be discreet. I don't suppose you've heard anything from your parents yet?'

He shook his head, and the strain showed in the tightness around his eyes. 'No. I just checked my messages, but there's nothing.'

She'd changed her sandals for walking boots at the hotel earlier, and they provided firm support for her ankle so that it only protested lightly on the walk down Scrub Road, four hundred metres or so. Past the corner of Spring Street, where she'd endured a year in the miserable house after Mick's dismissal from Marrayin. Past the park at the waterhole, where the town's teenagers had gathered on summer evenings. Where Mark and Paula had pretended to be an item; where Gil Gillespie's daughter apparently had been conceived, somewhere in the trees beyond.

The old timber house that Bella O'Connell and her father used to live in had changed in the intervening years, but the roses he'd planted for his wife in the shade of a vine-covered trellis were still there. Roses in Dungirri's hot climate had always struck Jenn as a grandly romantic but impractical gesture. They'd proved her wrong, though, surviving more than thirty years.

She could hear voices and the high-pitched laughter of children coming from the backyard, but she hardly knew Ryan, and hadn't seen Beth in years until this week – so instead of opening the gate and walking uninvited in to the yard, she rang the bell at the front door. Beyond the security screen the door was open, the short passageway dull compared to the bright sunlight outside.

A screen door at the back of the house banged closed, and Beth hurried to answer the bell, her face relaxing into a broad smile as she recognised Jenn.

'Jenn! Come on through. We're out the back, where it's cooler.'

In the garden three young girls played in a wading pool, protected from the sun by a tree and a large shade-cloth awning off the garage. They paused and watched as she came out on to the veranda until, reassured by their mother's presence just behind her, they resumed their game with the plastic floating bath toys that bobbed in the water around them.

Not just a play space, the backyard had some raised garden beds with a range of vegetables and herbs, and half a dozen chooks foraging lazily among them. Clothes – mostly T-shirts and shorts in assorted sizes – danced in the breeze on the rotary clothesline, and on one side of the open double garage a few pieces of weight-training equipment found usable space among tools and timber.

At the table on the veranda, Ryan Wilson greeted her with a broad grin. 'Jenn Barrett. Jeez, girl, you've hardly changed a bit.'

Even though she'd heard about his accident a few years ago, a rugby tackle gone wrong, seeing him in the wheelchair still came as a shock. She leaned down to kiss his cheek and he wrapped a strong arm around her shoulder in a hug. 'Good to see you, Jenn.' He caught hold of her hand as she straightened up. 'I'm so sorry about Jim. He was a good mate. A good man. We're all going to miss him.'

A good mate. She preferred the simple, sincere words to any flowery condolences.

Sitting at the table with Ryan and Beth, sipping iced fruit juice, she could have been enjoying any pleasant weekend afternoon with friends. Except for the news she had to share.

She waited until Beth had brought out a plate of biscuits and sat down again before she began. 'You'll want to know . . . Mark asked me to tell you. There's been another incident. At his place.' She had their total attention and Beth's hand slipped into Ryan's. There was no easy way to say it, so she simply told them what happened. 'He noticed one of the dogs sniffing at his car. He thought there might be an animal under it, so he checked. And found a car bomb.'

'Oh, my Lord,' Beth breathed, closing her eyes, and Jenn knew it was a prayer.

'He's okay. He's at the police station with Steve and Kris, and the Sydney detective has just arrived. They'll keep him protected now.' She sounded more assured than she felt, and she had to put her glass down on the table to steady it.

'What the f—, heck is going on, Jenn?' Ryan demanded. 'Jim, Doc Russell, Schmidty, a Molotov cocktail and now this?'

'It seems as though Mark's resignation has opened a can of worms.' It was a cliché, but maybe 'worm' wasn't such a bad descriptor for sexual predators and blackmailers.

'Last night Wolfgang slipped me a memory stick containing photos,' she explained. 'There are images of Mark's accident that – well, that raise a lot of questions. And there are other images,

234

going back almost forty years.' She kept her voice low, aware of the children not far away, seemingly absorbed in their play. 'Disturbing images of sexual activity, mostly women in positions that could be bondage and S-and-M activities but more likely suggest coercion, maybe even rape. We went to his place this morning to ask him about them, but he died before he could say much.' She raised the glass to her lips, took a sip and continued, 'Have either of you ever heard mention of a club called Bohème?'

'Bohème as in Bohemian?' Beth asked. When Jenn nodded, she glanced over at her children and said, 'I can't say I know anything really. But when I was seventeen or so – it was after Mark's accident – my mother came to my room one night for a talk. I always thought it was just, you know, that I was getting older, going out with the crowd sometimes. But she warned me – it seemed to really worry her – she warned me not to get involved with any Bohemians. I was a bit surprised, because I thought she meant hippies and she's not the type to be so judgemental. But she said it several times.'

So, Sylvia Fletcher had known about the Bohème Club. But how? From Caroline? If Mark's parents didn't respond to his messages soon, Jenn would visit Sylvia.

'I don't know much either,' Ryan said slowly. 'But there were a few rumours. I left school early, did casual work here and there before I went on the boxing circuit. Some of the guys I knew reckoned they wanted to get work with—' He hesitated. 'With certain employers, because rumour had it there were extra rewards for good work. Nudge-nudge-wink-wink kind of rewards. I assumed they meant booze or drugs, but "Bohemian girls" were mentioned a few times. I wasn't a saint by any stretch of the imagination, but I didn't want to get mixed up with anything illegal, and I steered clear of . . . of that employer.'

'Dan Flanagan?' Jenn asked outright.

He nodded. 'Yeah. There were benefits if he liked you, but I saw more than a few guys employed by him who ended up broken. Some OD'd, some ended up in hospital, some left town and have never been back. Nothing they could ever prove, of course, even if any of them wanted to give evidence. It's the way he always worked, right up until Gil came back to town and the mafia cousins got too ambitious. There's a few people coming forward now, enough to put Flanagan's sons away, but they were only ever his tools, just like everyone else. Unless they turn on him, he'll probably get off scot-free.'

Not if I have anything to do with it. The thought must have shown on her face, because concern tightened Ryan's face and he added, 'Tread carefully, Jenn. Very carefully. Flanagan is a dangerous bastard. Best leave it all to the police.'

Be careful, Wolfgang had said, and now he was dead. And Mark would have been dead but for a quirk of luck.

Yes, she'd be careful. But the police were over-stretched, and she couldn't rely on them to ask the questions – her questions – that needed answers.

⁂

'You shouldn't be standing at that window,' Kris scolded, coming into the kitchen with her laptop and a notepad. 'Anyone hiding in the scrub out there could see you.'

He stepped to one side so that the gingham curtain mostly blocked any view of him, but from where he could still see down the road to Beth's place. Jenn had been there for more than an hour while he'd been questioned by the very thorough Detective Haddad.

'I might—' *call Beth*, he'd been about to say when he saw Beth's car back out of the driveway.

'Do whatever you like,' Kris said. 'Just stay inside and out of sight. I have to go and make some calls, but I'll just be in the station. I contacted Jeanie. She's finishing with the lunch clean-up at the pub and she'll be on her way shortly.'

Staying inside chafed his already restless mood. He craved the outdoors, and the long list of work he should be getting on with at Marrayin worried him. He'd planned to go back after he'd had lunch with Jenn and work for the rest of the day, but the murder attempt had well and truly stymied that. With Jim gone, there was no-one to keep an eye on things, and Mark was reluctant to ask anyone else to go out there when there might still be danger. He had to hope that the water pumps were working in the various water troughs, that the dams had not dried up in the heat, and that the cattle still had sufficient feed in the dry paddocks. Salvaging belongings from the homestead wreckage could probably wait another day or two, as long as no summer storms rolled in.

Beth's car slowed approaching the main street, and although it passed out of sight he heard it turn towards the station, and breathed easier when she drove into Kris's driveway. Jenn called out a goodbye, greeted Rosie, and moments later tapped on the back door.

'You survived the interrogation?' she asked as he let her in.

'We came to a cordial allegiance,' he said. 'She's thorough, Jenn. She won't make mistakes. Did Beth or Ryan have any information to help?'

She pulled out two chairs at the table, sat on one and propped her booted foot on the other. 'They'd heard things that rang true with our suspicions, but nothing specific. Ryan purposely avoided any involvement with Flanagan, although rumours about the benefits for good work included "Bohemian girls". And not long after your accident Sylvia Fletcher warned Beth to stay away from Bohemians.'

'Sylvia knows.'

'She knows *something*,' Jenn corrected. 'But what Beth recalls of the warning is pretty vague.'

Vague. From Mark's knowledge of the Fletchers, that sounded like the devout Catholic Sylvia, with her natural innocence and naivety, wasn't quite sure what she was warning Beth about.

He filled Kris's electric kettle and flicked it on. He didn't expect her fridge to yield much – he'd known her for five years and cooking wasn't one of her strengths – but was pleasantly surprised to see cold meats and cheese. He suspected Gil's influence. His half-starved stomach rumbled.

'Have you eaten?' he asked Jenn. 'I'm going to make up a couple of sandwiches.'

'Some sourdough bread at the pub, that's all. I didn't get time for lunch, although it looked a lot better than I expected for the Dungirri pub. So, I could go a sandwich, thanks.'

While he sliced the loaf of bread he found on the bench he explained: 'Deb is the chef, and a good one. She and Liam, the bar manager, worked with Gil in Sydney, and came up here with him. They stayed here when he went into witness protection, and since Nancy Butler hasn't been able to sell the pub – Stan died earlier this year – Deb and Liam stepped in to keep it open. Jeanie's been helping them out.'

'A town this size without a pub – it would be a death knell.'

'Yes.' Just one of his many concerns about the town's future. 'George and Eleni Pappas want to sell the shop and retire, too.' He slid her sandwich on to a plate and passed it to her, lightening the gloomy talk with a teasing, 'I don't suppose you want to move back to town and buy a shop or a pub?'

She laughed outright. 'Me counting lollies or pulling beers? Nope, not going to happen. But what about you? I can see you as the friendly local publican. Might be a good investment for the family company.'

So much for dispelling the gloom. He sat at the table with his sandwich in front of him, his appetite receding. 'Strelitz Pastoral has been over-extended for a long time. My father's rivalry with Dan Flanagan stretched the company's resources too far years ago. It's been a constant battle to get it back into the black ever since I took over, and it's not there yet. You know the usual story – borrowings too high, drought, flood and bad seasons reducing income.' And now it would be even more difficult, without his parliamentary salary to supplement the running costs, let alone rebuild the homestead.

'Can you sell some land?'

'I could any time – to Dan Flanagan. A couple of Chinese companies have been sniffing around the district and there are mining companies around, too. But I'd much prefer to sell to someone who is going to manage the land sustainably and invest in agricultural production for this country.'

'Land, gas and water,' she commented. 'The problems are everywhere. I sometimes wish there was more I could do, beyond making people aware.'

Stay here and rebuild Marrayin with me. The wish formed unbidden in his thoughts, the wild rush of hope immediately doused by brutal rationality. Yes, they'd resumed a friendship, despite the shadow of Paula's death. He had to be grateful for that, content with that. Even if he could make sense of what he felt now, why he felt it, they had little in common in adulthood beyond, perhaps, nostalgia for an adolescent attraction and friendship, and a commitment to finding the truth about the past.

Jenn was her own person, always had been, always would be. Proud, independent – a wild bird that flew high and far and rarely settled for long.

'The Dungirri Progress Association has developed a plan to revitalise the town, and presented a proposal to a prospective buyer for the pub. If things go ahead as the Association hopes, perhaps you could encourage any lifestyle reporters you know to come out and feature the town, later in the year.'

She stopped with her sandwich halfway to her mouth, and lowered her hands to the table again. 'Okay, some things make sense now. I heard Gillespie ask Liam for figures the other night, and he walked behind the bar like he owned the place. Is he going to buy the pub?'

Mark fervently hoped so, for the sake of the town, and for Kris and Gil. Liam and Deb had asked Mark for his feedback on the business plan they'd put together for Gil, and he'd made a few suggestions, given his encouragement. But it wasn't his decision to make, or his place to comment. 'You'd have to ask him that, Jenn.'

'Maybe I will. From the crowd there at lunchtime, the prospect of him buying doesn't seem unpopular.'

'Liam and Deb have done a great job these past couple of months. But give Gil time. He only came out of witness protection and returned again a week ago.'

಄

When Jim had picked Jenn up off the floor, bruised, bleeding and crying after Mick's beating on the day after Paula's death, he had taken her to Jeanie Menotti.

The few days she'd stayed with Jeanie in the flat above the Truck Stop Café were something of a blur, but she did remember Jeanie's gentle care of her and her down-to-earth common sense. A safe harbour, emotionally and physically, for a battered young soul, and practical help in fetching her clothes and books from Mick's house and giving her a lift to Birraga to catch the bus out of the district for good after the funeral.

Jeanie was the type of person who glued a community together, someone people knew they could turn to in need. Compassionate, empathetic, non-judgemental, she'd always been a friend to those who needed one, and Jenn could only imagine the secrets she held in trust.

When Jeanie arrived at the police cottage she greeted Mark with a motherly kiss on the cheek and Jenn with a warm embrace.

'You've done so well, Jenn. Congratulations on all your achievements.' Jeanie gripped her hand tightly between two arthritis-gnarled hands, her blue eyes shining into Jenn's. 'Your parents raised a fine young woman, and would be so, so proud to see the kind of journalist you've become. We're all very proud of our Dungirri girl.'

Jenn's eyes moistened. Jeanie had known her parents, so her assurance that they would be proud mattered, went beyond the empty words others had said throughout her life. And seeing Jeanie again somehow brought the memory of her parents closer, a connection of friendship as much as history. Jeanie had known her father all his life, and his parents before him; she'd known Jenn's mother only since her marriage, but they'd become friends on Dungirri visits and Susannah had spoken of her liking and respect for the older woman.

When this mess was untangled, Mark safe, the truth uncovered, perhaps she could come back to Dungirri and spend some time with Jeanie, find out more about her parents through Jeanie's eyes.

Come back to Dungirri? Jenn momentarily reeled at the thought. Not one she'd ever expected to entertain without some compulsion.

She dismissed it to concentrate on the here and now. When they were seated at Kris's kitchen table – more comfortable than the sterile interview room – she broached the reason they'd asked her to come. 'Jeanie, we need your help. I think Kris told you that Wolfgang Schmidt was shot this morning?'

Jeannie nodded, tight-lipped. 'I knew him a little. I knew Marta better.'

'Wolfgang gave me some photos. Most are not his own work – they're more . . . disturbing. Some go back a long time. There are photos of the accident too – not only was Gil framed, but it looks like the car was interfered with, and that caused the crash. But that was covered up in the reports. We think there's a connection between the earlier photos and the accident cover-up, but we're not sure how or what.'

Mark poured tea from the pot he'd made. 'Jeanie, I can't get on to my mother at the moment. Did she ever talk to you about . . . about a group or a club called Bohème?'

'Ah . . . Bohème.' Jeanie leaned back in her chair, clasping the mug he'd passed her. 'It still rears its ugly head.'

Jenn stirred sugar into her own tea, watching the older woman's troubled face. 'What can you tell us?'

She and Mark stayed silent while Jeanie arranged her thoughts. Although the stifling heat outside warmed the room, the sweet tea soothed in a familiar, calming way.

'In the sixties, early seventies . . . you weren't born then, you mightn't understand what it was like. Change was everywhere. Students rioted in Paris, astronauts landed on the moon, there were mass demonstrations against Vietnam, and Woodstock and increasing wealth convinced a generation that they could do anything, be anything. You might not believe it to look at them now,' she said with a wry smile, 'but many of your parents' generation had something of a wild youth, experimenting with alcohol, drugs, sex. They were the first generation in Australia to have easy access to university education, and many of the locals went to the city to study. The pill enabled sexual freedom, and magazines – everyone – talked about sex in a way that we never had before. Birraga was no different from anywhere else. Young people went to uni, travelled more, and came back with new ideas and a taste for adventure. And so Bohème was born.'

'Do you know who was involved in it?' Mark asked.

'I'm a little older,' she said, 'and I already had everything I ever wanted in Aldo. But no-one in Bohème invited ordinary folk like us. It was a small, private social group – not even a formal club – and it involved young people from wealthier backgrounds. Professionals, grazing families, business people.'

'People with money to spend,' Jenn said, adding, 'or to be separated from.'

'Yes. It started out happily enough. Social gatherings, parties and . . . excitement, you could say, of various sorts. But as things got darker, people tried to leave – and found that what had happened there would continue to haunt them.'

'There are some photographs of my parents, and of my mother,' Mark said. 'Before I was born, and much later – not long before my accident. She got caught in it, didn't she?'

Jeanie looked down at her hands clasped in front of her, and the clock on the wall ticked off several seconds. 'Mark, you will have to ask your mother about those photographs. It's her story to tell, not mine.'

If Jeanie held a confidence she kept it. But maybe if she knew what was at stake . . . Jenn reached over and covered the woman's hand with hers. 'Jeanie, Mark's sent messages to Caroline, but she's in the wilds of Bolivia. We can't wait until she gets back to civilisation. Not only was Wolfgang murdered this morning, but Mark nearly was, too – someone planted a bomb under his car.'

'Oh dear God,' Jeanie murmured, reaching with her spare hand to take Mark's.

'Doctor Russell, Wolfgang, Mark – someone is trying to silence people with a connection to the accident,' Jenn urged. 'We need to know who was behind the club, the blackmail, and probably the cover-up of the accident. I think Caroline would forgive a breach of confidence to protect her son, don't you?'

Jeanie considered for a long moment, holding both their hands, before she squeezed them gently and withdrew. A sip of tea, a deep breath in, and she spoke. 'I don't know the whole story. As I understand it, when she was young – around the time she started seeing your father, Mark – her own father, Charlie Napier, was deeply in debt, facing bankruptcy, and she succumbed to pressure from someone for sexual favours in return for leniency on the debt. I don't know who he was, but he introduced her to the club.'

Jenn exchanged a glance with Mark. Gerard McCarty, bank manager. Gerard McCarty, in the old photo with his arm around an uneasy Caroline, and Len looking on, angry. A puzzle piece fitted neatly into place.

'My father followed her there, didn't he?' Mark asked, his voice strained.

'I don't know about that, but there was trouble of some sort. Your parents married not long after, and your Napier grandparents sold up their property around that time and retired.'

'Granddad Napier spent a lot of time out at Lightning Ridge with Pop Josef after he retired. He said it kept him away from the bookmakers. Gambling's a nasty addiction.'

'It is,' Jeanie agreed. 'Sadly, Charlie Napier's not the first and won't be the last to have lost a farm that way.' She took another sip of tea. 'Anyway, to get back to your parents, Mark, years later, after they'd developed Marrayin into a successful property and expanded into more property, your mother asked me, in a roundabout way, if I knew any ways to deter a blackmailer. I'd managed to extricate the Truck Stop Café from Flanagan's protection-money racket, and I told her how – by gathering evidence and holding it over him.'

'You had evidence against Dan Flanagan?' Jenn asked, unable to keep the hope from lighting her voice.

'Not specifically against Dan, no. He kept a safe distance and did everything through bully boys. That's why he's still walking free when his sons are in prison,' she replied, a hard edge on her usually gentle tone. 'But with Gil's help I collected enough to hold Flanagan's boys off.'

An unlikely crime-fighting duo, the compassionate elderly woman and the rough teen, but Jeanie's story correlated with Gil's information. In her memories of the cafe, Jenn recalled the taciturn youth who'd worked to fill tanks and keep the place clean while the rest of the teens ate hamburgers and laughed at the tables . . . yes, she could see how that partnership, that loyalty had developed.

'Did my mother say what the blackmail was?' Mark asked.

Always 'my mother', Jenn noticed, and rarely if ever 'Mum'.

'No, she didn't say specifically, but it was something that went back to the early trouble, and she was afraid for your father, willing to do anything to protect him. But the price was high, requiring regular "payments", and she was desperate to get out of it. I advised her to go to the police, but she said she couldn't, that they'd destroy Len. That was a couple of weeks before your accident, Mark.'

Mark's face was drawn, anger in his clenched hands, his white knuckles. But he kept his voice low and even. 'Was Flanagan behind it?'

'It was no secret that your parents and Dan were rivals, in the legal side of Dan's businesses, anyway. But I remember her saying that there were far more dangerous criminals than thugs like Dan.'

Worse than Dan? Jenn thought of the photographs, and shuddered. 'Do you know what she did to get out of it?'

Again Jeanie considered her answer. 'I knew Marta Schmidt a little, and I knew there was more to Wolfgang than he let on. Marta hinted that he'd taken on the Bohème Club. I suggested to Caroline that she contact them. I didn't see her alone for some weeks after that, until after you'd come back from hospital in Newcastle, Mark. But she said she'd resolved it, and she never mentioned it again.'

'*Blackmail . . . hurt Marta.*' Wolfgang's words echoed in Jenn's mind. A threat to Marta would have been reason enough for him to take on the club, to get his hands on the photographs he'd taught Dan to develop long ago, and to gather evidence in surveillance photographs. And if he'd known that Caroline was being blackmailed, perhaps it wasn't surprising that he'd taken photos of Mark's accident. Assumptions, yes, and she had no proof connecting it all yet, but it made a logical sense, fitted all they knew.

Caroline might have 'resolved' her problem with Wolfgang's assistance, but questions still tugged at Jenn. Was it resolved before the accident, or after? Did she resolve it permanently? Did Len know? And did it have anything to do with Caroline and Len leaving Dungirri and handing everything over to Mark when he finished university? That had struck her as strange, for a fit and healthy couple barely near retirement age.

But if Caroline had endured forced sex – damn it, call it what it was, *rape* – that would be reason enough for any woman to want to leave the district. Jenn's stomach churned. They might be getting closer to answers, but none of them were easy to bear.

Jenn still had questions for Jeanie, and although she wasn't sure she wanted to hear the answers she sucked in a breath and asked, 'Do you know if . . . if my father ever had anything to do with Dan Flanagan?'

Jeanie turned her teaspoon over on the table and took a long time to answer. 'I think he did some work for him. Before he joined the army. It was decades ago, Jenn. He ran a little wild like many young men, but he straightened out and made your grandparents proud.'

Aware of Mark near her, his wordless gaze reading her intention and giving her courage, she asked, 'Do you believe my father did it, Jeanie? Killed my mother?'

Jeanie sat up straighter, her hand warm over Jenn's. 'I believe he was a good man, Jenn. I don't know what happened or why, but he loved your mother and you. I've never doubted that.'

I've never doubted that . . . The words eased some of the ache in her heart, and made her more determined to find the truth, clear her father's name.

Jeanie embraced her affectionately before she left. 'Don't go running away again without coming to see me. And,' she drew Jenn's head down and kissed her forehead, as if in benediction, 'be careful, and look after each other.'

❦

While Jenn worked through the photos, creating a spreadsheet of dates, initials and other details, Mark made lists, laying the names out in groups – everyone who might have been involved in the accident and its aftermath, police, medical, legal, each name notated with position titles, current whereabouts and other notes. Bill Franklin topped the list of police, Will Cooper the list of paramedics. Where he didn't know names, he noted positions, such as Deputy Coroner, nurses at the hospital, other patients.

When he finished with those lists, he started a new one: Flanagan associates and friends. People who worked for Flanagan. People who worked with him – other graziers, suppliers, business people who didn't seem to mind the company. People who attended his Christmas drinks, usually reported in the social page of the Birraga *Gazette*.

Gerard McCarty topped that list. Mark added Larry Dolan from the *Gazette*. There had certainly been more advertising of Flanagan's transport and irrigation operations in the *Gazette* after Clem Lockrey's retirement as managing editor.

And all the time he made notes, Jenn worked at the other end of the table, every now and again glancing up, making a comment. But she didn't recognise anyone else in the photographs. 'Whoever took these photos was either very cautious,' she commented, 'or just not interested in faces.'

Steve returned in the late afternoon, and brought Mark's laptop with him. 'Forensics have finished at your place, and I thought you might need this.'

'Thanks. Any news?'

'Good news is, there are prints on the tape on the explosives. The bad news is, they're not Flanagan's. Forensics will run them overnight and maybe we'll get an answer in the morning if they're on file. In the meantime, you're staying here tonight. Haddad and the Feds want you protected.'

'Here?' Mark hesitated. 'I could go to the pub.'

'Nope. Not secure enough, and there's no-one spare to stand guard. Kris says you can have the guest bed. Apparently Gil will be down later – no prizes for guessing where he's sleeping – and I'm going to crash on the couch. In a police station with the three of us and your dogs outside, you should be safe enough for tonight.'

The continued inactivity and restriction on his movements grated, making him uneasy, and he had to consciously stop himself from pacing around the rooms of Kris's small residence. Patience. Focus. Work. Research.

At least with his laptop returned he had something to do with his restless mind. He booted it up and connected to the internet via Kris's wireless. First task: check his email. He scrolled the lists of messages in the Marrayin and his personal accounts. Still nothing from his parents. *Damn it.* If they'd been flooded in to the village by heavy rains it might be days before they received his messages.

Second task: he typed 'Gerard McCarty' into the search engine. Too many results, with many professional, presumably

250

respectable men filling the top few pages – but no bankers. He narrowed the search terms to New South Wales, then on a whim added Queensland. On the second page of results, the summary sentence of a news report caught his eye: Gerard McCarty, wanted for questioning on suspicion of rape and murder. He opened the link, and the report – dated four years ago – included an image. As the image slowly loaded, he found himself looking into the cold, smirking eyes of the man photographed with Dan Flanagan eighteen years ago.

FOURTEEN

She was well outnumbered, three against one. She would have argued, held her ground – but the trouble was, they were right.

She rubbed Rosie's ears. 'Guess I'll be staying here tonight, Rosie girl,' she murmured. 'It does make more sense than being alone in the hotel.'

So much for peace and quiet and space to think without a horde of others around. So much for time to sort through some ragged, confusing-as-hell emotions.

The screen door squeaked. Steve, not Mark. He sat on the back step beside her and launched straight into round two of ordering her about.

'Listen, Jenn. McCarty's been on the run for four years and you can bet he's in this up to his bloody neck. He might have a chance of beating one accusation of rape and murder, but if he knows that you – we – have the photos, and if we can get Caroline and the other women to testify, he's looking at life.

You're potentially as big a target as Mark. And I don't want to have to identify your remains, so stop being a stubborn idiot and use your brain.'

'Are you always this much of a bossy bastard or are you making a special effort to impress me?' She aimed for a mocking tone but in truth she wasn't feeling it, and the edge of teasing showed.

He glanced sideways at her, that playboy grin not far away. 'Sweetheart, if I thought I had any chance this side of hell of making that kind of impression on you, you'd know about it. But I don't do lost causes.'

A lost cause? Well, yes, as far as Steve was concerned, she was. She'd come to like the guy and his mildly flirtatious ways and to respect the serious dedication beneath it, but the flutter in her heartbeat, the awareness of him, the tingle on her skin and catch in her breath? No, none of that had happened. Wasn't going to happen. Not with Steve. A part of her wished it would because that might be a whole lot less complicated than . . . No, she wouldn't even *think* that. Not Mark. Nothing but a little nostalgia with Mark.

She decided against trying to respond to Steve's bait and flipped back to the real issue. 'I was just telling Rosie here that I'd be staying the night. I wasn't so much suffering from a bout of stupidity as a mild oh-shit-oh-shit-oh-shit attack. So, don't go thinking it was your persuasive charm that made me agree, okay? Rosie's my witness.'

'And probably more intelligent than half the witnesses I see on the stand,' he said. 'But now, can I persuade you to come inside? That scrub out there has hidden snipers before.'

With the vision of Wolfgang bleeding to death still fresh in her mind, she didn't need further convincing.

Afternoon darkened into evening. All of them continued to work, think, research; Steve and Kris in the police station, Jenn and Mark in the marginally more spacious kitchen. She finished indexing the date and initial codes of the photos and started trying to match Birraga or Dungirri names to the faceless or blindfolded women. There was one that might have been Marta – MS – a woman bound in a chair and flinching, the antithesis of Wolfgang's reverent work.

Others she couldn't be sure of. Wealthier women, Jeanie had said, and the haircuts, artfully coloured lips and smooth skin in the images confirmed they were women with the time and money to look after their appearance. She concentrated on the time period she remembered best, trying to recall the women featured in the *Gazette*'s social pages, the ones who'd had the money to make regular visits to Vanna's beauty salon next door.

The mayor's wife? He'd been a slimy pig but she'd been a sweet if nervy woman. Initials – tick. Body type and hair – yes, probable.

Sally Duncan from the Birraga Boutique? Initials – tick. Body type and long wavy hair – yes.

Sharon Rennie, a daughter of the family who owned the local, long-established department store? Initials – tick. Body type and pageboy hair cut – yes.

'Bastards.' She pushed the laptop away, nausea roiling in her gut. At the end of the table Mark looked up from his own work. 'It wasn't just your mother, Mark. There's at least three other prominent women of similar age in there. Maybe more.

Bohème got its dirty claws into at least half the best businesses in town.'

'Take a break, Jenn. You've been at it for ages.'

Take a break and do what? 'No, I should keep going with this. If you can give me the names of some of the women from grazing families, I can check for them.'

He came to her end of the table, reached over and closed the laptop screen. 'Take a break. You've been staring at the screen too long, and there's a limit to the amount of horror a person can take in at one time.'

'Yes, I know. Horror's part of my business, remember?' And she crafted it into thirty-second sound bites, two-minute reports, or longer features that kept the hardest-hitting facts for the climax after easing the reader or viewer in. 'I should be used to this kind of shit. I've uncovered enough of it.'

'Maybe not so close to home. People you know. That's always worse.' Standing behind her, he drew her back in her chair and began to massage the tight, hard muscles of her neck and shoulders. 'Take a break,' he repeated. 'This cement means you've been working too long.'

She closed her eyes, accepting the gift, letting his firm fingers work gradually, increasingly, into the knots. Maybe he was right. Not just about the cemented muscles. About horror being worse when it was people you knew. She'd seen plenty of evil – corruption that made her cynical, violence that sickened her, poverty that made her despair, and natural disasters that left her feeling powerless, tiny and vulnerable in the face of the planet's physical forces. But each time, after a few days, after filing her reports, she could walk away from the strangers whose lives she'd glimpsed for a short while.

The August day when Sally Duncan had been planning her boutique's spring sale and enquired about advertising rates in the *Gazette* office – had that been before or after she'd gone to the room with the long drapes and the metal chair?

When Caroline had driven to the place where she'd knelt naked on the carpet, what had she worn? The well-cut jeans and tailored shirt she often wore for quick trips to town? The blue linen dress for lunch with her friends? Had Len known where she was going, and why, or had she made up a story, forced to lie? Had she scrubbed her body all over when she got home and then pretended over dinner with her husband and son that everything was fine?

That son's hands paused on Jenn's shoulders. 'You're tensing up. Is this hurting? Do you want me to stop?'

'No. It's okay. I just lost the zen thoughts there for a while. Will your hands hold out for a minute or two more?' Two minutes wouldn't make much difference to the state of her neck and shoulders, but she could get herself together in two minutes, defeat the urge to cry, and be ready to face him and pretend that she could deal with everything – including him – without falling apart and taking more from him than a shoulder massage.

❧

Being confined in a four-room house made him edgy. Mark lingered at the printer in Kris's spare bedroom-cum-study, staring at the pages in his hand without seeing them. He rubbed the rock-hard muscles at the back of his own neck, tense after hours of being cooped up inside, of considering all the possibilities of the past darkness, of working at the same table as Jenn. His offer to massage her shoulders had been every bit as much for him as for her – to ease her pain, to touch her, and to stand behind her so she couldn't see how deeply she affected him. All the promise, all the potential she'd had at seventeen flowered now as an adult – her intelligence, her perseverance, the passion for justice that blazed in her eyes.

If things had been different . . . He cursed the circumstances that had brought her back into his life now, now when he had a cloud over his head, when he was bound here by honour and commitment to help Dungirri – his community – recover from traumatic years and rebuild its shattered identity. Even if he was not charged over Paula's death, Jenn's life and career lay elsewhere, and he was not free to be with her.

He'd gripped the pages in his hand so tightly they'd creased in long untidy folds. He wished it was Flanagan's neck he'd had his hands around.

Did that make him little better than Flanagan? He didn't know, but the anger and violence within him simmered and he had to deliberately focus to slow his breathing, to open his fists, to smooth out the papers and return to the others – to Jenn – with some semblance of calm.

Gil arrived, bringing with him bread, steaks and salad from the pub kitchen, and he prepared a meal while the rest of them gathered around the table and shared progress and news.

'Leah's banging her head against a brick wall trying to get more resources on the ground,' Steve reported. 'So, tomorrow I'm officially back on the team. At least if I get shot in the line of duty tomorrow I'll be covered by workers' comp, but we'd better try to avoid the shooting stuff tonight, right?'

'I'll second that,' Mark volunteered, re-joining them at the table. They'd put away computers, reshuffled seats for everyone to fit, and he took the vacant seat next to Jenn. Maybe he should have taken the one furthest away instead of being so close that their thighs were only inches apart and he could almost feel the warmth of her body. Every small move distracted him, and he had to concentrate to follow the discussion. But she was part of it, animated and engaged with the intellectual puzzle, despite her fatigue.

'Jenn, I passed along your information about the women you've possibly identified,' Steve continued, going through his notes. 'Leah wants to visit them in the morning, and she wants you to go with her, Kris, as you're the local sexual assault specialist.'

'Did the forensic team find anything else at Wolfgang's place?' Jenn asked.

'His artwork is neatly catalogued in cabinets in the studio. But there's a storage space under the darkroom floor with a whole lot more photographs and negatives, and I doubt they're his work. They'll take some time to go through, but this is a copy of one that fell out of the pile while forensics were packing them up.'

Steve passed the photo across the table to them and Jenn took it, placing it so Mark could see it.

A black-and-white photo, almost cartoonish, with an oversized head added clumsily to the image of a beaten woman's body, the face young, pretty . . . and familiar. Jenn made a small sound of shock, and with disgust Mark turned the photo face down, and shoved it back to Steve.

'It's Barbara Russell,' he said, and Gil stilled for an instant at the bench, then spun around, knife in hand, and reached across Steve for the photo. 'Just her face, edited on. Poorly edited.'

Mark watched the knife gripped in Gil's hand, but he had himself under control. Almost. If Flanagan had been there, he'd have been a dead man. And Mark wasn't at all sure he wouldn't have helped.

'It's a threat,' Gil said harshly, tossing the photo back on the table. 'You'll probably find a copy in the doc's papers somewhere. That'll be how they gained his compliance.'

He turned away again, but the knife clattered into the sink, and he grasped the edges of the bench, breathing through clenched teeth. Kris went to him and put her hand on his shoulder, then his arm came around her and pulled her close to his side.

Glad for them and what they'd found together, Mark nevertheless had to stifle a wave of envy. Beside him Jenn held herself stiffly in her seat, closed off and unreachable. Except her intellect wouldn't be silenced.

'Maybe the doc knew,' she said, thinking aloud. 'Maybe he knew about the women and what went on at the club. Because that image would have a lot more impact if he knew how real it could become. I can't imagine many women confiding in him, but if there'd been injuries, unwanted pregnancies, emotional distress he might have guessed something of it.'

And done whatever he had to do to protect his daughter from the same fate. Like signing a blood-alcohol sample with the wrong name. Mark's anger at the old doctor eased down a few notches.

He still had questions about how Wolfgang had obtained – or stolen – those photographs and from whom, but they weren't his main concern. Men who preyed on beautiful women were, and the need to protect the woman sitting beside him who'd become involved and wouldn't step back from searching for answers. 'Did you track down any more information on Gerard McCarty?' he asked Steve.

'Yes, I'm getting to that.' Steve shuffled a couple of pages of notes. 'Okay, McCarty left here not quite eighteen years ago – a couple of weeks after the accident. He transferred to a similar position in a larger branch of the same bank on the Gold Coast. He resigned from there three years later. Then he set up a business as a financial consultant and paid cash for a million-dollar house on forty hectares in the hinterland. He liked to entertain, was well respected and had interests in several property-development companies. He was questioned about the disappearance of a woman five years ago, brought along a top lawyer, refused a DNA test without a warrant, then walked out of the police station without being charged – and hasn't been seen since. Her body was found in bushland a week later. And,' he grimaced, 'you don't want the details of that.'

Gil had resumed cooking and the steaks sizzled on the hot grill, making Mark's stomach take a queasy roll.

Gil put a salad bowl in the centre of the table and threw a glance at Steve. 'After dinner,' he said, with a slight emphasis on *after*, 'see if there's any connection between McCarty and

Vanna Flanagan. She's been up on the Gold Coast ever since she left Dan, which was around that time.'

Mark watched Gil's face. He'd been inadvertently involved in the business run by Vanna's mafia brothers in the city, and had discovered their local connection. 'Do you think McCarty got her caught up in this, too?' Mark asked.

Gil shrugged. 'Maybe. I don't know enough about her. But there's a coincidence there. Rumour has it she took Dan to the cleaners in the divorce settlement. She certainly expanded her empire – the network of salons, spas, whatever you call them, across the country, and what's now a large modelling agency.'

Steve shoved his notes to one side. 'The Feds have been looking into all of that in the investigation of the Flanagan businesses since the sons' arrests. But she's not involved in the family companies now; she came up clean.'

Gil snorted.

Jenn suddenly sat forward, her hands on the table. 'What if we've been underestimating her? She's a link. Her salon back then was probably a link. The place where Birraga's wealthy women went, relaxed, unwound – and talked. She would know them all. McCarty would have known their financial status. Women aren't always victims. Sometimes,' her eyes locked on Steve's and she used the words Jeanie had quoted earlier, 'sometimes there are far more dangerous criminals than thugs like Dan.'

It was after midnight, and only small sounds were audible in the quiet of the house. The rattle of a chain on the wooden veranda as one of the dogs changed position. Steve's low, deep breathing from the couch in the living room. The sound of Mark turning in his sleep on the blow-up vinyl mattress. Only silence from the next room, where Kris and Gil slept.

Jenn didn't know what had woken her. She must have drifted off to sleep at last but it had taken a long time to still her brain enough to relax. Now she lay in Kris's guest bed, the sheet half over her, and listened for any sound that didn't belong.

Frogs in the creek, the low call of a mopoke owl – years since she'd heard that – and the high-pitched buzz of a mosquito circling just outside her room.

She pulled the sheet up over her bare arms and scratched an itch on her wrist. A feasting mozzie. Yes, that would be enough to wake her. Nothing to worry about – except the itch. She turned over, settled the pillow and made sure the sheet protected her shoulders before she closed her eyes again.

Explosion . . . fire erupting . . . flames, flames all around him . . . she ran, fell, pain in knees and hands and ankle . . . crawled, crying . . . couldn't get to him . . . couldn't save him . . . cried out again . . . and again—

'Jenn? Jenn, it's okay. You're dreaming. You're safe.'

Quiet voice. A dark head, a weird green glow on the face . . . She closed and opened her eyes again. Mark. Mark in the dull light of the bedroom. The green glow from the power light on the printer.

The nightmare still lurking in the cobwebs of sleep, she pushed herself up to sit and shook her head to try to wake up. 'Sorry. Bad dream. Thought . . .' *Thought you were burning to death in a car.* No surprises that her subconscious had thrown that at her.

'I had one too,' he whispered. 'I was going to get a glass of water. Do you want one?'

Her throat as dry as if she'd been trying to scream in her sleep, she nodded. 'Thanks.' Water would be good but . . . Bathroom. That would help her settle again. She tossed the sheet off and swung her feet to the floor, following him out the door.

When she came back the green glow from the printer reflected off a glass left for her on the bedside table, and Mark stood silhouetted against the window, sipping from a glass in his hands, tall and muscular and yes, breathtaking in a rumpled T-shirt and jeans. The floorboards cool against her bare feet, she crossed to Mark and laid her hand on his arm.

Aware of the others sleeping just metres away, she kept her voice to a whisper. 'Thanks. You always were a rock when I needed you.'

He smiled just a little. 'Everyone needs someone to lean on once in a while.'

'Who do you lean on?'

'Friends. Kris. Ryan and Beth. You.'

'I left. That's not much of a friend.'

He touched her then, brushing the back of his fingers against her cheek, the caress resonating deep within her. 'You were there when I needed you, growing up. My parents were . . . distracted, but you believed in me, understood the things I cared about. You mattered, Jenn.'

A small piece of her heart defrosted. And cracked in pain. 'I wasn't there for you after the accident. I had to go.'

'I know. And you'll go again.'

'Yes.'

Yes, she'd go. She took a step away from him. Better to keep her distance now and resist the temptation to lay her head against his shoulder. She didn't need him, didn't need the reassurance of his strength or the reminder of the affection and intimacy they'd once shared. She didn't want the pain of leaving him again intensified by becoming too close. She'd learned the hard way, last time, that having memories of love didn't make the parting easier to bear.

At least he didn't have the memories, and she didn't plan on giving him new ones.

'I'm sorry I woke you,' she whispered, retreating to politeness.

'You didn't. Bad dreams woke me.'

After too many disturbed nights and enough emotional turmoil to break a weaker man? Not surprising. 'You need to sleep, Mark. You're exhausted. We're both exhausted, with too much scope for nightmares. Go back to bed and think of dogs and count your cattle and you'll drift off.' She gave him a light kiss on the cheek, noticing the sensuality of his unshaven jaw, the faint salty scent of maleness, and was hit hard by desire and the longing to slide into his arms and be surrounded by his strength.

She took another step back. *Go*, she pleaded silently. *Go and don't let me give in to temptation to invite you to share this bed and hold me while we sleep.*

His fingers brushed her face again, and she almost wished he were flirtatious and cheeky like Steve because she could have dealt with that far more easily than this quiet intensity, the *presence* of him and his eyes focused on her. 'You go back to sleep too, Jenn. I won't be far away if you need me. If ever you need me.'

He left the room, his footsteps silent on the wooden floorboards and she stayed by the window, staring out into the darkness.

From the living room, she heard the faint rustle of the bedclothes, the soft squeak of the mattress against the floor as Mark lay down again. Alone.

She went to her own bed, pulled the sheet up around her shoulders, rolled on to her side and curled up. Alone.

Her choice, her decision, but regret curled up with her, and she didn't sleep until she allowed herself to imagine being held, safe in the arms of a man who demanded nothing of her and who cared enough to let her go.

༚

He lay flat on his back, wide awake and staring at the century-old pressed-metal ceiling. The ornate floral pattern didn't replace the image of Jenn's face. Jenn, looking up at him, wide-eyed and undecided. She'd wanted him to stay. He'd wanted to stay. And yet . . .

And yet he'd left her there. He hadn't drawn her against him, held her and kissed her and comforted her, body to body.

Sex? Yes, he thought about sex. His body thought about sex. But she didn't want sex, and beyond a basic pheromone reaction, neither did he. Not right now. He wanted more than physical intimacy from her. Sex with her – making love with her – would be wondrous, but not without emotional intimacy. And emotional intimacy still scared her. She'd walled off her heart in self-protection decades ago and strode through life, needing no-one.

He wasn't in a position to offer her much, anyway, and maybe in a few days, when they'd tracked down the killer and untangled the old crimes and new, when the intensity receded to normal, maybe then he'd be able to put their relationship into its proper perspective – an old friendship, a fondness and affection for a woman he respected.

He closed his eyes and let his mind relax, drifting towards sleep. In the semi-awake, semi-asleep stage the neurons wandered along their many paths, unmarshalled by conscious reason, freeing thoughts, ideas, memories and fears filed in various parts of his brain into a buzzing flicker of subconscious voices and images. Things to do. Parliamentary questions. His old dog, Sammy, loping across a paddock. Jenn, frowning over her homework. Insurance policies. Flames. A blue hair scrunchie caught up in a tangled cotton blanket. Sun streaming into the shearers' kitchen and Jenn laughing and reaching back with one hand to drag her wet hair out of its scrunchie.

His eyes shot open again, and he tried to grasp the wisps of memory. Jenn – yes he remembered that day in the shearers' kitchen. Sammy – much loved, long gone, his marker a cairn of stones and a painted tile. The scrunchie, in the room in the shearers' quarters he'd set up as a study and bolthole. The old camp bed he lay on while reading and listening to music, the desk with his books.

He could see himself standing there, holding the scrunchie, puzzling over its presence. It took a moment to pin the memory down. In those first few days home from the hospital, his brain was still healing from the injury and sometimes foggy, making it harder to come to terms with Paula's death, with the gaping hole in his memory, with Jenn's absence and with the news that he'd become Paula's boyfriend. A scrunchie from a girl's hair caught up in the rumpled blanket? The only conclusion to draw at the time was that he'd lost his sense and maybe even his virginity with Paula in those days he couldn't remember.

But Jenn remembered those days, and the only girl he'd ever dreamed about sleeping with, making love with back then, was her. Paula had never featured in his youthful fantasies, and he doubted he'd ever featured in hers.

Whereas Jenn . . . Jenn still featured in his dreams. Every few months through all those years, he'd woken in the night, having dreamed of her in his bed, in his arms, in his life. There'd been other women every now and then, even a couple of relationships, but he'd never dreamed of those women the way he dreamed of Jenn.

He turned over and tried to relax the tension in his body. All this time he'd told himself that he'd dreamed of Jenn because he saw her name in the newspapers, her face on the television. That was all.

He must have slept, because he woke suddenly in the first light of dawn to a car's engine revving in the street, a fast brake, and the dogs on the veranda barking in warning.

Steve swore, car doors slammed outside and footsteps sounded on the veranda steps, Dash barking loudly, Maggie growling.

Alert and wary, Mark rolled off the air mattress and pushed to his feet as someone knocked hard and repeatedly on the front door.

'Officer, please, it is urgent. Please open.'

Kris hurried past and joined Steve near the front door as Jenn came out of the bedroom. Mark gently pushed her back, out of the line of sight of the door. Gil came and stood beside them.

Kris checked through the spyhole and nodded at Steve. 'It's okay. It's a couple of tourists I've met.'

The young couple stood on the doorstep, dishevelled and tense. The young man spoke first, his English accented with a soft Scandinavian lilt. 'Officers, there is a murder. A man shot. At Ghost Hill campground. Two hours ago, but we hid, could not come earlier. There was a car, and shouting, and then the gunshots. The killers did not leave straightaway, so we waited in hiding. When they did, we went to help the man – but he was dead. We did not touch, we left him, came straight here, but see this.' The young man passed his phone to Steve. 'I took his photo. We do not know his name, but perhaps you know him?'

Steve looked hard at the phone image, then passed it to Kris. Mark saw her frown, studying it for a moment before looking back at him. 'Mark, you remember faces well.' She handed him the phone.

In death, the man's face was slack, sightless eyes staring up beneath sparse grey hair, jowls fat around his neck. In his sixties perhaps, or older. Mark tried to imagine the face with movement and life, and recognition crystallised.

Mark handed the phone to Gil. 'Yes, I know who that is.'

Gil glanced at the image and nodded.

'Please, wait here for just a moment,' Kris said to the tourist couple. 'I'll take you through to the station shortly to get the details from you.'

She half-shut the door and the five of them gathered in the kitchen, all eyes on Mark and Gil.

'Okay, so who is it?' Steve asked.

'It's Bill Franklin,' Mark said. 'The old sergeant.' The man who'd framed Gil and written a false accident report. At the very least.

Gil said nothing, his dark eyes narrowed.

'The Northern Territory coppers thought he was dead,' Steve said.

Mark thrust his hands into his jeans pocket and leaned on the kitchen table. 'He is now. He had a lot to lose with the reopened investigation. That might be why he was here. But the big question is: who killed him?'

crea

After the abrupt awakening the morning crawled by in uncertainty and restlessness, waiting for news. There was no chance to find a few minutes alone with Mark; the tourists had to be calmed and were invited for breakfast, and then Leah Haddad arrived with her team in quick response to Steve's call, and the small station overflowed with police and forensic officers.

Jenn had to admire the detective's focus. Leah held a quick briefing with Steve and Kris and despatched them to the scene, then interviewed the young couple, called Mark in for some questions and background information and within a very short time was ready to head out to the campground. Before she left she joined Jenn in the kitchen, a young constable behind her.

'I've asked Mark to come with us, because he knows that area well,' she said. 'So, Constable Riordan will stay with you for now.' She paused for a second, hesitation that might have been uncertainty. 'I have a favour to ask you, Jenn. Our media team is flat-out with something else, and the regional media officer has appendicitis – and I need to get a media statement out covering yesterday and this morning. You'd know the kind of thing well – could you possibly draft something up if you have the time? I'd be very grateful.'

Jenn had the time. She had hours to fill, stuck in the cottage with the young probationary constable, who took her duties so seriously that she followed Jenn from room to room. The media statement – how many thousands of these had she read during her career? – took only a short time, bland facts and standard declarations of resources allocated to the continuing investigations and the Crime Stoppers contact number for anyone with information.

She collected the page from the printer in the bedroom and handed it to the constable, Tenita, standing in the doorway.

'Tell me what you think,' she said, not because she needed any reassurance herself, but because the young woman seemed as bored and restless as she was.

Jenn then sat back down at her computer and opened a new document. She should write something. Something other than a bland media statement. She was a journalist in the middle of a series of crimes in a town she'd once known and she should record . . .

Record what? Events? She'd done that, in the single page Tenita was reading. Distant, objective statements of fact, circumstance and intentions. Easy.

She rested her fingers on the keyboard. Could she stand back enough from herself to observe realities and impacts? She had no plans to report anything for now – in fact, avoiding the media was her preference – but maybe there could be a feature article down the track. The effect on a small community. The experience of being caught up in crime after crime. Someone she cared about threatened.

Any number of potential angles came to her. But the page remained empty.

&

Steve returned several hours later.

'I dropped Mark at Ward's store,' he said, propping against the kitchen bench, more relaxed than he'd been earlier. 'He's getting some supplies for Marrayin. He's worried about things being neglected out there and wants to get back.'

'But—' Jenn glanced at Tenita. 'Is there someone with him?'

'Nope. Good news is, the vic's definitely Franklin. Our Danish friends said he was already camping out there when they arrived yesterday morning. And the portable scanner confirmed that his fingerprints are a match to the ones on Mark's gate on Friday, and yesterday's explosives tape.'

Jenn pushed aside her laptop as relief and worry battled for dominance. 'Franklin tried to kill him?'

'That's what the evidence says. Oh, and the man's a fool. Any cop – hell, any crim – worth their salt knows that if you're going to stand on a damp garden in boots with a distinctive print while garrotting a man, you should toss those boots and get a new pair.'

A fool? Or a man panicking? 'So, he tried to get the report on Friday and failed, silenced Doc Russell on Saturday, and since Mark was away from home on Saturday night he wired his car?'

'That all fits. There's nothing yet to connect him with the attack in Birraga, but I'm still not convinced that was a murder attempt.' Steve grabbed a glass from the drainer and filled it with water. 'Anyway, Mark's prepared to take the risk and wants to look after things at his place.'

'Do you know yet who shot Franklin?' He couldn't. Not so soon. So, there was still a murderer out there.

'It wasn't Dan Flanagan. He was in Birraga hospital all night with angina, so he's in the clear. Again.' He gulped a few mouthfuls of water. 'Look, I know what you're thinking. But I can tell you that Franklin – his death was execution-style. His prints may well be linked to a drug seizure a while back. He has to have been living off the grid, so to speak, and drug running would make sense. But if you piss off the wrong people in that game, there's no need for a pension fund.'

'So, you don't think it's connected?'

His mouth curved into a small grin. 'Oh, all things are connected, Grasshopper, in one way or another. And I may be spectacularly wrong. Wouldn't be the first time. I can still argue a case for protection for you. That's up to you.'

Another day holed up inside? 'No. Thank you. There are some things I need to do.'

He smiled, and this time it wasn't a cheeky grin but a warm smile of friendship. 'Mark said to ask you if you could give him and the dogs a lift to Marrayin. If you want to. Otherwise he'll call Karl and hitch a ride with him.'

If she wanted to? She had plenty of unanswered questions, but that wasn't one of them. Although the answer frightened her. She and Mark were a team, she reasoned, actively searching for the truth, and when they found it she could leave Dungirri with her heart intact. Mostly.

The sun hot on her skin, she walked the block down the main street to Ward's Rural Supplies, the first in the row of century-old shops, the rest of them empty. She pushed the door open, an electric buzzer sounding instead of the jingle of bells she expected. That had changed. Little else seemed to have altered. Tools, stock tags, marking rings, ropes and other supplies on the first few shelves; drenches, weed killers and other chemicals beyond, and deeper into the store stacks of dog food, rolls of wire, fence strainers and star posts.

There was less stock now than there used to be, and instead of Joe Ward, a young woman rang up the stack of items on the counter.

'On the account, Mark?' she asked, casting a quick, curious smile at Jenn.

Mark's smile lasted a good second longer but he gave his attention back to the woman and answered, 'Yes, thanks, Mel. Do you remember Jenn Barrett?'

Mel. She had to be Melinda Ward. Not six years old anymore. Tall and capable in jeans and a cotton drill shirt, with strong hands that had probably hefted many a twenty-kilo bag of feed.

'Hi, Mel,' she greeted her politely. But reluctant to get bogged in conversation with the woman when she'd scarcely remembered the child, she turned to Mark. 'I'll go and get the car from the pub. Won't be long.'

The empty shopfronts she walked past each evoked memories. The bakery and milk bar. The barber's shop. The butcher's shop. All gone, and only George and Eleni's corner store across from the pub providing groceries now.

If Dungirri lost the pub, the town would die.

She left her gear in her room, and was upstairs for only a few minutes, but when she came down she found the local police constable, out of uniform, standing near her car. She'd seen him at the Russells' on Saturday morning and out at Wolfgang's yesterday. A young Indigenous man with a serious attitude and an easy manner with his colleagues. Adam, she'd heard him called.

'Hi. Steve just phoned, asked me to check your car before you drive it. Can't see any signs of interference around or under it but let's be sure, hey? You wanna pop the bonnet?'

Checking her car – she hadn't given it a thought. Grateful to Steve and to Adam, she unlocked the door and leaned in to pull the bonnet lever. Adam propped it open and spent long moments examining the engine and surrounds.

'You seem to know what you're doing,' she commented.

'Yeah. I was a mechanic for a few years.' He dropped the bonnet and pressed it down closed. 'She's clear of any surprises. Explosive ones, anyway.'

She thanked him, and he sauntered off down the road. Although he'd assured her the car was all right, she still hesitated when she put the key in the ignition. The engine hummed to life, and she exhaled a long breath.

Mark waited out the front of Ward's, a couple of sacks of dog food at his feet, and a few tarps and ropes. Once loaded, they collected the dogs from the police cottage, and with the three animals lying on the back seat she reversed out the driveway and turned the car towards Marrayin.

So far their conversation had been practical, about tarps and dogs and Melinda running the store after her father's death. Nothing about their discussion in the night or the connection between them that refused to be ignored. She kept her eyes on the road and the conversation away from that particular emotional minefield.

'You're confident you're safe at home?' she asked.

'Yes. Pretty much. Franklin's dead, and his prints are sound evidence he was the one out there. He was out there, and he had motivation.'

She gripped the steering wheel tightly, the black ribbon of road blurring slightly in front of her. 'So, he killed Jim.'

'We might never know exactly what happened, Jenn. But he left him unconscious in a burning room. That's close enough to attempted murder.'

And for that, she hated the former police sergeant. But hate was destructive and she made herself consider reason and motivation instead. 'I just don't understand why he would have come back. If he'd faked his death and has been living anonymously for the past few years, why did he risk it?'

'Could be any number of reasons, I guess. He'd been in the police service for his entire career. Maybe he wanted to reappear and claim his superannuation pension.'

'If the truth about his role in the corruption came out, he wouldn't be able to.'

'Yes. That's purely conjecture, of course. And we don't know for sure what he was searching for at Marrayin. He probably knew I had the police report, but perhaps he also knew there were photos in existence. Or if my mother had gathered information to hold over Flanagan, he might have been looking for that.'

She turned into the driveway and drove up between the long avenue of trees. The damaged homestead was quiet but for the flapping of the police tape in the breeze and the sounds of cattle in the distance.

Although the kitchen and the east wing had escaped mostly unscathed, sections of the roof were damaged and open to the elements. Not that the weather – huge blue skies and harsh sunlight – threatened more damage yet, but Jenn remembered how quickly a summer storm could come up in the evenings.

It took more than an hour to drag the tarpaulins over the roofline on each side and secure them to the veranda posts, Mark up the ladder and clambering on the roof, Jenn below holding ropes and hoping every moment that the beams were still strong enough to hold.

He'd lent her a hat but by the time it was done they were both hot, sunburned and sweaty. Mark splashed water over his head at the tank stand and she followed suit, drinking long from cupped hands to quench her thirst.

With water dripping on to his damp shirt, Mark slid his hat back on. 'I had to put some cattle in the scrub paddock the other day but they need moving to better water. Ground's rough there and they'll need rounding up, so I'll ride. How's the foot?' Despite the years and the worries, his grin took her right back to their teens. 'Do you want to saddle up and join me?'

On horseback through the bush with Mark? Oh, she was tempted. Memories of times she'd loved, felt alive, caught her imagination. But reality intruded and doused the short flight of fancy with practicality. 'It's better, but not that much better. I haven't ridden for years. Give me something I can do in the car or on a quad bike, though, and I'll do it.'

He didn't tell her to rest and take it easy, or doubt her abilities despite the years she'd been away from this place. 'Could you check the dam in the creek paddock? I was out there a few days ago and it's getting low.'

When she nodded he added, 'Take Dash with you, if you like. She's only just started, not ready yet for serious work.'

The quad bike was a smoother ride than the old one she remembered and although she took it slowly, re-acquainting herself to the controls and the feel of a quad, most of it came flooding back quickly and her nerves evaporated.

The creek had only a trickle of water in it but the small dam still held enough for the stock, and enough for Dash to burn some energy swimming to the sticks she threw into the centre of it.

How many times had she been here with Mark? Sitting beside him in the shade of this old eucalypt at the end of a long day, while he threw sticks for his dog, Sammy. Quiet, peaceful, his contentment both a salve and an abrasion on her own restless, unhappy spirit. She loved this land, Mark's land, but she didn't understand it as he did; as steward and guardian, attuned to the rhythms, the ebb and flow of water, the wind, the heat and soil, the complex web of plants, animals, insects and weather.

Dash bounded back and dropped the stick at her feet, shaking herself vigorously and showering her with water and mud. Jenn signalled her up on to the back of the quad and they headed towards the homestead. Closing a gate behind her, she paused and watched from the rise on the far side of the wool-shed paddock the mob of cattle moving out of the scrub, the single horseman guiding them along. For years she'd ridden those paddocks with him, and she knew exactly how he and a horse worked together. Perfectly.

He'd excelled as a member of parliament, representing his electorate with energy and dedication, but this, here – man and horse and the land and beasts to nurture and keep – this was where he belonged. He'd managed Marrayin and the other properties sustainably for more than a decade, respecting the land and its needs, taking a leadership role in the farming community even before his election.

As she left the quad bike in the shed, she heard the canter of a horse, its whinny as the rider dismounted, and Mark was there, sweaty, dusty, those rich brown eyes lit with energy and joy, the mare nuzzling him, dogs at his feet. At home. Lean and muscled and so damned attractive that the rush of desire caught her by surprise and she only barely stopped herself from gaping.

Fingers gripped around her heart and squeezed and she muttered something about seeing him up at the house and walked away, unable to think clearly.

When he returned from releasing the mare into her paddock, Jenn took a jug of tank water out on the terrace, and they sat together, their backs to the house, the paddocks rolling down to the river in front of them, the dogs flopping to relax in the shade, tongues lolling out.

Mark leaned forward, his elbows on his knees, his hands clasping the glass. 'I remembered something last night,' he said. 'I remembered that when I came out of hospital after the accident, I went down to the shearers' quarters and my old room there.'

She stilled.

He tilted his head around to look at her. 'Apparently, in those days that have been erased from my memory, a girl lost a hair scrunchie on the bed down there. And it's pretty unsettling to have no recollection of how, although I can guess. And it's worrying not to know . . . not to know if what happened hurt her in some way. I assumed it was Paula, because I was told she and I got together. But that in itself puzzled me until the other day. And now I'm more concerned that it wasn't Paula. That it was you, and that I may have hurt you – and that perhaps that's why you left.'

Her face heated – a blush for heaven's sake – and she didn't know what to say, words scattering in her thoughts, elusive. How could she respond? How could she hide, protect herself?

The light breeze skimmed her face. Dash snapped at a fly and missed. The late-afternoon sunlight made long shadows of the trees lining the paddocks and the rivers.

And he waited silently.

Protect herself? From Mark?

All the careful words and phrases she might gather as emotional armour were meaningless, inadequate. Mark deserved nothing but honesty, and for the first time in a long, long time she spoke without vetting the words, without caution, silencing her intellect and laying her emotions bare.

'Paula and I were planning to leave for Melbourne that week. I had a great-aunt there, batty as all heck, but she had a big house and was happy for us to live with her. It was all arranged. But I wanted . . . I wanted to be with you before I left. So that I'd have that to remember you by. So, yes, it was me. And you. The first time for both of us. Gentle and sweet and more beautiful than I ever dreamed.' She met his gaze steadily. 'And then I told you I was leaving. I'm the one who did the hurting, Mark. Not you.'

He reached over, brushed a thumb against her cheek, a fleeting, so-soft touch. 'I loved you, Jenn. But I always knew you'd leave. I'm glad I had the courage to show you that before you went. I just wish I had a memory of it.'

'Maybe I'm glad that you don't. I never gave back to you a fraction of what you gave me. Maybe you'd remember that and hate me.'

'One afternoon change years? I doubt it. All the rest of that time is firmly in my memory, Jenn.'

Fear edged its way forward again, and she wasn't quite sure which emotional shield to use to keep it in its place. 'I wish sometimes that . . . that I could forget you. It was half our lifetimes ago. You're supposed to be back there as just a fond remembrance of youth. But you don't stay firmly in your place.'

What did it say about her choice in men that none of them made her as happy, as whole, as an eighteen-year-old youth had? She forged on blindly, unsure where she was going. 'You should be married, Mark. Sharing this place with a partner. Begetting

Marrayin heirs and putting them on ponies and teaching them the relative strengths of Angus and Hereford cattle.'

She couldn't quite read his expression: part closed, part amused, part . . . sad? 'I'm not. Yet. I haven't had much time for a personal life these past six years. There's always too much else that needs doing.'

'You should put yourself and what you want first sometimes. You don't have to save the world every day.'

Now there was definite amusement. 'Speak for yourself. Do you ever put yourself and your needs first?'

Her needs? She needed to step away from this intimacy, keep it from going any further. In an echo of that long-ago afternoon she had to make the break with him again.

'The network's correspondent position in Moscow will be vacant at the end of next month,' she said brusquely. 'I've put my hand up for it. The paperwork's not through yet but I don't expect any problems. I've worked out of Moscow a few times, and I have some good contacts in the region.'

'Moscow.' He took a mouthful of water and his gaze returned to the landscape in front of them.

Uncertain what to say, she kept her eyes forward to the view. The vista of dry brown paddocks, the wool shed and shearers' quarters and the darker grey–green line of trees at the river, the vibrant blue sky crowning it all with the light starting to shift to gold as the sun dropped lower in the western sky.

'The job's based in Moscow but it covers Eastern Europe and Central Asia.' Where there were steppes and plains and mountains and stunning views and hard-working people . . . and nowhere she belonged.

'Sounds like you'll be busy,' Mark said, and although his words were perfectly courteous they lacked energy. When he rose and faced her, his eyes were shadowed, hiding his thoughts. 'Just keep in touch, okay?'

'I will.' She stood up, too, busying herself with gathering their glasses and the jug, the quiet interlude between them over. If there was never another one, at least she'd told him the truth, put things right between them as best she could.

Dash danced around his feet and he leaned over to scratch her head. 'With no refrigeration I don't have enough food here to offer you a decent meal,' he said, changing the topic evenly. 'How about we go back to Dungirri and after I shower in hot water I'll shout you dinner at the pub to thank you for your help?'

'Thank you. I'd like that.'

'Good.'

She laughed at something Karl said, the serious lines of her face relaxing, mischief dancing in her eyes as she quipped back at him, and the others joined in the laughter at Karl's good-natured expense.

Mark hardly listened to the conversation flowing around the table. His senses overloaded with Jenn beside him, and it was all he could do not to stare at her, not to drink it all in – the sound of her voice, her too-scarce laughter, the profile of her face, animated by the easy company, the subtle scents of shampoo and some light perfume.

Mark had envisaged a quiet dinner with Jenn in the courtyard; not a romantic gesture with half of Dungirri around to see, merely a chance to talk. A chance to spend time with her before she walked out of his life again. But he'd forgotten that Monday night usually saw some of the SES team share a meal after training – the younger, single ones without kids. Officially single, although there were definitely relationships developing. Karl and Gemma, the new young teacher at the Dungirri school. And Karl's brother, Eric, back from uni for the summer break and Melinda Ward. Adam, off-duty for the night, and Keisha, the teaching assistant.

Accepting the invitation to join their table proved a good decision, Jenn relaxing for perhaps the first time since she'd returned. The conversation was light-hearted and irreverent, avoiding serious topics. But the open affection between the three couples, the body language and the simmering energy of sensuality and love all served to remind Mark of what he didn't have, and he had to clamp down a surge of envy.

When they eventually called it a night, drifting away in pairs, he stayed at the table with Jenn, the conversation from the bar a hum in the background.

The liveliness fading, she stared down at the empty glass in her hands, fiddling with the edge of it.

He didn't touch her, not here in public. All evening he'd tried to hide his awareness of her, the way she occupied his thoughts. He wanted to hold his feelings for her privately so that when she left there'd be no awkward questions from others, no pitying looks, no mumbled condolences.

He'd left his gear in her room when he'd showered, but going back up there now to retrieve it, into her small, private space, didn't seem a good idea. He drained his glass of water. 'It's getting late,' he said. 'I should go.'

'You'll need to come and get your bag,' she said quietly.

He took their empty glasses back to the bar, and was a minute behind her going up the stairs. He doubted that anyone in the bar noticed. Good. Neither of them needed any misplaced assumptions or gossip.

In her room, she drew the curtain across the French door to the veranda. He paused in the doorway, his pulse a drumbeat in his head. She was beautiful, with her hair falling loose, the sheer white fabric of her shirt over the curve of her shoulder, the collar framing the delicate nape of her neck. Beautiful and serious and thoughtful.

His bag containing his sweat-stained clothes and shaving kit sat neatly by the door. He should just pick it up, say goodbye and leave.

'Mark . . .' She stopped. A sad half-smile softened her face. 'Nothing like seeing all that young love to make a person wish . . . well, wish that everything wasn't so complicated. Wish that maybe time could roll backwards.'

He spoke quietly, carefully. 'Wish that he could remember an afternoon, long ago.'

'Yes. Maybe. I'm sorry, Mark. I'm sorry I can't be . . .' She stopped again, and gave a small, self-deprecating laugh. 'You were supposed to be out of my system half a lifetime ago. Maybe when all this is over you can come and visit me in Moscow and we can have a wild weekend together. And then we can forget each other and move on.'

Desperate hope took flight and collided immediately into the brick wall of reality. 'Maybe in a year or so,' he conceded, clinging to the frail remnants of hope. Definitely without the *forget each other and move on*. 'I have to stay here, Jenn. I can't walk away from Dungirri, from this community when it's been through so much trauma. Not when some of it is my doing. I have to stay and see it through.'

'I know.'

She did understand him, because she didn't argue the point. She stood close to him, only feet from the bed, and if he was a man without a conscience or into casual sex he could easily have manipulated her uncertainty, the loneliness and yearning she'd half-admitted to, and persuade her into bed. But he wasn't that kind of man, and he didn't want that kind of sex.

He bent his head and brushed her mouth with his, felt her initial shock dissolve so that she sought his mouth again. He cupped her face with his hands and kissed her one more time, light, brief, gentle and full of all he couldn't say.

Then he stepped away from her, before the rush of need and desire and longing overpowered him. He had a cloud over his head, an uncertain future, and responsibilities that stood between him and her.

'I'm going, Jenn. But not because I want to. You understand that, don't you?'

She nodded without words.

'I'll phone you tomorrow,' he promised, before he turned on his heel, picked up his bag and walked out.

❧

She dreamed of him. Her subconscious ignored her body's need for deep, restorative sleep and instead kept neurons firing and nerves on edge with dream after dream, alternating between nightmares of flames, explosions and guns and altogether different dreams of naked skin, passion, and a man who held her close and kissed her and overwhelmed her with tenderness, broke her heart with gentleness.

When she woke for the umpteenth time, at around seven, she gave up trying to sleep. Untangling herself from the twisted sheets she rolled out of bed, blinking grainy eyes until the room came properly into focus. A shaft of sunlight angled in through the gap between the curtains and already the heat was building. She pulled the last clean clothes – jeans, tank top, blue cotton shirt – out of the bag she'd hastily packed the other night, less than two hours after she'd flown home from Tashkent.

Practicalities. The pile of grubby, smoke-stained clothes stuffed in a plastic bag in the corner might come good with a run through a washing machine. Presumably the pub had one somewhere. But she added a trip into Birraga to her mental list. Most people probably went to Dubbo or Moree to shop for clothes but surely she'd be able to get another pair of jeans and some basic T-shirts in Birraga.

She took her laptop down to breakfast. Snagging the best table in the courtyard – under the spreading branches of the kurrajong tree – she accessed her emails and the major news sites while she ate. The police statement she'd written for Leah yesterday formed the basis for each of the brief reports; it didn't seem as though any of the newspapers or television stations had sent anyone to cover the murders. Yet. No-one had connected the dots she'd been very careful not to join in the bland police statement. Not because she wanted the story herself – quite the opposite. She hadn't told her boss the location of her urgent family business, but one of the emails she had to deal with had come from him – a tactful enquiry about whether she was related to the Dungirri Barretts. She replied but told him she was too involved to report on any of the events; too involved to be objective. If he wanted a report he should send someone else – but with Franklin no longer a threat and the latest sports scandal the media frenzy of the day, she doubted he would.

Too involved to be objective. Her gaze drifted to the table she'd shared with Mark and the others last night. *Mark.* The turmoil of confusing emotions swirled again as it did every time she thought of him – and even when she didn't. It was there, underlying everything, a constant sense of drowning in him even as he seemed the only solidity she could count on.

She pushed aside her empty cup and closed her laptop. Practicalities. But as she climbed the stairs to her room to collect her things, something niggling at the back of her mind broke through. The blood-alcohol reading. The *Gazette* had reported it as 0.14. That was *high*. That was a count that would have a young man reeling, obviously drunk. Mark might have only reached the legal age days before, but out here moderate amounts of alcohol were part of life, and although the pub had been strict, no-one blinked when the older teenagers had a beer at a barbecue, or shared a six-pack between a group of friends at the waterhole. She'd never known Mark to have more than one beer, and he didn't touch alcohol when he was driving. Paula wouldn't have got into the car with him if he'd been drunk.

She enjoyed a wine cooler now and then but with an alcoholic father she knew too well the impairment of intoxication.

Realisation hit. The blood-alcohol reading couldn't have been Mark's. Even if he'd gone on some kind of bender that afternoon after he'd dropped her home, Paula would have stopped him driving.

As she walked down the short corridor to her room, she passed the open door of another room, and caught a glimpse of the head forensic officer – Sandy, she recalled someone calling him – closing up a laptop bag with one hand while he spoke on the phone.

'I took a metal detector out to the original accident site at first light this morning,' he was saying, and she paused as she put her key into her door. 'Picked up a couple of wheel nuts and bolts buried in the sand beside the road. I'll have to clean them up further, but at least one of them suggests deliberate weakening. I know, sir, but it's a country road, a dry climate. Metal lasts decades. If the bolt type matches the make and model of the vehicle, then combined with the photographic evidence there's strong evidence that the vehicle was tampered with.'

She let herself into her room and quietly closed the door behind her. *Strong evidence.* Loosened wheel nuts, maybe damaged wheel bolts. Swerve hard to avoid a kangaroo, lose a wheel . . . and lose control.

That afternoon, long ago, Mark had parked his car in the usual place in town, in the shade of the gum trees at the waterhole. Away from the activity of Dungirri's main street, and off the road far enough for someone to get to it, unnoticed.

And the evidence was building that someone had tried to harm him, back then.

She couldn't tell Mark what she'd overheard. But they both needed to go into Birraga later in the day, among other things to finish their statements about the explosion, and if they drove in together, perhaps Steve would give him an update and the official word about it.

⚬

Driving to Birraga and back, buying groceries and finalising their statements about the explosion? Two hours, he figured. Two hours with Jenn in town, and then maybe . . . maybe he'd be able to make some sense, some meaning of the connection that still bound them together. Maybe find some peace for the yearning that had been with him for so long.

She'd been distracted when she came to get him. So distracted that she'd acknowledged it with a shaky laugh, made some excuse about being tired, and handed him the car keys.

A few kilometres beyond Ghost Hill, he slowed for a rough section, where the road awaited repair. But the truck that had come up behind him didn't, swinging out into the other lane and drawing up alongside him.

'Idiot,' Mark muttered, slowing still further to let it pass.

Instead, the truck veered over, slamming against the side of their car, the force of the hit jarring through his body, sending the car off its course. Jenn cried out and grabbed the dashboard.

With no clear verge, and too many trees lining the road, Mark fought to keep the wheel steady and the vehicle on the edge of the bitumen. He couldn't see the driver's face, but he did see his hand, mimicking a gun shooting at him, as the truck veered over and scraped along the side of the car.

He swore. If he stopped, so could the truck, and that might put them in more danger. He'd have to accelerate. He had more power than the truck, could pull ahead and out of its range. He pressed his foot down.

Mark braced to keep control on an upcoming bend, hoping for a good grip on the road. As the acceleration kicked in and he pulled ahead of the truck, he heard the answering roar of its engine . . . and saw the school bus rounding the bend, travelling straight towards the truck.

The school bus.

With no choice, he yanked the steering wheel over, sending the car off the road towards the trees.

For long, slow microseconds his senses sped into overdrive. The gnarled trunk of the huge tree in front of them. Jenn's sharp gasp. The grip on the steering wheel as he angled it, desperate to hit the tree on his side, not hers. His voice in his head, drumming, 'Not Jenn. Please, not Jenn.' The white explosion of the airbag. The crunch of the bullbar against thick wood. The hard band of the seatbelt, ramming into his chest. And more distant, the squeal of brakes on bitumen, and the harsh scream of metal tearing as the school bus and the truck collided.

FIFTEEN

She was alive. Alive and conscious and breathing, and despite the general undefined ache of her jarred body, in that first few seconds after the car stopped, she identified no major pain.

Mark moved, pushing aside the airbag to switch off the ignition, unclipping his seatbelt.

'Are you hurt, Jenn?' She heard the tremor in his voice.

'No.'

'The school bus . . . we have to . . . I'll get you out.' He pushed on his door, and when it didn't open he shoved hard against it, but still it stayed closed.

Her movements sluggish, requiring concentration, she unclipped her seatbelt, found the door latch and with an effort managed to open her door. The car was at an angle, leaning to the driver's side, the front wheel up on a log. Maybe that had saved them from worse injury, slowing the car before it hit the tree at a lesser angle.

She clambered out, her legs unsteady on the rough ground among stones and dead branches. Even with the boots supporting her ankle the sloping ground sent pain shooting up her leg.

Mark scrambled out on her side. He gripped her arm, looked into her eyes. 'Are you okay?'

'Yes. Just shaken.' Very shaken. So shaken she wanted to sink to the ground.

But he didn't let her. 'Jenn, the bus.' The harsh urgency of his voice penetrated through the whirling cloud in her brain. 'It'll be the primary school kids. The district swimming carnival was in Birraga today.'

The enormity of his words sunk in, and she registered the scene beyond their car, the bus almost on its side, the cabin torn. 'Oh, God.'

'Yes.'

Kids. Injuries. Probably many of them. She gulped in a breath. 'I'm okay,' she said. 'I've done advanced first aid.'

He nodded, and they set off at a run. The bus had come to rest on the opposite side of the road, knocked to its side, the front of the cab crumpled. Forcing her legs to work, desperately disciplining her thoughts against panic, she followed as quickly as she could.

A little further down the road, finally back on the side it should have been, the truck had rammed into another tree. A stream of smoke came from the engine and Mark bypassed the bus and ran directly for the truck, unclipping the fire extinguisher from the side of the truck with rapid, sure movements. He was already spraying the truck's engine when Jenn reached the bus.

There was movement inside, children crying, a repetitive, high-pitched scream, and the sound of breaking glass coming from the rear of the vehicle.

The driver was beyond help, and it made more sense to go in through the large, back exit. It was Beth at the back of the bus, bloodied and dishevelled, tears streaming down her face, kicking out the glass in the window from inside.

'It won't open,' she said, through the hole she'd made, kicking again. 'The window won't bloody open.'

'It's okay, Beth. Mark and I are here. And there'll be help coming very soon.'

Even as she said the words, her eyes adjusted to the duller light inside the bus, to see the tangled mess of swimming bags, brightly coloured towels, shattered glass, broken seats and bloodied children, and she knew she'd lied. It wasn't okay. Nothing about this could be *okay*.

✧

Mark extinguished the small fire, climbed on to the step and reached into the cab to switch off the ignition. The identity of the driver who'd tried to run him off the road hit him like a blow to the gut.

Mick Barrett.

Mark stared at Mick's bloodied, lifeless face, battling the tumult of anger, wanting to swear, yell, close his eyes and be anywhere but here.

Mick had tried to run them off the road, and now he was dead, and a busload of children were smashed on the road.

Another child on the bus joined in the screaming, the sound

piercing through Mark's anger, clearing the blankness in his brain and jolting it into action. Police, ambulances, rescue services – the kids needed all of them. He jumped down to the road and pulled out his phone. With no time to waste trying to explain locations and requirements to a distant triple-0 operator, he dialled Kris's number. Kris could report it quickly, and coordinate everything.

He cut across her greeting the second she answered. 'Kris, listen to me: the school bus and a truck have crashed, about two kilometres west of the Ghost Hill turn-off. It's major, Kris. If there's a disaster plan, get it into action, now.'

'How bad, Mark?'

'Very.' His heart raced as he watched Jenn bash more glass from the back window with a kid's shoe. But his first priority was to make sure Kris understood the situation. 'Get every ambulance in the district, and all the rescue teams. The bus hit the side of the truck, and has tipped over. It's the Dungirri school kids, Kris. Multiple injuries, and at least one fatality – the truck driver. It was Mick Barrett. Jenn's with me, and we'll do what we can, but get help here urgently.'

He disconnected without waiting for her answer.

He reached the bus and took in the sea of wreckage, glass and bleeding children, and he prayed that it was better than it appeared.

He could see Jenn inside, hear her voice, low and reassuring, among the groans and cries. Two boys were crawling to the back window, whimpering and wincing on the broken glass, and he helped them climb out. Braden Pappas and Calum Barrett. Both twelve years old, both usually cheeky and lively boys, and both bleeding from various scrapes and bruises. But alive and moving and at first glance at least, mostly okay.

'Sit down in the shade there, boys. Don't go walking around. There'll be help here very soon.'

'Will my mum come?' Calum asked, wiping a bloodied hand across his nose.

'Yes, mate, she'll be on her way soon, I bet.' Somehow they'd have to cope with all the panicked parents who would rush here as soon as word of the accident spread – and that wouldn't take long.

With the bus tipped on its side, children were sprawled over seats, some lying on the smashed glass of the side windows. He knew the Dungirri school statistics: two teachers, one teacher's aide, and thirty-one kids aged five to twelve, from Dungirri and the nearby Friday Creek Aboriginal community. And he knew almost every one of them. The staff, Gemma and Keisha; Simone Callaghan, the head teacher who'd transferred from Sydney to be closer to her husband, working further north on the gas fields; and the kids . . . most of them children of his friends. Kids he'd watched grow from babies to children.

He scrambled inside. For a moment, the scene in front of him paralysed his brain and his breathing. Too many injured to know where to start. But he had to think clearly. They'd all need to be brought out and the back exit was the clearest. Wrapping a towel around his fist, he bashed out the rest of the glass in the window.

'Thanks.' Jenn came up behind him as he finished, a balancing hand against the roof of the bus. Pale, her shirt and hands already smeared with blood, she spoke quietly but urgently. 'Beth says we need to triage. If we can get the least-injured out, that will give us some more room to deal with the more serious ones.'

'Bad?' he asked.

She bit her lip and nodded. 'A few might be critical. But thank God for seatbelts.' She waved a hand back down the bus. 'Beth's arm's fractured, but her girls will be okay. If you can help her outside, she can look after the ones out there until other paramedics get here. Then we can decide who else can be moved.'

His chest tightened again. Of course Beth would be on the school excursion with her girls. She sat on the remains of a window halfway down the bus, cradling an hysterical child with her uninjured arm, her two older daughters huddled close into her, sobbing.

'Take Alicia away from here.' Beth signalled with a glance to where Simone, the head teacher – who was also Alicia's mother – lay unconscious, bleeding from a head wound.

He lifted the girl from Beth's lap, but she fought him, pounding on his chest and crying for her mother. Beth struggled to push herself to her feet, but with his arms full with the distraught child, he couldn't assist her. He hated seeing her in pain, hated his powerlessness.

Just nine years old, Beth's eldest, his goddaughter, looked up at him, searching for guidance. He kept his voice firm and even. 'Tanya, your mum needs a hand up. That's right. That's good. Now, hold on to Emmy's hand. Good girl.'

Alicia still struggled in his arms, and as he made his way towards the exit, Beth and her girls following behind, he tried to decide the next course of action. With her arm fractured,

Beth couldn't hold on to the girl any longer, but in her current state Alicia might just run back to the bus. There were too many hurt kids, and not enough uninjured adults to deal with them.

The sound of a car arriving lifted his hopes as he clambered out of the bus. Too soon for emergency services, probably just someone travelling between the two towns, but the more help the better at this stage.

Jeanie Menotti slammed the door of her car and ran across the road. She took one look at the bus, turned to Mark and Beth and said, 'Tell me what you need done.'

'Stay out here with Beth, and help with the kids. Emergency services are coming. Can you take Alicia for me?'

She sat down on a nearby log, and held out her arms. 'Injured?' she asked, as Mark passed the girl to her.

'Her mother is.'

She held the girl close, one hand stroking her head, and started rocking slowly, talking to her in her low, loving tones.

Beth sat on the ground, checking over Braden and Calum, Tanya and Emma close by. Mark handed her his phone. 'Call Ryan. Tell him you and the girls aren't badly hurt.'

That would at least save Ryan some anxiety. Other parents wouldn't be so fortunate. He returned to the bus, and stepped back into the nightmare to help Jenn.

ॐ

Nothing in her first-aid training or her experience of reporting disasters had prepared her for the reality of being first on a scene with dozens of injured. The cramped space, the absence of even basic equipment, the heart-rending cries of children and the staggering responsibility of it all sent waves of panic that Jenn fought to quell.

Focus. One child at a time.

The seatbelts had limited the injuries from the initial impact, but the toppling bus had thrown its occupants around, and many of the kids had fallen awkwardly, tangled in their seatbelts. Fractures, head injuries, possibly internal injuries, bruises and cuts from shattered glass . . . some would walk out of the bus, all would need medical assessment, and some she was scared for.

In that first, long half-hour before paramedics arrived, Jenn worked her way down the bus and concentrated on staunching blood flow on a couple of children and one of the teachers, and getting the lesser injured out of the cramped conditions. She wouldn't risk moving those with potential internal or spinal injuries, or having someone trip over them.

After he carried or guided each child out, Mark returned to her side. He knew everyone's name, talked with them in calm tones, his presence reassuring, his hands gentle. And each time he returned, the light touch of his hand on her shoulder kept her grounded and reminded her she was not coping alone.

Kris, another police car and the Dungirri SES arrived first, followed a short while later by the two ambulances from Birraga and more police. Never more relieved, Jenn left the cramped space inside the bus to the people with skills and equipment.

The road filled with emergency vehicles, flashing lights and people, some in uniform, some not. While Kris and other officers kept order in the traffic, ensuring access for the ambulances due to arrive from around the district, a few older men rigged a couple of tarpaulins from the trees, creating shade from the hot sun for the injured.

She recognised Calum, kneeling on the ground by a small boy, arms around him as he struggled and cried. Ollie, who had trouble with too much noise and movement.

She had no clue what to do, but they were her small cousins and she couldn't do *nothing*.

'Calum,' she said, touching his arm. 'I'm Aunty Jenn, we met the other day. Tell me what Ollie needs.'

Calum's face crumpled. 'He needs Mum. He needs Mum and I can't find Dana.'

A twelve-year-old kid trying to carry a huge responsibility. But not running, as she wanted to run.

She knelt on the ground and took Ollie's hand. His eyes were screwed shut and he rocked as he struggled. She could see no sign of major injury. But what should she say to a totally stressed child? 'Ollie, I'm Aunty Jenn. I know this is all scary for you. I'm going to pick you up and carry you somewhere quieter, okay?'

He must have been five or six, one of the little ones, light enough still for her to carry a short distance away, and although he struggled and kicked she managed to keep his arms pressed close to her.

'Calum, do you know Mark? He's just over there. Go and ask him to help you find Dana.'

She kept hold of Ollie, turning his face away from the scene. She might have tried talking to him but if he didn't like noise . . . she tried humming a lullaby, a song her mother had taught her, the melody gentle and soothing. Gradually he quietened, and when Mark brought over Calum and a teary Dana with a dressing on her arm, Jenn stayed with them, sitting on the dirt by the road in the shade, reassuring them while police, emergency services and frantic parents arrived in a constant buzz of movement and noise.

When Chloe arrived, Calum recognised her car and flagged her down before she reached the bus. She dropped to her knees beside her children, tears running down her cheeks, trying to hug them and inspect them for injuries all at once, pulling them back into her arms, all together, and telling them again and again how much she loved them.

No longer needed there, Jenn left the children in her care. Her cousins would be all right. Other children might not be so fortunate.

When she offered help, a paramedic asked her to squeeze into a cramped space in the bus and hold an IV bottle for one of the children. Cody, someone told her, so she held his small hand and talked to him although he was barely conscious. Cody Pappas, the name on the nearby lunchbox read.

She didn't know how long she knelt there with Andrew and Erin's son in the stuffy heat, thick with the odour of blood. She couldn't cry, couldn't fall apart, not here. They all needed her to be strong: Cody, the children, their parents, the emergency-services teams working around her – especially those still trying to release Gemma, the young teacher, from the crumpled front of the bus. She had an IV drip now, and pain meds, and was conscious and clung to Karl who stayed with her in the wreck, holding her hand, telling her she'd be on the Royal Flying

Doctor Service plane to Sydney as soon as the rescue team cut apart the bus to get to her.

A paramedic tapped her on the shoulder. 'We can take him out now. His parents are just outside.'

Her legs cramped, she stumbled out of the way, out of the bus. Someone helped her through the window, on to the ground. Andrew. She didn't know what to say but managed a weak smile of thanks and staggered a few metres away, so Cody's parents wouldn't see her fall apart and think the worst. She pressed her hand against her mouth, stifling the sobs.

Arms steadied her, closed around her. Mark. She hid her face in his shoulder and gulped for even breaths.

'The kids are all alive, Jenn,' he said. 'Mostly minor injuries. We'll all get through this, okay?'

She nodded, wanting to believe him.

'Mark?' The voice came from a short distance away.

Steve. More formal than usual. She turned to see him, his face grey, his shirt dirty and blood spattered.

'Mark, there's a major-incident investigator being flown in from Sydney, due in fifteen minutes, and he's going to want to interview you. It's a double fatality. And it's standard procedure that, since your vehicle was involved in the accident, you have to be breathalysed.'

Breathalyser. Investigation. Fatalities. The implications of the words made her reel. They'd want someone to blame. Both the other drivers were dead, and Mark was already under a cloud.

From the paleness of Mark's face as he nodded wordlessly, the same thought had occurred to him.

'The accident was not Mark's fault, Steve,' Jenn insisted. 'And he hasn't been drinking.'

Steve's sharp glance reminded her that he was both Mark's friend and a police officer. 'That's why I've asked Leah Haddad – a neutral person – to breathalyse you, Mark. She'll also take you into Birraga for the formal interview and blood samples if necessary. We'll make sure our facts are fully documented. I suggest we go find her right now. The national media has already scrambled, and we'll have TV choppers landing any minute. The last thing we need is a photo of you blowing into the breathalyser on the front page of every newspaper tomorrow.'

SIXTEEN

The investigator's offsider interviewed Jenn thoroughly, pinning down every small detail, every aspect of the drive between Marrayin and the accident. Inconsequential things, such as whether the radio was on, whether the windows were open, through to the more significant ones – how many times the truck hit the car, how hard it hit, when the car started to swerve off the road, how Mark had tried to avert the accident. Presumably so he could check her story against Mark's for consistency.

Then he asked her about Mick. She hadn't realised, in the chaos and urgency of the crash scene, who had driven the truck. Steve told her, on the drive to Birraga, after Leah had insisted that she and Mark be transported separately.

'He was my uncle. For five years he was my guardian until I left town when I was seventeen. He was an emotionally and sometimes physically abusive alcoholic, and I did not set eyes on him again until Saturday morning, when he assaulted me. Karl Sauer and Mark witnessed that assault.'

'Did you report this assault to the police?'

'I discussed it with Sergeant Matthews shortly afterwards, but I decided against making a formal complaint. Now I regret that decision.' If she'd reported the assault, perhaps Mick would have been arrested, or at least formally warned to keep away from her. Would that have been enough to stop him from waiting on the Birraga road near Mark's place for the car half the town knew she was driving? Had he been waiting for her or for Mark?

She was nauseous and thirsty, her head ached, and although she'd washed as best she could in the police station bathroom she still had blood on her clothes and the smell of it in her nostrils. But she owed it to the kids on the bus, to the Dungirri community, to help the police get to the truth of the accident.

'Sergeant, my uncle was drinking and quite irrational in his anger towards me and towards Mark on Saturday morning. I believe he hated me for being alive instead of his daughter. He behaved in a similar way immediately after her death, which was one of the reasons I left and didn't come back until now. Now, please, unless you have more questions, I'd like to see Mark, and then go to the hospital.'

Suddenly all concern, he asked, 'Are you injured? In pain? You should have informed me.'

'I'm okay. But I'm worried about my young cousins. And my friends' children.' *And Mark.* Especially Mark. At the crash site he'd been constantly on the go, a calm and reassuring presence everywhere, looking after injured children, connecting parents with kids, keeping track in all the confusion and activity of the names of children and which towns the ambulances were taking them to, liaising with the incident controller to avoid two kids from the same family being sent to different places. He knew all those kids and their parents. Although he didn't show it, the stress must have been immense. And then to be interviewed at length . . .

'I think Mr Strelitz may be some time,' the sergeant said. 'If you wait in the reception area, I'll have someone drive you to the hospital.'

With officers still out at the accident site, the police station was almost deserted and it was Steve who found her waiting on the hard plastic chair. He collapsed into the chair beside her. 'Mark's still with the Inquisitor. Would you like to wait in my office or go to the hospital?'

The Inquisitor? That didn't bode well. 'I'll wait. It may be chaos still at the hospital.'

'What makes you think it's not chaos in my office?'

It *was* chaos, with files and papers all over the desk, but at least there were no injured children, and the chair he emptied for her was more comfortable than the ones in the reception area.

'Listen, Jenn, I haven't had time to tell you the latest development. I had Larry Dolan from the *Gazette* on my list of people to talk to but I haven't been able to get on to him. But the Inverell cops contacted us this morning. A man walked into their station yesterday with a box of photos. He said they were evidence the police needed and he had more in the car. He didn't come back in and a while later the cop wandered out and found a vintage sports car stacked with boxes of photographs.'

'Larry?'

'His car. No sign of him, though. Turns out he cleared out his bank accounts before he went to the police station.'

'He's disappeared?'

'So far. After making sure the police would get the photographs. We'll put out an alert for him.'

'The photographs?'

'From the few they scanned and sent, I'd say it might be the original prints of the Bohème pictures. But there're thousands of them, apparently. We went out to Dolan's place early this afternoon. Found the storeroom where they'd been kept. But we also found hard drives full of images of a nastier sort. We've given them straight over to the Feds.'

Nasty images that the Feds investigated – there was only one likely interpretation of that. 'Child pornography?'

'Yeah. We don't know for sure it's Larry's, though. And we didn't see any production equipment or kiddy things in the house. Some guys just consume it, don't create it.'

Certainty settled in the pit of her stomach, along with the sorrow of disillusionment. All the cheek, the showy car, the boyish charm – all hiding a dark and terrible addiction.

'If someone found out about the porn they could have held it over him.'

'That's what I'm thinking. Dan Flanagan's place has been searched several times since his sons were arrested, all his records seized for examination. The slippery bastard doesn't keep anything incriminating near him. I'm wondering how many other caches of evidence we'd find if we searched the whole town.'

'Wolfgang worked part-time for the *Gazette*. I wouldn't have said he and Larry were friends, though. But he must have got the photos from Larry, somehow.'

'Yep. Although whether or not Larry knew is anyone's guess.' Steve picked up a pen from his desk and rotated it in his fingers. 'Interesting thing about your mate Wolfgang, though. We're trying to track down his next of kin, and we're not having much luck so far. Other than a local bank account connected to his photographic website and paying his household bills, there's astonishingly little evidence that Mr Schmidt existed.'

Schmidt. Smith. Pick a common name, one shared with thousands of others, and travel to the other side of the world. There would be a story there, behind the man. Her journalistic curiosity already picked at a few threads . . . no. Maybe one day, but not now.

They both started at the sound of a door opening down the corridor. Male voices.

'We'll be in touch, Mr Strelitz. Thank you for your cooperation.'

She was on her feet and out the door in seconds. Mark walked towards her down the corridor. Exhaustion dragged at his shoulders but he smiled at her. Uncaring who watched, she walked into his arms and held him tightly, and she wasn't sure if she gave strength or took it or if they created it, together.

'There's no problems, Jenn. They just have to go by the book and ask every question. You know, in case those pesky journalists ask awkward questions.'

She understood, respected the process, even if she and Mark had been the focus of it tonight. But she also knew how easily prejudice or corruption or even incompetence could twist things, obscure the truth, damage lives, and she'd been afraid.

Steve pulled his door shut, jingling car keys. 'I'm going home to my well-deserved bed,' he announced behind them. 'You two are welcome to cras—' He caught the word and corrected it, '*Stay* in my spare room if you like.'

Mark let Jenn answer. 'Thanks,' she said. 'But I need to go to the hospital first.' Mark nodded, and she continued, 'Can you drop us off there?'

'Not a prob. My place is just opposite. Probably the closest parking anyway, with all the crowd tonight.' He twisted a key off the key ring and tossed it to her. 'I won't wait up. Just let yourselves in when you're ready.'

⁊

At Birraga hospital the whole community had swung into action, and Mark could see that despite the scope of the crisis immediate needs were being met. He had the count in his head: two seriously injured adults and two children airlifted to Sydney or Newcastle; nine children with fractures and other injuries sent by ambulance to other towns, including two to Tamworth. Which left twenty children and two adults to be assessed and treated at Birraga – a small hospital with fourteen beds and an aged-care wing with ten.

The small parking area overflowed, and cars were parked all along the adjacent street. In the sporting oval across the road the lights lit it to daylight, and an ambulance waited while the rescue helicopter, rotors loud, came in to land.

308

Not a good sign. It meant another child with serious injuries, another family who'd have to travel, find accommodation, juggle jobs and kids and commitments for days or weeks.

The emergency department overflowed into the foyer and the garden, with parents, children, high-school siblings, grandparents and others filling the few tables and garden seats, some sitting on the grass, some standing. On the wide lawn beyond, council staff had almost finished erecting a marquee, the hospital auxiliary had an urn going and Rotary members unloaded chairs from a truck.

The Birraga mayor hurried through the throng to the admin block, where the boardroom lights were on. If a crisis meeting wasn't already in progress, it should be.

Mark touched Jenn on the shoulder. 'I'm going to the boardroom. There's federal services they can access, federal funds.'

For a moment, confusion registered in her eyes. 'Why?'

'There isn't anyone else yet and I can get to the right people, fast. Go and find Chloe and the kids. I'll find you in a little while.'

He bent and kissed her lips, a brief touch but one she returned, a caress he needed and maybe she needed to maintain their strength.

Then he left her and strode towards the boardroom to gatecrash a meeting that four days ago he would have been invited to. It didn't matter that he no longer held the role. He had knowledge and skills to help. And this scene – the crowd of families and traumatised and injured kids and teachers being treated for injuries – was only the beginning of a long road to recovery.

CරE

The media were there. Not a huge scrum, yet – not all the outlets had choppers on hand to fly people into a town with no airport – but there were enough.

She'd come in with Mark across the lawn, avoiding the front entrance of the hospital because of the cameras and microphones. They hadn't seen her yet. Two men, one with a camera on his shoulder, made their way into the garden from the back, past the marquee, into the groups of families. The guy without the camera thrust a microphone into George Pappas's face as he stood in the queue for coffee.

No. Not while she could do something about it.

She marched over to him and took the microphone out of his hands even as George tried to stutter an answer. George, who had two injured grandkids here and Cody on his way to Tamworth with broken ribs and possibly other internal injuries.

'Have some damned respect.' She would have snapped the words but the camera swung to her. 'These people have injured children.'

The older guy's eyes widened in recognition. 'Jesus. Jennifer Barrett.' His quick glance took in her blood-smeared clothes and the mess of her hair. 'You were involved in this?'

With the camera already on her, the cameraman focused closer.

'Yes. This is my old home town. Go back out the front. In ten minutes I will be out there to give a statement to the media and answer questions. I'm sure the mayor, who's in a crisis meeting in the boardroom now, will have another statement for you not long afterwards. There'll be plenty to report.' Yes, she'd dumped

310

the mayor in it, but if he had any sense he should already be jotting notes for a media statement. 'Now, leave these people alone. This is not good journalism. If I see you back around here I'll have the local police remove you.'

She watched to make sure they left, then she took out her phone and opened the social-media feed she hadn't looked at for days. Yes, there was already a Birraga hashtag. She thumbed a quick message, added the tag and pressed send. Out the front, they'd be watching the stream for any snippets to enliven reports. Her message would be well spread and they'd all be waiting within minutes.

Basic rule of journalism: avoid becoming the news. Okay, she'd just broken that. But her eyewitness account – even a careful one, kept to generalities – would provide good filler for the news-hungry media feeding a twenty-four-hour cycle and maybe keep the pressure off the shocked and worried Dungirri families, at least for tonight. Praise for emergency services, some non-specific information about injuries and the shock to the community, and some Dungirri background; there'd be plenty of sound bites in that.

⚬

Somewhere around midnight the sense of urgency and shock started to fade. Some children were allowed home, grandparents and friends took away siblings, the children who remained were settling, some of them asleep, all of them assessed and treated as required.

Jenn sat in an armchair in a darkened room with Chloe and her family, but it was Alicia, the school teacher's daughter, who slept on her lap. Alicia's father had yet to arrive from the gas fields up north in Queensland, but he'd be there soon. Jenn didn't envy him the long drive to his daughter, knowing that his wife was in Sydney undergoing surgery, another nine hours' drive away.

Mark returned, walking softly and dropping to kneel at Jenn's side. 'It's arranged. Harry from Birraga Air Charter can fly Alicia and her father to Bankstown first thing in the morning. They'll get there before he could make it if he drove.'

Just one more thing he'd taken care of, using his local knowledge and contacts, finding solutions and reducing the impossible stresses. Jenn could see he was as exhausted as she was.

A figure loomed in the doorway, hesitating until his eyes focused in the dimness; a big man in work clothes, hands clenching at his sides until he saw Alicia on Jenn's lap. He cried silently as he took his daughter carefully from her, a tear dropping to her cheek as he kissed it. Alicia stirred. 'Daddy?'

'Yes, sweetie, I'm here. Daddy's here.'

Mark signalled with a tilt of his head to the door and Jenn nodded. She'd done all she could for now. With whispered farewells to Chloe, they left the room and walked along the hushed corridor.

Passing through the emergency reception area to the night exit they met Rhonda from the emergency department.

'Are you heading home now?' Rhonda asked, reaching for her bag and hooking it on her shoulder. 'I'll walk out with you. I need to get my other shoes from the car. My feet aren't what they used to be.'

'It's been a long night,' Mark said. 'Your team deserves medals for their work.'

Her brain fuzzy with exhaustion, Jenn barely listened to the polite conversation between Mark and Rhonda as she walked between them out of the hospital. Rhonda's car must have been parked a fair way down the street, because they were almost at the corner across from Steve's house when Rhonda stopped and reached into her bag.

Three men walking towards them came near and Rhonda's face caught the light from the streetlamp as she smiled. Smiling, but with nothing warm or kind in it.

Mark tried to pull Jenn aside as she saw the guns, but the men instantly closed in, pressing a weapon into her chest.

'You've been working too hard, Jenn and Mark, with all your investigating,' Rhonda said, and she took a syringe from her bag as one of the men grabbed Jenn's arm and tugged it out straight. 'I'll give you a little something to help you sleep. And my friends will take you to a nice, quiet place where you can rest undisturbed.'

'Bitch,' Jenn said as the needle went into her arm. 'They'll find you. It's all unravelling and you'll be . . .' But it was her mind that was unravelling, as the drug took effect, taking her words and her thoughts. She sagged against Mark, and he caught her, holding her against him.

'Let her go,' she heard him say loudly. 'You've got me. I'm who you want. But leave her here.'

No, she tried to say.

'No,' someone else said. 'She wants both of you. She's got jobs for both of you.'

SEVENTEEN

He couldn't hold Jenn's dead weight and fight. With a gun at her back and two on him he didn't dare struggle. His brain raced for options.

She wants both of you, one of the men had said. *She*. Rhonda had always had beautiful skin, perfect make-up, short but manicured fingernails despite her nursing work. She was a Birraga local, and he'd often seen her around town, aware of her face and name and nodding a greeting in passing in the way of small communities. But now a faint memory surfaced. When her children were still young, before she'd returned to nursing full-time, she'd worked for Vanna Flanagan. *'Oh, hello, Mark. This is Rhonda from Vanna's salon. Could you let your mother know that her appointment for the Bohème treatment is on Monday at nine?'*

Anger burning in his gut, he watched Rhonda's eyes. 'Jenn's right. The police know about Vanna and are planning raids.

It's all about to collapse. If you leave now, you might have a chance of escaping.'

A tiny hint of doubt or fear flickered in her eyes. But not enough. She took another syringe from her bag and he couldn't drop Jenn to struggle and avoid the man's grip on his arm, pushing up his shirt sleeve.

'You can tell Vanna all about the raids when you wake up,' Rhonda said, and he felt the sting as the needle slid in.

❦

Jenn crawled to consciousness, her head pounding and the light too bright on her eyes when she forced them open. She screwed them shut again. Her arms were uncomfortable and she tried to move them but bands tightened around her wrists.

A rush of fear jerked her wide awake.

A small, sparse room, painted white. Sunlight slanting in through a narrow window, covered by a simple curtain. She could see the outline of a security grille shadowed through it.

She was curled up on a narrow bed and her hands were cuffed to the metal frame. Panic surged and the nausea bubbled again as the Bohème images flashed through her mind. But no, she wasn't blindfolded, she still wore her clothes and her booted feet were free. She breathed just a fraction more easily.

Her head spun as she struggled to sit up, twisting her body uncomfortably, the movement of her hands limited by the cuffs. She had to huddle awkwardly in the corner, but at least from this angle she could see the room better. Small. Just the bed with its musty mattress, a narrow cupboard, and an old wooden chair against the wall beside it. Cobwebs draped from the corners of the dusty walls. No pictures, no old calendars, just a single nail on the wall. One old-style wooden door, shut. A lock on it that was much more modern. She leaned over to see the floor. Bare wood. The bedframe was old but shiny bolts, much newer, bolted it to the floor.

Hopelessness sucking her strength, she let her head fall back against the wall, her thoughts racing . . .

Convent.

A small, sparsely furnished room. A nail where a crucifix might have hung. A convent.

'Oh fuck, oh fuck, oh fuck,' she murmured.

She slowed her breathing, enough to listen for sounds. Nothing but some birdsong outside. No traffic, no voices – definitely not the convent beside Saint Joseph's school in the middle of Birraga.

The faint tap of footsteps grew louder than the birdsong, until they stopped outside the door. A key slid into the lock with a faint metallic rasp and it clicked open. A man she recognised as one of her kidnappers stepped in, and in a soft swish of fabric and the click of high heels a woman followed him.

Jenn doubted that it was merely skin-care products that had ensured Vanna Flanagan scarcely looked any older despite the years since she'd seen her. She had to be well into her sixties, probably older, but her sculpted, smooth face was a convincing advertisement for her business.

'Good morning, Jennifer,' she said briskly. 'I hope you've found the accommodation . . . contemplative.'

Vanna's smooth face betrayed no expression, and Jenn didn't plan on showing her own fear. 'Very contemplative, Mrs Flanagan. Thank you.'

The man placed the chair in the centre of the room and Vanna sat, just out of reach. 'Are you right-handed or left-handed, Jennifer?'

Vanna held a spiral-bound notebook and pen in her hand. Jenn went with the truth. 'Right-handed.'

Vanna nodded to the man and he released Jenn's right hand from the cuffs, leaving her left hand trapped, checking it was secure before he stepped back.

Vanna handed her the notebook and pen.

'You're going to write a feature article, Jennifer. One of your strong, well-evidenced accounts of corruption and vice. This one will be about a politician who has led a double life. Mark's been very good at that, hasn't he? Who'd have guessed the extent of his corruption and manipulation? You could throw in something personal there – those drugs he experimented with at eighteen. Maybe that's why you refused to go to Birraga with him and your cousin that tragic night.'

An article damning Mark. Nausea threatened again but she kept her voice steady. 'You want me to destroy Mark's reputation?'

'Yes. You're good, Jennifer, and a trusted source. You'll make it headline news across the country.'

'And if I don't write it?'

'That would be rather stupid. And you're not. You understand perfectly well that you have to be useful to me to stay alive.'

Yes, Jenn understood that. 'What I don't understand is why you're involved in this. What you hope to achieve.'

'Cleaning up my ex's mess and protecting my interests, of course. He's sloppy and impatient, and he's always thought with his dick more often than not. Him and his stupid friends.'

Information. Information meant power, and chained up to the bed she needed all the power she could get. 'You mean Gerard McCarty?'

Vanna raised an elegant eyebrow. 'You have been busy, haven't you? But Gerard at least has his uses – a sharp brain with finances, despite his predilections for violence. Quite a weakness, really, now that he's not as controlled as he was. So, just a word between us girls, sweetie – I'd keep cooperating if I were you. Stay useful to me. I could use your skills and give you a luxurious life, if you want it. Much better than traipsing through disease-ridden disaster zones.'

'Work with you?' She tried to hide her disgust.

Vanna waved a casual hand. 'A favour here and there. Nothing difficult.'

Favours. Yes, so much corruption worked on the twin currencies of favours and fear. At least the disease-ridden disaster zones were honest work.

'I'll think about,' she lied.

Vanna laughed. 'Oh, Jennifer, you are so like your father, you know. You're not very good at lying. Which is unfortunate, because I don't have much use for all that straitlaced honour.'

Jenn gripped the pen in her hand tightly. 'You knew my father?'

'Oh darling, yes, I knew your father. He did some landscaping work for me when he was young and brawny and quite delicious, really. But he ran away and met your mother. A pity, because he was actually quite good in bed and I'd rather have had you for a daughter than the stupid lumps of offspring Dan made.'

Bile burned Jenn's throat, harsh and bitter, but she wouldn't give Vanna the pleasure of seeing her throw up.

'Did Dan kill him?'

'Dan?' She snorted indelicately. 'Dan didn't have any say in who I took as a lover. Doesn't have any say in anything. Oh, I know he swans around like a big man, but you and I, Jennifer, we both know where the real power is. He was never anything more than a tool.'

Vanna. Vanna Flanagan, nee Russo, sister of key figures in the Calabrian mafia in Sydney. But everyone had overlooked her because she was a woman who lived out in a rural area and ran unthreatening beauty salons. *There are far more dangerous criminals than thugs like Dan.*

And Jenn was looking right at her.

Think, think, *think*.

'Did you kill them? My parents?'

'Sorry, sweetie, but it had to be done. Your father developed too much conscience and became a threat.'

Jenn closed her eyes, rage burning red in front of them. She'd have happily killed Vanna there on the spot, if she could have, but she needed to focus. She needed to stay alive.

'What have you done with Mark?' she asked. A risky question, but if she was going to have any chance of talking her way out of this, she needed to know.

Vanna smiled, with all the enjoyment of a purring cat. 'The sainted Mark? He's busy writing his confession.'

He was alive. Jenn kept her face still so that her relief wouldn't show. 'His confession?'

'Yes. Rather apt to do it here, I suppose. It was an enclosed convent, a silent order, nice and isolated from the world, although I'm sure the priests came to visit and hear whatever tedious sins the sisters confessed. The last one died in the 1960s, though, and there's been plenty of sinning and little confessing here since then.'

A silent order, long gone. Would anyone remember the convent's existence, more than forty years on?

Yes. Hope surged. Yes, if this building housed the Bohème Club. Caroline Strelitz and the other women she'd identified in the photographs – Steve and Leah and Kris had their names – would know where it is. Steve would have known, as soon as he woke this morning, that she and Mark weren't where they were supposed to be.

She could write the damned article Vanna wanted, but not in a hurry. If she could stretch it out, that might give the police more time to find them. And if she knew where Mark was, they'd both stand a better chance.

'If I'm going to write a convincing article for you, it will have to be consistent with Mark's confession,' she said.

'I'll make sure you see a copy,' Vanna told her with a deadly cold smile. 'I'll return in an hour for the draft. Ensure you put your email address and password on it, so that I can deal with any queries for you.'

The lock clicked into place as they left.

An hour. She had an hour, a ballpoint pen and a notebook bound with a spiral of wire. A selection of basic weapons, and a burning, powerful anger.

❧

Vanna allowed Mark a laptop to write his confession – his own laptop, which he'd left yesterday afternoon in the cottage, before the bus accident. He checked for a wireless signal but, as expected, found nothing.

In the room with the patterned carpet his mother had knelt on, he was instructed to confess to his lies, to his drunkenness causing the original accident and Paula's death, to knowing that his parents had paid to keep it quiet. Vanna had given him a concise list of other vices to include. A drug habit. A working relationship with Dan, participating with him in bribery, corruption and extortion. Anger with Dan for ruining his life.

'You're saying that you want me to implicate your ex-husband?' he clarified.

Cold, calm and deadly, Vanna crossed one elegant leg over the other in the armchair, two metres from the steel chair he was chained to. 'Of course. He and his associates have been far too careless. I'm putting a stop to that now. His death at your hands will finally tidy up this mess of his.'

So that's how she planned it – for the police to find his confession, and two dead bodies.

'Where is Jenn?' he asked.

Vanna smiled. 'She's doing some work for me for a while. We're due to leave in an hour, Mark. If you get that confession polished before then I might let you see her before we go. If you don't, I might rethink my plans about taking her.'

Her goon locked the door behind them as they left. Mark balanced the laptop on his knees with his cuffed hands. Jenn was still there, still alive. He began to type. He wrote as he'd been instructed, the confession of a man torn by guilt and addiction, no longer able to bear it. The anger he expressed for Dan Flanagan wasn't a lie. His sorrow and regrets – yes, there was a core of truth in that. At the end, he typed his full name: Mark Joseph Alexander Strelitz. His parents and Jenn would know, maybe even Kris or Steve would pick the deliberate misspelling of his middle name: Joseph instead of his grandfather's Josef. He hoped, if he didn't make it, that it would be enough to raise their suspicions and prompt them to ask questions.

He closed the laptop, rested his cuffed hands on it, and steadied his breathing. He had to be ready to take advantage of any opportunity they gave him. They had him at a disadvantage now, but Jenn was still there, somewhere, and he'd snatch any chance to fight to save her. Whatever it took, whatever it cost – he'd fight, kill, die if it gave her a chance to escape them.

C&

Vanna refused to let her see Mark. Not bothering with any further pretence of feeling, she merely took the pages Jenn had drafted and began reading them as she turned to leave the room, pausing at the door to throw an order back to her offsider. 'Restrain her and take her to the van. He'll be here soon and he wants her ready to go.'

The guard grinned wolfishly and opened the door of the cupboard. Fear squeezed Jenn's lungs when she glimpsed the contents – chains, leather bonds, hoods. She didn't know where Mark was, even whether he was still alive. She had only minutes before she'd be helpless, stuffed in the back of a van and driven away.

The guard didn't notice the scratches on the handcuff as he bent to unlock it, or the coil of wire stuffed under the pillow that she'd used to try to unpick it.

An open door, and a pen they'd forgotten about. And Vanna still within hearing, only metres down the passage. Just as he clicked the cuff loose from the bed, she closed the fingers of her right hand around the pen, gripped it tightly, and plunged it into his neck, ramming her left hand over his mouth. He gasped but she covered it with a cry of her own, as if protesting, struggling. Then she rammed his head hard against the wall. If he was faking unconsciousness he was doing it well. She didn't have to fake her sobs.

She couldn't find the handgun he'd had last night, but she took his key ring. She paused at the door, then checked the corridor. No sign of Vanna. Three closed doors like hers on either side of the passage. If Mark was behind one of them . . . no, Vanna's heels had only come down this way to her room. There was a door at the end of the corridor behind her, but ahead of her Vanna's heels had tapped around a bend in the corridor.

She tried the door and it opened. Fresh air, light, and two cement steps to the overgrown grass of a yard with a crooked clothesline and a small cleared area surrounded by trees.

The rumble of an engine was coming closer, and she heard tyres crunch on a gravel track. She peered around the corner of the building: one car at the front, and one dark van, plus the car arriving through the scrub. She hadn't seen or heard anyone except Vanna and the single guard, but this car meant at least one extra.

Three at least against her. But Mark with her, if she could find him. If he was still alive. He had to be alive.

The car stopped and its doors opened. Dan Flanagan. Gerard McCarty. Walking into the house like two mates about to have a good time.

From a different angle she would probably recognise the front door. The scrubby forest surrounding the house beyond the small clearing would provide good cover for a photographer.

She crept around the back of the building, and stopped when she heard laughter coming from inside. As she came closer to the floor-to-ceiling window she heard Vanna's voice, and the laughter died.

'You've screwed up again, Dan. If you hadn't brought Franklin back, this whole mess could have been smoothed over.'

'He's an idiot. Now he's getting old and careless. And I didn't tell him to—' The voice broke off abruptly.

'Didn't tell him to do what, Dan?'

Mark's voice. Mark, alive and in that room. Speaking with complete authority. Even if he were bound and about to die he would still retain the self-control, the natural command. He would not cower before them.

Dan tried to laugh it off. 'He always went off half-cocked. That's what started this thing years ago. He was supposed to give your parents a warning and instead he almost killed you.'

'Franklin sabotaged my car? Loosened the wheel nuts?'

'Oh yes, that was Franklin.' Vanna sounded bored. 'And then he panicked when he saw the accident because these dickheads had told him you were not to be touched. So, he thought it was a good idea to frame Gillespie. If he hadn't come up with that idiotic scheme, you'd have walked away from any charge and I'd have dealt with Gillespie rather more quietly and effectively, instead of having to get Rhonda to pull some blood from an old alky.'

These dickheads? Was she talking about Flanagan? And who? McCarty? And why the hell wasn't Mark to be touched?

Mark's voice came from close to the window. 'So, now you're going to *deal* with us all to wipe the whole slate clean, aren't you, Vanna? Just me and Dan or McCarty as well?'

'What?' Flanagan's voice, Jenn thought. Rising in volume and tone. 'What do you mean? *Vanna?*'

'They're going to kill you, Dan.' Mark, still so even and calm. 'Or at least I am. Before I shoot myself.'

'Oh Jesus, Vanna, you can't.'

He cried out and Jenn heard a thump. But no gunshot.

She looked around, desperate for something, anything to use as a weapon. Two bricks on the ground nearby alongside some cracked terracotta pots. She stuffed some pieces of terracotta in her pockets and took a brick in each hand. She drew in a deep breath and flung the first brick at the window as hard as she could, hoping desperately that Mark wasn't standing next to it. The glass shattered and she followed it with the other brick, aimed at the remaining window. Then she ran as bullets fired from the room. But instead of running to the trees she ran back to the door she'd left through, keeping close to the house.

∞

Police? Mark thought as he jerked away from the shattering glass. But the brick that landed on the floor inches from his feet probably wasn't police equipment. McCarty and the guard spun away from him and fired their guns out the remains of the window as Vanna wiped blood off her cheek and swore and Dan gripped the edge of the table and started to haul himself up.

No orders from police were shouted, no rush of officers, but they'd unchained him from the chair a few minutes before and he was no longer helpless.

McCarty, with his gun still in his hand, jumped through the window frame and started towards the trees.

One guard with a gun remained, and Vanna, both looking to the window. Dan was still reeling from the blow to his head. Mark raised his eyes at him. A man scared for his life could become an ally. The laptop sat on the table just inches away but as Mark shifted his feet slightly to find a better stance, he caught a shadow at the half-open door. *Jenn? Police?*

He moved, grabbing the laptop and flinging it sideways towards the guard's head, then leapt after it with his cuffed hands raised to strike. As he hit the ground with the man, he was vaguely aware of Dan moving, of Vanna's shout, of Jenn rushing in. He rolled with the guard, grappling for the gun.

Someone screamed and a gun fired. Rolling over the guard, Mark grabbed the guy's head and pounded it against the floor, and out of the corner of his eye he saw McCarty in the window, gun aimed towards him. McCarty fired once as Mark grabbed the guard's gun. He squeezed the shot as McCarty fired again, and pain erupted in his side as the man fell.

'Mark!'

He staggered to his feet, ripping the handcuff keys from the guard's belt. Vanna had Jenn by the hair but Jenn's fingers gripped Vanna's face, digging in near her eyes, and with one hand she dragged a rock down the older woman's face.

Mark grabbed Vanna and flung her into the table, following with a hard blow across her bleeding face. She tried to kick away but Dan, on the floor beside his feet, grabbed her leg, dragging it down with his weight as he pulled himself up.

McCarty was stirring, the guard starting to moan.

'Mark! We have to go!' Jenn yelled, grabbing his arm.

Dan shoved him aside and started to pound his ex-wife's face.

With all his concern for Jenn and no sympathy for either Flanagan, Mark didn't hesitate to leave them to each other and McCarty.

The gun held awkwardly in one cuffed hand, he pressed the other hand against the damp burning at his side and followed Jenn as she darted out of the room and across a hallway to the open front door.

'There's another guard, somewhere,' she said, pausing for an instant to check beyond the door. 'We have to get to the trees.' She glanced back and her eyes dropped to the blood staining his hand. 'You're hurt. Oh fuck, oh shit.'

'It's okay. Just run. I'll be right behind you.'

'No. I won't leave you.'

He tucked the gun into the waistband of his jeans, then grabbed her hand and set off, forcing his legs to run, each hard step on the ground jarring pain through him. The dark blur of trees ahead was the only thing in his vision, and he kept going, because if he stopped, Jenn would stop.

He heard a shot.

He couldn't let her stop.

In the trees it was cooler, the light not as harsh, and they slowed but kept moving, deeper, deeper into the cover. His side ached, but he was still upright, still walking.

Jenn breathed heavily and Mark's own breath rose in gasps. He thought they'd come about a kilometre from the house, and ahead the trees seemed to thin out. The mix of mulga, native cypress and eucalypt was dry and scrubby but he steered Jenn towards one of the few larger red gums that dotted through the shorter growth.

He leaned his back against the broad trunk, grateful for its support. Jenn immediately moved his bloodied hand aside and pulled up his shirt, wiping away blood with the bottom of it.

'It's not bad,' he told her. 'Just caught me on the side. I think the bleeding's stopped.'

'Not quite yet, it hasn't.'

Probably because he'd been running, pumping blood through his body – and out of the wound. She uncuffed his hands, helped him tug his shirt off over his head and then hastily folded it into a pad, wrapping the sleeves around him to tie it on.

She straightened up, steadying herself with one hand against the tree, and he didn't miss the catch in her breath.

'Are you okay?' he asked sharply. He'd assumed she was, because she'd run without stopping, making good speed, but he had no idea what she'd endured in the hours since their abduction. Her shirt still bloodied from the bus accident and from his blood, her hair dishevelled, she looked like she'd been through hell but he couldn't see signs of external injury.

'I'm fine. Just a twinge from my ankle and a bit woozy from the drug and no food. Do you know what time it is? How long were we out?'

He'd bet her ankle more than twinged. Practical, uncomplaining and focused – just as she'd always been when it mattered. His captors had taken his watch and phone but the sun had already passed its highest point before they unchained him. 'It's early afternoon. Maybe one or two o'clock.' And getting hotter, which worried him. Weakened physically by the after-effects of the sedatives, the heat and lack of water would make them even more vulnerable.

'Do you know where we are?' Jenn asked.

'No. I'm guessing west, because of this mulga. West of Dungirri, certainly. West of Birraga, maybe. A lot of the land around Birraga is cleared but there are a few pockets of scrub,' Mark said. 'Let's keep moving,' he suggested. 'We might be able to see more once we're out of this.'

He pushed himself away from the tree and took her hand. But as they stepped out from the protection of the broad trunk, a bullet gouged into the bark of a cypress pine, passing just inches from Jenn.

EIGHTEEN

Her hand gripped tightly in his, Mark led her on a zigzag path through the trees. Her head pounded, branches whipped her face and her ankle jarred every time she leapt over a rock or a fallen log, but somehow she managed to stay on her feet despite the rough ground.

She heard four more shots, and saw two of them strike nearby.

She didn't turn her head to see their pursuer but she heard him crashing through the bush. She kept her gaze focused on the ground in front of her boots, desperate not to trip and fall.

But she almost stumbled when Mark stopped abruptly. Lifting her head, she saw the landscape opening up in front of them – cleared paddocks, only a tree here and there. No cover.

'There's a road over there,' Mark said. 'And I think there's a vehicle coming.'

They set off again, twisting along the edge of the trees, and she caught glimpses of the dirt road. But she'd lost her sense of direction, and she wasn't sure whether they'd run away from the convent or had zigzagged back towards it, didn't know whether that track went through the trees and reached the convent, or somewhere entirely different.

The sound of their pursuer's footfalls receded, but twice more shots were fired. He was still out there, looking for them, but now he was some distance behind them.

When the man fired another shot, Mark stopped, pushing her behind a large tree, withdrawing the gun from the waistband of his jeans. 'You go on. I think those are police cars on the road. If they are, see if you can get their attention. I'll wait here and keep this guy off your tail.'

She wanted to protest, but as she opened her mouth he cut off her words with a brief, hard kiss. 'Go, Jenn. I'll see you soon.'

If he hadn't looked so grey and exhausted, if the wound on his side wasn't still seeping, she'd have argued with him. But he must be almost at the end of his endurance and it *did* make sense for her to run for help. Besides, of the two of them, he'd always been a far better shot.

He stepped out to cover her, firing a shot into the trees behind her as she sprinted towards the road, dodging through the edge of the scrub.

She could see the cars through the trees. Four cars. Relief flooded her to see the police markings. They'd stopped on the road and at least half a dozen officers in protective gear spilled out, taking defensive positions behind open doors, weapons drawn. She skidded to a halt thirty metres away as one of the windscreens shattered. The shot had come from in front of her, not behind her.

Two gunmen now, armed police ready to fire – and she was in the middle. She dropped down into a crouch, her breath coming in hard gasps from the run and her ankle throbbing. For long seconds she froze, undecided. Then she forced in a deep breath and stepped out into the open. Waving her arms to attract the police she screamed, 'We're here! Mark's hurt!' before she dropped low to the ground again.

In the protective gear and helmets she didn't recognise the first two who came running but she knew the third, a few metres behind them. Steve. He crouched beside her and wrapped an arm around her shoulder. 'Jenn, it's okay, there's an ambulance not far away. Where's Mark?'

She wanted to collapse with the relief but she had to tell them what she knew. 'Mark's back that way a little. Gunshot in the side. He's walking but he's lost blood. There's at least two gunmen – one beyond Mark, one over that way. Five people, total, but I don't know where they all are. Dan Flanagan, Vanna, McCarty and two others. Some might be dead or injured at the convent.'

'Go find Mark,' he ordered the two others.

She started to scramble to her feet to go with them but Steve pulled her back down. 'Stay here. We're going to run for the car in a minute.' He spoke briefly on the radio, passing on her information, ordering the officers by the cars to proceed with caution.

In the distance she heard over her thudding pulse the beat of a helicopter, coming closer. The police by the cars fanned out and began to move forward.

'Okay, Jenn – can you make a last dash for the cars with me?'

'Mark—'

They heard a shout, then a second call in return. Steve's radio hissed and a man's voice reported, 'Mr Strelitz located. Ambulance required.'

Ambulance required? Had he collapsed? Been shot again? She didn't wait for Steve but leapt to her feet and blundered back into the trees, running towards the movement she could see in the direction she'd left him. Running to Mark.

He sat on the ground, his back against a tree, eyes closed, one of the officers hunkered beside him pressing the makeshift pad against the wound, the other standing guard, weapon ready.

As she dropped to her knees, his eyes shot open. 'I'll be fine, Jenn,' he said, reaching with one hand to grip hers. 'But you need to get somewhere safer than here.' He looked up at Steve. 'Get her out of here, Steve. Please.'

Emotions crashing around her, she shook her head in a wordless refusal. Always, his first thoughts were for others, but no way would she leave without him. She knelt on the ground on the dead leaves and twigs and dirt and fought back tears, fought for control of herself. She couldn't cry. She *wouldn't* cry. She had to hold it together, get through the rest of this. Be strong enough to love him. Strong enough to leave him. Because he could have died and she had no knowledge or ability to deal with how lost and vulnerable that made her feel.

∽

Birraga hospital. Again. A young doctor she didn't recognise – she'd have remembered the purple spiked hair and the nose stud – took her in hand while Morag Cameron directed Mark's gurney to an examination cubicle and pulled the curtains closed.

'I'm Abby,' the young woman said, kindness in her eyes as she skimmed over Jenn's grubby, scratched, bloodied appearance. 'I've come up from Dubbo hospital to help out. Let's check you over and see how you are.'

Jenn ran her gaze around the emergency room. 'Rhonda – the nurse—'

'In police custody.' Abby's arm on her shoulder gently steered her towards a bed. 'She's no threat to you now. Hop up on the bed here. Is it okay if I take your blood pressure and examine you? You've got a fair few scratches and bruises.'

Her attention still half on the curtained cubicle beyond, Jenn acquiesced to the doctor's request. Disproving the stereotypes of the stud and the spikes, the young woman's compassion and professionalism impressed her, and almost enabled her to unwind some of the tension that still gripped her.

'The Dungirri children – how are they doing?' Jenn asked while the blood pressure cuff tightened around her arm.

'Most went home this morning. We've still got two in, for observation for a little longer. The children who were taken to other towns are all doing well. The two teachers who were flown to Sydney are listed as serious, but that's better than critical.' She noted the monitor readings on the chart. 'I'd like to put in a cannula, give you a litre or two of fluid. Is that all right?'

The familiar panic fluttered in Jenn's chest. 'I'm not . . . I don't want to stay. I'm not hurt and this place . . .' *Reduces me to a scared kid.*

'I don't think you'll need to stay overnight. But if you can manage an hour or so while we rehydrate you, you'll feel a lot better. And I can get you a cup of tea and some food if you feel up to it.'

An hour or so – she could do that. An hour or so and she should know how Mark was, should have her composure back after the adrenaline crash. Some fluids, a cup of tea and some sustenance and she might even feel human again.

cℛ

Steve arrived as the young doctor attached the second bag of intravenous fluid to Mark's drip. He hadn't needed a transfusion, and for that he was grateful. Jenn fidgeted, restless in the chair beside his bed, unable to settle. She had some colour back in her face and she'd eaten a light meal but she refused a second litre of fluid for herself and he knew she itched to escape.

He didn't blame her. He, too, wanted to be out of here, somewhere quiet and peaceful. Alone with Jenn.

Steve dragged a chair over and collapsed into it. 'You two are looking a whole lot better. And I've got good news for you. McCarty and the two other guys are in custody. They're on their way to Dubbo hospital but one of the guys is wide awake and talking fast. Dan and Vanna – they won't hurt anyone again.'

'They're dead?' Mark asked. He knew the answer but needed to hear it.

'Yes. Dan bashed Vanna pretty badly. She didn't make it. It seems that McCarty shot Dan, trying to stop him, and Dan was dead when we got there.'

Vanna and Dan both dead. Mark wished he could feel more relieved. They wouldn't harm anyone else now, but the repercussions of their decades of influence in the district would take a long time to alleviate. Too many damaged people, too much damaged trust. How could lives and relationships be healed?

'How did you find us?' he asked Steve, because that question might be easier to answer.

'Your parents emailed me late last night, Mark. You've probably got one as well. They're on their way back and will be here tomorrow morning, but they attached a full statement. The convent's on one of the original Flanagan holdings; Sister Brigid said that Dan's great-grandfather donated the land for it. First thing this morning Kris spoke with a couple of the women you identified and they told us exactly where it was. They all have similar stories to your mother's.'

His mouth still dry, Mark asked, 'Which is?'

'Back when all this started, in the seventies, your folks went to the club a few times. Apparently it seemed pretty harmless then – music, some drugs, no-one raising an eyebrow about sex. But they met McCarty, and he blackmailed your mother over her father's debts, and the sex and domination frightened her. When Len found out there was a fight, him against McCarty, Flanagan and a few others. He was knocked out, doesn't remember the end of it. But years later, when your parents and Flanagan were deep in business rivalry, photographs were sent to Caroline. Photos of Len in bed with a woman who was tied up and beaten, along with newspaper reports of police finding her body a week after the fight, and threats to send the photo and witness statements to the police unless your mother complied with their demands. It seems that McCarty and Flanagan got their kicks from power games. Your father was besting them in business but they took sexual control over his wife. And they enjoyed it.'

A spike of red-hot fury made it through Mark's numbness. 'Bastards.'

'No. That's too mild a word for them,' Jenn said, her eyes glinting with anger.

'The prints on the bottle used for the Molotov cocktail – they're Mick's,' Steve continued. 'We found a phone on him and there are calls – a number of them – between that phone and Vanna's. The truck he was driving when he tried to run you off the road is an old one that used to be registered to Flanagan's Transport.'

'Vanna manipulated him?'

Mark saw the tension in Jenn's face. 'It's not hard to manipulate a mad alcoholic,' she said. 'And he never had much of a moral compass. I'm not sad he's dead.'

'Can't say I am, either,' Steve said. He glanced at his watch. 'I'm going to have to go. We'll need to get statements from you both, but that can wait until tomorrow. Oh, one last thing – Mark, I can tell you officially that there will be no charges over the initial accident and Paula Barrett's death. Everything we have strongly suggests the vehicle was tampered with and that's why you lost control of it. There's no evidence of culpability on your part. The Assistant Commissioner will make a public statement announcing it later today.'

'But the blood-alcohol report – was it mine? I was here, in the hospital that night.'

'And so was Rhonda,' Jenn answered instead of Steve. 'Vanna told me that she got the blood from "an old alky". But I knew before then that it couldn't have been yours. It was too high a reading. You'd have been slurring, unsteady on your feet. Paula would never have gone in a car with you if that had been the case.'

Steve nodded in agreement. 'Gil says he saw no sign of impairment, Mark, and I have two witnesses who've come forward and said you were playing street cricket with them that evening, totally sober, before you left to pick up Paula. So you can rest easy on that now. I know I will.'

After Steve left, Mark strugged to find some clarity in the complex whirring of his thoughts. He hadn't caused the accident – but he still carried responsibility for the events of the previous days. 'I'm sorry, Jenn. All this has happened because I resigned so publicly. If I'd done it differently . . . If I'd done it quietly, you'd never have been at risk. No-one would have died. Mick wouldn't have harmed anyone.'

'And the truth would still be buried.' She reached over and took his hand. 'You did what was right. You're not responsible for Mick's actions or anyone else's. There are women who will get some justice now. Gil has justice. Paula has justice.'

More grateful than he could express for her support, he rubbed his thumb gently against her hand. 'And you?'

'I have answers. About Paula. Even about my parents' deaths. Vanna admitted that she killed them. But, Mark . . .' She gripped his hand tighter. 'I still have a lot of questions. About myself. And some of them are as scary as hell. I need to take a little time to work through them.'

He had questions, too. Mostly about Jenn; about what they were to each other and what they could become. But he understood her need for time. The bond between them had lasted for eighteen years. He could wait another few weeks or months until they came to a decision about their futures.

The tougher question, the one haunting him since Vanna's comment about him being untouchable, was which man – Dan Flanagan, Gerard McCarty or Len Strelitz – had fathered him?

He remembered the date and year code on the first image of his mother with McCarty. Nine months before his birth. A month before his parents' marriage. McCarty had coerced her, and who knew what else had happened. And Dan Flanagan had always called him *son* . . .

NINETEEN

Mark was silent as the constable drove them towards Dungirri in the evening light. Jenn sat beside him in the back seat, and told the constable not to take the turn-off to Marrayin.

'You need to sleep, Mark,' she said quietly when he realised they'd passed the turn. 'You're exhausted. We're both exhausted, with too much scope for nightmares. You can't be alone at Marrayin.' For her own need, as much as for his, she drew on her courage. 'There's a comfortable double bed at the pub. Are we friends enough to simply hold each other and sleep?'

She saw the tiny pause in his breathing, the slow exhale. 'Yes. If that's what you want.'

She entwined her fingers in his and rested her forehead against his shoulder, trusting him with her vulnerability in a way she'd trusted few others. 'It is. Just tonight. I know I'm asking a lot of you, but I don't want to face the nightmares alone.'

'I'll be there, Jenn,' he murmured into her hair. 'Close your eyes and sleep and I'll be right there beside you.'

And she could hear Mark's heart, feel the soft fabric of his T-shirt, the warmth of his arms around her, one hand gently cradling her head against him. Always and never, except for a few stolen moments that had to last.

⳥

She breathed deeply and slowly in her sleep, his shoulder her pillow, chestnut hair falling loosely over his arm that held her close to his side. Her hand rested lightly on his chest, and he enfolded it in his, her fingers instinctively curling into his. The sunlight streamed through the gap in the curtains. His parents would be here shortly but he was reluctant to break this moment, to wake Jenn and start the day and face others and lose the quiet joy of just being with her.

But he had to.

The wound in his side ached as he showered and dressed in borrowed clothes, but not as badly as the ache in his heart as Jenn withdrew from him. Although she kissed and hugged him before they went downstairs to meet up with his parents, it was affection, not love; any deeper feelings she might have had were hidden behind the smile that didn't make it to her eyes, and they went down the stairs side by side but not touching.

His parents waited in the courtyard, deserted at this hour of the morning although a tray with coffee cups and a plunger sat untouched on the table.

They embraced him, both of them, hard and tight and his mother's tears dampened his cheek as she kissed him.

His father cleared his throat. 'Mark, Jenn – I don't know how to apologise, what to say. I'm not the man you are, son. I should have faced them years ago. I should have gone to the police and faced the investigation, whatever it brought. But I didn't – and Caroline, you, so many others have paid for that. I don't deserve her. I don't deserve you.'

The pain and guilt in his father's eyes were familiar, but deeper now, and Mark recognised it for the load he'd always carried – maybe even the reason for the constant drive to serve others.

'I made my choices,' Caroline reproved her husband. 'You didn't make me do what I did, didn't know until afterwards. But I'm okay. I survived.' And she smiled, but it was forced and brave and never made it to her eyes.

'But I should have gone to the police then,' Len objected, and Mark wondered how often they'd gone around and around the same arguments. 'We might have had enough, with Wolfgang's help, to cast doubt on them.'

'There would have been false witnesses, Dad. They would have convicted and imprisoned you. Or worse. You know that. And that would have left Mum at their complete mercy. I don't know that I'd have done anything different.'

'You *did* do something different.' Len lifted his head high and met his gaze steadily. 'You went to the police and requested they reopen the investigation into Paula's death, despite what it might cost you. I've always been proud to be your father, but never more so than when I heard that.'

His father. Len's earnest gaze held his; brown eyes, eyelids creased at the edges, short once-brown hair framing an oval face.

342

Mark's last doubt evaporated. He didn't need a DNA test to see the resemblance. He carried Len's genes, not any other man's.

❧

Mark stayed by Jenn's side throughout the long day and the whole time awareness of him strummed constantly through her, winding her tight. They gave their statements to Leah Haddad at the Dungirri police station, and afterwards Kris made them coffee in her kitchen and told them the unofficial news – of more documents found, and multiple versions of the image with Len and the murdered woman, but each with a different man. Half a dozen women blackmailed, at least, and Jenn wondered how many more traumatised lives McCarty and Flanagan had left.

She went with Mark and Caroline and Len out to Marrayin to survey the damaged homestead, but despite the confessions of the morning, they all kept discussions practical, focused on repairs and rebuilding, avoiding the personal and the painful. Emotionally exhausted, Jenn was grateful for that, and she stayed on the edges of the conversation, watching Mark's quiet, realistic planning for the gradual rebuilding of his home. It would take him months, and she wouldn't be here when it was done.

In the afternoon she went with Mark to a meeting in the pub to discuss the town's strategy for supporting the children and families in the wake of the bus accident. Although Frank Williams chaired it, Mark's unobtrusive leadership helped to keep the meeting on track, moving forward, his suggestions couched in terms that acknowledged the skills and built the confidence of others, so that they never seemed like his ideas. Although she watched from the sidelines, she found herself suggesting the format for a media release and agreeing to write it.

The official meeting closed, plans agreed on, but everyone seemed to stay on for a meal, for the affirmation of the sense of community. They made her welcome, too, tried to draw her in, but she craved time alone with Mark, and always, always, there were people around them and between them. His people, his community. He belonged there, committed to them, in a way she could never belong.

When night's darkness spread over the town, they climbed the stairs to her room at the pub, and Mark drew her close into his arms. Very close. He bent his head and rested his forehead against hers.

'You said a few days ago that I should put what I want first more often,' he said. 'This is what I want, Jenn.' He kissed her, slowly, deeply, and desire and need overcame fear so that she wrapped her arms around his neck and responded without hesitation.

'Your side . . .'

'It's okay,' he said against her mouth.

She wanted to lose herself in sex, in passion and heat and lust. But he didn't let her. Every slow, exquisitely tender kiss that he trailed across her mouth, the nape of her neck, on the pulse at her throat, asked for her awareness, her focus. She couldn't slide into an oblivion of physical pleasure. With every touch of his mouth, every caress, Mark gave himself to her, and asked the same in return.

Asked, not demanded. Did he know how that scared her? How she'd played and laughed and had sex with other men but had never let them get close? How she'd never again found the joy of the long-ago afternoon with him?

His fingers brushed the swell of her breast through the light fabric of her shirt, pausing on the fluttering pulse of her heart.

Her body craved more; his hands, his mouth on her breast, his skin against hers and him with her, complete in her. Her heart recognised the question he asked. She kissed his mouth, long and gentle and uncertain.

'Do you know how strong you are, Jenn?' he murmured. 'Strong and beautiful and courageous.'

Courageous and strong . . . was she? Was she brave enough to believe him, to let go and trust him, trust herself?

He held her close against his body, work-hardened lean muscle, firm arms around her that would not let her fall, his heart beating beneath her cheek, sure and even.

She slid her hand between them, slipped three buttons of his shirt open and placed her palm over his heart, his skin warm under hers.

Courage. She pushed aside his shirt and rested her forehead against his bare chest while she drew breath, and then trailed kisses up to find his mouth again.

She found enough courage to hold back nothing – not her pleasure, not her emotion, not her desire to caress and touch and love his body, to accept the gifts of his hands and mouth and skin, the generosity of his heart, his love. Naked, they tumbled on to the cool white sheets of the bed, the pace intensely slow, every moment, every movement, every touch deliberate, aware. Intimate. When he'd caressed her almost to the edge of exquisite bliss, she gently pushed him to his back on the bed, held his hands captive by his sides, and, uncaring that her eyes filled with moisture, that she couldn't form a coherent word, she held his gaze, taking him inside her, focusing on his pleasure until her own desire blurred and there was nothing but the two of them and the depth of his eyes, and she cried out as the wave took hold of her, aware of nothing but ecstasy and Mark and the strength of his hands and falling with him, on to him, wrapped in the strength of him.

♋

He held her as she slept, whispering assurances when her body tensed and her breath hitched in her dreams, keeping her safe as best he could from the fears lurking in her subconscious. He loved her as he'd loved no-one else, the love of their youth deeper now, enriched by all they'd learned and become, by the possibility of what they could become, together. His heart belonged to her, and there would never be anyone else for him.

But he had no illusions. The nightmares of her past still haunted her, scars that hadn't healed holding her back from giving herself fully, risking her heart and her love. She would leave again.

He watched her eyelids flicker, brushed a kiss across her lips and she stirred and snuggled closer into him with a contented sigh. In her heart, she trusted him and loved him. He had no doubt of it. If he could ease her fears, help her discover her own strengths, there might be a future for them.

He planned to fight for that future. He planned to love her so gently, so deeply, that she'd always remember the joy of it. Although he couldn't leave Dungirri yet, in a few months, when the children and their parents no longer carried trauma in their eyes, when school reopened in the new year and the teachers returned from hospital, when the town could see hope and happiness again – then he could go to Moscow.

He had skills, experience and knowledge beyond running Marrayin – he could build a career for himself wherever she was. And though he'd miss the sunrises over Marrayin's paddocks and the contentment of his work there, the prospect of life away from his home unsettled him far less than the prospect of life without Jenn. His grandparents had built a new life together, far from their home. He could do the same with Jenn – if he could persuade her to trust her heart.

⚬

Four days later – four quiet days with Mark out at Marrayin, absorbed in the rhythms of companionable work during the day and nights together that almost tore apart her resolve – she delivered the eulogy for Jim. In the peace of the Dungirri cemetery among the trees, most of the town gathered for the simple service and she read the words Paul and Sean had written. They stood beside her, Sean's handcuffs hardly visible under the long sleeves of his good shirt, the prison guard a respectful distance behind.

Their words summed up the unassuming, well-lived life of a man who loved the land and worked hard, earning respect and friendship. Then they lowered him to rest in the earth next to his wife, and Paul and Chloe and then Calum dropped in some gum leaves, and Sean stood for a few moments, looking down, tears escaping.

'I'll try to make you proud, Dad,' Jenn heard him murmur.

She stepped forward, then dropped her own small branch of leaves. *I know I'm running away again, Jim. I wish I had your strength. I wish I had Mark's strength.*

Mark waited at the back of the crowd. She'd come to the cemetery alone, before the service, to sit by the graves of her parents and Paula, and to see Paul and Sean when they arrived.

Throughout the short service she'd been aware of Mark, his intense eyes, his gentle smile of support.

Now she walked to him. He bent his head and kissed her cheek.

'You're worried. I saw you texting on your phone.'

'Yes. There was an earthquake in Indonesia this morning. I'm booked on a six a.m. flight from Sydney tomorrow. I'll drive to Dubbo shortly, and catch a flight from there late this afternoon.'

'So, you're going again.' He swallowed hard. 'Already. Will you come back?'

'Yes.' Some time. She couldn't promise him when. 'Mark, I know I'm running away. I know I've done that a lot of my life. That's one of those uncomfortable questions I'll be contemplating while I'm gone. Mark, I don't know . . . I don't know if I can do this. I'm scared and I need to find out if I'm strong enough to love anyone enough.'

He drew her into his arms. 'I know you need to do this. I won't stop you. But believe me, Jenn – if you don't come back here, I'll come and find you.'

She held him close, reluctant to move, and wished she could be as sure as him.

TWENTY

In a plastic tent in a field of hundreds of plastic tents Jenn watched a mother feed her baby while rain poured down, spattering on the plastic, sending rivers of water and mud all around them. The woman, who'd lost everything she owned in the earthquake, smiled at her child and stroked his forehead, and thanked Jenn in fractured English for the baby clothes she'd brought.

Jenn stuffed her camera back into its waterproof bag under her perspiration-drenched raincoat and left the tent, heading out into the monsoonal rain and the cloying heat. The inadequate tents provided little shelter for the thousands displaced by the earthquake. There was a story there, a story about suffering and bureaucracy and the struggle back to normality.

There were other stories, too, about families and love and courage and the determination to overcome hurdles and achieve dreams. They were the ones that kept coming to her.

She passed a father walking hand in hand with his child, a little girl about the same age as Alicia, and Jenn caught herself thinking of the Dungirri children again. She turned and stood in the teeming rain watching the progress of the father and daughter until they ducked into a tent further down the row.

She would never see them again, never know how they fared, never know their names and dreams and stories beyond the first few days of this disaster.

She was an observer, not a participant, and that was growing increasingly unsatisfying. As she walked back to her car, the understanding that had been pushing at her for days took a clear shape.

She'd lived her dreams, achieved her goals. All that she'd been able to imagine at seventeen, she'd worked her butt off for and made happen. Now, at thirty-five, what dreams did she have? What goals? The vague dream of being good enough to win the respect of a major prize for her journalism – but what the hell did it matter if she never won a Pulitzer?

She could research to uncover truths, find answers to unasked questions; she could weave words with talent and skill to relate facts clearly, to inform, to persuade, to raise consciousness and evoke anger or sorrow. All these things she could do well, and she was proud of her skill, of upholding good journalistic ethics and working to make the world better, more informed. Her work *mattered*.

But she hadn't let much else matter.

She'd run away from everyone she cared about and buried herself in work. Head work, not heart work. Maybe it was time – past time – to stop observing and reporting and start living. Time to stop running away to avoid risking pain and sorrow. She hadn't avoided the sorrow anyway, and it had been laced with regrets.

The driver opened the car door for her.

'The airport now, Miss?'

'Yes. Thank you. It's time to go home.'

TWENTY-ONE

She drove into Dungirri on another hot, dry day, the wind stirring dust devils on the dirt road ahead of her as she wound through the last of the scrub. Coming out of the trees to cross the low bridge over the creek, she caught sight of the large cloud of smoke to the north of town.

Bushfire. A bushfire in the scrub, the humidity so low the air crackled, and the wind coming from the north – driving the fire towards Dungirri.

Still kilometres away yet. She hoped. She'd never been much good at estimating distances, let alone when the horizon was shrouded in smoke. She'd lived five years in this district and she'd never forgotten the risks, the way the locals kept a constant watch on the horizon through the summer months, the ever-present awareness of temperature, humidity and wind.

On Scrub Road, just beyond Ryan and Beth's home, an SES

crew was setting up a road block and a police car edged past it. Going to evacuate people? Perhaps. Not a good sign.

She hadn't expected to see Christmas lights strung across the main street, or the painted nativity scene filling the window of one of the empty shops. A very Australian Santa in singlet and Stubbies relaxed in a rocking chair surrounded by Australian animals in the next window, and she saw several large posters advertising a carols service.

Dungirri was fulfilling its plans of giving the children a Christmas to celebrate, a Christmas to heal.

She drove on past the pub. Cars and utes were parked all along the road outside the Rural Fire Service shed, just beyond the showground. She found a spot towards the end of the line of vehicles and pulled in to park.

So much for driving straight to Marrayin and Mark. Although she'd sent an email to tell him she was leaving Indonesia, she hadn't told him of her spur-of-the-moment decision to hire a car at the airport this morning. He wouldn't expect her until tomorrow.

He was in the RFS. With a fire burning in the scrub she wouldn't find him at home. She could phone him – but that would warn him of her arrival, and for some reason she couldn't entirely fathom, she wanted to see him, watch his unguarded reaction when he saw her.

The RFS shed – extended several times since her day – bustled with activity. Two RFS utes were parked out front but the large bays that housed the tankers were empty. Several guys sorted equipment and others were erecting a tent beside the shed and setting up trestle tables.

The door of the control room stood open and as she approached she could see familiar faces inside. Jeanie Menotti caught sight of her, her face blossoming with a sudden, wide smile.

'Jenn! Welcome back. If you've got nothing better to do, I could use your help.'

'I was going to Marrayin, but I guess Mark's not there.'

'No.' Jeanie nodded to the map on the wall, marked with pins and string. 'He's in sector one on Dungirri One Bravo. Paul's on Dungirri Two Alpha protecting Friday Creek. We've got two Birraga crews as well and there are others from the region on their way. This could be a bad one, Jenn. There's a wind shift forecast but if it doesn't come in time Dungirri itself might be in trouble.'

'What do you need me to do?'

'Phone calls. We need to get on to all the landholders in this area and make sure they're aware, find out if they're evacuating or staying to defend their places.'

At one end of the room, she made phone call after phone call, but every time the RFS radio on the other side of the room crackled, she held her breath, listening for any news of Dungirri One Bravo.

She stopped breathing when the radio crackled loudly and a panicked male voice burst through. 'Emergency! The road's blocked – we're trapped. The fire's jumping the break everywhere . . .' A pause came, voices in the background, and then Mark's voice, deep and even. 'Firecom, this is two-seven-one-five on Dungirri One Bravo, calling an emergency sitrep.' Clear and concise, he proceeded with the situation report according to standard operating procedures. And the calmness and clarity terrified Jenn more with each word. 'We are on Toms Creek Road, at the Woolshed Gully fire trail. The road is blocked by trees to the west and the fire has jumped the firebreak to the east. All the crew are in the tanker, and we have five hundred litres of water remaining. We are commencing emergency procedures now. Please confirm receipt of sitrep.'

Commencing emergency procedures. The bland words stood for a nightmare. Taking refuge in a truck from a firestorm. Six fire-fighters, all volunteers, crowding under blankets in the cab of the tanker while the world burned around them.

Jenn stood, frozen on her feet, her pulse thudding in her head. *Mark.*

'Confirmed, Dungirri One Bravo.' Ryan, the radio officer, spoke as evenly as Mark had, although his face had faded to grey and sweat beaded on his forehead. 'We will despatch units to your assistance. Take care and good luck, mate.'

Someone swore the minute the radio went quiet, and someone else slammed a fist into the wall.

'Don't think it,' Jeanie ordered, her voice so harsh that everyone in the room turned to her. Her gaze swept around them all. 'You pray, or send them strong thoughts, or hold them in the light, or whatever works for you, but *do not* panic and imagine the worst. Mark knows what he's doing; he'll make sure they follow the procedures. They have plenty of water, so the protective sprays on the tanker will last a while.'

One part of Jenn's brain heard and acknowledged the logic. Another part screamed.

No. No. No. No, he couldn't die. Couldn't *be* dying right now. Because she couldn't bear it if he died. Couldn't bear it if he died and never knew that she'd come to her senses and come back. If she never had the chance to tell him she loved him and finally, *finally* wasn't afraid to feel it.

The minutes dragged past, tension holding them silent except for the voices on the radio, arranging assistance, although no truck could get close to them straightaway.

Jeanie's arm came around her shoulders and they stood together, unmoving, all attention on the radio.

Ten minutes. Fifteen minutes. Twenty.

The radio crackled again and Mark's voice came into the room, a little croaky and breathless, but still even. 'Control, Dungirri One Bravo portable. Sitrep – we're all okay. Repeat, everyone's okay. The tanker is heavily damaged, but no major injuries. We are sheltering in a burned-out area approximately twenty-five metres east of the tanker. Please confirm receipt of sitrep.'

'Confirmed, Dungirri One Bravo,' Ryan said. 'Thank God. We'll have someone in to pick you up in ten minutes.'

The rescue truck brought them in an hour or so later and Jenn found him, leaning against a wall outside, gulping down a bottle of water, red-eyed from smoke and exhaustion. His yellow uniform jacket lay on the ground at his feet, his helmet beside it.

His wide, weary smile when he saw her melted away any uncertainties, and struck her heart. Oblivious to all the people around, she walked straight to him, and when he reached out and pulled her close she went without hesitation, burying her head in his shoulder, breathing in the smoke and sweat and reality of him. Hip to hip, shoulder to chest, his cheek resting on her head, she fitted there with him, encompassed, belonging.

'You came back,' he said at last.

'Yes.' She took a deep breath. 'I hope you're willing to help me with my new research project.'

'Which is?' Underneath the hint of teasing, she heard a hitch of uncertainty.

'Researching stories about life, and courage, community and friendship, and strength and love,' she told him. 'I figure there's probably a fair few out here in regional Australia that need telling. And maybe my skills can be useful here in Dungirri.'

He gently lifted her chin to look into her face. 'So, you're staying for a while?'

'Yes. I'm staying for a while. I've taken six months' leave of absence. It seems as though that's enough time to learn some things I need to learn, and to decide . . . decide if there's a future here for me.'

He brushed a strand of hair back from her face, and smiled, light dancing in the warmth of his eyes.

'I've missed you, Jenn. Not just these long, last two weeks, but the eighteen years before that. Count on me to help you with this research project. As much as you want. Anything you need.'

She cupped his face with her hands and he met her kiss, long and slow and breathtakingly tender, that gentleness, the strength of him, the centre of him.

A burst of laughter nearby brought them back to reality and a fire-fighter slapped Mark on the shoulder as a group of them passed. Andrew Pappas, grinning widely, although he'd been on that truck with Mark facing death not so long ago.

'Free food at the pub for emergency services,' Andrew told them. 'You two coming?'

Mark's warm eyes smiled at her. 'I don't know about you, but I'm starving. Shall we go?'

'I'm not an emergency worker.'

He reached down to pick up his jacket and helmet. 'I hear you've been working the phones for hours.' He put his helmet on to her head with a grin. 'You're one of us, Jenn.'

Arms around each other, they followed their friends along the road through the dust and the heat, the dry leaves swirling in the promised wind change, towards the pub and the town with enough heart and strength and determination to survive, whatever the odds.

Bronwyn Parry grew up surrounded by books, with a fascination for places, people and their stories. Bronwyn's first novel, *As Darkness Falls*, won a prestigious Romance Writers of America Golden Heart Award for best romantic suspense manuscript in 2007. Her second novel, *Dark Country*, was named the Favourite Romantic Suspense Novel of 2009 by the Australian Romance Readers Association (ARRA) and in 2010 was a finalist in the Romance Writers of America RITA Awards – the Oscars of romance writing. *Dead Heat* was named the Favourite Romantic Suspense Novel in 2013 by the ARRA and was a finalist in the RITA Awards. An occasional academic, Bronwyn's active interest in fiction and its readership is reflected in her PhD research and she is passionate about the richness, diversity and value of popular fiction. Bronwyn lives in the New England tablelands in New South Wales and loves to travel in Australia's wild places.

www.bronwynparry.com

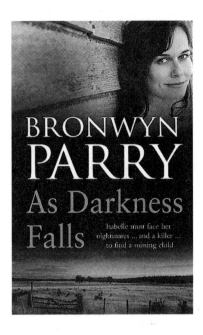

Haunted by her past, Detective Isabelle O'Connell is recalled to duty to investigate the abduction of a child from her home town. She and DCI Alec Goddard have only days to find the girl alive, with few clues, a town filled with suspects and a vast wilderness to search. It quickly becomes a game of cat and mouse, with Isabelle directly in the killer's sights.

For Isabelle, this case is already personal. For Alec, his best intentions to keep it purely professional soon dissolve as his anguish over Isabelle's safety moves beyond concern for a colleague. Their mutual attraction leaves them both vulnerable to their private nightmares – nightmares the killer ruthlessly exploits.

'an impressive debut' *The Australian Women's Weekly*

'a strong debut from an author who could be a future star'
Australian Bookseller & Publisher

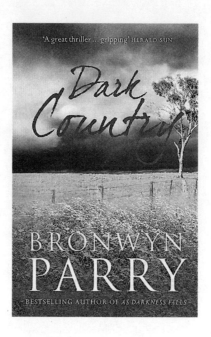

Most people in the small town of Dungirri have considered Morgan 'Gil' Gillespie a murderer for eighteen years, so he expects no welcome on his return. What he doesn't expect is the discovery of a woman's tortured body in the boot of his car, and new accusations of murder.

Wearied by too many deaths and doubting her own skills, local police sergeant Kris Matthews isn't sure if Gil is a decent man wronged by life, or a brutal criminal she should be locking up. But she does know that he is not guilty of this murder because she is his alibi . . .

Between organised crime, police corruption and the town's hatred, Gil has nowhere to hide. He needs to work out who's behind the murder before his enemies try to harm the few people he cares about. Kris is determined to help him, but will their search for the truth make her the next target?

'loyalty and romance combine with all the action to make a memorable story' *Woman's Day*

'Nuanced . . . intriguing' *Weekend Australian*

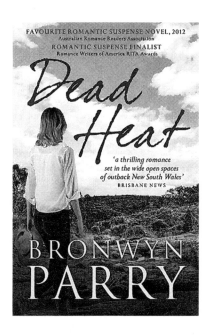

Dead Heat

'a thrilling romance
set in the wide open spaces
of outback New South Wales'
BRISBANE NEWS

BRONWYN
PARRY

National Parks Ranger Jo Lockwood is often alone in the wilderness, and she likes it that way – until she discovers the body of a man, brutally murdered.

Detective Nick Matheson's posting to country New South Wales after years working undercover is supposed to be an uneventful return to normal duties. But he knows organised crime from the inside out and suspects that this victim is not an isolated murder.

As the body count starts mounting, Nick's past and present collide, threatening the people he cares about most.

Jo is determined to do everything she can to help the investigation but she has seen the killer's face and now she's his next target.

Trapped in the rugged outback, pursued by hunters who can't afford to fail, Nick and Jo will need to trust each other and act quickly if they want to survive.

'a thrilling romance set in the wide open spaces of outback New South Wales' *Brisbane News*